THE TEMPEST'S SOUL

Published by: Fox Tale Publishing

Cover Design | Map | Interior Formatting | Typesetting by: Fox Tale Publishing

Map Border Design: Alderdoodle @ alderdoodle.co.uk

Conceptual Edit by: Kasey LeAlma

Line Edit by: Lana Staux

Copy Edit by: Enchanted Ink Publishing

Proofread by: Green Spark Publishing

First edition 2024

ISBN: 978-1-964131-00-9 (paperback)
ISBN: 978-1-964131-01-6 (ebook)

WWW.AUTHORBRITTANYMRILEY.COM

For my mom,
who always encouraged me
to write and follow my dreams.

BRITTANY M. RILEY

THE TEMPEST'S SOUL

A DIVINE TEMPEST NOVEL

FOX TALE PUBLISHING

AUTHOR'S NOTE

The Tempest's Soul contains elements of the following:

- On page consensual sex
- Murder, violence, and gore
- Abuse
- A missing/kidnapped child
- Cannibalism (accidental and mentioned)

NASCENT SEA
SERPENTINE MOUNTAINS
MYTHBEL
TIRUHM
THISTLEWALL
REINA'S WOODS
DUSMIR
RIVENGLEN
KINGDOM OF VALARYN
RYSEER
EVERDAWN COAST

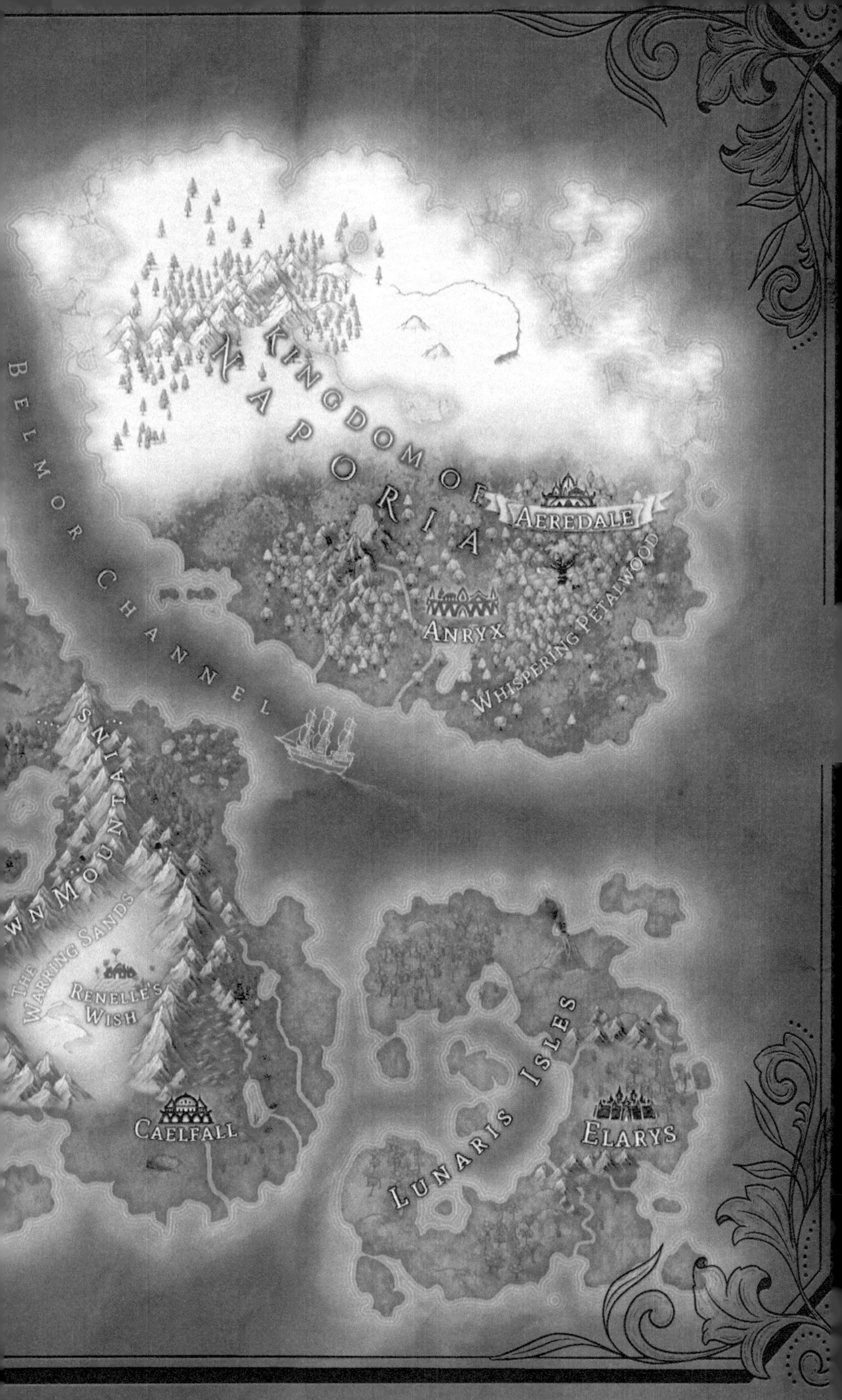

KINGDOM OF NAPORIA
AEREDALE
ANRYX
WHISPERING PETALWOOD
BELMOR CHANNEL
SNIW MOUNTAINS
THE WARRING SANDS
RENELLE'S WISH
CAELFALL
LUNARIS ISLES
ELARYS

Sign up for my newsletter

Be the first to know about new book releases, behind the scenes, and more!

Pronunciation Guide

Ahrea: Ah-ray-uh

Caelus: Kay-less/Kay-luss

Dusmir: Dus-meer

Corrin: Core-in

Eira: I-rah

Esprit: Eh-spree

Evryn: Ev-ren

Labryn: La-brin

Maelynn: May-lynn

Navryn: Nah-vren

Oerban: Or-baan

Perrin: Pear-in

Reina: Ray-nuh

Renelle: Ren-ell

Ryseer: Rye-seer

Saios: Sigh-ohs

Tenebrae: Teh-nuh-bray

Thanally: Th-anne-uh-lee

Tiruhm: Teer-rum

Valaryn: Vah-lah-ren

Wrynal: Wry-nahl

Gods of the Realm

Ahrea
Goddess of Luck and Freedom

Maelynn
Goddess of Night and Dreams

Oerban
God of Day and Contracts

Saios
God of Life and New Beginnings

Evryn
God of Abundance and Virtue

Thanally
Goddess of Death and Spirits

Reina
Goddess of Love and Remembrance

The Twins, Wrynal and Renelle
God of Vengeance and Goddess of Mercy

The Forgotten, Navryn
Goddess of Harmony and Chaos

1

The alabaster gods peered down at me, and moonlight shone through the glass ceiling, illuminating their judgmental stares. For a place of tranquility, meditation in the center of the Chamber of Gods always left my hair on end. No matter how long I sat in the middle of the room with my legs tucked neatly underneath me, inhaling the muggy scent of incense, it didn't change that I never heard the gods speak.

The Divine were meant to be able to commune with them, often hearing their will or prophecies during meditation, but they never spoke to me. Not that I blamed them. Their "gift" had caused more problems for me than it fixed. They probably didn't want anything to do with a Divine who was a disappointment.

I tapped my finger against my thigh and huffed. *I wish they'd take the tempest back.*

My hair fell forward, blocking the stare of the goddess of luck and freedom, and the tightness in my chest eased.

A vase shattered, and my gaze snapped to the crumbled pieces on the mosaic-tiled floor below the statue of Oerban. Two small feet peeked out beside the bottom of the statue, along with a tuft of curly chestnut hair not quite concealed by the statue's leg.

I smiled. How would the god of day and contracts have felt about a boy hiding behind his statue?

Teeg stepped out, a sheepish grin on his round face.

"You've been told not to be in here," I said.

"But you're in here all the time."

I sighed. Ever since he came to live at the temple of Ahrea, he'd been like a little brother to me. "You should be in bed."

The stone doors of the chamber scraped against the floor behind me.

"Eira, you will do something with Tryssa, or I will," the high priestess shouted, her footsteps clicking against the polished tiles. "There isn't another temple who will take her. It'll be the streets, with the reputation she's earning."

"Hide," I whispered to Teeg.

He darted behind the statue of Oerban again—no feet or hair to be seen. Teeg knew we would both suffer if she found him here.

Klareth stopped in the center of the chamber a few feet from where I knelt.

I pushed myself up on numb legs and smoothed out the soft fabric of my ice-blue gown over my curves, facing her.

Her black hair, in her usual too-tight bun, pulled her face taut and smoothed out the wrinkles of her forehead. Her traditional gray robes accentuated her thin, angular form. In her youth, she might have been pretty, but with her reddened neck, it looked as though she might breathe fire like the dragons of near myth.

"What did she do this time?" I asked, pulling my long, dark hair over my shoulder.

Her nostrils flared. "Does it matter?"

I clenched my teeth, running my fingers through the length of my hair and shifting my weight, legs tingling with the movement. "No, but—"

"Tryssa decided it would be best to replace another girl's bathing oil with an enchanted one. The girl lost all her hair," she bit out.

The corner of my lips twitched despite my best effort to fight smiling. Klareth caught the slight uptilt. Her hand shot out and grabbed my wrist, and her sharp nails dug into my skin. "At twenty-one, I expect better from you, but you're just like that ridiculous orphan girl."

I flinched at her words.

Klareth smiled wickedly, the slightest wrinkle forming around her eyes.

Lightning sparked at my fingertips, tingling my skin, and I clenched my hand to conceal it.

Her eyes darted in my hand's direction, and I stiffened. She definitely hadn't missed that little slip of my "gift."

"I—I'll talk to her," I said, heart beating rapidly.

"You will. Otherwise, you'll be the one to suffer the consequences." Klareth's gaze slid past me toward the various statues. "You can't even meditate without causing a mess." She released my wrist and placed her hands on my shoulders, forcing me to turn around. She pointed at the broken vase on the floor. "Clean up after yourself." Her thin hands released me, and her footsteps clacked as she exited the Chamber of Gods.

The doors clanged shut behind her, and I caressed the sore reddened indentations around my wrist. They were nothing compared to the high priestess's favorite form of punishment.

Shuffling sounded behind me, and a moment later, Teeg collided into me, wrapping his arms around my hips. He sniffled, and I tousled his curly hair. "Don't worry," I said.

He looked up at me, eyes glistening. "She won't take you away again, will she?"

There wasn't a simple answer I could give him. Not one that would quell his fear, anyway. I forced a smile and said, "Let's clean this up and get you to your room."

"I got it!" Teeg said. He ran over to the broken vase and placed his hand on one of the shards.

"Careful!" I called.

The pieces began to move and weave themselves back together, attaching to the one he touched. In seconds, the broken vase was once again whole, sitting beside Oerban's feet.

I smiled. "Now, time for bed."

He took my hand, and we passed acolytes as we made our way through the stone halls of the temple. Most started in the opposite direction, avoiding me. A few stared, concern marring their features at the sight of Teeg holding my hand as they murmured about the disappearances throughout the kingdom.

I ignored their implications.

Teeg had long since stopped asking why none of them were friendly to me like they were with him. Their fear of the lightning coursing through my body didn't stop me from getting Teeg to his room and tucking him into bed, though.

He asked for the same story he'd been asking for since I'd first told it to him, the very one my mother used to tell me of a girl who loved her sister very much. He nodded off before I finished, and I kissed his forehead. I closed the door with a soft click, careful not to disturb him, though he'd always been a heavy sleeper.

The nosy acolytes were nowhere to be seen in the hall outside his room, and I made my way to the temple courtyard, heading for Tryssa's room.

Moonlight glistened off the running water of the fountain in the center. The stone woman in the fountain's center depicted Ahrea, goddess of luck and freedom. Her stone form sat with her head back, water flowing down the length of her hair. Her eyes were closed, and her full lips tilted into a smile.

At one time, I truly believed myself lucky—free. It was ironic that I'd ended up in the unluckiest of places with little freedoms. I sighed, running my hand over the engraving of little butterflies on the stone lip of the fountain. I missed my aunt's silly parties that she'd forced me to attend now that I had no way back to her.

A pulling sensation in my stomach forced my attention to the doors of the Chamber of Gods across the way. They were open.

I tilted my head. *I'm sure I closed them.*

Before continuing to Tryssa's room, I approached them. My chest tightened and sweat built on the back of my neck.

The pull intensified, coaxing me to go inside. It was like there was a rope tied around my waist and it was trying to drag me in. I ignored it and the building tightness in my throat and tugged the stone doors closed.

The tightness eased, and I let out a heavy sigh.

My fingers slid down the smooth lotus engraved in the stone doors, and I shook my head. All the hours I'd spent inside the chamber, begging to be freed from the Divine gift I'd been blessed with, had to be getting to me.

2

Tryssa's room was the last on the left in the girls' dormitory in the west wing of the temple. I passed doors decorated in paint and wreaths of flowers, stopping in front of her plain wooden one. She'd never answer when I'd ask if leaving it bare was intentional. Part of me guessed she didn't want to stay.

I tapped my knuckles against the door.

No answer.

"I know you're in there," I cooed, knocking again. "I'm sure Klareth has already given you a mouthful."

The lock clicked, and the door creaked open. Big brown eyes peered up at me through the small crack. Strands of thick, dark curls framed her heart-shaped face.

Tryssa glared at me. "She always sends you."

"If you don't want to see me, you shouldn't get into trouble." I smiled. "Can I come in?"

She rolled her eyes and pulled the door open the rest of the way. "As if I have a choice." She flopped onto the bed face-first.

I stepped inside, closing the door behind me.

Her faintly lit room had only what she absolutely needed. Tomes on history and the gods lined a single shelf on the floor-to-ceiling bookcase. The acolytes took the orphans living in the temple out to buy anything they wanted. But whatever Tryssa bought wasn't in this room.

"You should decorate more," I said.

She ignored me and asked, voice muffled by pillows, "What's the speech this time?"

I leaned against her small desk near the window, careful not to disturb the neat stack of papers. "Klareth told me about the bathing oil. The girl's hair will grow back, but I imagine you had a reason for what you did?"

She pushed herself up and pulled her knees to her chest. "Emi is a bully. She thinks she's better than everyone. She learns what happened to the other girls' parents. Uses it against them so she can take their stuff."

"And none of the acolytes step in?"

She shook her head, squeezing her legs.

My blood sparked, the tempest rising to the surface, and I gripped the desk to keep my hands steady. Why were they allowing that to continue? I closed my eyes.

Breathe. In. Out. In front of Tryssa is the last place to lose control.

As Divine, I should've had final say on matters at the temple and should've had authority to punish Emi. But Klareth bonded herself to me with an imitation of the *tenebrae* bond—a bond meant to make her my protector. All it did was make it so I couldn't harm her with the lightning coursing through me and allowed her to have free rein over the temple of Ahrea.

I may have never wanted the responsibility of the temple, but with the choice removed, I played peacekeeper as often as I could, even if it meant suffering the consequences.

I opened my eyes and pushed away from the desk and approached Tryssa's bed. Kneeling, I said, "I know you're trying to help, but you can't keep getting into trouble. There's only so much I can do to keep Klareth . . ." I squeezed her heavy gray blanket. "Keep her content."

Tryssa scoffed and stared out her window. "The other girls are scared of you," she said, changing the subject. "I tell them they shouldn't be. That you're nice, but . . ."

I smiled. "Don't concern yourself with that." I stood and started for the door. "I'll see what I can do, but keep your head down and stay out of trouble. Let me or Marus know if something is going on. Better to let us deal with it *and* Klareth."

The sound of rustling blankets sounded behind me. "Eira . . ."

I turned to face her.

She was lying on her side now, facing me. "We've all heard the thunder. Seen the lightning on a clear day. It's why the others are scared of you. How come you're never like that when you're here?"

My stomach turned, and I took a shaky breath. "Get some sleep," I said, then stepped out into the empty hall, closing the door behind me.

I sucked in a deep breath of the cool, quiet air and leaned against Tryssa's door. Holding my hands palm up, I discharged a fraction of lightning. Tendrils of the blue-white energy danced between my fingers.

The Tempest—my Divine title and my Divine gift. The gods' chosen for their power. Lightning festered within me, longing for release. Even when I was calm, it itched to be free. A constant check and balance, trying to stay within the storm's eye. One wrong lapse of emotion—one too-strong flare of frustration or anger—and I would slip out of the eye and into chaos.

I drew in the tendrils of lightning, the sparks dissipating, and started for the library.

The tempest writhed beneath the surface, prodding for an escape, the small discharge not enough to sate it. "All the power of a storm at my fingertips and nothing to show for it," I muttered. *Just calming techniques and hours wasted meditating.*

I TOOK A DETOUR through the serene temple garden—the perfect place to hide, making it one of my favorite places. It hid an entrance to the hall that led past the kitchen and to the library. The everflame lamps in the kitchen were doused, so I ducked inside to grab a bottle of wine—the one other thing that helped keep the tempest in check. Though any sort of alcohol would've done the trick.

Alcohol was the closest thing to muffling the storm I'd found. I grabbed a bottle of red wine and two wineglasses, and continued through the empty halls.

Using my hip, I pushed through the gilded double doors of the library emblazoned with symbols representing each god and goddess. The scent of books and parchment filled the air as I ambled through the rows of tall shelves toward the nearly hidden study Marus claimed as his office.

The temple of Ahrea's library was his little corner of the world. He adored language and knowledge, though his age was often a point of criticism from the grumpy old scholars long past their prime.

I didn't bother knocking before entering the secluded study in the far back of the library. Marus sat on a worn couch that had seen better days, feet propped up on the rectangle cedar table in front of him. He'd tied back his long blond hair and had abandoned his coat on the back of the couch, leaving him in a patterned brown waistcoat and with the sleeves of his white shirt rolled up to the elbows.

"Klareth would be fuming if she knew you had your feet on the table," I said, placing the wine bottle and two glasses between the scattered books. "And with your shoes on? She might finally blow a vessel."

He peered at me past his square glasses and smiled. "Sounds like I may do everyone a favor if she found out."

I laughed. "Maybe so."

He closed his book, placing it on the cushion next to him, and pushed his glasses up the long bridge of his nose. With his high cheekbones and narrow face, he could have almost passed for one of the fey. His russet-colored eyes drifted to the bottle. "I was wondering when you'd get here." He glanced at the clock, which read one in the morning. "Klareth have you meditating again?"

I plopped down in the armchair that matched the couch. "Something like that."

He stood, grabbing the bottle of wine to open it. "Do tell."

"She interrupted. Apparently, Tryssa got her hands on enchanted bath oil. Emi doesn't have hair anymore. I'm sure you can imagine Klareth's fury."

Marus laughed, warm and infectious. The sound brought a smile to my face. "I can't believe she'd do that." He removed the cork from the bottle. "Wait. Actually, I can. But what did Tryssa have to say?" he asked.

"Emi is terrible."

He raised a brow.

I rolled my eyes. "Fine. Emi may be blackmailing the other girls."

He poured a healthy amount of wine into both glasses and handed me one. "Quite the accusation."

I took the glass and a long drink, letting the acidic sweetness coat my mouth and settle deep in my stomach. "Which is why I have another reason for my visit."

"You want me to monitor her?"

I nodded, biting the corner of my lip.

"That's a demure look, even for you."

"I'm sor—"

"We both know how everyone acts around you, and far be it from me to help a friend in need."

I lowered my wineglass and stared into the crimson liquid. Marus often made it easy to forget that I was a Divine around him—that I was the Tempest. Yet he'd also been the one to notice the weather anomalies caused by the outbursts of my power and had tracked me down in the dwarven city of Tiruhm.

I raised the glass, taking a long swallow of wine. "If there's ever anything I can do for you, tell me."

"Helping me research the Divine and their gifts is more than enough. Watching out for some mishap between the kids is the least I can do."

I smiled and tilted my glass to his, and they clinked together. "As promised." *Not that I have much to offer.*

Using my gift was too dangerous around him. It'd be too easy to accidentally kill him if I wasn't careful. My account of my abilities and the occasional observation was all he had to go off of. But he'd promised he'd use his findings to help future Divine, so I did what I could.

Quick, heavy footsteps sounded in the library, and Marus shot me a questioning look.

I shook my head. It was too late for anyone to be visiting aside from Klareth, but the footsteps didn't match the click of her heels. *Roan?*

I shot up, placing my glass down without a sound. Him finding me in the library would be just as bad as Klareth. I cracked open the door of the study but didn't spot anyone. Tiptoeing, I slipped out and hid behind a bookshelf in the shadows.

The footsteps grew closer, and I peeked out.

Malik strode toward the study, his usual combat leathers replaced with a fine tunic of green and gold. The sword at his hip remained, and he'd tucked his loose pants into knee-high boots that likely concealed more weapons. Beside him, Selena looked almost out of place with her soft face and dark, tight curls.

My heart raced. *Malik only visits the temple for one reason.* I stepped out into the open.

The hard lines of Malik's face softened, his green eyes somber. Someone had to be injured.

"Where are they?" I asked.

Marus stepped up beside me, wine still in hand. His eyes narrowed at Malik.

"The guildhall," Malik said.

I nodded, already heading for the library's exit, not caring about the possibility of Klareth's punishment if she found out that I was gone or using the only good that came from the lightning I wielded—the ability to heal.

3

Malik led us to the Copper Jackals' guildhall looming at the end of Copper Alley. The street had picked up the not-so-clever name as the guild grew and members established businesses along either side. Everflame lamps decorated the white stone walls of the large guildhall. Most of the members lived in this building, using it as a home.

After nightfall, only members could enter, but several remained active throughout the night to keep the city and surrounding villages safe in place of the five High Houses. Most believed they'd forgone their duty to the people of the Kingdom of Valaryn. Truthfully, if it weren't for the Copper Jackals taking up residence in Dusmir, the city wouldn't have grown as much as it had.

We made it up the steps leading to the entrance, and Malik

placed his palm against the enchanted golden-jackal motif in the center of the door. The eyes glowed amber, and the door swung open on its own.

Two sweeping staircases framed the large foyer, and corridors led left and right, deeper into the guildhall. We veered right down the hall leading to their infirmary, somewhere I'd grown all too familiar with.

I couldn't help but wonder what had happened since Malik only called on me for severe injuries. The less frequently he needed me, the less likely it was that Klareth would find out what I did for the Copper Jackals.

Malik pushed open the door to the infirmary. A stringent medicinal scent stung my nose, and I blinked, my eyes adjusting to the blinding bright light from silver everflame lamps.

Three unfamiliar faces watched me. I thanked the gods that not all the beds were full and liked to think it meant others I'd healed had learned from their near-death experience.

I stepped closer to the bed farthest from the door, and the blood drained from my face.

The guild leader, Veth, pressed her hands to a young woman's wound, holding in the intestines threatening to spill free. A bloody pink loop had escaped her efforts. Blood pooled on the white floors, leaving the woman's skin ashen. Each breath she took was ragged as her chest sank in.

It was a miracle the woman even hung on to life.

"Hurry," Veth said. Tired, dark crescents cradled her emerald eyes.

Swallowing hard, I knelt beside both of them and placed my hand along the girl's stomach and took a deep breath, closing my eyes. I imagined a glowing silver thread connecting my soul to hers. A sliver of vibrant life remained along the woman's thread, barely a blip. I sighed, anxiety easing. But the only thing standing between the woman and death was me.

I released my hold on the lightning. It tickled my fingers, twining around them. I didn't need to open my eyes to know that it now skated across the woman, seeking the wound.

Her thread of life grew shorter.

No!

I pushed more lightning from within me toward her gaping abdomen, willing the mending to hasten. The thread bobbed again, the light blinking out for a second and then returning. My jaw clenched, and then I gasped, her pain rushing into me, sharp and vicious.

Her warm, sticky skin burned like fire against my cold hands, the healing process leeching their warmth. I sucked in a heaving breath.

The bit of thread flickered, then glowed with life again, and I smiled. *She's going to be okay.*

I opened my eyes and pulled my hand away, drawing the energy back. A little pink scar of new flesh had replaced the gaping wound. By tomorrow, it would be gone. Only the people in the room would know anything was amiss.

If the wound hadn't healed fast enough, she would've died, and there would've been nothing I could do. Each Divine's ability to heal was unique. Lightning expedited the natural healing process, making fatal wounds tricky.

Veth placed her hand on mine. "Thank you," she whispered.

I stood and then nodded at the Copper Jackals' leader. The world around me wobbled, her half-fey beauty blurring. I steadied myself on the bed. "Someone had to," I said.

"Rest here as long as you need."

I started to nod again but thought better of it. "Thanks, but I'm fine," I lied.

Veth frowned, and the sharp angles of her face softened.

"You worry too much," I said, keeping my hand on the edge of the bed. Sure of myself, I let go but stumbled with my second step. Marus placed a steadying hand on the small of my back and took my hand in the other.

"You really should rest," he whispered, guiding me out of the room.

"And lose this bit of freedom?"

"My quarters before you go," Malik interrupted outside the doorway.

I sighed.

Malik likely wanted to discuss me joining the Copper Jackals. Again. But it'd be after he saw to it that each injured member's family was informed of their status. It could be hours before he was ready to talk.

"Find me at the Sleeping Alligator," I said, waving him off.

His sharp glare cut through the blurry haze. Before he could argue, I started down the hall, Marus sticking close by and assisting as best he could. He ensured I didn't fall but knew better than to hover like a mother hen.

Even with his help, my balance failed me, and I stumbled into a wall. If anyone saw me, they would likely think I'd had one drink too many and that Marus was helping me home. Only a few people knew about what I did for the Copper Jackals, and it was better that way. Having the entire city beg the resident Divine to heal them would be hard to hide from Klareth.

Getting down the steps outside the guildhall tested me; it had to be Ahrea's luck that I didn't tumble down them. *Or maybe I should thank Marus.* He stopped me a few times and made me wait until I was steady before moving down another step.

"You should take it easy," Marus said.

"That's what Esteban's tavern is for." A drink would dull the throbbing in my head.

Marus groaned and continued to follow for a few minutes before asking, "Are you sure you'll be all right?"

My balance steadied on the level street, and the cool air eased the dizziness and my pounding head. "I feel better by the minute."

His brow pinched together, but he conceded. "I'll be at the library if you need me."

I nodded and suspected it was only because I'd be with Esteban that he'd relented.

Keeping my focus on putting one foot in front of the other, my mind continued to clear from the intense healing, and the relentless itch of lightning had dampened. Lethal wounds always drained the buzzing energy from the power I'd been gifted.

The Sleeping Alligator came into view, but coming out of a nearby restaurant was Klareth's husband, Roan Beris. His coppery hair shone in the lamplight of the street. He held the hand of a smiling child. In the dark, I couldn't be certain if it was an orphan from the temple.

I ducked into the alley between the tavern and the blacksmith before he spotted me.

Roan blocked any further view of the child, gesturing as they headed toward the temple. Klareth often liked to treat her favorites to meals outside of the bland food within the temple but didn't always have time to do so herself, and she often asked her husband to do so in her stead. That was most likely what he'd been doing.

They rounded a corner, and I waited an extra minute before peeking out of the alley and dashing for the Sleeping Alligator.

I pushed on the door of the tavern and met resistance, so I squeezed through the crack, tumbling into a muscled chest. Stepping back, I recognized the broad-shouldered member of the Copper Jackals who often worked for Esteban. He bore a copper pin of a jackal's head on his open tunic, which revealed muscled dark brown skin.

He smiled down at me and said, "Careful. Wouldn't want you to piss off the wrong guy."

I smiled back. "Peacekeeping for Esteban tonight?"

He nodded, scanning the tavern patrons who were drinking, dancing, and eating their fill. "If Esteban didn't offer such a nice deal, it'd be a different story."

A fight broke out on the other end of where we were, and the broad-shouldered man darted off. Over his shoulder he shouted, "Be careful, girlie."

Esteban's tavern was very . . . dwarven.

The interior and furnishings were mostly iron. A large forge stood in the far corner like a fountain of molten iron, giving the space a perpetual smoky, metallic scent. A couple of dwarves stood in front of the forge, crafting steins for the bar. The forge functioned the way a fireplace would in an average tavern, only it was far more dangerous.

I sat at the iron countertop. Esteban wandered over a moment later, stepping up behind the counter on the landing that had been built for dwarves and gnomish alike. His brown-red beard speckled with gray hairs was braided, with a decorative bead holding it together at the bottom. He studied me. "You look like you've had a shit night, girl." He pushed a wineglass in front of me that had a familiar berry-sweet scent.

I beamed at it, taking the drink. The wine was a special brew he'd made for me. He claimed it was too sweet for his average clientele, but he'd used his skill with dwarven ale making to craft the decadent vintage.

I gulped down the first swallow of the smooth, tart wine. "And you're looking as lovely as ever."

"You're pale," he said.

I waved off his concern. "I'm always pale."

He frowned.

I took another long drink. "I didn't sleep much," I lied.

Esteban scoffed, wiping down the counter. "Take care of yourself, girl. I don't have much I care for."

My eyes dropped to the red-berry wine swirling in the wineglass. Esteban was the closest I had to family aside from my aunt and cousin, strange as it was. He used to belong to a performing troupe that visited every year for the Lunar Dream festival in the winter before my parents passed. Happenstance brought us back together. Those simpler days were long gone, but I still held those childhood memories close to my heart.

"I'll avoid any undo recklessness," I said.

He rolled his golden-brown eyes. "Direct some of that reckless behavior at freeing yourself from that temple, and live your life, girl."

Before I could reply, the kitchen staff called Esteban away.

I sipped the wine, letting the sweetness coat my mouth before swallowing, and tried not to think about what he'd said. As the Tempest, I wasn't sure I'd ever be free.

I spun around, surveying the tavern patrons. My white-haired acquaintance—the magnate who supplied the Copper Jackals—was nowhere to be seen, and I sighed. Keiran and I only got to see each other when we happened to cross paths in the tavern, but it'd been a few weeks since I last saw him.

Leaning back against the counter in my seat, I finished the wine. Looks darted my way here and there. I flashed them a thin-lipped smile, and their eyes wandered away with expressions of embarrassment. I doubt they had expected me to notice them.

A barmaid with dark braided hair filled my glass, and I savored another sip, the sweetness warming my throat and spreading as it went down.

A man slid onto the stool beside me and whistled, and I shot him a glare, straightening.

He grinned, crinkling his twisted nose. He looked as though he needed a bath. "And I thought it was just the dwarven ale that was good." He slurred his words, and from how he grappled the counter to stay upright, I could tell he'd had a few too many. He took in a slow eyeful, his gaze lingering on my chest.

An arm wrapped around my waist from the other side. I yelped, drawing attention from a few nearby patrons, who quickly went back to their drinks and conversations with their companions.

The man with the twisted nose stepped closer.

I wriggled in the grasp of the sour-breathed man who'd grabbed me, and glanced toward the kitchen, but there wasn't anyone there.

Lucky for the intoxicated men, the storm inside was a dull thrum against my skin and not a threat to them. Unlucky for me.

"You're a pretty thing," the man holding me said.

I elbowed him, and his grip loosened enough for me to slide out of my seat. I stepped away, but one of them grabbed me from behind, their grasp pinning my arms at my sides. A hand slid toward my breasts, and nausea built in my stomach.

A shaggy-haired man stepped in front of me—the sour-breathed man. His rough fingers brushed against my cheek, and his eyes stilled as they met mine. Mismatched eyes weren't common, after all. I used his pause to try to kick him between the legs, but he pressed himself against me before I could. He grinned, revealing a missing tooth as his gaze shifted from my deep blue eye to the burnt umber one. "Be a sweetheart and play with us."

Between the drinks I'd had and my waning energy from healing a lethal wound, my physical strength wasn't at its peak. I tried slipping my hand to the dagger I kept strapped to my thigh, but it wasn't there. *Dammit, I didn't grab it before leaving the temple.*

"It doesn't look like she's enjoying herself." I peered over the man's shoulder to the savage-laced voice.

My gaze met his, and I couldn't look away.

Eyes the color of dark storm clouds ready to burst reminded me so much of the tempest that writhed in my body and under my skin, waiting to break free—I hated the color for that but found myself trapped in them all the same. His gaze promised violence.

The shaggy-haired man's calloused fingers ran along my cheek again, and I jerked away.

From behind me, the stale alcohol on the other man's breath carried his words. "Mind your business, asshole."

Those storm-cloud eyes darkened, and he stalked forward, a wolf in a den of prey. Each step he took was full of deadly intent.

They released me and both scurried off, seeming to finally notice the promise in his voice and eyes. The one with the twisted nose tripped, stumbling to the floor, and his friend abandoned him.

I turned back to the man who had saved me. No, not *saved*. He'd simply scared off the brutes. I didn't need to be saved.

"A thank-you would be nice," he said, taking the drunkard's seat next to me and placing an iron mug on the counter. Lamplight gleamed off his artfully messy dark hair.

"Excuse me? I didn't ask you to do anything."

The corners of his lips rose, lazy and full of arrogance. "But didn't you? It would have been a shame if those men had their way with you." He paused, but when I didn't respond, he added, voice smooth like decadent chocolate, "The name is Caelus, by the way. Since you still haven't asked."

I blinked a few times, not sure what to say.

"The tavern keep and you seem to be on good terms."

It was common knowledge that Esteban and I were close. I'd never seen this man before, and I certainly would have remembered him for his looks alone. "Everyone around here knows that Esteban isn't *just* a tavern keep. Anyone who thinks less of him is either crass or uneducated."

His smile changed. Some of that arrogance slipped and filled with warmth. He was handsome, with high cheekbones and a sharp jawline. Before he could catch me staring, I took another drink.

"And you're clearly not of the uneducated sort," he mused, playing with the rim of his mug.

"Clearly."

"And what can I call the woman who is clearly not of the uneducated sort and who didn't ask for my help and is the most beautiful person in the room?"

My mouth would have fallen open if I hadn't filled it with another sip of wine. I swallowed hard. "Excuse me?"

His gaze swept over me, that smile still in place. "I'm asking for your name." He gestured to the room and said, "But before I came to be in your company, anyone who hasn't been otherwise occupied has admired you. Even those who *were* otherwise occupied stole a glance."

"And how do you know that?"

He leaned in and whispered, "I watched them as you stumbled in."

"So, you're a stalker?"

He laughed, the sound rich and inviting, and my chest tightened. I hated his laugh. Not because of the warm sound, but because I wasn't allowed these moments. Klareth kept me at her whim in the temple. Experiencing pleasant, flirty moments was near heart wrenching, knowing my life wouldn't—*couldn't*—be normal.

"Some might say so," he said finally. "I'd like to think I'm simply quite . . . perceptive."

"That's a fancy way of saying you enjoy watching people."

He shrugged and sipped from his cup. "Perhaps. Do you often visit the tavern? Or is it to see the owner?" he asked.

"That's quite the personal question for someone you just met."

"Fair enough," he said, scanning the room. He smiled. "What about your favorite food? Harmless enough?"

A laugh escaped at the absurdly basic question. "I suppose. I love sweets. Especially chocolate. The baker on Copper Alley makes the best chocolate-filled pastries."

From the corner of my eye, a familiar head of ebony hair that fell in dark curtains around a square face came closer, and my smile fell. *Alissa.* Klareth's assistant.

My heart sped up, but Alissa turned and walked to the far side of the tavern, shooting glares at anyone who was too close. The rapid beating eased for the moment. *Did she notice me?* I couldn't take any chances. She may be on the other side of the room, but after what Caelus said about people admiring me, I didn't want to take any chances.

I jolted up and reached out for the counter to keep steady, my head spinning again. Esteban must have changed how he brewed the wine and made it stronger. I only made it a handful of steps before I tripped. Caelus's hand wrapped around my arm and pulled me against his warm, hard chest. The act sent my vision whirling, but it was Caelus who led me closer to the exit and, subsequently, closer to Alissa.

"Running off?" he asked in a teasing tone.

I peeked around him. I'd lost Alissa in the group of patrons. "Not exactly."

He watched my gaze shift back to him. "Then running from someone?" He was so close. The smell of leather, spring rain, and citrus broke through the stuffy tavern air. His breath caressed my cheek, and it sent warm little tingles through my body. *When did he get this close?*

"More like avoiding. For now."

Something flashed across his eyes that I didn't catch before he was closer, his lips on the verge of brushing against mine. "Perhaps I can help?" he asked.

I blinked, my body too warm. "H-help?"

"I'm rather good at making escapes, my lady."

"Don't call me that," I hissed. "If anyone heard you, they might think poorly of you. The High Houses aren't exactly beloved here."

Caelus smiled lazily. "Of course. We wouldn't want that." He peeked over his shoulder, then turned back to me. "But you're running out of time if you want my help."

I tried to look past him, but it was impossible. He was too close, and his broad shoulders blocked prying eyes. It was an oddly sweet gesture for a total stranger.

I clenched my hands against my sides, and my gaze landed on Caelus again. He watched me with intense dark eyes, waiting.

Alissa didn't always inform Klareth. Why did I even care if she caught me? It wouldn't be the first time, but I didn't want to take the chance of being subjected to hours of torment either. Maybe it was because I knew I shouldn't be here. Was I running from the loneliness in my room at the temple? Before I could talk myself into being reckless and staying, I nodded.

Caelus didn't waste any time leading me out of the tavern. He glanced over his shoulder once more, and I wondered how he knew whom I was avoiding. He pulled me to his side after a moment and headed straight for the exit, not even bothering to stick to the edges of the crowd. I stiffened as we snaked through the throng of people.

He must have noticed when my muscles tensed, because he leaned down and said, "It's easier to go unnoticed when you're one of many."

We were approaching the exit when suddenly I heard, "Eira? Is that you?"

Caelus intercepted her, and I ducked into a nearby broom closet. I heard him say, "My, I never expected to see someone as lovely as you here tonight. Care to sit with me?"

Alissa didn't say anything for a moment. I wondered what kind of expression he got from a line like that. My mouth dried at the thought. I had no claim to him. Alissa wasn't one to swoon over a man simply because of some pretty words and a pretty face, though.

"Excuse me, but I thought I saw a friend," Alissa said.

"Oh, you'll have to excuse me, then. I didn't mean to intrude. It seems you were mistaken about your friend." There was a pause. "Let me buy you an apology drink on the chance that I caused you to miss them."

I waited several minutes before popping out of the closet. I turned to make my escape when I came face-first with Malik's chest. Stumbling back a step, I looked up at him. Dark coppery-brown strands of hair fell over his eyes, casting a shadow over the harsh lines of his face and adding to his expression of a man who was forever on the edge of exploding at the first person who said something wrong. Without saying a word, he turned on his heel and stepped outside.

I kept a fair distance as I followed him into the cool night air that calmed my flushed cheeks.

4

Malik led the way to the Temple of Ahrea, only the sounds of nighttime frivolity around us. He walked with his back straight, shoulders tense. *He's pissed.* But was it pissed that I'd left, or was it because I'd gone to the tavern? Knowing him, it could be both.

While Malik—the Second of the Copper Jackals—was revered as well as feared in Dusmir, the only person he listened to was his sister, and Veth could be a pushover for her little brother.

There were stories about his esprit—the soul's magic essence, according to Marus. People whispered that Malik could curse someone with a look or inflict hours of torture in a second. Considering esprit was a reflection of the soul manifested, it made sense, but it scared people as much as it made them respect him.

But Malik protected Dusmir when the king and his council—the Dawn Conclave, made up of the five sworn High Houses—didn't. Though I should say four: the Quinns died in a fire nearly fourteen years ago. He wanted me to join their guild and leave the temple. The high priestess ensured that wasn't possible.

It was a shame the king and the Dawn Conclave opposed the formation of guilds. They made keeping the kingdom safe easier on them. But since they couldn't control the guilds as they did their armies, it likely grated on them. And there was concern the king could change the laws surrounding guilds. Too bad for the king that the guilds made it hard by operating within the law.

He stopped at the temple's limestone steps, and I bumped into him, stumbling back a bit. I smiled sheepishly and ran my fingers through the length of my hair. He crossed his arms, leaning against the stone railing, and I watched a lotus floating in the nearby pond.

"Naomi owes you her life, and I owe you for coming." He sighed. "I've heard Klareth has been extra bitchy lately. You can still leave. Join the guild."

I shook my head. "You know I can't."

His brows pinched together. "Then need I remind you of your promise?" To his credit, Malik kept his tone even.

I bit my inner cheek. "I haven't forgotten."

Malik had been the one to bring Teeg to the temple a year and a half ago. He'd sought me out and demanded that I keep him as far from Klareth as possible. Funny, considering I was the person Klareth kept leashed nearby. Malik wouldn't answer when I'd asked why. Not even Veth would tell me, but I promised all the same.

He faced the empty street, his expression bored despite his tense posture. "A small town to the west reported disappearances. Everyone we found was dead." He kicked a stray rock. "Naomi must have Ahrea's luck to have made it back here alive with that wound."

A bitter taste filled my mouth.

King Olbecht and the High Houses never used any resources investigating the increasing number of disappearances over the past few years, leaving the Copper Jackals and Midnight Wolves to pick up their slack. Neither guild had gleaned much. If only they'd put aside their rivalry and work together, they might make headway in figuring out why.

"Did she come back alone?" I asked.

"Her team is dead, if that's what you're asking."

My hands fell to my sides, and my gaze drifted back to the lone lotus in the pond.

"Go inside. Remember to keep that bit—"

"Watch what you say about the high priestess, Second," came Alissa's sickeningly sweet voice.

She stopped a careful distance from Malik, her face flushed, and I couldn't help but wonder what Caelus had said to her.

Her sharp eyes landed on me. "And you should be in your room or the Chamber of Gods, Tempest."

At least she hadn't seen me at the tavern. Great, now I'd have to thank Caelus. *If I ever see him again.*

"I was just heading inside," I said, taking a step past where Malik leaned against the railing.

He tipped forward, whispering, "Keep the boy safe, Tempest."

I focused on continuing to walk as though he'd said nothing, but my shoulders bore the weight of his request. Every time Malik used my title, I felt like he expected more—like his words were that of the people of Dusmir. *Maybe they are.*

But why did I care what he thought? The people viewed the Divine as beacons of hope. Yet I was as good as helpless, unable to use my abilities to help as often as I wanted because of a bond that leashed me to Klareth. And really, I couldn't use the tempest for anything other than healing people behind Klareth's back.

I wanted to run back into the tavern and enjoy the night. Talk to Caelus. Pretend I could do more. But I endured with heavy steps, until I was inside the large, cold temple and back to my room.

There was no sense in letting myself believe that I could have what everyone took for granted. Not while I was here, and not while Klareth lived. I would be stuck in the temple for decades. My mind wandered to my brief conversation with Caelus. His handsome features and charm lingered until I drifted off.

5

I pushed myself out of bed, my temples throbbing thanks to the wine and lingering effects of healing a lethal wound. Morning light peeked through the sheer curtains, and I winced at the brightness.

A knock came, and without waiting for a response, Alissa entered, her petite frame nearly taken out by the door shutting behind her. She carried various bathing oils and soaps in her thin arms, the same as every morning.

Klareth's assistant proceeded to run hot water and gathered my clothes to help me get ready for the day, as if I were a child unable to bathe and dress myself. I believed she sent Alissa to assess what I'd been up to the night before. Not that Alissa didn't already have an idea.

Before she could step forward to help, I stripped myself bare and headed for the bathing chamber attached to my room. I dipped into the warm water, savoring the heat and letting it seep into my skin. Content to let the water leave me flush and pruned, I leaned my head back.

But Alissa wouldn't have it. She burst in and started washing my hair. It was all I'd let her do, though. Once she finished, I proceeded to clean myself, the sound of splashing water filling the room.

Years ago, I thought maybe Klareth had sent her to give me a friend. The two of us could've almost passed for sisters, aside from her eyes and the shape of her face. I wasn't sure who stopped trying to make idle chitchat first: me or Alissa. But it seemed we had a silent, unspoken agreement that it was better for both of us to get the morning over with as fast as possible.

With a deep breath, I rose from the water. Alissa wrapped a towel around me and fled the room. A moment later, she returned with dark pants and a close-cut tunic for morning training with Selena.

Once dressed, Alissa led me to the training grounds near the courtyard. She left before Selena came into view, deeming me capable of finding the rest of the way on my own. My shoulders relaxed, and I brushed my hand over my long braid.

Selena stood next to the two targets lined up several feet away, a chest full of weapons beside her. Her dark hair was in rows of braids, and sweat glimmered across her warm brown skin. Her soft features were a stunning contrast to the twin swords she wore strapped to her hips and the daggers sheathed along her sides.

Kids who showed promise with esprit were training with acolytes nearby. Teeg broke away from their group to join us. He ran past Selena, who ruffled his curls, before skidding to a stop in front of me.

I hugged him and asked, "Shouldn't you be with your group?"

He gave me a toothy grin. "I'm ahead of all of them."

I glanced at the cluster of kids struggling to manifest their esprit. One's hair stood straight up, and the others laughed. "Stay out of trouble."

He nodded and began practicing with his esprit while Selena launched into a series of warm-up stretches, instructing me to follow along. I bent forward, touching my toes. A small blade lifted from the trunk into the air. A smile tugged on my lips at the use of his esprit, but Selena scolded him. He giggled, growing a vine around her ankles so she couldn't chase him.

I straightened, and Selena glared at him until he retracted the vine. I shot him a look that said, *Behave*, and he rolled his eyes. At least he knew better than to push.

While Teeg practiced and was generally less disruptive, Selena and I finished stretching and started sparring hand to hand.

I got into the stance she'd taught me, and Selena circled me. I waited for her to make a move, for any hint of what she might do. An eye movement or a shift of her hips. Her eyes darted down, and she swept her leg, causing me to tumble to the ground.

"Gotta be faster, Eira," she said, smiling. "And work on your landing. You need to bounce back up."

I pushed myself up, and she described how to absorb the landing so there was less impact. We tried again and again. I lasted longer each time, before she inevitably put me right back on my ass. Bruises were no doubt in my future.

After a short break, Selena gave me a handful of throwing daggers.

"Gotta keep up that skill," she said with a wink.

I lined up to the target several feet away. I pulled in a deep breath and let the blade fly with a flick of my wrist. It hit the center. I repeated with two more, and Teeg applauded.

Selena threw at the target next to mine. Her blades hit their mark but sank deeper into the target than my own. With a grin, she said, "Esprit makes the difference."

I headed for the target to retrieve the blades. She used her abilities freely, but it was better to keep my own locked tight.

"None of the acolytes can hit the middle!" Teeg called, running up beside me.

"And how do you know that? Aren't the kids supposed to be in classes when the acolytes are practicing?"

His cheeks flushed. "I was headed to class when I saw it!"

I laughed and pulled the blades free. "Of course."

"Why do they train?" he asked.

I bit my inner lip and debated whether he was too young to learn about the Abyss. "Because sometimes creatures from the Abyss slip through to Marunia."

He sucked in a breath. "What's that?"

Of course he'd want to know more. "Marunia is our realm, and the Abyss is a place of monsters," I said, walking across the training yard toward Selena.

"That sounds fake."

"Monsters from the Abyss are very real," Selena said, joining us. She rolled up her sleeve, revealing a jagged scar.

His eyes widened.

"Now, get back to your practice before you get in trouble, kiddo," Selena said.

Teeg nodded and started manipulating water while creating invisible barriers of air around those he wanted to protect from being soaked.

Selena held out a sword to me.

I raised a brow. "Is today special or . . . ?"

Selena smiled. "Take the damn sword before I change my mind."

She usually stuck to daggers after I'd slashed her leg by accident with a sword. She must have gotten over it, so I took the blade.

I got into position, and she came up behind me, adjusting my stance and widening my feet. Then she ran me through drills. *No sparring, then.* I frowned but performed the defensive techniques without complaint. Selena went on and on about how proper form made a difference in both power and stability. Once I'd gotten the pattern down, she joined. "You won't have time to think in an actual fight. Hone the muscle memory now, and you'll thank me later."

It was close to lunch when we started cooldown stretches.

Coated in sweat and feeling like I needed another bath didn't dampen the otherwise calm tranquility inside me, thanks to the physical release. That inner sense of normalcy brought me back to what Malik said the night before. It wasn't new for him to distrust Klareth, but it was rare for him to explicitly say so. Usually, it came out in his tone or choice of words.

Then there were the doors to the Chamber of Gods being open and that strange pull, as though I needed to go inside. *Could the two be related?* It would be a stretch, and Malik had no way of knowing about it. Whatever his concerns were had to be due to what happened to Naomi.

A crash caused me to jerk up from my bent position. In the corridor connected to the courtyard, an acolyte crouched over a slew of broken dishes at their feet. She was apologizing profusely to someone while frantically swiping up the bits of broken ceramic. I left Selena to assist the acolyte before she shredded her hands.

"Let me help." I bent down and gathered pieces of a broken plate.

"Did you make it back before being caught?"

I glanced up right at Caelus. My eyes widened, and a broken chunk fell from my fingers. What was he doing here?

"Tempest! You needn't worry. I can take care of this," said the acolyte, not paying any mind to the man beside me.

I stopped the acolyte from grabbing a sharp piece. "Go get a broom, please."

She nodded and darted down the hall.

"Tempest? Well, it's better than nothing," he said, a hand on his hip.

I stood, facing him. The way the midday light caused his dark gray eyes to glitter as if they were storm clouds streaked with lightning didn't infuriate me as much as I expected. Instead, I found myself enamored.

"Unless you plan on telling me your name now?" he asked.

That broke my stupor, and my face flushed. There was no way he didn't notice. "Don't talk openly about last night. And why are you here?"

He held up a tome on the history of runes as if that answered my question. Most people went to the small athenaeum in the city for books, so why was he here? "The temple library requires permission to view their books."

He smiled. "I know."

I shot him a questioning look. In the past seven years I'd lived here, no one had received access to the records and tomes kept inside the temple other than the priests and acolytes.

A string of curse words followed by a slam against the stone floor of the corridor drew my attention. "Marus!" I called.

He leaned against the wall, clutching his foot.

Selena entered the corridor, and her musical laugh echoed throughout it.

I ran over to him, but he was glaring at where Selena stood. Embedded in his foot was a two-inch piece of ceramic. Blood seeped from the wound at a slow pace. Below him was a book, a drop of blood now on the hardcover.

"Gods, help me. Why is the floor covered in broken ceramic?" His eyes were fuming.

"Stop squirming. I need to pull this out."

"Ah. Yes. So I can bleed onto the poor book some more."

A hand dipped down, grabbing the book. I turned, and Caelus was next to me. I hadn't even noticed that he had followed.

"Good. You two have met. Now, if you'd be a dear, this pain is quite unbearable."

I rolled my eyes. "It's not killing you." *Wait. He knows Caelus?*

"He's holed up in a library all day," Selena said behind us. "A tap on the shoulder probably hurts him."

Marus gave her a look that might have been frightening if it were anyone else.

Selena giggled. "I'll go find some bandages."

I started to pull the shard from Marus's foot, but he grabbed my wrist and shook his head. "At least get me somewhere comfortable before you go poking and prodding."

I smiled and pulled one of his arms over my shoulder to support him.

"Let me," Caelus said, pulling his other arm over his shoulder.

"I can get him to the library. You can continue with your business."

"Seeing as my business is with your friend and he favors the library, I believe I'll continue assisting him."

My cheeks flushed, and together, we helped Marus hobble to the library. It was clear after a few steps that nothing I was doing was truly helping, though. Caelus took over most of Marus's weight even while keeping the book he'd been carrying tucked underneath an arm.

I didn't know what to make of Caelus and his sudden appearance at the temple. Much less that he and Marus would be working together. Would he tell someone we met at Esteban's tavern last night?

Once in front of the library, I broke away and held the doors open for the two of them. Marus scrambled for his favorite worn couch and lay down, propping his injured foot up on the arm.

Caelus sat in the armchair and opened the book he'd been carrying.

Marus covered his eyes with the back of his arm, looking so much like a damsel in distress that I wanted to laugh. I stepped around and examined his wounded foot. The amount of blood seeping from the wound made it seem serious, but the small bit of ceramic was barely wedged into the flesh. It'd take almost nothing to heal. There would be no need for bandages, so I pulled the shard free.

"What happened to giving warnings?" Marus whined.

I smiled. In my mind, that thread of life appeared, connecting Marus and I. Arcs of azure energy slithered free from my fingers, reaching for the minor cut, and the flesh started mending together.

"Divine power," Caelus murmured beside me.

I jolted, the lightning falling free. There hadn't been a sound indicating he'd moved, let alone come to stand beside me. Thankfully, the cut had healed enough that it was no longer bleeding.

The way Caelus looked at me was different. He didn't appear afraid of it—more like intrigued instead—but lines of confusion were present on his forehead. I wanted to ask what he was thinking, but it seemed inappropriate since we barely knew each other.

A bell tolled, signaling that it was after lunch.

"Shit," I said. *I'm late.*

Marus peeked out from under his arm. "Hurry, Eira."

"Watch over him," I said to Caelus. "He can be a bit of a baby when he's injured."

"That's no way to speak of your friends!"

One corner of Caelus's lips lifted in a lazy smirk.

I smiled and turned to leave. Caelus's stare warmed my back, and it took all my will to keep walking. "As you wish, *Eira.*"

6

A few days later, I darted through the corridors, morning light sifting through the windows. Gods, why had Alissa let me oversleep? I was running late. *Again.* Hopefully, Klareth would be late too. From time to time, matters in the temple would call for her attention, and while she hated it, as high priestess, it couldn't be helped if she was late occasionally.

Rounding a corner, I skidded to a stop before I ran face-first into Caelus.

"It seems your tardiness is becoming a habit, Eira," he said.

"Sorry." As much as I wanted to ask him about how he came to be Marus's research assistant, I didn't have time. That didn't wholly stop me from taking one quick second to admire the way the sun lit his eyes to a lighter gray and the way his dark clothes, with their dark red-orange accents, clung to his muscular body. I forced myself to step around him.

A hand wrapped around my arm, pulling me to a gentle stop and sending a thrill along my bare skin. "Trying to run away again?" he asked.

I turned, face-to-face with him. "Late, not away." *It isn't quite a lie, at least.*

Caelus glanced up over my head, and I swiveled around to look in the same direction. A second later, the rustles of Klareth's robes and the click of her heels against stone sounded. She stalked through the hall toward us, and I tried to pull away from Caelus to go to her, but he wouldn't budge.

Klareth grabbed my other arm. Her fingers dug into my skin, her touch not giving the same heady thrill that Caelus's had. Her face was neutral, but her angry red neck gave her away. She attempted to yank me along with her, but Caelus's grip kept me in place.

My face heated.

Caelus glared at her, and his grip tightened but didn't hurt.

Klareth narrowed her eyes at the sight of his hand on my other arm.

I looked between the two of them, and my face burned hotter. It was probably a bit selfish, but I didn't want him to know how horrible she could be. I tugged the arm Caelus was holding. His eyes met mine, and I wasn't sure what he saw in them, but he gave me a small nod and released me.

Klareth took the opportunity and pulled me along with her. I looked back and shot Caelus an apologetic half smile and shrugged. Klareth yanked my arm, forcing me to face forward, and

I could feel his gaze piercing my back.

"And good day to you, too, high priestess," he called.

Klareth remained silent on our trek through the temple to the secluded chamber that contained the grand statue of Ahrea. The chamber was for those who wished to seek her guidance in solitude. Beneath Ahrea's statue was a hidden stairwell that led down to the Pools of Divinity—one of several allegedly divine pools of water across the kingdom.

With each step down into the sacred cavern, Klareth's fingers tightened their hold, as if she hoped to brand my skin.

We reached the bottom of the stairs, and she released me, leaving red indents behind. Man-made steps that led down into the pool were several feet away. The water cast us and the rocky walls in a turquoise luminescence, but the shade made Klareth look sickly.

Her eyes narrowed on me. I remained still, body tense. She circled me for a moment, taking in every detail.

I'd gotten dressed in a rush, and my clothes weren't the usual silk Klareth insisted on. She'd said because the gods deserve the opulence, but I found it to be a waste of otherwise fine fabric. I doubted the gods cared about the clothes I wore. But within the pool was considered the closest to the gods Divine could be.

"Strip," the high priestess commanded.

Dumbfounded, I stared at her. I couldn't have heard her right. "Here?"

"You certainly can't go into the pool wearing those ratty clothes."

I wanted to avoid a repeat of a few nights ago, so I removed my clothing, placing them neatly on a nearby rock, and waited for her next command while fighting the urge to cover my breasts.

"Step into the water. Meditate. Try to *hear* the gods for once."

It was the same thing she always ordered, but I'd received nothing from the gods besides my gift. I stepped into the ever-warm water, and bubbles prickled against my skin. I made my way in until the water came just above my breasts.

She remained along the rocky edge of the pool. Never touching the water. Never stepping inside. The pool was a haven in that way.

Closing my eyes, I took a deep breath in, letting it slowly release through my mouth, and focused on the bubbles against my skin, letting my thoughts drift away.

I wasn't sure how much time passed, with only the sound of water flowing into the pool from a small waterfall and the occasional drip from the stalactites echoing throughout the cavern.

Footsteps descended the stairs into the cavern. A moment later, Roan asked, "Anything?"

"Of course not. She'd be better off a whore than one chosen by the gods," Klareth huffed.

Lightning tickled my fingertips, and I opened my eyes, facing the waterfall. *No, no. Not now.*

The heavy stare of Klareth and her husband bore into my back.

"And her 'gift' is as volatile as ever," Roan murmured. His heavy footsteps receded up the stairs.

My shoulders tensed. I took another deep breath in and held it before releasing it. A calm mind kept the lightning at bay. I did my best to push Klareth's comment away and out of my mind. I wasn't sure how long had passed, but soon the ruffle of robes and clicking steps withdrew, leaving me alone.

Klareth's comment rushed back in. *Better off a whore.* I'd never lived up to her expectations of a Divine. Perhaps she was right, but that wasn't the life I'd been given. And when I didn't live up to her expectations, she found gratification in my punishments.

I let out a sigh and ran my arm through the water. *Is Caelus with Marus now?* Marus's foot would still be sore since I'd been interrupted while healing him. I smiled. They'd probably be arguing since Marus and pain did not mix well—not that a librarian often experienced many injuries.

My thoughts drifted to the sacred water. In history, the Divine came to the pool for guidance, but nothing ever came to me. The water was always warm and inviting, yet they never pushed me closer to the gods like Klareth wanted.

The high priestess wanted proof that I was connected to the gods—that I was truly Divine, as if my power wasn't proof enough. She said it would be even better if I spoke with one directly, and demanded that I ask if the gods had abandoned us. Klareth refused to answer when I asked why. More than once, she'd punished me for questioning her. Marus believed her curiosity was because of the state of the realm, but I wasn't so sure.

Even so, I tried, fruitless as it may be. My questions for the gods went further than what she wanted to know, though. Why had I ended up bound to her? Why wouldn't they protect me from her punishments? How long would they let the High Houses continue to ignore the needs of the people?

Take heart. The wolf of the moon's shadow is with you.

I stilled.

Careful not to disturb the water, I scanned the cavern. There wasn't anyone there. "I must be hearing things now," I murmured.

The gods had never spoken before. Now wouldn't be any different.

The sound of the waterfall filled the space, and one hour turned into two. Then three. Finally, Alissa retrieved me. She had a sleeveless gown in tow. I slipped it on and hurried out of the cavern. She asked if I had any news, and I shook my head. The gods didn't care now, if they hadn't in all these years.

My stomach grumbled thanks to a missed lunch and no pity from Alissa. I sat in an oversize armchair, legs tucked underneath me, in the small study I'd been given, waiting for Marus. Normally, he would already be present for my lessons on prophecies. Klareth thought it might help me connect with the gods. But he hadn't arrived yet.

Peacebloom tea sat on the round table in front of me, floral notes wafting into the air, but it was too hot to be enjoyable. I leaned my head back against the chair and closed my heavy eyelids. While all I'd done was soak in the Pools of Divinity, waiting for an answer that wouldn't come, exhaustion had still bored its way into my bones.

The door opened, causing the air to stir with citrus. I sat up, and Caelus walked in with a large stack of papers in his arms.

My eyes widened, and I flushed at the sight of him.

"Marus sent me." He smirked, the look far too mischievous to be innocent. "Claimed his foot was killing him." Caelus plopped down a tower of pages on the table between us. "He also told me to bring this," he said, pulling out something wrapped in cloth.

I took it, the sweet scent of chocolate coming from within, and unwrapped it carefully. The decadent filling oozed out from the center. I wasted no time and picked it up, savoring the delicious and milky-smooth sweetness.

"You're eating rather . . . voraciously," he said, taking a seat on the small faded couch.

My cheeks burned, and I placed the remainder of the pastry back onto the cloth and wiped my mouth. "I missed lunch," I said, wrapping the rest carefully.

He watched as if it were the most interesting thing he'd ever seen.

"How exactly are you helping Marus?" I asked.

He raised a brow. "From what little time I've spent with him, I thought you two were close."

"We are."

Caelus eyed me, but I couldn't quite read his expression. "He placed a request to the king for a temporary assistant for help with researching and learning to use runes."

An icy chill filled my veins at the mention of runes, and my hand went to my wrist to fight it, rubbing the smooth skin. Klareth employed runes as her favorite method of punishment.

His annoyingly *perceptive* eyes flicked to the hand on my wrist. "The request claimed it was to help the Divine in Dusmir. Far be it from the king to deny a request involving the Tempest."

I forced my hand from my wrist and onto the armrest. "So, are you an expert on them?"

"It's a subject I've researched for Prince Alpheus."

My eyes widened. "You know the prince?"

He sighed and his gaze fell to my messy oak desk. "The prince would likely call the two of us friends, but I never know what he's thinking." Before I could ask more about their relationship, he said,

"But runes require a soft and elegant touch. I'm sure you're familiar." He winked at me.

My face flushed, burning away the chill from before.

Caelus's lips twitched up, but he didn't give me a chance to ask what that meant. "The Tempest is often associated with trials that bring about great change. Why are you cloistered to the temple, *Eira*?"

The way he said my name caught me off guard. His mouth took its time forming the word, as if he savored it. He'd said it with such care and thoughtfulness.

My mouth wouldn't form words. Not that there was a good answer to that question. Certainly not an easy one.

Having Klareth bonded as my pseudo-*tenebrae* kept me here, but it wasn't common knowledge. A Divine's *tenebrae* was a protector. They were rare, another gift from the gods. The bond she'd forced on me was from a ritual—unlike a true *tenebrae* bond—and protected her more than me.

"My Divine 'gift' came later in my life than what's typical," I said finally. "At least, so says Marus. For now, it seems best to keep away from crowds." My cheeks reddened at the accidental admission of my fear and the half-truth.

He stood. "Fearing your power only gives it control over you. Claim it."

I glanced at the door beyond him, not ready for him to leave. "Do you struggle with the power from esprit?"

He smirked. "I used to." He pushed one of the pages toward me. "This prophecy is a favorite in Ryseer. Some believe it has already come and gone. I've always found it intriguing."

I looked at the recorded prophecy. It was from five hundred years ago. How could it not have passed already?

I glanced up to ask Caelus, but he was already gone. All that remained was the faint waft of citrus. I hadn't heard him leave.

I turned my attention back to the slip of paper. It was a handful of lines that meant . . . nothing.

> *Jaded and lost, seeking gold.*
> *Full of Abyssal ire and seeking dominion.*
> *Dreams of the unknown follow.*
> *Nations fall in flame without resolve.*
> *To quell it, one must strike stone and restore*
> *the balance of harmony and chaos.*
> *Only with fortune's favor, dawn's light, and*
> *the moon's shadow could all be saved.*

I frowned, thinking back to all my history lessons.

Before the current kingdom, the nation fell and was rebuilt by King Calbert after he'd slain Efrain and united the continent under one kingdom. It had been on the dawn of the summer solstice. Efrain's mind had given way to madness—many thought through influence from the Abyss. He'd lost himself to it and only cared about gaining power. The prophecy fit. Did people think that it referred to something else? Something that was to come?

I read the prophecy over and over until I had it memorized.

Teeg found me when it was time for dinner, and he dragged me along with him to the dining hall to sit with him and Tryssa.

7

I saw Caelus in passing over the next couple of weeks, but other than simple pleasantries, there was never enough time to ask him about that prophecy or why anyone would believe it.

Some part of me shouldn't have hoped for him to return to my study during my lessons, if only to chat for a moment or two. Partly because I had questions, but I also enjoyed his company. It helped that he was nice to look at too.

The alabaster statues of the gods stared down at me once again. I sat on a small ornate pillow in the Chamber of Gods, legs tucked underneath me, tingling with numbness. Moonlight poured in from the glass ceiling above, and the incense left the air muggy. The prophecy still sat in the back of my mind, and I hoped sitting among the statues might provide . . . something.

Nothing came.

"Silent meditation doesn't suit you."

I whirled around in the direction of the voice from where I knelt.

Clad in black, Caelus strolled toward me. He wore a deep crimson tunic tucked into his pants underneath his black coat. The color complemented him. His eyes met mine. I loathed how the moonlight caused his eyes to glitter like levin-streaked storm clouds, but I couldn't look away from them. "Sneaking up on people is frowned upon," I said.

"My apologies, Tempest. I thought you heard me."

I gave him a confused look, and he laughed.

"Calling me *Tempest* doesn't suit you either. Why the formality? No one else is here."

"True."

Not really an answer. I rolled my eyes and looked at the statue of Ahrea. Her expression always appeared sad to me. "The prophecy you had me read . . . why would people believe it hasn't come to pass?"

"There are whispers of it in Ryseer. Perhaps because it's the capital. Perhaps because King Olbecht isn't always known for his kindness."

I faced him. He was staring at Oerban, hands in his pockets. No one in Dusmir complained about the king. Were we that far removed, or had we simply forgotten because the Dawn Conclave didn't care for those under their charge?

His gaze fell to me again. "You seem shocked."

"I just didn't expect that."

He faced the gods again. "Everything here is . . . different from the royal city."

"Tell me about Ryseer."

He mused for a moment. "It's lovely. There's a cliff overlooking the sea and the city. Children play in the white sands along the coastline. The river that flows through it is the clearest blue." His eyes darkened when he turned to me. "Your left eye reminds me of it."

My face flushed, and I focused on Ahrea, hoping to hide it. I knew if I looked at him, he would be smiling. Deep down, I cursed myself for feeling flustered. Maybe it was because I wanted to stare at him more often than not. Except for when my face was likely red as a tomato.

"Any burning questions?" The amusement in his tone wasn't lost.

I was silent for a moment, hoping I looked thoughtful rather than flustered. "The study of runes. How's it going?"

"Well enough. Though I'm afraid my knowledge is more limited than your good friend hoped."

"Eira!" Klareth shouted.

Blood drained from my face. I knew that tone. Slowly, I stood and turned to face her. Her hair was spun tightly atop her head. Even from so far, I could see the fire in her eyes. Today was a special kind of livid—one she reserved for me.

Caelus's stare was a brand on the back of my neck.

Her eyes darted from me to Caelus, that rage burning hotter. "Leave us," she said, her fiery gaze never leaving his.

He started to walk past but swiveled on a heel and reached out, twirling a strand of my hair around one of his long, elegant fingers. "It's quite the honor, I hear, to even stand before you, Tempest." Knowing flashed through his storm-cloud eyes. But he couldn't know what she was about to do, could he? Then there was question and concern in those eyes—neither of which I could answer.

Klareth's hands clenched, and her jaw flexed. She was no longer hiding her emotions well.

There was no way out of this. "If you'd be so kind, we'd like some privacy," I said, voice barely a whisper.

His forehead pinched together, and my hair slipped from his fingers.

He stood there, eyes never leaving mine, as though he was still searching for something in them. Gods, I begged he would listen and leave. But if he didn't . . . I pushed away the thought.

I wasn't sure if he'd heard me, but he finally said, "Apologies." He pivoted, heading for the exit. From the door, he added, "I'll see you later."

Those four words. I knew he meant them. I watched his retreating back, my stomach knotting. Those words made some useless part of me hope he would stop what was to come.

But he disappeared through that doorway.

Klareth stalked forward, her shoes clicking along the polished mosaic floor. My palms were sweating as I waited for what she might do. Her fingers wrapped around my arm, her nails digging into the flesh, and she dragged me from the Chamber of Gods. I stumbled behind her, struggling to keep upright on my numb legs while Ahrea's sorrowful stare pierced my back.

Luck and freedom had never been my ally.

KLARETH DRAGGED ME BY the arm through the empty late-night halls of the temple toward the abandoned wing. I wasn't sure what had sent her into a rage. Alissa may have waited to tell her about the night she saw me. Or Klareth could have decided that it was the perfect time to punish me for what she perceived as misdeeds. Healing Marus's foot wouldn't have gone unnoticed by her, either, and I knew she would be livid once she learned of it. All mixed with my inability to speak with the gods was a recipe for her wrath.

Teeg called, "Eira! Come pla—" He cut himself off, and his eyes widened at the sight of Klareth yanking me along behind her. She pulled me past him, and his cheeks blanched.

"Your room. Now!" Klareth said to him.

I didn't see if Teeg listened or hear his retreating footsteps. I squeezed my eyes shut. *Please listen.*

We stopped inside an abandoned room on the opposite side of the temple away from the kids' dormitories. Beams along the ceiling had collapsed, and the scent of molded wood filled the air. She closed the door behind us, and my stomach knotted, a sour taste filling my mouth.

She headed for an old dresser next to another door, which looked ready to fall off its hinge. The clank of shackles sounded behind me. "What have you been up to, my dear Eira?" Klareth asked.

It wasn't the first time she'd brought me here, asked me what I'd been up to or what wrongdoings I needed to confess to.

"If you tell the truth and beg, perhaps I'll be generous."

My face flamed at the memories of the times I had apologized and pleaded for her not to place those rune-carved manacles around my wrists.

But I'd never confess to healing those who needed me.

When I didn't answer, she yanked my arms behind me and

fastened the cold iron cuffs around my wrists. Cool sweat ran down my neck, but I didn't fight her. There was no point in it. She'd made sure the tempest within me was useless against her years ago, thanks to that fake *tenebrae*-bonding ritual. Had the Copper Jackals' enchanter known Klareth's intentions all those years ago, when I'd been too young to consent to it? Too young to see the malice tainting Klareth's soul?

I begged the gods who'd made me a Divine for a way out. The gods who gave me a gift that was impossible to control yet impossible to use to save myself because of that poor imitation of a *tenebrae* bond meant to protect me. Surely they didn't condone what was to come. *Right?*

"Tell me. What lies has that scholar's assistant been whispering to you?"

"Lies?" What was she talking about?

"After everything I've done for you, you worthless girl. Going out and attempting to play as if you're one of the gods and healing wounds." She pushed my hair over one shoulder, then ran her long, sharp nails down my neck. "Being late. Fraternizing with that man."

I jerked away from her touch involuntarily. "I haven't done anything," I lied.

Her nails pressed into my neck enough to sting but not enough to draw blood. The runes along the shackles activated, stirring the lightning within me. "I wish I didn't have to do this," she whispered.

The power coursing through me began to writhe. Even though I couldn't see the cuffs, I knew as each rune lit up. The storms within grew more restless and ready to escape with each one. But it wouldn't—couldn't.

"You'd do well to rethink keeping secrets from me."

Lightning crackled across my skin, burning but never marring. No, Klareth couldn't let that happen, or everyone would know. The runes redirected the esprit—letting it free, but not truly.

The arcs snaked up my arm to my neck and down my body. Everywhere burned and it only got hotter, until my insides were molten too. I screamed, the sound ripping through the back of my throat. My knees cracked against the rotting wood floor, and Klareth shoved a cloth in my mouth.

"Think before you're late or run off and heal someone again. Think before pretending you are like the gods." She left, not looking back.

Tears streaked my face, but not just from the pain. The lightning pulsed and throbbed within me. My body writhed helplessly.

Help. I wanted to scream it to anyone who might hear. But I couldn't. Eventually, darkness came.

I awoke briefly from unconsciousness, my mind no longer able to protect me from the boiling pain coursing through every inch of my body, unsure of how much time had passed.

From where I'd collapsed into myself on the floor, I opened my eyes and looked toward the exit. But my mind created the illusion that Caelus was there. His dark, tousled hair had fallen over his forehead, and one side of his full lips was tilted up. Concern quickly replaced that teasing expression. Seeing him caused my heart to race, and I clamped my eyes shut, not wanting to see something so untrue that it was a different kind of pain—the kind that twisted my heart and threatened to rip it out.

It was wishful and pathetic to want him to save me. Wishful to even think he might be able to. I'd lost my chance the moment he left. Yet some deep-seated part of me had wanted him to save me from everything.

But that wasn't the reality. Right now, he would be with Marus in the library. They would be reviewing some sort of research. Probably arguing if Marus's foot was still sore.

But that man. He had interrupted Klareth. Delayed the inevitable like some small gift. Maybe it was a gift—the best the gods could do, or maybe the best they *would* do.

8

Small hands shook me awake, and I peeled open my heavy eyelids and blinked several times before the haze cleared. My temples throbbed, and I caressed my aching head, pushing up off the grimy stone floor with the other hand. The shackles were no longer cuffed around my wrists, and beside me was Teeg. *Had he managed to remove them somehow, or did Caelus?*

"You shouldn't be here," I said, voice hoarse.

Teeg sniffled. "Tryssa's missing. I've looked everywhere for her."

I did my best to give him a reassuring smile. "Go to Marus, tell him she's missing, and stay with him. I'll look for her."

He wrapped his arms around my neck, nearly pulling me over, and squeezed.

I hugged him back and ruffled his hair. "Hurry, before

someone sees you."

He smiled up at me and nodded. He darted off, leaving me alone.

Next to that worn dresser, the door had been left open. An everflame torch shone past it. That tugging sensation washed through me, urging me to go inside, the same as it had when I'd seen the door to the Chamber of Gods open nights ago.

Keeping quiet, I peeked inside. Steps led deep beneath the temple. I made my way down, torches lighting the way, and stepped in a sticky jade-colored puddle with a bare foot. It reminded me of blood, but thicker.

Small beaded green drops were every few steps along the dusty floor. The dark stone walls became rough the farther down I went. At the bottom, limestone had been carved into recesses along the walls and the floor, and there was a sarcophagus in each.

Was this an alternate route into the catacombs? But why?

I continued past the carved recesses. Each held a former servant of the temple. Some were ancient and offered no dates or markings to indicate when they'd died.

Avoiding another green drop, I peered down the narrow hallway. There were two options: left or right. I followed the lit torches to the left.

My nose crinkled at the stench that filled the hall. A strange mixture of sweetness and . . . decay. I tripped on a dip in the floor, cursing the dim torchlight. Using one hand along the wall to maintain my balance, I continued. More of those small jade drops were scattered along the path, and the potent odor of decay grew with each step.

I neared a large alcove with stone doors, and voices filtered through it. I slowed my pace and stepped carefully to keep quiet, unsure of how deep into the catacombs I was and who might be inside them.

One door was slightly ajar, and the faint sound of Klareth's voice came from within. I stilled and tried to remember if she had any deceased family entombed in the temple, but came up blank. I stepped toward the cracked doorway until the voices were clear.

"You've been a nuisance long enough. You're out of luck. Lord Ebonhammer doesn't need you."

Lord Ebonhammer? I knew of him. He was part of the Dawn Conclave from the dwarven city of Tiruhm.

A whimper sounded. "Please. Let me go," Tryssa cried.

My hand curled into a fist against the stone, and my heart raced. I stepped closer, flattening myself against the door.

Tryssa sobbed over what sounded like chains clanking against stone.

I peeked inside.

The room was bathed in a faint green glow that originated from a large jade-like crystal sitting in place of where a sarcophagus would've been. On the back wall, Tryssa was suspended by the same rune-carved manacles Klareth used on me. Tryssa's head hung low, and blood trickled down her chin.

Klareth stood in front of her, a knife in one hand.

Along the walls were other small bodies, broken and bloodied. Had Klareth been killing other children down here? Gods, why? *What's going on?*

I spotted a pedestal near the large crystal. Books, bottles of strange liquid, a dagger, torn papers, and smaller crystals laid atop it. *Rituals?*

Klareth was the high priestess. She would have had to spend years in service to the temple, praying to Ahrea to gain her position.

No matter how I thought of it, I couldn't figure her out. Did this have something to do with why she wanted to know if the gods had abandoned the realm?

Tryssa whimpered again. "Please . . ."

Her broken, begging voice shattered my soul. She was just a teenage girl who wanted to help others, keep things fair. Nothing she ever did truly harmed anyone. I had to do something. But what? The bond wouldn't let me harm Klareth with lightning, and I wasn't confident I wouldn't hurt Tryssa in the process even if I could.

Klareth stepped toward her again and pressed the flat side of the blade beneath her chin, lifting her head slightly. "Quiet. Unlike the Golden Child, you're dispensable."

Golden Child? I'd never heard that before—but I pushed that information aside.

I darted inside. There wasn't time to think of a better plan. Tryssa's gaze connected with mine, and her eyes widened.

"Stop." My voice came out weaker than I wanted, sounding more like a plea than a command.

Klareth turned, lowering the dagger precariously closer to Tryssa's neck. Her eyes lit up with amusement and disdain. "And here I thought you'd be unconscious until morning. How did you remove the shackles?"

"Let her go."

She lowered the blade, tapping her nails against it. "Her soul must be collected. Just like the others."

Collecting souls? I needed to keep Klareth away from Tryssa.

"Please. I'll . . . I'll do anything," I said, stepping closer to them.

Klareth sighed. "You already do everything I want exceptionally poorly. Being blessed as a Divine was wasted on you. But it's what I don't want you doing that is the problem." She held up a pair of the shackles. "Even after using these. It shouldn't have to be this way."

I flinched at the sight of the iron cuffs, and her vicious grin grew. I'd always felt I deserved whatever punishment she doled out for the tiniest of misgivings—for being unable to control my volatile power—after I'd accidentally killed my best friend years ago. But had it been because she hadn't been made Divine? Or was it that she wanted control over one?

Klareth looked at Tryssa again, her lips curling into a snarl. "Until your soul is marked, you will stay in line, or more will follow."

I took another step forward, but before I could respond, Klareth whirled and sliced the blade across Tryssa's throat.

My levin-coated hands flew to my throat, strangling my scream. Tears burned my eyes. Tryssa had been laughing and smiling with Teeg earlier. They'd been happy together, annoying Marus to no end.

I couldn't tear my gaze away. Blood poured from her neck. I shuffled back, bumping into the pedestal, sending books and crystals tumbling to the ground. I jerked around to find the dagger teetering on the edge.

Selena's training kicked in. I grabbed the blade and hurled it at Klareth's heart.

Klareth's mouth opened in shock, her blade slipping from her fingers. Her hand wrapped around the dagger protruding from her chest, but blood blossomed on her robes. Later, I might consider how proud Selena would have been that I had aimed for the heart and hit my mark.

I rushed to Tryssa's limp, bloodied body hanging from the chains. Blood ran from the wound in her throat, no longer spurting as it had been. She wouldn't—couldn't—die.

"I'm so sorry," I said, a sob breaking free.

Tears slipped down my cheeks, and my chest ached at the sight of her. I placed my forehead to hers and my hands on her pale cheeks. *Focus.* I took a deep breath in, holding it for a few seconds before letting it out.

But no matter how hard I tried, her thread wouldn't appear. The healing power couldn't connect to her soul.

"No, no, no," I whispered, running my thumb along her still-warm skin. Her face was losing color, and her eyes had dulled.

Her life was gone, and for what? Because that bitch wanted to prove a point.

I straightened, and my arms fell to my sides, my gaze drifting to where Klareth lay. I'd killed her.

An unfamiliar sorrow had brimmed in her typically hate-filled eyes before her body went still.

What have I done?

People would know something happened when they didn't see her after a day or two. Who would take over her duties? Her husband wouldn't be able to.

And the kids . . . would they know I'd killed her? They wouldn't be wrong to think so, but it was as though I'd proved her right: they *should* fear me.

New tears welled up in my eyes. *What am I going to do?*

"I'm sorry," I said again, and ran from the room, leaving Tryssa's and Klareth's limp bodies.

My bare feet pounded against the dirty catacomb floor, stirring dust into the air. I followed the torches and found the stairs leading out. I ascended the steps by twos, and moonlight peeked in from above. The exit led into the Chamber of Gods. The stares of each alabaster statue pierced through me, and my body froze, meeting each of their judgmental gazes. My chest tightened and the lump in my throat grew.

What did the gods think? Would they strip away my Divine power, leaving me nothing? That's what I'd wanted since I'd killed *him*. But not like this. Not for killing her.

My body shook, and my eyes halted on Ahrea. Tears streamed down my face. "I'm sorry. I-I didn't mean to. I just . . ."

I shook my head and ran. I couldn't stay in that room—couldn't stand to have the gods staring, judging me. Not after killing someone else. I truly wasn't worthy of the gift they'd given me.

I wrenched open the exit and collided with a hard chest. The scent of leather, rain, and citrus surrounded me. I looked up, and Caelus's deep gray eyes stared back. His full lips turned down, and his brows knitted together as he took in my appearance.

"Are you hurt?" Caelus asked, voice low.

I glanced down. Splotches of blood and dust covered my gown, but none of it was mine. Not that he knew. His only concern was whether I'd been hurt. My panicked heart swelled. I shook my head.

His features softened. "Are you okay?"

Fresh tears escaped. I couldn't bring myself to say what happened. It was all too new, too fresh. Tears escalated to sobs, and I buried my face in his chest. I'd killed her for what she'd done. And Tryssa hadn't deserved any of that.

Caelus's arms tightened around me. "You're safe," he said. "Breathe." He rubbed soothing circles along my back.

Safe. I wasn't so sure. The watchful eyes of the gods weighed on me.

He held me until my sobs subsided. Normally, I wouldn't have been comfortable crying into the chest of a man I barely knew, no matter how fond of him I'd grown in such a short time. But it felt *right.* Everything about being held by him had a sensation of *rightness* to it. Maybe later I would consider how wrong it was to want to be held by this man—protected by him—while I cried over everything that had brought me to this point.

His rough hands cupped my tear-streaked face, lifting it to meet his gaze. "What happened?"

The question I was dreading most.

I couldn't possibly tell him I'd killed the high priestess. What would he think of me? I had no idea how he'd react. Even if Klareth had deserved it, was it right?

"Eira?" His voice was gentle. Careful.

Tears stung my eyes once again. I wanted to trust him, but I didn't know him. "I can't."

My vision was blurred, but I didn't miss the hurt that washed over his expression in a blink before it hardened. "You're covered in blood, and you're telling me you're fine? I'm sorry, but that's bullshit. Something happened. Tell me. I can help you."

"I need Marus. Please."

His jaw tensed, but he nodded. "He's in the library. Let's go before anyone wakes."

9

Caelus pushed open the gilded library doors, and we made our way through the rows of shelves. The warm light of the high-hanging chandeliers shone on his hair, revealing that it wasn't quite black, but a dark brown. In the wake of the events in the catacombs, it seemed like an odd thing to notice, but I couldn't tear my gaze away.

I hated not telling him about what had happened. Hated the hurt in his eyes when I'd told him I couldn't. But I knew I could trust Marus in a way that I wasn't sure I could with Caelus.

Voices drew my attention at the back of the library near Marus's private study. One was Marus. And the other was . . . *Gods, not him.*

I tugged Caelus into a shadowy row of shelves and pushed him behind me. I flattened against the shelf and peeked around the corner.

"Where is she?" Roan boomed.

An exasperated sigh escaped Marus, and a book slammed shut. "I already told you I haven't the faintest idea, sir. She was at dinner and then left for her room. After that, your guess is as good as mine."

Caelus's warmth pressed into my back, and he leaned in, whispering, "Is he looking for you?"

I turned and came face-to-face with him. With the slightest movement, our lips would brush against one another. "I don't know," I said.

"And what of my wife?" Roan asked.

"Surely you can keep up with your wife, sir."

"You don't fool me, scholar. Befriending the Tempest wasn't your job. And if you see that worthless excuse for a Divine, alert me. Immediately."

Footsteps stormed toward the row of shelves Caelus and I were between. I pushed him back and flattened myself against the shelf, hiding in the shadows. Caelus pressed his body flush against mine. My heart raced, and it had nothing to do with Roan possibly discovering me—us. Our eyes latched on to one another, and I fought the urge to shove him away and pull him closer all at the same time. The footsteps faded, but Caelus's expression remained unreadable in the shadows.

The doors to the library slammed. I jumped. The shelf wobbled, and a few books clunked to the floor. More footsteps were heading toward us. Caelus didn't move, caging me between him and the shelf.

The footsteps halted. "For gods' sake." Marus let out a deep sigh. "This is a library. Take the foreplay outside!" His voice was harsh, tired.

Caelus pushed away, but his heat lingered. "Sorry to disappoint," he said.

I took a deep breath, inhaling his scent mixed with the musty smell of books, and stepped forward.

Marus's eyes drifted over my blood-covered gown. He headed straight for me. "Eira, what happened?"

I opened my mouth to speak, but nothing came. My eyes drifted to Caelus. What could I say while he was there?

Marus followed my gaze and said, "Follow me before Roan returns." He turned on a heel and faced Caelus. "We'll pick up tomorrow," he said, dismissing him.

Caelus's jaw flexed, but he said nothing and exited the library.

I followed Marus to his private study.

Inside, I stood in front of the couch, unwilling to ruin the fabric with my bloodstained clothes, the fire behind me warm.

He made for a cabinet and pulled out a decanter of whiskey I'd only seen him drink from once before. He poured a glass and offered it to me. I grabbed it by instinct and cradled it in my hands. Marus poured another for himself before nudging me to sit. I obeyed.

Tryssa was gone. Klareth was dead. *I killed her.* And I had no idea what would happen next. Marus sat next to me and wrapped his arm around my shoulder, and silent tears trickled down my cheeks. The amber liquid in the glass sloshed in my trembling hands.

"Tell me you aren't hurt," he said after my shaking eased.

"I'm fine." My words were hollow.

"Drink. Then tell me what happened."

I took a sip of the whiskey and welcomed the warm, bitter burn as it moved low into my stomach. I stared down at the burgundy rug, focusing on a golden lotus sewn into a corner. "Klareth took me for her . . . favorite punishment. Teeg found me and told me Tryssa was missing. I sent him to you." My eyes widened. "Where is he?"

"He's in bed. The late night caught up with him."

I nodded and continued, "I found her. She was in the catacombs with Klareth. She killed Tryssa." Marus's arm tightened around me. "Tryssa's still down there. I tried to heal her, but . . ." I closed my eyes to keep more tears from spilling free.

"I'll have her retrieved."

"I killed Klareth," I blurted out, before I lost the nerve to say it aloud.

He said nothing.

I cast him a sidelong glance. Marus opened his mouth to speak but faltered and instead finished the contents of his glass. He took a deep breath and said, "I didn't expect that. Gods, she had it coming—but if I'm being honest, Eira, there will be ramifications. The temple will be in disarray once the news spreads. Roan is already in an uproar looking for you."

"I know. But what was I supposed to do?" I asked. "And what about the gods?"

Marus sighed and rubbed his hand along my shoulder. "I don't know. But I'll help however I can. If the gods haven't acted, I doubt they will. Perhaps they didn't condone her acts either." He paused and set his empty glass on the table. "The guild owes you several favors. Veth and Malik despise Klareth. They may be able to keep your name out of it with a mock investigation." He looked me over and added, "But right now, you need to get cleaned up."

"There's something else," I said. "She spoke of Lord Ebonhammer and mentioned the 'Golden Child.' None of it made sense."

Thoughtfulness took over his expression. "I'll look into it after contacting the guild tomorrow. But you need rest, Eira."

Marus was right. I hated that all I could do was bathe and sleep until morning, and I wasn't sure sleep would even come despite the exhaustion.

He smiled lightly. "You're acting high priestess of the temple now. Exciting times."

My chest tightened, and I sipped the whiskey. Another title I didn't want. I'd never wanted it. Overseeing the temple was left to me as a Divine without a high priest or priestess, though. Even if almost everyone in the temple feared me.

Klareth's husband might *try* to claim the status of high priest, but he'd be rejected. He was nothing to the temple. His authority would mean little.

But if my word as Tempest meant anything, then . . . "I want you to do it."

Marus blinked at me, confused.

"As Divine—the Tempest—I want you to be high priest."

"You can't be serious. I'm a scholar. Far from a priest, let alone a *high* priest." He stood and began pacing in front of the fire.

With Klareth dead, my word as a Divine was all it took to appoint him as high priest, and no one would fight it. He knew that just as well as I did.

No one would be better suited than Marus. He spent his life studying anything there was to know about the gods. All his time researching the Divine would be invaluable to any other temples seeking his counsel. The children we cared for adored him, even if they annoyed him endlessly when he wanted nothing more than to be left to his reading.

He was perfect for it, unlike me.

I nodded. "Please?"

"Consider it with a clear head after you've rested."

There was one last thing. "What about Roan?"

He sat beside me again, his face weary. "Klareth's death is enough to have him removed from the premises. He was only her husband, not a priest of the temple. I'm sure Veth and Malik will help with him too."

I pulled myself from the couch, fighting the desire to collapse onto it and hide away from everything.

I made it to the doorway, and Marus said, "The Tempests in history bring about great change. I don't think you are any different."

The words were so like what Caelus had said before, but I wasn't sure I believed them.

10

"Come on, Eira," Dorian said, his skin slick with sweat from working outside. "Don't be that way."

Lightning tipped my fingers, and my heart raced. "You told her! After you said you wouldn't."

He reached out, his face full of remorse. "But she's your family."

The pounding on the door grew louder, and Aunt Celeste called my name. She was here to drag me back to that gala, where she would pretend to care I existed. Pretend to love me.

I hadn't wanted to go. He'd known that.

Dorian took my hand, and lightning slithered from my skin and arced up his arm. His hand locked around mine. I shook my head, trying to jerk away. The lightning subsided, and he crumpled to the floor.

I jerked up from my bed. Cold sweat made the silk sheet cling to my naked body. I'd stripped off the bloodied dress and bathed away the grime and tears of the previous night before climbing straight into bed. Late-morning sunlight shone through my round bedroom window. Marus had probably thought it best to let me sleep in.

With a huff, I lay back and draped my arm over my eyes. Killing Dorian that day had been an accident. The memories of him from the dream faded, only for the events from last night to come swelling back to the surface.

Killing Klareth had been different. I'd chosen to kill her. It had been so easy, and I almost wished I had done it sooner. Tryssa would still be alive if I had. But both their deaths haunted me all the same.

I turned onto my side and faced the wood-panel wall, pulling the sheet over my shoulder. It did little to warm my body from the chill of the nightmare, but I was content to spend the rest of my day in bed and hiding away.

Yet I would need to face what I'd done, eventually.

Marus seemed to have a plan to keep me from being implicated in Klareth's murder, at least, even if it was a lie. Not that she would be missed. He wouldn't let the temple have any additional reasons to be afraid of me.

There was a knock at the door, and I groaned, trying to ignore it.

Another knock. This time the lock clicked, and the door opened.

I sat up, clenching the sheet to my chest, and faced the door, expecting Marus, Alissa, or even Esteban. Instead, Caelus was there, in a fitted deep red tunic. He strode in with a tray of food and a pitcher in his hands and set them down on the oval cedar table in front of the small fireplace. On a plate was another of those chocolate pastries and sliced fruit.

"You shouldn't be in here," I said.

He smiled all too playfully. "Sulking doesn't suit you."

I frowned.

Caelus took in the room and picked up the narrow vase from the table, eyeing the single lavender rose in it. He sighed when I didn't acknowledge him further. "That was my attempt at a joke."

"Why are you here?" I asked, lying back and covering my eyes with an arm. Last night he'd been comforting. Gods, even now, his presence eased the dread of facing the day. But I wanted to be alone.

"There's no water," he said after a moment.

I sighed, removing my arm. He was still looking at the rose. "Why are you here?" I asked, ignoring his statement.

He set the vase down without a sound and faced me. "Marus sent me. Thought you might be lonely." He strode toward the bed. "And you need to eat."

"You're free to go. I'll eat later."

"You see"—the edge of the bed shifted—"I don't believe that for a moment."

I glared at him.

His grin was full of mischievous arrogance.

"I said you could go," I reminded him.

"But you didn't specify where to. Problem?"

I turned away and closed my eyes. *Fine. Let him sit there.* He'd leave eventually. When he did, I'd take the time to get ready and indulge in the pastry at my leisure.

"Do you always sleep naked?" he asked.

My eyes flew open. The sheet had dipped low, revealing the upper swell of my breasts. My face heated. I tugged it up, closing my eyes again. Gods, surely he would leave. Or at least sit in silence.

"And do you always sleep with a dagger stashed in your bedside table?"

How did he— My gaze fell to the drawer I'd left open, revealing the dagger. He'd seen me in that bloody gown last night. Would he think I'd killed Klareth, between that and the blade? Not that he would have been wrong, but . . .

The bed shifted, and Caelus pulled the blade from the table and dangled it in front of me. "That got your attention," he said. "Why is it you have a dagger in your room? Should I be worried, since they announced the high priestess is dead this morning?"

I shot up and out of the bed and grabbed his wrist. His eyes widened, and I squeezed, freeing the blade from his hand. It landed on the bed. I grabbed it and pointed it at him. "Unless you've forgotten, I train with Selena. The dagger was a gift."

His mouth parted a fraction, and his eyes churned, traveling down—down to where the sheet had fallen away, revealing my naked body. He stared for a moment before he tore his gaze away. My face burned, and he smirked. "You're rather ill-tempered this morning," he all but purred.

"If you have questions, you should ask Marus."

Caelus grabbed my wrist, mimicking the move I'd used, and pulled me to him. Surprise loosened my grip, and I attempted to back away but stumbled. His other arm wrapped around my waist, pressing my breasts against his hard chest. He released my wrist and threw the dagger, the tip sinking into the wooden shelf several feet away. "I found you covered in blood coming up from the catacombs, where she was found dead. And you're trained by a member of the Copper Jackals. Suspicious, isn't it?"

Heat flooded my senses, and his warmth seeped in. Caelus's words should have worried me. But with my chest flush against his, all my focus was on his muscled body and his thumb caressing the skin near the underside of my breast.

"Still want me to go?"

Yes? No?

I shoved him away before I made another reckless decision. Thank the gods his eyes remained on mine. I yanked the sheet over myself. "Leave." Figuring out what to do about the temple and about the Golden Child with Marus was all that mattered.

He laughed and stepped away. "Get dressed. Marus wants to see you. If you insist on not eating, we'll go now." As an afterthought, he added, "Malik is with him."

"I don't need an escort."

"I never said you did."

He hadn't, but my thoughts were scattered. I couldn't help but notice he didn't seem appalled at having a dagger pointed at him. He was Marus's assistant. Another scholar. But he'd disarmed me as easily as I had him—more easily, if I was being truthful. "You're not just a scholar, are you?"

He smirked. "I'm whatever I'm needed to be, Eira."

He didn't elaborate, turning and exiting the room instead. After the door closed, there was no sound of footsteps fading away.

A heavy sigh escaped me. There was no point in staying in bed now.

WE PASSED THROUGH THE gardens on the way to the library. I glanced at the stone doors to the Chamber of Gods as we passed them, unable to stop myself. The doors were closed, and that tug I'd felt was gone. Had what Klareth had been doing and that tugging sensation been connected somehow? My stomach turned at the thought.

I paused and Caelus looked over his shoulder at me.

Before he could make another assumption—albeit an accurate one—I hurried past. Staying near the chamber was only an ugly reminder of what had happened, and it was bad enough Caelus already had a decent guess about the events that occurred in the catacombs. He just didn't know it was true yet.

We came to a stop at the library doors, which were gilded with a symbol for each of the gods in gold and silver. It was a reminder that the gods could decide I was unworthy of the power they'd gifted me.

Caelus pushed open the doors. He held one open, waiting. The musky smells of books and parchment were enough to bring a little ease in my shoulders.

Marus was in his study with Malik. "Finally, you're here," Marus said. He looked over his glasses in our direction, his expression grim. "I'm afraid I have something difficult to tell you. Teeg is missing, and so is Roan."

My heart raced. "Since when? Did he take Teeg?"

"You had one order," Malik interjected from where he stood across from Marus.

I scowled at him. "Does healing your wounded not count, then?"

Malik glowered.

"Placing the blame purely on a Divine is not becoming of a guild leader," Marus said.

"She knew what I requested of her."

"Guild leader?" I asked. But Veth was the guild leader of the Copper Jackals. I looked to Marus, seated on his couch, for answers, but he was focused on Malik.

When neither answered, Caelus leaned in and whispered, "Veth was found dead last night. Poisoned."

Marus frowned, and his gaze drifted to the open bottle of wine on the rectangular table. "The fault doesn't fall to Eira alone."

"It doesn't matter whose fault it is. Find the damn boy."

"Does 'Golden Child' mean anything to you?" I asked, recalling Klareth's words.

Malik stiffened, facing me slowly. "What do you know?"

I told them of Klareth's mentions of Lord Ebonhammer needing the Golden Child and where I'd been when she'd said it, though I omitted that it'd been me who killed her.

Malik sat in an armchair that matched Marus's worn couch and leaned forward, elbows on his knees. "The Golden Child is born once every one thousand years. They're born with a font of esprit and can accomplish amazing feats comparable to that of a Divine. Perhaps more so. But because of their overflowing esprit, they're easily influenced. It could make them go mad from the power inside of them or be manipulated into a destructive force." He cast a hard gaze at me. "That is why I left Teeg in your care, Tempest. You are good. Kind. A positive influence for him."

Teeg was the Golden Child. His talent with esprit made sense now. He'd been able to use it with ease. "But why would Lord

Ebonhammer want him?"

"I have no doubts that the Dawn Conclave and the king suspect a Golden Child is alive. Klareth must have been working with Travok Ebonhammer to locate him. The bitch always wanted renown. Teeg needs to be located," Malik said.

"Let me," I blurted out.

Malik's expression hardened. "You failed me once. Why wouldn't it happen again?"

He had no reason to believe in me, but I wouldn't sit back and let someone use Teeg. Not after watching Tryssa die and being helpless to stop it. "He's like a brother to me. Let me help him."

Malik considered this for several moments, but it was Caelus who spoke. "I'll go with her. As crown's guard, I may have a few connections in Tiruhm."

Facing Caelus, my eyes widened. "Crown's guard?"

He smiled, arms behind his back. "Among my other duties, yes."

From the corner of my eye, Marus's brows lifted. It must have been the first he was hearing of it as well. "Why would the king send one of the crown's guard as my assistant?" Marus asked.

"I knew about runes," Caelus answered, as if it explained everything.

11

We decided we'd leave the next morning, giving me time to pack. Not that I had much to bring. My gaze drifted toward the bookshelf in my room, the dagger still impaled in the side. My mother's book sat on the top shelf—a story about a mother who'd been gifted a daughter by the gods. The daughter had mismatched eyes like mine, making it my favorite when I was a child. It was the same story that Teeg requested almost every night of the girl who loved her sister. I grabbed it, stuffing it away, before yanking free the dagger.

On my way out of the room, my eyes stopped on the vase containing the rose Caelus had been looking at. It was empty. The rose had been a gift from Marus. I'd learned it didn't need attention when I'd forgotten to water it. After a week, not a single petal had shriveled or fallen. I'd checked over my room for the rose but didn't find it, so I had continued packing.

That night, I found Marus in his study and brought up my concerns of being found unworthy by the gods again.

Marus said, "Klareth wasn't innocent. I don't know about her personal life, but she killed Tryssa. And there were other bodies."

He was right. Klareth hadn't been innocent. That chamber within the catacombs covered in ritual markings and littered with limp corpses removed any semblance of innocence. Had she sent other children to Lord Ebonhammer—those she thought might be the Golden Child? A bitter taste filled my mouth.

Marus stood and pulled a necklace from his pocket. "Wear this. It may bring you peace and perhaps a little luck." A silver lotus with a moonstone embedded in the center dangled from the chain. The lotus was the flower of the goddess of luck and freedom's symbol. He helped me with the clasp.

Once it was around my neck, I held it up. "Just because she wasn't innocent, that doesn't make it right. Does it?"

He picked up his wineglass from the coffee table. "That is for you to decide, Eira. I am sure the gods are more understanding than you give them credit for."

"Do you think she's been partly responsible for the disappearances? Several of the missing have been children."

"I'm afraid we can't rule it out. But you're leaving the temple and venturing to Tiruhm. You wanted to speak with the Inquisitive in the past, and Klareth wouldn't let you, right?"

I nodded.

"Perhaps speaking with another Divine will give you some answers."

At one time, I'd wanted to do that. But stories implied the Inquisitive didn't sit still and the Refulgent rarely left Ryseer. She might not even be in Tiruhm. "Oh, did you take the rose you gave me?"

Marus shook his head.

I'd have to ask Alissa, then, and I hadn't seen her since Klareth's death was announced. But there would be time for that when I returned.

All that was left to do before morning was assign someone to look over the temple.

Thankfully, Marus agreed, but only if I sought out a replacement for him. As acting high priest, he planned to allow Malik to investigate the catacombs. Their interests were tied primarily to the glowing emerald stone, according to Marus.

I avoided the Chamber of Gods and headed back to my room to sleep. That didn't stop the judgmental stare of the statues penetrating through the stone doors, all of them seeming to wait to see what I would do.

The next morning, Selena and, to my surprise, Alissa met with me. Together, they presented several sets of clothes imbued by the Copper Jackals' enchanter to offer protection. They appeared to be a variation of traditional robes, a way to honor my time with the temple while appearing, as Selena put it, "more fashionable."

I made my way to the outskirts of the city, cobalt swaths of fabric swishing between my legs. At least the clothes were less cumbersome than the dresses or robes. With a cloak, I'd look like anyone else.

The last time I'd gone somewhere new, it'd been to come here. But now I was leaving, headed right back to the city I'd left and the grieving mother—Dorian's—I'd abandoned.

Caelus adjusted the bags strapped to a beautiful large black horse near the city's edge beneath an oak tree. A golden-jackal emblem on the bridle gleamed in the sunlight. It was the first time I'd seen him since he revealed his status as a crown's guard. He didn't seem unlike the scholar's assistant I'd gotten to know over the past few weeks, yet he was wholly different at the same time.

His movements seemed more graceful, sure. Then there was the black leather he wore and the weapons neatly strapped to him. There were no fewer than three daggers that I could see, and he slid a sheathed sword into a strap along the saddle. *Has everything been an act? What did he think could happen on this trip? Or did being overly prepared come with being a crown's guard?*

As I continued toward Caelus, none of the townspeople paid me any mind.

I sighed. We had a lot of ground to cover, and it would be a few days before we'd arrive. I wasn't looking forward to the hours of travel on horseback.

But Caelus only had one horse—not two.

"Is there some sort of mistake?" I asked.

He faced me, raising a questioning brow.

I gestured toward the animal. "With the horses."

He patted the horse's neck, his lips twitching up. "Malik said you didn't know how to ride."

It was bad enough I was stuck with him, his handsome face, and his charm. Being that close? I couldn't afford that kind of distraction.

Especially after learning he'd been keeping his role a secret and that he possibly knew I'd killed Klareth. Gods, if he went to the catacombs after he saw me that night, there would be no other obvious explanation. And he was right on top of all of it.

"But that look on your face isn't too thrilled."

I frowned. How could I get out of it?

"Good. You haven't left yet," a voice called out behind me.

I turned around.

Esteban was pushing his way through the busy cobbled street.

"Esteban?" Everyone had been busy after Klareth's and Veth's deaths, so I didn't expect a chance to give Esteban a goodbye.

"I'll join you in a few days. Malik told me what you're doing, and I won't be letting you run off too far on your own, girl."

He knew I wouldn't be alone, but I didn't point that out. "Any news about Veth's death?" I asked.

Esteban shook his head. "Malik asked me to stay for now. He hopes to find something soon."

Klareth's and Veth's deaths occurring on the same night had likely sent the guild into an upheaval. "I'll miss you," I said, kneeling down and hugging him.

He wrapped his arms around me, squeezing. "You're a soft one," he laughed. "And I'll be sure to bring some of that wine you like."

I smiled and nodded against his shoulder.

He let go and took a step back, looking toward Caelus. "I don't much trust you, but keep her safe."

Caelus nodded. "With my life."

Esteban turned and headed toward Copper Alley.

I watched until he disappeared into the crowd. Dusmir had

become my home, in a way. It'd be strange not to see anyone from the temple or sneak out. Even the routines Klareth had put me through would be gone.

I turned to face my current dilemma of trying to avoid riding one horse with Caelus. But it was such a stupid thing to care about, given everything. Teeg was missing, Tryssa died barely a day ago. My stomach dropped. *And I killed Klareth.*

Caelus placed a hand on my shoulder. "It's time to get going."

I didn't protest the arrangement and placed a foot in the stirrup. We didn't have the time it would take for me to learn how to ride properly on the way. Even if Malik thought that Teeg would remain unharmed, that didn't mean it was wise to take longer than necessary.

Caelus helped me onto the horse. He swung up behind me, and I did my best to stay straight and avoid leaning against him. Within seconds, we were off.

Caelus followed the worn dirt road that connected Dusmir to a trading town. Colors shifted from green to yellow and orange, and leaves fell like snow in the slightest autumn breeze. Midday sunlight poured through the various cedar and oak trees. The chilly air seeped deep, all the way into my bones, despite my cloak.

Once I found Teeg, he'd still need someone to keep him safe. But could that really be me? Malik was better suited to it, even if his personality was less than friendly on a good day.

I sighed.

The Golden Child. Teeg seemed like an ordinary boy. Nothing stood out about him, despite his prowess with esprit. He blended in. I'd envied it at the temple.

Maybe Teeg and I weren't so different. We shared the burden of having a power neither of us asked for. People would try to use him once they knew the Golden Child was alive; I knew it wouldn't stay hidden for long.

I hoped our journey would remain quiet. Calm. That we would avoid running into any creatures from the Abyss or otherwise and arrive in Tiruhm safely.

Then there was the man sitting behind me, whom I was avoiding all contact with. And failing, given our circumstance atop the horse.

All the questions I had for him seemed off-limits now. Everything he'd said about the king was at odds with his position—a position he so carefully avoided mentioning. And it was none of my business.

But why did he choose to come with me? If he completed his assignment with Marus, he would need to go back to Ryseer, wouldn't he? The whole situation was confusing. So we rode in awkward silence.

"Something on your mind?" Caelus asked eventually.

"Nothing at all."

"Really? Because I'm certain I've heard you sigh at least five times in the past hour."

Have I? "I don't know what you're talking about."

He chuckled behind me. "We'll be on the road for a while longer. If you need to rest, lean against me."

"I'm fine," I lied. Truthfully, I hadn't expected riding to be so uncomfortable. Muscles I didn't know I had were sore. My lower back ached from sitting straight to avoid exactly what he was suggesting. *But leaning against him would be warmer.*

"I overheard you with Esteban. How well did you know Veth?"

I frowned. Other than wanting me to join the guild, I didn't know much about her. "She was always kind to me," I offered.

"It's best not to mistake kindness as virtuous."

I squeezed the pommel of the saddle. "And how well could you have known her?" Veth had never mentioned having a contact within Ryseer, but she had little reason to share that with me.

A light breeze blew my hair into my face. He tucked the loose strands behind my ear, his fingers grazing my cheek. "I spoke to her a couple of times. She reminded me of someone who was once kind. I learned the hard way not to be so trusting."

I snapped my mouth shut.

Veth and I had interacted a few times. She was kind, but I knew her agenda was to get me to join the Copper Jackals. Maybe Caelus was right, but I'd never know now that she was gone. *Would Malik even let me join the guild without Veth?*

"Why aren't you headed back to Ryseer?" I asked, changing the subject.

He adjusted the reins. "Officially, I completed my task in Dusmir. But with the disappearances and discovery that Klareth, a high priestess, was involved with sending a child—*children*—to Lord Ebonhammer, it'd be negligent to return to the royal city without investigating." He sighed, blowing a stray strand of my black hair forward. "Besides, Tiruhm was the last place my sister was seen."

Sister? That surprised me. I couldn't imagine him in a brotherly role. "And you think Lord Ebonhammer may be involved?"

"Anything is possible. She tends to be a snoop—sticking her nose where it doesn't belong."

"Do you think she was sent there like Teeg?"

He sighed once more. "I'm doubtful. She's nearly an adult and was in Ryseer when I left. But I intend to find her."

I pulled my cloak tighter around me. Could the Dawn Conclave have been involved in the increasing disappearances? Surely the Copper Jackals would have learned if they were. Then again, maybe not. They weren't on good terms with the High Houses. And if the Midnight Wolves ever learned anything, they were unlikely to share information with the Copper Jackals. They'd rather focus on their rivalry.

But we needed to speak with Lord Ebonhammer. Hopefully, a Divine could gain an audience. Then there was Caelus. As a crown's guard, he might have sway to see him.

I wanted to help Caelus find his sister too. I prayed to Wrynal's twin, Renelle, goddess of mercy, that she remained safe.

THE SUN SANK, AND dark clouds took over the sky by the time I finally caved and leaned into Caelus's hard chest. His heat enveloped me, sending warm tingles through my body. A sound of relief escaped.

He chuckled. It rumbled through me, and I was grateful he couldn't see my embarrassment.

"I'm surprised you volunteered for this," he said.

"Someone had to go. The Copper Jackals are busy enough with Veth's death and protecting Dusmir."

"Teeg is important. I'm sure someone else would have gone."

"It would have been wrong not to help. Especially since I wasn't able to protect him from Klareth."

"Ah, yes. The dead high bitch. You know, I never liked her, and

Marus never had a kind word about her either. Obviously, none of this is your fault."

But wasn't it? In the end, I'd killed her. It just wasn't before Teeg was put in danger. Having Divine power hadn't helped—the gods hadn't either. Maybe Klareth wanting to know if they'd abandoned us had merit. I chose not to voice that to Caelus.

I tugged the hood of my cloak up moments before the rain fell, and a wolf howled in the distance. Caelus eased the horse into a canter. Buildings peppered the landscape along the horizon. The sprawling fields and tree lines were replaced with pastures of livestock and growing crops as we neared the town.

The tempest beneath my skin purred in response to the rain and thunder, and my shoulders relaxed. It always rose to the surface to greet storms, calling to the Divine power within me. The lightning inside me *liked* the rain and the thunder and always left me with a sense of calm.

We stopped in front of an inn. The dark wooden structure appeared newer among the homes and storefronts. Caelus helped me down from the horse, and the stable-hand whisked it away after Caelus paid him.

Inside, people drank and gambled, hiding away from the downpour. The rowdiness wasn't unlike the Sleeping Alligator, but I missed the warmth of the forge. I smiled, thinking of Esteban and how he might like the small inn, even if he'd suggest his own improvements.

I abandoned Caelus and ordered a glass of wine at the bar. I took a long drink of the cheap, sour wine that reminded me of vinegar. Esteban's sweet vintage really had been a luxury.

"If I recall, you had wine the night we met," Caelus said, joining me.

I tapped my fingers along the glass. "It helps." I took another drink. "But Esteban's is better."

He leaned forward, elbows on the counter. "What does it help?"

"Oh. I . . . The lightning . . . Well, it isn't always easy to control." I averted my gaze back to the wineglass. "Did you get the rooms?" I asked, avoiding the subject.

He nodded and headed for the stairs. I followed, sipping the wine, until we stopped in front of one of several doors. He unlocked it and pushed it open. I stepped inside, but Caelus followed me and sat on the bed.

"This was the only room," Caelus said.

My grip tightened on the wineglass stem. The shoddy bed, barely big enough for two people, was in the center. A small bedside table sat on both sides. There was a door that led to an attached bathing room, and there wasn't enough space for either of us to sleep on the floor comfortably.

He smirked in that odd mischievous yet arrogant way. "You look like you could use more of that wine."

I looked away and drained the rest.

"Your integrity is safe, *Tempest*."

My face flamed. "I'm not concerned about that." It wasn't as though I didn't *want* to or that I thought he would try anything without my consent, but sharing a bed was something I'd never done. The most I'd managed was kissing. Klareth's punishment for having sex wouldn't have been worth even trying. But to share with Caelus? Handsome, with-easy-to-get-lost-in-eyes Caelus? I fought the urge to chew the corner of my lip.

He stood and crossed the short distance between us, leaving the slightest bit of space. Dark storm-cloud eyes stared into mine. "Bathe first. I'll get us food." His fingers brushed mine, slipping the wineglass from my hand. He stepped around me with enough grace so that our bodies didn't collide in the cramped quarters.

Of course I'd be stuck with him, and I was finding it harder and harder to ignore how handsome he was.

I did as he said and scrubbed away the day. In the bathing chamber, I stared at the black silk nightdress. Regret filled me for not bringing along a robe or more modest clothing to sleep in. What I owned was limited since I wasn't supposed to leave the temple.

I twisted my hair between my hands, my gaze shifting to the clothes I'd stripped off. But it didn't matter what I wore. Caelus had seen my naked body when I'd nearly assaulted him in my room. He had even been a sort of gentleman about it, considering he'd kept his eyes on mine instead of wandering—after he'd gotten an eyeful.

Before I could talk myself out of it, I slipped on the little dress, letting it fall to the middle of my thighs. With a deep breath, I pulled open the door to the bedroom. My skin prickled in the cool bedroom air. Caelus sat on the bed with a tray of food he was picking at, the black leather he'd been wearing abandoned. A full glass of wine was on the bedside table nearest me.

"I was beginning to wor—" His eyes darkened.

Flattered. I think that's how I should have felt when a man's eyes heated—not that I had much experience with such things. I pulled my hair forward, twisting it, as if it was some sort of shield between us.

"Well, you certainly didn't drown."

"What?" I breathed.

He stood, clearing his throat. "You took so long I was beginning to worry you may have drowned."

I got into the bed, thankful for the warm blankets. "I doubt that was a serious concern."

"Crazier things have happened," Caelus said, stepping toward the bathing chamber and pulling off his dark tunic. The muscles of his back and shoulders constricted and moved, and I thanked the gods he wasn't facing me, because I couldn't tear my gaze away.

The door closed, leaving my body flushed.

While he bathed, I eyed the tray and laughed at the single small chocolate pastry. I ate and sipped the wine and tried not to think about how thoughtful Caelus had been. With nothing better to do, I braided my damp hair. Once it was done, I laid back against the wooden headboard and closed my eyes, taking a deep breath.

The reality that Caelus and I would share a bed grew closer. It was such a mundane thing I'd spent years longing for but never able to have because of Klareth.

We'd just be sleeping, but even that would be the most—well, second-most—intimate thing I'd ever done. Nearly assaulting Caelus while I'd been naked might have been number one.

The door of the bathing room opened, and I jumped. My attention flew to him. His tanned skin and lean muscles were on full display. My eyes lingered on the taut lines of his stomach and trailed down to the indents of his hips that disappeared beneath linen pants that hung low.

"Tell me something," he said, drawing my gaze up to his lazy smirk. "What has your face so red?" His eyes glittered with amusement.

He knows exactly why. I looked away. "I'm not sure I know what you're talking about."

"Certainly not."

I slid down into the bed and turned onto my side, away from him, and closed my eyes again. The bed shifted in front of me—on Caelus's side—and the blankets lifted slightly. There'd been no sound of footsteps indicating he'd moved.

Caelus said, "I'm not sure facing this way has the desired effect you were hoping for."

In turning away, I was facing exactly where he would be.

"Pretending to sleep didn't work last time."

I sighed, opening my eyes. Caelus was on his side, his head propped on a fist. "Do you need something?" I asked.

"Not particularly."

I studied his face. Light stubble lined his jaw, and his eyes crinkled slightly when he grinned. "You have a lot of leeway for a crown's guard."

He raised a brow. "I assume you're referring to the fact I'm not headed straight back to the king."

I nodded against the pillow.

His fingers tapped along his leg. "My position as crown's guard is higher than most. It grants me a degree of freedom others don't have to investigate matters that may be of interest to the king." He shifted, lying back on the bed. "This one happens to involve you and my sister."

I hadn't expected such an honest answer. To be so close to the king likely meant he had many secrets—ones he couldn't share. Would he tell the king about Teeg being the Golden Child?

He turned his head to me. "Why do you drink to control your esprit? Doesn't seem like the most effective way."

I drew in my bottom lip. "I wouldn't have called Klareth the best of mentors."

"And what would you have called her?"

There wasn't a simple answer to that.

When I didn't respond, he said, "We'll work on your skills. It shouldn't be too difficult on horseback. Before you know it, you'll be a full-fledged lightning bug."

I repressed a laugh. "Lightning bug?"

He shrugged. "It's fitting, isn't it?"

I shook my head and turned away. "Good luck with your lessons. I'm not sure it's meant to be tamed."

"Start with believing in yourself."

In all the years I'd struggled to control the tempest, I'd never been given a reason to believe it could be. Tomorrow Caelus would see how much of a lost cause I was.

12

Light filtered through the window, and I pushed back the sheet, cool crisp air giving me relief from the too-hot covers. The sleep-addled haze faded enough for me to notice that I wasn't lying on my pillow; my head rested on Caelus's hard chest as it rose and fell softly. *He's still asleep. Thank gods.*

My hand lay on his stomach, and I fought the itch to trail my fingers along the toned muscles. His arm was wrapped around my waist, and one of his legs was tucked between mine.

The scene seemed wholly inappropriate. Maybe it was because I was a Divine or because Klareth's punishment had never been worth the risk.

It was early morning, and I wasn't sure how to escape without waking him. Instead, I went with the adult thing to do—pretend to still be sleeping.

I wasn't sure how much time passed before he stirred. His finger made idle shapes on my waist. After several moments, it became quite clear that he wasn't going to "wake" me up.

Stifling the urge to sigh, I shifted and opened my eyes.

"Finally tired of pretending? If you wanted to use me as a pillow, all you had to do was ask."

My face burned, and I slapped his chest, groaning. I headed for the bathing room, closing the door behind me.

Chuckling erupted behind the closed door.

Once we were both dressed and ready for the road, I waited outside the inn while Caelus retrieved the horse. Which was fine by me. After being indecently wrapped around all those hard muscles and waking up to his handsome face, I wanted a little space. More like, a lot of space. But that wouldn't happen while we were traveling.

I couldn't afford distractions. Not until I found Teeg.

Caelus returned with his black horse, and the sight of it made me groan inwardly. My body wasn't used to riding for long hours. My muscles were sore, and my back had barely recovered overnight from the day before.

"What's his name?" I asked, delaying the inevitable.

He raised a brow and patted the horse's neck. "Kast."

I stepped up. Kast smelled as though he'd had a bath. My fingers brushed through his coarse mane. He grunted softly and I smiled. "He's beautiful."

Caelus helped me up and then seated himself behind me. "If I didn't know any better, I'd think you're trying to make me jealous."

WE TOOK A BREAK to stretch our legs and let Kast drink from a river, and I combed my fingers through the horse's mane to avoid moving my aching muscles.

"It'd be better if you walked around," Caelus said, stretching in the shade of a nearby cedar.

I frowned. "I'm content over here with Kast."

He laughed. "How about practicing your power?"

It wasn't really a question, since I'd agreed to try last night. And I doubted there was anything I could say to this man to get out of it. Not sure what he had in mind, I reluctantly nodded.

He smiled. "I was thinking—"

"That must be new for you."

"You'd be surprised." He plucked a handful of leaves from a shrub with red berries. "Your Divine title is Tempest, but storms are more than thunder and lightning. There's also wind and rain." He made a motion with his hand, and a breeze stirred the leaves, sending them whirling upward in a small circle. Citrus filled the area—his scent. "Air is harmless in comparison."

"That's nice in theory," I said, patting the thick neck of the horse as it drank from the river. "But that doesn't explain how to do it, assuming I even can."

"It's about visualization and letting esprit flow through you. Simply believe the power is yours. Over time, it'll become second nature."

I fought a smile. "You sound like you've taught others before."

He stiffened. "My friends tell me my talents are wasted as a crown's guard and I should be an instructor."

98

"But . . . ?"

Caelus's gaze fell to the flowing river. "A story for another day. For now, focus. Visualize."

Visualization was easy enough. It was how I healed people for the Copper Jackals—the only thing I felt confident in my ability to do. "The power of gods shouldn't be played with."

"Except that it is *yours*."

"The gods choose Divine. Nothing about *this* is mine."

He sighed. "You were born with it. It's up to you to embrace it."

I pulled my dark cloak tightly around me. Being born with it didn't make it my power. But he couldn't understand. "Is hand motioning necessary?"

"No, but it does help beginners direct their esprit. It may be helpful to you."

Doing as he said, I imagined the leaves moving in the same way he had. I twisted my hand in a swirling motion, mimicking Caelus.

Nothing happened. "I feel like a fool," I muttered under my breath.

"You're far from it," he said, now standing behind me. "Try again."

When did he move? I hadn't heard him.

Doing the hand motion again, I pictured the leaves whirling in a circle only a few inches above the ground. Nothing happened.

"Again," Caelus whispered against my ear. Warmth seeped through my veins.

"I'm doing exactly what you said."

"But you're not doing the most important part," he murmured.

My heart raced, and I took several steps away before turning to face him. "I'm doing exactly what you said." I repeated, balling my hands into fists. "The leaves aren't moving. We don't even know if I can control the air."

Those infuriating eyes filled with amusement. "Then why did they lift once you became flustered?"

He was right; the leaves were now swirling around me. I took a slow, deep breath in and let it out, releasing the frustration within as I'd been taught. They glided to the ground. "Is that what you wanted?" I asked.

He shrugged. "No, but it proves you can do it. We'll keep practicing."

I wasn't certain I knew how to do as he asked, but I nodded all the same.

I'd never been given any reason to believe in the power I'd been gifted, especially as it wasn't mine, but the gods. It always seemed like some cruel joke that they had gifted me esprit so volatile, knowing it wouldn't be easy to control . . . if I could control it at all. That didn't stop me from hoping that maybe—just maybe—I could manage it.

Caelus's body grew rigid, and he uttered, "People are approaching."

Rustling sounded a moment later, and out popped three individuals. Each bore a silver wolf pin on their chest. The signet of the Midnight Wolves. But what were they doing so close to Dusmir?

A woman with muddy brown hair and a large frame stepped forward first. "Fancy meeting two copper pups out here. Heard your guild leader died."

They thought we were both with the Copper Jackals? *The jackal emblem.* Someone must have seen it on the bridle in the trading town.

"That's none of your concern," Caelus said, placing himself between me and the Midnight Wolves.

The man to her right, who had a scar along the side of his face, snarled.

I'd heard stories that the members of the Midnight Wolves and the leader of their guild could be cruel, often starting fights. I peered around Caelus to keep an eye on them and hoped that wouldn't be the case here. "Excuse me. We're not looking for any trouble," I said, then winced at my lame attempt to avoid confrontation.

The woman eyed me up and down. "What do we have here? Maybe we should take you back to the guild, make you one of ours."

I took a step back. That only caused her to grin wildly.

"We'll be on our way. Isn't that right?" Caelus asked, glancing at me.

I nodded and took a step toward Kast.

"Fuck," Caelus said, before the world around me shifted.

I stumbled forward, no longer standing where I'd been. I faced Caelus. He stood where I had been, near the horse. An arrow protruded from his chest, near his left shoulder. His face contorted.

I turned. Another arrow flew at me. Citrus wind whirled around me and sent the arrow careening toward a tree. Caelus saved me.

With his right hand, Caelus unsheathed a dagger and stalked toward the woman. She drew her sword and then advanced, slashing at him. He pivoted, avoiding her attacks. She groaned and scowled at him. Caelus dashed forward, one hand grabbing her wrist. The hand holding his dagger lunged toward her chest.

I started to shout—to stop him from killing her—but a burly arm wrapped around me. A hand slammed down over my mouth before I could scream. The man began pulling me away into the trees. "Perrin was right about you," a rough male voice said.

I dug my heels into the ground, trying to stop him. He didn't slow, continuing to drag me farther away. I squirmed in his grasp, but my cloak hindered my ability to free myself. He adjusted his grip, trapping me against his chest. With aching muscles, I kicked at his knees, but his hold didn't loosen.

My heart thundered. The tingling power wanted to be free. I clamped my eyes shut. *Breathe.* I didn't want another death on my conscience, but I couldn't let him take me.

He removed the hand covering my mouth.

I started to scream, but cool metal pressed against my throat, squelching it.

"I would hate to ruin that pretty face," he said against my ear.

My breath hitched. Any semblance of calm ceased.

"Come and may—" he started.

My fingertips prickled. I inhaled a deep breath to keep the tempest at bay. But the intensity of it grew and lightning broke free, snaking up my arm toward him.

He jerked and seized and then fell away, releasing me.

I collapsed forward, but quickly straightened and faced him. Arcing energy continued to race along my fingers.

The scar along the right side of his face disappeared beneath a thick beard. He grinned, making it seem to take up more space. "You're coming with me, little Divine."

Sounds of fighting behind me ceased. I fought the urge to turn around—to see if Caelus was alive. He was a crown's guard, but could he win three on one?

The scarred half-dwarf peered past me. "Seems time's running out."

I turned, but there wasn't anything through the cedars.

It was a bluff, and I fell for it.

Before I could turn back, he pinned me to the ground. A hot, shooting pain radiated below my shoulder blade. He pulled my head up by my hair. I tried reaching behind me, only to aggravate the wound. The lightning that had been my savior fizzled out, and my focus split between the pain in my back and the stinging sharp pull from my scalp.

The knife's sharp edge glided across the base of my throat. "Tsk. He finally noticed you were missing."

Caelus appeared in front of us. The arrow penetrating close to the shoulder was now broken in half. He focused on the man pinning me to the ground and stepped forward like a true wolf stalking its prey.

"Ah, ah. I wouldn't come closer if you don't want something to happen to the girl." He pressed the blade harder against my neck, breaking the skin. Air hissed through my teeth.

Caelus's jaw flexed. Then he vanished.

A grunt sounded behind me, and the grip on my hair loosened. I scrambled forward and pushed myself up. I whipped around, the lightning teeming at the surface now that I was free.

Caelus stood behind him. The man unsheathed the sword at his hip. He slashed at Caelus. Caelus sidestepped, pulling back his fist. It collided with the man's scarred face. Wind sent strands of my hair flying into my eyes. The scarred man flew several feet away, crashing into a tree. There was no movement from where he lay on the ground.

Caelus turned. In a single step, he stood in front of me. This time a gentle breeze stirred the air around us. It was the last thing that mattered, but I couldn't stop myself from blurting out, "The air smells like you."

One side of his lips raised, and he reached out, halting just before his blood-soaked fingers touched my cheek. "An unfortunate side effect of my esprit."

I thought of all the times I'd smelled citrus around him or before I saw him. He'd been using his esprit all along. "Nifty trick."

His eyes drifted down to the cut on my neck. "You're hurt."

I touched the tender cut at my throat; my fingers came back red and began to tremble. "What about you?"

He glanced at the remainder of the arrow sticking from his chest as if he'd forgotten all about it, then took my shaking hand. Tingling shot up my arm, and the storm beneath the surface calmed. I let him guide me back toward the horse and past the three bloodied bodies lying on the ground.

He reached into the saddlebag and pulled out two lavender rose petals and held them as though he thought they might break. I eyed them, unsure of his plan.

"May I?" he asked, gesturing toward me.

"What are you going to do?"

His thumb ran across a velvet petal. "It's from one of Reina's roses. It has the ability to heal wounds. Since it's yours, I thought you wouldn't mind."

"Mine?"

"You didn't know?"

"That's why it was missing," I said. I shook my head. "It was a gift from Marus."

"He gifted it without telling you? Intriguing."

Reina, the goddess of love and peace, had wanted to share her love with mortals, according to stories. She'd blessed a garden of roses in the mortal world. The petals from her roses could heal any wound. It explained why it hadn't needed water in years.

"We should use it on you," I said, reaching for one.

He eyed the shaft again. "I'll be fine. But you shouldn't have been hurt."

The concern in his eyes had me nodding my head. Even if he wouldn't use it on himself, I could heal any of his injuries.

He stepped forward and placed a petal against my throat, his fingers brushing against the sensitive skin. A faint light appeared and sank into the cut. Warmth spread through my body. He placed another against the wound below my shoulder blade. In seconds, all my injuries were healed, thanks to Reina's rose.

I reached for my neck, touching where the cut had once been. There was nothing left of it. I rotated my shoulder, and there wasn't any pain or tension there either.

"Let me take care of the arrow," I said.

He looked ready to protest but seemed to decide against it. He leaned against a cedar and took a deep breath.

I examined the arrow lodged in his chest, and I glanced at him. "I've never done this before," I admitted.

"Pull it fast. Slow will hurt more."

I nodded and placed a hand against his sternum for support, feeling the steady thumping of his heart. With a deep breath, I wrapped the other around the shaft and yanked.

A grunt of pain sounded from Caelus, and I imagined that thread connecting us. Arcs of bright blue light danced along my hand and across his torso.

His eyes flitted closed as he hissed in a breath. The flesh began to mend together. He tipped his head back against the tree. "So, healing a wound is easy, but believing the power is yours isn't?"

The lightning skittered across his chest as though it were drawn to him. "Like it was easy for you to kill those people?"

His eyes opened, landing on me. "They would have done the same, or worse, to me and you. Fuck, they were planning to, Eira."

I couldn't help thinking of what I'd done to Klareth—how I'd killed her as easily as he had killed the people who'd attacked us. "Does that make it right? To kill them?"

He placed his hand on mine, the beat of his heart thudding against it. "I've had to do terrible things in my life, Eira. Killing someone is never a simple choice. Humanity makes a difference. Some people lose theirs. Some aren't even born with it and live only to bring misery to others. Is it fair to let them live, knowing they'll go on to ruin someone else's life? Someone who can't defend themself?"

I didn't know how to answer that.

"Every death lingers—marks you in a new way. If it doesn't, maybe that's the time to be worried about, whether it's right or wrong."

If it lingers? Would that mean he wouldn't care if it was me who'd killed Klareth? He'd saved me. Bothered to care if I'd been hurt. There was good left in him, despite the deaths he'd caused here.

"You were right," I said. "When you said it was suspicious that Klareth is dead and that I'd come out of the same catacombs. No one else would have been down there."

"I know," he said, squeezing my hand. "You have nothing to worry about. What you did . . . She pushed you to that point over years, from what I could gather."

The lightning receded, but I didn't move, savoring the heat of his skin against my icy fingers. His heart thudded against my palm. "And why would you be gathering that kind of information?"

"A lonely Divine is as strange as it is intriguing."

13

Once we were back on the road, I relaxed against him, no longer fighting it. His warm hands rested against my hips to keep me in place as I drifted between sleep and wakefulness, battling the fatigue from healing Caelus's wound. Tingles ran through me at his touch, and the tempest within calmed.

A weight lifted from my shoulders after I'd told Caelus about Klareth. Killing her wasn't right, but it was comforting to know that perhaps it wasn't wrong either. It was for the gods to decide, and they hadn't acted.

But what kind of life had Caelus lived? As a crown's guard, I knew it was inevitable that he'd taken lives, but how many? I wasn't sure of the current state of the kingdom. The temple was uninterested in court politics, making information scarce. Klareth's involvement with

Lord Ebonhammer had been the newest information I'd learned in some time.

Until we arrived in Tiruhm, I wouldn't know why or how far their relationship went. Not that it mattered. Finding Teeg and keeping him out of the hands of the kingdom and the Dawn Conclave was my priority. I wouldn't let them use him in the same way I'd been used.

Over the next couple of nights, Caelus coerced me into attempting to create an orb of light, claiming that the Refulgent could do so with ease. Considering their power was light, it wasn't surprising. I envied the ease of their power as opposed to my own tempestuous gift. But I tried to do as he said since there would be little harm involved while we were separated.

At first, I could only make one about the size of a marble, and it quickly fizzled out, but I continued to focus on creating dense balls of contained levin until sweat beaded from my brow. He'd been satisfied with even the smallest progress, offering praises easily.

One night, I'd asked why he chose not to be an instructor. He was clearly suited for it, and before it had sounded as though his friends encouraged it. But he tensed and his tone shifted, becoming somber. He'd changed the subject, stating it was time to sleep, and I didn't pry despite my curiosity.

Caelus had placed his bedroll next to mine, leaving a few inches between us each night since we'd been attacked. He didn't seem keen to allow a repeat incident.

Each day, the Serpentine Mountains grew closer, and Caelus had me practice using a turquoise wolf fang attached to a leather cord he'd pulled from under his tunic. He wanted me to lift it and keep it suspended in the air.

After a few days, the fang floated above my palm easier than it had before. "How did you know about the rose?" I asked, hoping to distract myself from how close we were to Tiruhm.

"I had a paper cut when I touched it," he said.

I laughed and thought back to the morning he'd been in my room. I hadn't noticed the faint light, but I also hadn't been eager to look at or speak to him.

"Your laugh is beautiful," he murmured.

I tensed, and the turquoise fang fell into my palm. "So I've heard."

"And who would go around saying that to the most sheltered Divine in the Kingdom of Valaryn?"

I huffed. "It's hard to go unseen in a tavern."

"You're right. Everyone noticed when you came in that night."

I wrapped my hand around the fang pendant and smiled at the thought of our meeting. "You only noticed because of how *perceptive* you are."

His hand gripped my hip. "Would you rather I'd noticed because of how beautiful you are?"

I opened my mouth, but words wouldn't come. If I was being honest with myself, I would've wanted that to be the reason. But I couldn't allow him to distract me, and we'd be going our separate ways once I found Teeg. There was no point in fantasizing about something more between us.

As we neared the mountain that held Tiruhm, silence fell between us, and his hand slipped away. I shivered, wrapping my cloak tightly around me.

THE CITY BUILT INTO the mountain with snowcapped turrets took form in the fading sun, and a light layer of snow covered the northern landscape. We passed carts draped in canvas, vibrant colors peeking out from underneath. A stone path led up to the iron walls shaped into geometric angles. It was cold and uninviting compared to Esteban's tavern.

The closer we got to the entrance of Tiruhm, the harder it became to concentrate on making the fang float. The guards stationed at the gate were not all pure dwarvish. A stocky half-fey woman, her height no doubt influenced by her dwarven heritage, allowed us to pass through the dark-iron gates.

Caelus left me to stable the horse, and I took in the cold mountain city. Several buildings had been constructed with the dark metal, and those that weren't had been reinforced with it. People of all races bustled from shop to shop. A group of dwarven revelers putting up an archway of autumn leaves argued. It was the most color I'd seen, outside of what peeked out beneath the canvas-covered carts as we were coming into the city.

"They're preparing for the Frostfire Festival," Caelus said at my side.

I turned to him and said, "I'm ready to see Lord Ebonhammer."

"I'm not sure that's a good idea. We've just arrived, and the sun is setting. He has no reason to grant us an audience immediately unless it's urgent."

My hands clenched at my sides, and lightning prickled the tips of my fingers, not quite escaping. "Finding Teeg is urgent."

His gaze dipped to my hands, and I fought the urge to hide them like I would have from Klareth. "I agree. But Malik said that the High Houses have no reason to harm him. We have time."

I didn't want to wait. The sooner we found him, the sooner I could get him home—the sooner he would be safe. And how could Malik be sure they wouldn't harm him? "You'll take me now."

Caelus let out a heavy sigh and started walking. "Fine. But keep your expectations low, Tempest."

I frowned at the use of my title and followed behind him on the stone path, surprised it, too, wasn't metal.

Caelus guided us with a familiarity I envied. My time in Tiruhm had been spent with my aunt. Parts of my memory were clear and others smudged away. My aunt and cousin lived in the upper district with the wealthy or powerful, including Lord Ebonhammer.

We stopped in front of the wall surrounding the impractical iron castle. To gather the amount of ore for such an atrocious building would have taken generations. That wasn't even counting the time to construct it; esprit was likely to thank.

At the front gate of the wall surrounding the castle, there were two stocky dwarven guards. Their dark beards hung down to the middle of their bellies. Both were armed with swords and axes.

"I need to see Lord Ebonhammer," I said.

"Do you have an invitation?" the one on the left asked.

"I'm the Tempest," I tried, hoping my title would be a boon. "It's important."

"You cannot see Lord Ebonhammer without an invitation or authorization from King Olbecht."

I shot Caelus a look, hoping there was something he could do.

"I'm a crown's guard of the Sunburst Throne. She wishes to inquire about the whereabouts of a child."

The one on the right guffawed, not even entertaining the request.

"A lost child is not the concern of Lord Ebonhammer. Take it up with the Temple of Evryn."

Lightning stirred in my veins, and the wind picked up around me. Did Lord Ebonhammer often ignore requests from his people? Let alone from a Divine?

Before I could say anything, Caelus placed a hand on my shoulder, the warm heavy weight grounding. "We'll be leaving, then," he said, pressing his other hand into the small of my back to lead me away.

I took a deep breath in and waited until my lungs burned before releasing it. Once we were no longer within earshot of the two dwarven guards, I asked, "What am I going to do? He's the only lead we have. Klareth sent Teeg to Lord Ebonhammer, and we don't even know why."

"There are more ways than one to gain information, Eira."

I frowned. "Then what do you suggest, great crown's guard?"

The corner of his lips twitched up. "I have my methods. For now, it's getting late. We need somewhere to stay."

The sun had long since sunk, and the thought of my aunt and cousin surfaced again. "I have family here. They may let us stay with them. That house is too big for the two of them, anyway."

Caelus looked down at me, uncertainty written on his face. "It's worth a try."

I told him what I remembered about the location of Aunt Celeste's villa, and within minutes, he'd led us there. The same stone wall with ivy growing across the top encircled the property. Sweet floral scents from Aunt Celeste's garden that she maintained with esprit wafted into the street. I peeked through the iron gate, and there were no lights. Not even the flicker of a candle.

"They must be out. We can wait for them inside. Lora always stashed a spare key in the plant near the door."

I pushed open the unlocked gate and stepped into the small courtyard. Caelus followed. Flowers and well-manicured hedges surrounded us, as pristine as if it were a temperate spring day instead of the cold of the mountain city. The villa was made of dark stone with iron reinforcements, much like the rest of the city's buildings. Near the large double doors sat several potted plants that Lora would hide her key in when she'd sneak out.

I poked around in the flame azalea to the right. No luck. She must have learned that Aunt Celeste knew where she hid it. I turned to find Caelus poking around in another pot, equally unsuccessful.

After several minutes, Caelus said, "What if we try the door?"

I glanced over my shoulder at him. "It's locked. We'll have to come back or find this gods'-forsaken thing in one of the twenty plants."

"True, but we haven't simply tried the door."

I spun around, hands on my hips. "All right. Go ahead."

He gave me an arrogant look. A light breeze whisked past with the unmistakable scent of citrus. Without so much as resisting, the door pushed open. "I have many talents."

"You can't just pick the lock with your esprit!"

He gestured to the now-open door. "As you can see, I can."

"Does the king know you go around doing that?"

"Would you rather spend all night in the cold looking for that key?"

I snapped my mouth shut and pushed past him into the foyer.

A crooked portrait of Aunt Celeste and Lora greeted us. Their perfect blonde hair had been pulled up and little curls framed their near-identical faces. Lora's features were softer, with big eyes and rounded cheeks.

Tucked in the corner was a sculpture of Maelynn, goddess of night and dreams, covered in a thin layer of dust as though someone had merely forgotten to clean. Everflame lanterns flared to life, illuminating the floral wallpaper that screeched a reminder of times better off forgotten.

I checked the various rooms of the house. A forgotten teacup sat on a table in the sitting room, half-empty. There was an abandoned book on the floor in the den. A disheveled blanket draped across the couch in the living room. Jasmine withering in the kitchen from lack of water. Each a reminder that someone lived here but wasn't present and had left in a rush.

My heart thudded heavy in my chest with each step up the stairs. *Something isn't right.* I checked their rooms, and the beds were made, just as Aunt Celeste demanded. But clothes cluttered the floor near the closet, and drawers had been left open.

Aunt Celeste wouldn't have left her home in such a state. She prided herself on always keeping it pristine. She'd hire someone to clean while she was away. What was left of my family, as much as I detested Aunt Celeste, was gone like they'd vanished on a typical day.

In the middle of the den, my legs grew weak. A weight fell into my chest so heavy that breathing hurt. My vision blurred, tears welling in my eyes, not yet falling.

Teeg was still with Lord Ebonhammer. And my family was just . . . gone.

And what could I do?

Caelus cleared his throat. "Eira."

I didn't want to hear what he had to say. I needed to leave, search for them. Someone had to know what happened.

His hand wrapped around my arm, forcing me to face him. "Take a deep breath." A flicker of light in his eyes caused me to look down. Lightning arced haphazardly from my fingers and over my arms. I hadn't felt the prickle against my skin or the threat of it escaping.

"Let go," I begged.

His grip tightened. "Tell me what's wrong."

I started to reach for him with my other hand, but lightning was there, too, and I stopped short.

"You're afraid," he said.

Dorian's face popped into my mind, the agony that was smeared across it like a brand in my memory. A moment I'd regret for eternity. All over some stupid, petty argument. "Aunt Celeste would have never left her home like this," I whispered.

He held up my hand in front of me. "If you act out of fear, so will this."

I took in a long, slow breath and released it.

"You won't hurt me." As if to prove that he believed what he said, he took my empty hand covered in skittering blue-white arcs and laced his fingers with mine. He didn't wince or gasp. There wasn't even a flicker of discomfort from him. He smiled, and I stared into those eyes I hated. But I wasn't so sure I really did anymore.

14

The next morning, I summoned all my will and pushed myself out of the bed that had once been mine when I lived with my aunt. If I couldn't seek an audience with Lord Ebonhammer, there had to be some other way to find Teeg and someone who knew what had happened to Aunt Celeste and Lora. And as much as I hated to admit it, those useless guards were right to suggest checking the Temple of Evryn.

The smell of cooked bacon filled the air the closer I got to the kitchen. I turned the corner and froze at the sight of Caelus in front of the stove. Of all the things I'd learned about Caelus, knowing that he looked comfortable cooking was among the most surprising.

I stopped in front of a platter of eggs, bacon, and toast on the island.

"Do you need help?" I asked.

He didn't look at me. "I think I can manage a simple breakfast." He cracked two eggs and dropped them into a pan, then shot me a glance. "Eat."

I sat and started with the bacon.

After last night, I wasn't sure how to act around him. He was convinced that the lightning wouldn't hurt him, but I wasn't so confident. "Is this something you do often?"

He slid the cooked eggs onto another plate. "My sister is a terrible cook, so I had to learn." He poured himself a steaming cup of tea, the deep, smoky aroma filling the space between us. "Care for some?"

I nodded.

He placed the steaming cup in front of me before pouring another.

I took a sip, the bitter flavor filling my mouth, and then added several spoonfuls of sugar. Caelus smirked but didn't comment.

When he sat, he wasted no time eating. I wanted to ask if he knew some way to gain an audience with Lord Ebonhammer—yesterday had proved a direct approach wouldn't work. But watching him, I decided not to. Enjoying a quiet breakfast with him felt easy . . . simple. A joy that I couldn't quite give up. I smiled to myself and picked up my fork.

Once we finished, I took my dishes to the sink and began scrubbing them.

"What's your plan?" he asked, leaning against the counter next to me with a small towel.

I sighed and handed him the cleaned plate before starting on the next. "The temple, I think. I'm not sure what they'll know, but I can take care of Marus's request."

He dried the plate and placed it in the cabinet. "It's a start. I won't be joining you, however. There's a few things I need to look into."

The cup slipped from my fingers, and I quickly reached for it, thankful it didn't break. I'd forgotten that while he might be here to help me, he was also here to find his sister.

"I trust you'll be able to find your way around?" he asked.

I gave him the next cleaned dish, and he was smiling as if he knew my thoughts. "I lived here once. I think I'll be fine."

He laughed and dried the plate before starting for the door. "Stay safe, and I'll see you later, Tempest," he called out, the door shutting silently behind him.

The statement was innocent but made my heart flutter. When had anyone who didn't want to use me planned to see me later, other than Marus, Teeg, or Esteban?

I got ready and headed out into the sunny streets of the upper district. Overnight, color had been added to the city. Banners in shades of autumn flew, contrasting the dusting of snow along the cobbled streets. The smell of buttery baked goods filled the air, and children played in the fresh powder.

I stopped in front of a familiar faded red door. Through the window, I saw the white-streaked black braids of Dorian's mother, Ina Anwir. She looked the same as she had so many years ago, her half-fey blood slowing her aging. Dorian's family had been a major source of love in my childhood, but they hated me after that day.

I wanted to knock—to apologize—but I turned away. Ina deserved to live without a reminder of her son's death standing in front of her.

I made it a few feet before a light feminine voice called out, "Eira?"

I turned, and Ina stood in her doorway, wearing an apron smeared with clay, a sheen of sweat on her brown skin. She stepped toward me. "It's really you," she said in disbelief.

I clasped my hands in front of me, not sure what to do with them. "I'm sorry. I shou—"

Ina darted forward and pulled me into her arms. "Nonsense. We miss Dorian dearly, but we lost you too." She stepped back and cupped my cheeks. Her vibrant brown eyes searched my mismatched ones.

I stared at her, eyes wide and tears welling up.

Ina smiled and dropped her hands. "Tell me how you've been."

"But after everything . . ."

"We love you too. Love doesn't simply disappear because of one terrible deed. Much less because of an accident. Dorian wouldn't have wanted us to abandon you either."

Of course it would be Dorian's will that led their actions to continue to look out for me, but I'd run away to the temple with Klareth and Marus. I'd thought it would be better, but I'd been wrong.

I smiled at her. "I've been better." There was a lot I could say, but Ina didn't need all the details. "Actually, have you seen Aunt Celeste? Or maybe Lora? Neither were home last night."

She shook her head. "I don't think I've seen them in about a week, sweetie. They left with a man with reddish hair. But it's not unusual for your aunt to go to galas in Ryseer with men. She'd never miss the Frostfire Festival, though. Give her a day or two, and I'm sure she'll be back."

I nodded, not entirely sure she was right. It didn't explain why the house hadn't been cleaned or the items left out of place. Before I missed my chance, I asked, "Have you heard anything about Lord Ebonhammer?"

"Oh?" she said, intrigued. "Finally interested in boys? I've heard his son is quite handsome."

"What?" I shook my head. "No. Have you heard anything that might be negative or unseemly?"

Her features contorted, confused. "I don't expect anyone from the Dawn Conclave to be perfect, but nothing out of the ordinary. Why?"

"It's been a while since I've been in the city. I'm curious about what's changed."

She didn't look like she believed me, but she didn't push it any further. "It's been the same as always. Oh, but you need to come have dinner if you can! Gavriel will be back for the festival. He'll be glad to see you."

"I'll try, but I should get going."

"Of course." She pulled me in for another hug, and before she released me, she said, "I'm so glad you're back. I've spent all these years worried about you, or that you hated us or yourself for what happened."

I blinked back the tears of happiness, or maybe relief, threatening to fall. "I could never hate you or Gavriel."

We parted ways, and I navigated the city using my faded memory as a guide. But the day I'd killed Dorian flooded in.

Aunt Celeste had thrown another party. She'd wanted me there, as always, to act as her prized possession—a Divine, but also a charity case since she'd taken me in. I'd snuck over to Dorian's only to find out he'd told her I was planning to not attend.

I'd been furious and thought he'd understood I didn't claim her as my family. That I'd chosen him and his parents because they cared about me. Loved me. I'd accidentally sent a deadly shock through him when he touched my arm, and I never expected Ina and Gavriel to continue to love me after that. *How could they?*

But Ina had been glad to see me.

I shook my head and let out a sigh. It made me wonder if I'd been too harsh with Aunt Celeste when I was younger. Expected too much from the woman who never signed up to care for her dead sister's child. I wondered if it would be possible to reconcile with her too.

My muddled memory led me to an enormous statue of a gnome. An ear pointed out of the hood of his cloak, almost horizontal, and his legs were short and stubby. Strapped to his sides were two daggers that were like swords for his size.

"Admiring the legendary hero Valton?" asked a man behind me.

I spun around, my hand drifting toward the concealed dagger at my thigh. A man, no older than his midtwenties, stood watching me. His straight white hair landed just below his shoulders, framing his slender face. With sapphire eyes that sparkled in the sun, he was striking. But he looked familiar somehow.

He smiled, tucking his hands into the pockets of his fine trousers, and looked up at the statue. "Dragons are fearsome, indeed, but only to those who do not take heed. Valton understood, and so he relied on a mystic hood. Now he stands stout and proud, despite now being laid underground." He looked back at me and waited.

I raised a brow.

His expression filled with amusement.

He thrust his arm toward me. "Vinnie the Storyteller," he said.

I shook his hand.

"Most know of me. It's quite the shock you don't," he said, releasing his hold.

People parted around us, and Keiran, magnate and supplier for the Copper Jackals, stepped up beside Vinnie. "I see you've met my favorite guest of the Sleeping Alligator. But your story was less than thrilling."

He slung an arm around Vinnie's shoulders and flashed me an inviting smile, his attention fixed on me as it had been the last few times we'd met. When I'd first seen him at Esteban's tavern, his wavy white hair had been astonishing for a man that looked no older than twenty-five.

Next to each other, the two were clearly related. They were almost identical in height, and their eyes were nearly the same shade of blue. But the sun shone against the waves of Keiran's shorter hair, revealing silvery strands among the white.

Vinnie scoffed, crossing his arms. "People find stories related to history boring, unfortunately. And I doubt you've come all the way to the city to balk at some statue of a long-dead hero."

I touched the lotus necklace Marus gave me. "Not exactly."

"I'm not sure what a beautiful soul such as you has found herself up to, but our assistance is yours," Keiran said.

"I'm trying to get to the temple."

"Perfect. We have business there."

"We do?" Vinnie asked.

Keiran ignored him and offered me his arm. "Shall we?"

I shifted my weight. "Are you certain?"

"It would be an honor to assist you," Keiran said, smiling.

I looped my arm through his, and he began leading us through the busy city.

"Did Keiran really never mention me?" Vinnie asked on my left after a moment.

I shook my head. "I can't say he's ever mentioned much outside of his work." He'd always asked about me and my role as a Divine at the temple when he visited Dusmir.

Vinnie laughed. "I'm not surprised."

"You never mentioned you'd be in Tiruhm for the Frostfire Festival when I last visited," Keiran said.

"Perhaps she didn't want you to know."

Keiran's laugh rumbled through me. "Did you not, Eira?"

"It wasn't exactly planned," I said.

"I always thought you could do with a little spontaneity. Tell me, what has you visiting the temple?"

I pressed my lips together, not sure how I could explain that I'd killed the high priestess and needed to find an appropriate replacement. Or that Teeg was the Golden Child, who might be in the hands of Lord Ebonhammer, and he won't grant an audience.

Keiran flitted a look at me. "How about an easier question? Will you be joining the festivities? Our family hosts it every year."

"If you didn't mention me, I highly doubt you mentioned our brothers or sister."

"Perhaps it slipped my mind while in pleasant company." Keiran winked.

I smiled. "I don't think I'll have a chance to participate."

Disappointment filled his eyes. "No? It would have been a joy to have you there."

"Maybe next time," I offered, and his eyes brightened. While I couldn't be certain there wouldn't be time to have fun during the festival, it was better not to make false promises. If I could find Teeg before it was over, he'd probably want to play, though.

The two continued to wind through the streets with ease, and I wondered if they'd grown up in Tiruhm.

We stopped before a shimmering iridescent path. The path to the temple was fitting for the god of abundance and virtue. History often depicted Evryn as a dragon with scales nearly identical to that of the pathway. He created the dragons that once roamed the land with humans, but there had been fewer and fewer sightings of them over the years, becoming more like a myth. One hadn't been spotted in over a decade.

I walked down the path lined with jasmine archways, and it rippled like water. A heady sweet scent filled the air until we stood in an open grassy clearing. There was no snow, and it had become warmer, as if we were no longer in the cold mountain city.

An enormous dragon had been sculpted out of a stone, which shimmered a brilliant silvery white. Gold veined in and out around the base of the scales. The dragon appeared as though it were clinging on to the side of the mountain with its four massive legs. Two golden horns protruded from its head, and royal burning sapphires inlaid into the eyes stared back at me.

A stone bench sat in the circular space. The sun shone down through a canopy of trees. I had to stop to take it all in. It was beautiful and so unlike the temple of Ahrea. *Are all the temples so different?*

A single stairway led down, nearly blending into the jagged mountain wall, and I wanted so much to explore what lay hidden beneath.

Keiran gave me a gentle tug, pulling me from my stupor. "I'm not sure I've ever seen you quite so stunned."

"The temple is just so . . ." My gaze drifted back to the gemstone eyes of the dragon.

"Ahrea's temple was magnificent at one time, if my father is to be believed."

The sound of two conversing men finally drew my attention. Vinnie sat with a handsome bearded man in finely tailored clothing. Faint wrinkle-lined eyes a shade lighter than Vinnie's and Keiran's. While he appeared older than the two men I was with, it was only by a decade, maybe two.

Vinnie looked at me, still smiling at whatever the man had said.

"Meet our father," Keiran said as we approached the two of them. "He's quite knowledgeable about the temple."

Vinnie stood. "It's been a pleasure to make your acquaintance, Tempest." He waved over his shoulder and headed down the pathway we had entered from.

"I'll leave you in my father's hands." Keiran released my arm and briefly took my hand in his. "Until we meet again, my friend." He let my hand fall to my side before disappearing down the stairs I'd seen.

The older man chuckled beside me. "Those boys have always enjoyed making a swift exit. Sit, sit," he said, patting the bench.

I sat next to him. Butterflies fluttered among the jasmine arches, and two blue birds hopped into a small puddle nearby. Both were unusual, given the frigid climate of the mountain, but the cold didn't penetrate this small courtyard above the temple of Evryn below.

"Being the Tempest must be quite cumbersome for you. You

seem not at all like the Inquisitive. What is it that you require here?"

I'd always wondered what kind of gift she possessed for such a title. But I asked, "Are you the high priest here?"

He nodded. "For the time being."

"The high priestess of Ahrea's temple has passed. Is there anyone you know who could take over? For now, a scholar at the temple is acting as high priest, but—"

"Is this scholar someone you trust and believe will lead the temple kindly and fairly?"

I nodded.

"I see no need to have him replaced."

"But what if he doesn't want that responsibility?"

"Did he state such thoughts to you?"

Marus had only stated that he felt someone more suitable should be in his place.

A butterfly with shimmering blue wings fluttered closer, and he smiled, holding out a finger. The butterfly landed. "Then I think you have your high priest. You do not need someone else." His wise eyes met mine. "But that's not all that causes you distress, I think, Tempest. Your gift is not an easy one. But there are those who find peace in the middle of a storm." He chuckled. "I can see on your face that you don't believe that. Perhaps shift your perspective. Lightning can start a heart just as easily as it can stop one."

Use lightning to start a heart? It would require an immense amount of control. If it lashed out and came all at once, it would burn.

"Come. I think there is someone you should meet."

He stood, starting for the steps into the Temple of Evryn, and I followed.

It wasn't unlike the temple of Ahrea underneath, except for the bright silvery everflame that lit the sprawling halls and various chambers. We passed a garden of jasmine, no doubt maintained by esprit, surrounding a fountain that poured water from a dragon's maw.

The people we passed ignored us, and they weren't apprehensive—worried about someone harming them. Most even gave me a friendly nod in greeting before going about their daily business.

But the most unusual part was their clothing. There was no way to discern who was priest, priestess, or acolyte. They all wore whatever clothing they found most comfortable instead of robes.

I bit down on the corner of my lip. Every similarity had an opposite, and while I loved it, I also hated it. I'd been taken in by a temple with a high priestess who'd found nothing but disappointment in me—had hated me. In the short time I'd known this old man before me now, he'd been kinder and more open to the tempest than Klareth ever had.

We came to a door depicting the same dragon I'd seen outside. He tugged it open. The smell of books and parchment washed over me, and a lump formed in the back of my throat. It hadn't been that long since I last saw Marus, but it was the longest I'd ever gone without him—without my best friend.

I thanked the gods that he paused, letting me gape at their library and swallow away that lump.

Several people were studying and talking among the various tables, but he headed for the stairs going up. Among the rows of shelves lounged a woman, book in hand. Her little alcove bore several tables covered in tomes and scraps of paper. He cleared his throat, and the woman looked up, blonde waves shifting with the tilt of her head.

"It's a rare sight to see you among those who love knowledge," she said.

He smiled at her and motioned me forward. "Eira, this is Thalia."

She blinked a few times, staring at me, and then jumped up, abandoning the book she'd been reading. "It can't be," she whispered, her eyes widening.

She shuffled around the tables, almost tripping on her sunset-colored dress, which complemented her tawny beige skin. In seconds, she stood almost nose to nose with me. "You've got quite the gift, don't you? Let me guess . . ." She took my hands and turned them palm up and studied them as if she could see beyond the skin. "Of course! It's beautiful but caged deep within." Her big hazel eyes met mine. "Tempest, yes?"

I glanced back at Keiran's father for help, but he was smiling. I sighed and looked back to Thalia, nodding.

She smiled, looking delighted with herself. "You are quite lucky. Ahrea watches over you, though it is an odd gift for her to give. Lucky to have made it here as well, I've heard."

I pulled my hands from hers. "I'm far from lucky."

"No?" She tilted her head. "You escaped a burning city that otherwise had no survivors. You made it several towns over to find your aunt, despite your young age. Most seven-year-olds wouldn't make it more than a few days without help. And now you've found yourself here, alive and well. All rather lucky, if you ask me." She twirled a lock of her hair. "All luck from Ahrea."

I took a step back. Power tingled at the tips of my fingers. How could she know so much about me? I'd never met her. Mythbel burning was recorded history, but she had no way to know the rest.

Ahrea couldn't be watching over me either. At best, those were all coincidences. Being in the right place at the right time—or gods, even the wrong place and the wrong time. Not luck from a goddess.

"You don't believe it." She puffed out her full bottom lip in a pout. "But you should. I believe the gods are watching. Come." She turned on a heel.

I didn't follow. "How could you know all of that?"

She made it a few steps before turning back. She tucked a stray piece of her wavy hair behind an ear. "I'm a Divine too. You have a power far greater in strength, but knowledge is a unique power."

"What are you saying?"

She smiled in a way that reminded me of Marus. "If there's something I don't know . . . Well, let's just say spirits of the dead are quite helpful, among other things." She shrugged and started walking, her dress billowing behind her.

I glanced back toward the high priest, but he was gone. And he'd left me with the Inquisitive.

15

I followed Thalia downstairs, deep into the library. The people we passed didn't bat an eye at the two Divine strolling among them. I doubted they even knew I was the Tempest. And I wasn't sure I wanted them to.

Thank gods the storm is still quiet. Between healing Caelus's wound and the exhausting ride, I hadn't felt the tempest stirring. But I'd be lying if I said I didn't want to give Thalia a light zap because she was surer of herself in a way I would never be.

We descended into what appeared to be a sanctuary on the lowest level of the library. Shelves lined only three of the four walls, but on the back wall was a mural depicting the gods gathered together, sprawling mountains behind them. Each bore a smile, but there was a goddess among them who stood out. Her slim face was solemn, and her hair shimmered in a rainbow of color with each step I took toward it, like that of the path to enter the tranquil temple grounds above.

Once I stood in front of it, the image shifted. Chaos replaced the serene landscape. Smoke and fire surrounded them. A dragon with multicolored scales lay in the center among the other gods, the eyes lifeless. Blood pooled out from where I imagined the heart might be. I tilted my head, scanning the gods and goddesses.

The goddess from before had taken on the form of the late dragon.

"Everyone knows Evryn is creator and king of dragons," Thalia said. "Few consider that perhaps another assisted him."

"You're saying *that* dragon helped him?"

"Perhaps. But she's dead. I'm sure you've heard of the legendary heroes. The ones that fouled the great dragon war?"

I looked at the mural again, studying it closer. Lost in the smoke were the shadows of five figures. One was shorter than the rest. *Valton.*

"I assume your belief in the gods has wavered, despite being Divine. Or maybe you believe they should intervene more?"

"Who wouldn't want that?"

She ignored my question and said, "They've sealed away their ability to take a corporeal form for extended periods of time; otherwise, they may go mad."

"That isn't what's taught in the temples. How can you be sure?"

"I've spent my entire life studying Divine and the gods across Marunia."

I knew the Inquisitive never stayed in one place long, but if she'd been studying Divine and the gods, it certainly explained why.

"The last time they walked among mortals didn't end well, and they lost a dear friend and fellow goddess to the madness."

"Madness?" I asked, tearing my gaze away from the dead goddess.

"At one time, I think they truly wanted to live among mortals. But imagine a never-ending life and having to watch those mortals you created go to war, die of sickness, or believe they're right to the point of ruin. It would make anyone mad, eventually, wouldn't it?"

She shrugged as if the answer was no longer important. "But after Navryn was defeated, the gods and goddesses have not set foot among us for long periods at a time. When I found this, I also discovered that tablet. It seems they believe there is a balance, and instead rely on Divine to intervene and carry out what they no longer can."

Below the shifting mural was a tablet I hadn't noticed, written in an ancient script I couldn't decipher. "But what does this have to do with them watching?"

She smiled. "They may sleep, but there's evidence to suggest that they still care for us and wake to be among us from time to time. Otherwise, there wouldn't be the Divine to begin with."

I couldn't fault that belief. The Divine were chosen by the gods and wouldn't exist without them.

She continued, "Each also favors a particular gift. Oerban favors gifts of fire or light, for example." She smiled and practically bounced up to me, grabbing my hands again. "Yours is perhaps one of the rarest."

I tried to take a step back, but she held on tight.

"I think Ahrea is the source of your gift. It's unusual for her, but it seems she favors the unusual." She giggled. "Texts suggest she may like to gamble too. Fitting, for the goddess of luck."

I tugged my hands away, succeeding this time. "And what could she be gambling on with me?"

Her eyes sparkled when she looked up at me, like I was a new puzzle for her to figure out. "I don't know. She might not be. I only assume it to be Ahrea due to all your lucky circumstances. Either way, I think you should claim your power. It was a gift meant for you. You should discover for what purpose."

I faced the mural again—faced Ahrea. Loose strands of black hair plastered themselves along her face, and a tear trailed down her dirt-smudged cheek. Her once-pristine white gown was tattered.

"Are they all dragons?" I asked.

"If one believes there is truth in stories, then no. There are stories of Oerban and Maelynn taking the form of the sun and moon respectively, and Thanally taking the form of a snake."

When I looked at Thalia, she was watching me, that sparkle still in her eyes. "How would you suggest I claim my power?"

She beamed and tugged me along behind her and back up the stairs.

Seated side by side in her cozy alcove, Thalia studied my palms extensively. She said she'd learned palm reading and discovered that she could see the currents of the soul—part of what allowed people to harness esprit to begin with—using her own power. "It's almost like a second set of veins," she said. "They can be blocked, either because the person isn't strong enough or because they never accepted their ability."

To unlock it would mean accepting my gift and learning to harness it, or so she said. She instructed me to avoid negative thoughts about it. Be positive. Find good in it.

She wanted me to increase the frequency that I used my esprit, too, saying it would help ebb emotional outbursts. She gave me an earring, a smoky crystal that dangled in the shape of a teardrop, and Thalia claimed it had some residual power to assist me with the tempest.

When I asked how she knew, she simply said, "The spirits of the dead are helpful but often vague." But she didn't give me a chance to ask more about her ability to communicate with the dead, choosing to focus on helping me.

I told her about Caelus's theory about my ability to control not just lightning. She jumped up again and began instructing me to open and close doors and lift things with air. Thalia also instructed me through attempting to release my esprit harmlessly, letting it skitter across my body and then in a small area around me. I scorched a patch of the wooden library floor but otherwise managed to do it. She seemed giddy that I might be more powerful than she'd considered.

The weight in my chest lightened being with Thalia. I was in a little bubble of normalcy that I'd never experienced before, except with Marus. Even the urge to zap her had dissipated.

Her passion reminded me of him, but she had an eagerness to share it with others that he lacked. Where Marus preferred to write and publish his work, she found joy in verbalizing her knowledge to anyone who would listen. I told her that he was currently the high priest of Ahrea for the time being.

"Are you sure he needs to be replaced? You said he'd be perfect for it. Who cares if he wasn't a priest before?"

"I'm not sure it's right to take that choice from him."

She sat back in her chair, propping her head on a fist. "You know, there is a chance he has grown to enjoy the position. It's quite cozy, from what I hear. But I'll speak with the high priest of Evryn for you. When you return, ask him what it is he wants."

I laughed. "And if he doesn't want to be high priest?"

"Then I suppose I'll help you find someone suitable if the high priest here doesn't," she said, smiling.

Thalia continued instructing me on using my power, never pushing me to use the lightning. I tried a few more times, letting it skitter across my arms but nothing more. Once it got late, she walked me to the exit of the temple. I'd gotten distracted by her company. She was easy to be around, and part of me didn't want to leave. And I still hadn't asked her anything about the true reason I was in Tiruhm. Her gift made her the most likely to be helpful when it came to information.

I bit my lip, then asked, "Do you know if there's been any strange disappearances in Tiruhm?"

"The disappearances all over Marunia the past couple of years have all been inherently strange. They haven't found any of those missing. It's as though they've vanished. It'd be hard to say for sure if it's anything outside of what's become an unfortunate normal."

"And what of Lord Ebonhammer? I used to live in Tiruhm, but I haven't heard much about him."

"He's a recluse. More so than usual in the past few years. Though he is getting older. I imagine Iker will become the new Lord Ebonhammer soon."

I sighed in defeat. It'd been the last lead I had regarding Teeg and Lord Ebonhammer, and maybe why Klareth had sent Teeg to him.

We said our goodbyes, and I made my way through the quiet

streets toward my aunt's home, the waning crescent moon shining overhead. Between conversing with Thalia and meeting with Keiran and Vinnie, my mind had been preoccupied. Would Caelus wonder where I'd been all day?

Everything Thalia had proposed to better control my power had been similar to Caelus's suggestions. But I'd seen what that storm within could do firsthand if given the chance. My fists clenched at my sides, and I tried to push away the thought. Thinking like that was the opposite of what Thalia had suggested. I fingered the dangling earring, hoping it worked.

An icy voice broke through my thoughts. "I never expected to lay eyes on you, Lady Quinn."

I froze. *Quinn.* It was a name I'd abandoned.

A name I wanted nothing to do with.

A name easier forgotten.

A tall fey man stepped around me. "Going to continue pretending you died in the fire with your parents?" he asked. "I think we can skip the bullshit. You're standing right here, alive and well. The long-lost heir to House Quinn."

"Who are you?"

He circled me before placing a long arm around my shoulders. "Call me Perrin. With any luck, we can be friends. All you have to do is tell me why you and the king's pet are in the city?"

"King's pet?" *Caelus?* Why would this man want to know about him? "I don't know what you're talking about."

"Pity." His hand slid down my arm, leaving chills in its wake, but I remained still. A finger twirled a lock of my dark hair. "You look like your father." With his thumb and forefinger, he forced my gaze to his.

"Especially the lovely blue one. How no one else notices who you are with those eyes is a wonder."

I jerked my chin away from him and stepped back. "What do you want?"

He laughed, the sound cold. "I told you. Tell me what it is you two are doing in the city."

I scoffed, pulling away, and started walking. "I'm afraid that's none of your concern."

"We could have been such good friends," said the fading voice of Perrin.

The sound of footsteps trailed behind, and my heart sped up. Would he follow me? The sound continued, keeping pace, and my palms started sweating. I quickened my steps and made a turn. Glancing over my shoulder, I saw no one. Had Perrin been following me, or had it been my imagination?

I let out a shaky breath and continued to make my way to the villa.

How had Perrin known I was a Quinn? It couldn't actually have anything to do with how I looked or my eyes, could it?

I'd avoided reading the history that'd been written about my childhood home of Mythbel, preferring to leave that life behind. Even my aunt refused to refer to me using that name—she never once spoke of my parents. I'd become Eira Ortunis while living with her.

What could a seven-year-old of House Quinn do for the people, anyway? The king had reassigned the land to the remaining High Houses before I'd ever considered the possibility of claiming it or my true name.

The scents of leather, rain, and citrus wafted by on a breeze.

"I've been looking for you," Caelus said behind me.

I yelped, tripping over my feet. He grabbed my arm to steady me. A tingling shot through me, and I waved him off. "You shouldn't go poofing around."

"Poofing?" He laughed.

I relaxed at the sound, my racing heart easing.

"It's a little more complicated than that."

I stared up at him. His face showed no sign of suspicion or like he'd overheard my discussion with Perrin. *King's pet* rang through my mind, but I dismissed it. Guards, royal or otherwise, likely had people who disliked them and gave them derogatory nicknames.

"Hey," he breathed. The distance between us shrank. "Are you all right?"

I ran my fingers through my hair. "I'm fine," I said. "You said you were looking for me?"

He searched my face. "You're certain?" he asked, ignoring my attempt at changing the subject.

I rolled my eyes and continued walking toward my aunt's home. "You nearly scared me to death."

Caelus fell into step beside me. "Awful things tend to happen at night."

I looked down at my feet, my boots crunching in the light dusting of snow. Would he know Perrin? Did I even want to mention that man to him? Perrin knew me somehow. Caelus knowing about him could reveal my most closely guarded secret.

My foot slipped on a patch of ice, and I fell forward. Caelus caught me, pulling me into his muscled chest. "Though I didn't expect the very dangerous frozen puddles hidden in the night to be my main concern," he said, his warm breath coasting against my forehead. His arms wrapped around me, and heat pooled in my core.

I met his darkened eyes. "Do you spend much time saving women from frozen puddles? You seem very aware of how dangerous they are."

He smirked. "There are many women in Ryseer who wish I'd save them from a myriad of things. In fact, Kenzo enjoys teasing me about the audience of women who find their way to the training grounds. A surprising number of them need assistance so they don't hit the ground due to fainting."

I gently pushed away from him, laughing. "Is that true?"

His hand found mine, and he winked. Citrus wind enveloped us, and our surroundings shifted. The cold night was replaced by the soft glow of my aunt's fireplace in her den. "Unfortunately, it is."

I smiled, stepping away from him, his fingers slipping from mine as though he wasn't quite ready to let go. *Or that's my imagination.* "You never said you could take people with you."

Caelus smirked and picked up a silver cup from the nearby table. "It's draining. Luckily, I'll be sleeping soon. Learn anything today?"

"Not really. Thalia—the Inquisitive—said Lord Ebonhammer has become reclusive."

"Interesting. Perhaps it's for the best that she hasn't noticed anything."

As frustrating as it was, he was right. Noticing nothing was better than noticing odd behaviors.

Caelus sat on one of the expensive plush couches. "I have something for you." The warm glow of the fire illuminated a large paper on the coffee table that showed what appeared to be the layout of a building, or maybe an underground system.

"This?"

"You sound disappointed." He set his cup on the corner of the detailed drawing. "Getting a chance to speak with Lord Ebonhammer won't be easy. I want to help you." He leaned back and let out a long sigh. "He'll be hosting his annual Frostfire Ball at the end of the festival. It's the perfect opportunity to get in and out of his castle nearly unnoticed."

I sat across from him and examined the layout again. "I doubt he lets the entire city inside. Even if we get in, that doesn't guarantee an audience with him."

"I'll help you get your audience, but first we have to find a way inside."

I narrowed my eyes at him. "I'm guessing you can't get us in the way you brought us here?"

Caelus draped his arms across the back of the couch and propped a foot on a knee. "No. It's too much of a risk, and we chance using too much of my esprit getting in. Instead, I think we pretend to be together."

I gave him a confused look.

"Romantically," he added.

My mouth fell open.

He couldn't be serious. I'd never been *together* with anyone aside from a drunken kiss here and there. There was no way I could pull something like that off believably.

Then there was the etiquette expected of those attending such a fete. Any lessons I'd had as a child had faded along with that life. And there definitely wasn't a suitable dress lying around for a ball.

But a chance to meet with Travok Ebonhammer and find Teeg . . .

"It can't be that simple," I said. "He isn't going to let us waltz in because we're—"

"Madly, irrevocably in love?"

My mouth snapped shut, and I hoped my face didn't betray me. From the way his lips twitched up, I knew it had. "*Pretending* to be that," I muttered.

"We'll also need an invitation."

"And how are we getting that?"

"The festivities."

16

The morning started with a debate over whether there was a way besides pretending to be together—*romantically*. He repeated the sentiment—that it'd be easier to go unnoticed and that two people "madly in love" attending a ball was the perfect cover. Couples were bound to be looking for somewhere private.

"Any plans for today?" Caelus asked.

I shook my head and continued washing a plate. "Any reason?"

"For this to work, it'd be better if you were more comfortable around me."

I grabbed the cloth from his shoulder and started drying the clean dish. "I'm not uncomfortable around you." In a platonic sense, that was true. But I didn't want to be seen as naïve either.

He chuckled. "Humor me, then."

I tucked the plate into the cabinet. "What did you have in mind?"

He smirked and simply said, "You'll see."

I finished getting ready for the day, and before we left my aunt's home, he paused in the doorway. "You don't have to do this. We could find another way."

I bit the inside of my cheek and shook my head. "I can do it." *For Teeg.*

Caelus led the way to the city's center. Colorful tents lined the area for the Frostfire Festival. He stopped in front of one hosting a game that appeared simple: use a ball to knock over as many of the stacked bottles as possible. He handed me one and kept the other for himself.

I gestured to the display. "How, exactly, does this help?"

He lightly tossed up his ball, catching it with ease. "You need to loosen up a little."

I glared at him. "Are you saying I'm tense?"

He grinned and leaned in, whispering, "Unless you're interested in another activity couples often partake in to ease tension, this will have to do."

I backed away a step, my ears flaming. *Playing along, it is.* But I wasn't sure that playing a game would help.

He stepped up and threw, sending all the bottles tumbling over. *Show-off.*

After the bottles were reset, I aimed and threw, hitting them with ease. The air filled with citrus, and they came crashing down. I scowled at Caelus, but the man suspected nothing and handed him two ebony coins with Lord Ebonhammer's emblem—a chipped mountain with a shooting star—on them.

Under my breath, I said, "You cheated."

He laughed, stepping away.

I hurried after him. "I didn't need your help."

He leaned in close as we walked, and his warm breath caressed my ear as he whispered, "They cheat too. Makes it a fair game." His fingers twined with mine, fitting together. I started to step away at the unexpected touch, but the warmth of his hand tingled up my arm as he pulled me along to another booth.

It's just practice for the ball.

He stopped in front of a different game that had throwing knives with a few targets set up several feet away.

Two men were failing miserably, sending the sharp points flying in all directions. A dartboard would have been easier and less deadly. What were these people thinking? Before I could voice the question, Caelus offered me a handful of throwing knives, keeping half for himself.

"Is this how you woo women?"

He smirked. "On occasion." He drew the knife back, lining up his shot, and then threw it. The blade flew, hitting the target's center. "But given your reaction last time, I don't think I'll be wooing anyone with a dagger."

I narrowed my eyes at him, but my face burned at the memory of the morning after I'd killed Klareth.

Facing the target, I got into position and drew back my arm. I took a deep breath and threw the knife. It hit the center next to his.

"Strange for the high bitch to have you trained with weapons but not your power."

"Activity exhausted me. Exhaustion helps with . . ." I trailed off.

Caelus drew back again, the flex of his biceps visible even beneath the sleeves of his clothing. He released the blade, and it penetrated the center once again. "You find me distracting, don't you?"

My mouth went dry. "What?"

He chuckled. "You didn't finish your thought, Tempest."

I looked away, not wanting to see that infuriating smirk on his face.

I mentally palmed my forehead. Gods, I'd been too busy watching him. But we only had to pretend to be romantically involved. That didn't mean I had to pretend I didn't find him attractive. Maybe it didn't have to be as difficult as I was making it for myself.

I took a deep breath, readying the blade. "Being exhausted helps with the emotional outbursts of my power." I released it, hitting the center.

I didn't watch him this time, but his blade hit the center again.

We continued to take turns, neither missing. We'd drawn a small crowd around us. I started to aim my last knife.

"Lord Ebonhammer should remove House Quinn's portrait from the castle," said someone in the crowd.

My chest tightened as the dagger released, and it hit the edge of the target. I searched for the source of who'd spoken but didn't find them. Perrin had been the first and only person besides Esteban, Aunt Celeste, and her daughter to know who I was. *Could someone else recognize me?*

Caelus took my hand and pulled me away from the game and the small crowd. Thankfully, they were dispersing after my near miss.

Someone called out for us after only a few feet. He'd won thanks to my miss, and was offered a prize. I let Caelus handle it, wiping my sweaty palms on my pants.

People were enjoying their day, but I couldn't stop myself from listening to see if anyone else was talking about House Quinn. I hadn't gone searching for paintings of my parents and didn't know how commonplace they might be outside of Dusmir. Had they had their portraits added to books on the kingdom's history?

My breaths came swift and shallow. I didn't know what would happen if people found out I'd survived. Would they fault me for abandoning them? I'd been seven, but all they'd see would be the adult I'd grown into. It would be too much if people knew—too much to be a Divine and a sudden member of the Dawn Conclave. I wanted to wander off and hide away.

Before I could act on the thought, Caelus appeared, handing me a small brown bear. Blinking several times, I took it.

With his thumb and forefinger, Caelus lifted my gaze to his, his expression concerned. "Did something happen?"

I cradled the soft stuffed bear to my chest, my breaths slowing. "I'm fine," I lied. Finding Teeg and getting home were more important than who I was born as.

AFTER A FEW GAMES and a break for food, the sun was in the middle of the sky. I didn't hear anyone else speaking of the Quinns. I prayed to the gods it would be the last I'd hear of it so I could focus on the reason I'd come to Tiruhm in the first place.

We started over an iron bridge heading toward the city's slums. While the structure appeared sturdy, I stayed away from the edge overlooking a chasm.

"Why are we headed here, of all places?" I asked.

"There will be a specific event rewarding the invitation. My informant should have figured out which by now."

"An informant?"

"More like a gnome with an explosive personality."

The buildings that inhabited the slums of Tiruhm were not like the rest of the city. They were mostly made of wood and had seen better days. I wondered how they were still standing. Roofs looked like they were ready to cave in, and one home had a metal sheet covering part of a gaping hole.

Urine mixed with the rotten wood created an odor I wasn't sure I'd ever be able to wash away.

We stopped in front of a metal shack—the only iron building we'd seen. The smell had lessened, but I couldn't tell by how much, given how it stuck to my skin.

An explosion sounded from inside, and I reached for the door. Caelus grabbed my hand, and a shock rippled between us. "I wouldn't do that."

I didn't protest and stared at his fingers around mine. He didn't seem like he noticed the shock any of the times it'd occurred or act as though it even happened. Shouldn't it have hurt?

He pulled his hand from mine and rapped his knuckles against the door. The sounds of objects falling and being pulled and placed against metal sounded on the other side. I shot Caelus a questioning look, but he stared at the rusty metal, arms crossed, not at all concerned while waiting.

The door burst open with a plume of black smoke. I took a few steps back, coughing and trying to fan it away with no luck.

"Tall Boy! I see you're back. Got a guest with you too. Come in, come in," a soot covered gnome said. He came up to just below Caelus's knees in height and wore spectacles around large, softly pointed ears that protruded up. There were attachments I'd never seen before on his glasses. And his hair was . . . white? Gray? He was covered in so much soot, I couldn't be sure. He disappeared back inside before either of us said anything.

Caelus didn't hesitate, stepping into the shack.

I stayed outside, gaping at the scene. *Going inside this place has to be a mistake.*

A hand shot out, and I met those storm-colored eyes. "Coming?"

Curiosity had me placing my hand in his and letting him pull me inside. A static shock passed between us again, and I pulled away. Caelus shot me a confused look but said nothing.

An explosion had most certainly gone off in the little metal shack. Soot covered most of the surfaces, and the corner farthest from the door was charred. A table sat in the middle of the room before a forge that seemed to function as a fireplace and stove. Before it was a chair small enough for a child.

"I'm Stumbleduck!" He grabbed my hand and shook it.

My eyes widened at his name, but I accepted his handshake before I could be seen as rude.

Stumbleduck spun around, almost dragging me with him, but he let go. He examined the site of the explosion. "You're lucky you had a young lady with you, Tall Boy. Might not have disarmed the door otherwise."

"Disarmed the door?"

Caelus shrugged.

"Yes, disarm the door! I can't have just anyone wandering in."

"I find it hard to believe that anyone wants to wander in," Caelus said, wiping his finger along a soot-covered table.

I stood in disbelief, listening to the two of them. *Explosive* had been the perfect word to describe Stumbleduck. But somehow, he had information about which event Lord Ebonhammer planned to reward invitations through. Finding Teeg was in the hands of a crazy old gnome who exploded regularly, by the look of his home. *Is this Divine punishment?*

"About our visit," Caelus started.

"I know why you're here." Stumbleduck grabbed a hunk of iron in the shape of a small man and whirled around. "I won't be telling you anything."

"Excuse me?" I said.

Caelus stepped toward me, bending his head close to me. "Don't worry," he whispered. The warmth of his breath caressed my ear. I started to turn toward him, but he took another step forward, placing himself in front of me.

"I'm too old to care about a fool's errand." Stumbleduck pressed the chest of the iron man, and it opened.

"I forgot to mention why I need one of those invitations. We're planning to meet with Travok."

The little iron man came flying at Caelus. Too fast to see, Caelus pulled out a dagger and, with deadly aim, threw the blade at the doll. It went flying into the metal back wall of the shack. The doll shattered.

Caelus wrapped himself around me, turning me away from the explosion. Shards of shrapnel pelted around us. My ears rang, and I covered them, but the damage was already done. Smoke filled the room, sending me into a coughing fit, and my eyes burned. The door shot open, and a gust of wind blew the smoke out of the shack, leaving only the faint scent of gunpowder mixed with citrus.

The ringing faded, and it was then that I noticed Caelus's hand rubbing soothing circles along the middle of my back. Once my choking had subsided, I peeled away from him and faced the gnome. "You threw a bomb at us?"

"You're lucky I don't throw another! Out. Get out. Both of you."

"Alston," Caelus said.

Alston?

The gnome's eyes narrowed, becoming clearer than they were before. His hand went for another of those metal toys.

"I don't think so," I said, taking a step closer to the gnome. "I need to see Lord Ebonhammer. There's a child missing."

Stumbleduck looked at me—really looked at me. His eyes were still clear, and they turned downcast, attempting to hide whatever emotion flickered through them. But I saw it. It was the kind of immense sorrow that left an open wound deep in the chest. The kind I'd felt when my parents died. When I'd watched Klareth murder Tryssa. When I'd killed Dorian.

When he looked up, it was gone, that haze over his eyes once again. "The tall one behind you better make good on his promise." He went over to the dressers next to the bed and pulled out a sealed envelope and gave it to Caelus.

Without a word, Caelus ushered me out with a hand on the small of my back.

Away from the urine-tainted air, I asked, "Are you going to open it?"

He retrieved the envelope from his pocket and flipped it over in his hands, as though he was debating what to do. To my surprise, he turned and offered it to me.

I pried open the wax seal. Inside was a small card that read *Treasure Hunt*. At the bottom, it read *Two days*.

"Wait, we only have two days to prepare?" I asked.

He peeked at it. "Seems that way. We've got a lot of preparing to do if you want to be convincing," he said with a wink.

"But what does it mean by 'treasure hunt'?" I asked.

Caelus started walking again. "A game."

I followed him.

"But we won't know what the treasure is until the day of."

That wasn't much to go on, especially if the treasure ended up being something only citizens of Tiruhm would be familiar with.

17

The next morning, I rummaged through my aunt's home and the few belongings I'd brought with me for a gown that was appropriate for a ball. And there wasn't anything.

Caelus said it'd be held the night after the treasure hunt event. But the clothes that belonged to Aunt Celeste and Lora didn't fit me well enough, and I wasn't sure if there'd be time to get a suitable gown on such short notice.

I groaned and sent a burst of air toward the door of Lora's room, flinging it open.

"Glad to see you using your power," Caelus said in the hallway.

I jumped, not expecting him. He hadn't been in the house when I'd awoken.

"Where were you?" I blurted out.

He stepped toward me. "Miss me?"

I rolled my eyes. "That's not what I said."

He smiled in that stupid, arrogant way of his. "If we're going into Ebonhammer's iron castle, someone should get an idea of his security. I highly doubt that's a skill of yours, so I took it upon myself."

"No one thought it was strange that a man in dark clothes was skulking around?"

Caelus strode forward silently, until he stopped in front of me. "If they saw me, they might."

I fought against taking a step away from him. If we were going to be a convincing couple, I couldn't step back every time he got close, or it'd ruin the ruse. I crossed my arms and tilted my head back to meet his gaze. "How are you so sure they didn't?" I didn't know why I cared. But scouring the house for something to wear to that damned ball had me antsy.

Those stormy eyes filled with amusement. "Are you worried about me?"

Despite my previous conviction to avoid it, I took a step back, looking anywhere but at him. Had I been worried?

"Stepping back isn't what a lover would do," he reminded me.

I sighed. "We're in private," I said, and made to push past him.

He took my hand in his, and a tingling sensation darted through my arm. "Come with me," he said.

I raised a brow, praying to the gods that my face wasn't flushed.

He didn't elaborate, but I let him guide me down the stairs and out the front door.

Caelus continued to drag me through the city to one of Tiruhm's taverns known for their musicians. The outside had been crafted with a vibrant metal with a deep purple hue, as though they inlaid the alloy with crushed jewels. An elegant sign read *Forgesong*.

Inside, flowers decorated the tables and lanterns floated above, casting a warm, yellowed light. Even in the middle of the day, it was lively. People danced and drank in the large space in front of a wooden stage, where a dwarven musical troupe performed.

Caelus showed me to one of the small round tables, not explaining the purpose behind why we were here. We took a seat.

The song changed. Partnered pairs began the practiced movements of a waltz, but based on the looks of disappointment, they would've preferred to dance with wild abandon.

Dancing had been how I'd met Esteban, though. My mother and father adored their little troupe and paid them well. As a child, I'd frequently danced on their stage. Esteban recognized me from that time when I'd arrived in Dusmir.

"Are you familiar with any formal dances?" Caelus asked from where he sat across from me.

"Vaguely," I said. Those trained movements might have been more familiar if my family hadn't burned away.

"We'll need to practice, then."

I glanced at him. He watched the people, his finger tapping in time with the music. The warm light gleamed in his dark hair, revealing those bronze strands that made it warmer and not quite black. I wanted to reach out and touch it, wondering if it felt as soft as it looked. He turned his head to face me.

I diverted my attention back to the dancers, hoping he hadn't noticed I'd been staring.

"The owner is a family friend of the Ebonhammers. They'll head preparations for the ball. There are guests here likely to be attending as well," he said. "Seeing us now will help and make us less noticeable later. If nothing else, they might see us as a blossoming new relationship, allowing us to blend in once we're there."

I bit the inside of my cheek. A man twirled a woman away and gracefully switched partners. He had a point. New faces would stand out; familiar ones would blend in. Aunt Celeste had continued my lessons so that I wouldn't embarrass her at the parties she hosted. But it'd been years since I'd last danced.

"Are you certain we'll even have to?" I asked.

He lifted a lock of my black hair, drawing my attention back to him. There was a tilt to his lips, and he twirled my hair around his finger. "Afraid?"

"Not at all." I hoped that somewhere deep down, I'd retained some of the training. Tripping, stumbling, and stepping on his feet would be embarrassing.

"A drink or two may help if you're nervous."

I laughed. I wanted one, truthfully. "Should I drink on the day of the ball as well, then?"

"While it may help with our ruse, I'm doubtful it's wise."

I studied the dancers, memorizing their movements to the best of my ability. "You're a crown's guard. Do you often dance at formal occasions? Wouldn't it be a distraction from your duties?"

"If I'm in attendance with the king, it's expected."

The song ended, and before I could ask what that meant, Caelus stood, taking my hand and pulling me toward the throng of dancers. He placed one of my hands in his and the other on his shoulder. His arm wrapped around my waist, and a hand rested on the small of my back, leaving a hairsbreadth between us. The starting position reminded me of my parents dancing the Emberglow, a romantic dance between partners.

I looked up at him and hoped he didn't notice the sweat building on my palm. *I can do this.*

The song started, rhythmic and light, and I did my best to follow his lead. My eyes drifted down to our feet. I stumbled through the movements that held some vague familiarity but tripped over myself and bumped into a nearby table. I spun around to apologize only to be met with the dwarf who'd denied us entry into Lord Ebonhammer's castle. His drink spilled in his lap.

The dwarf scowled, muttering under his breath.

"Apologies," Caelus said, drawing me toward him and back into the crowd.

I stepped on Caelus's foot, and my eyes shot up at his groan.

"Eyes on me," he whispered.

I nodded, acutely aware of every part of our bodies that touched.

He led me through a turn, my feet almost tangling together. His arm came up above me. I steadied myself, regaining my footing. He stepped away and pulled me toward him in a short spin. The warmth of his hand met my back, and he guided me through another spin before pulling me into his hard body.

Our chests pressed together, the heat of him seeping through. My arms had a mind of their own and wrapped around his neck. His eyes widened and resembled an overcast sky at dusk in the dim lighting. There was a heady thrill in seeing him surprised for once.

His hands slid down my waist, stopping just above my hips. My gaze drifted to the distance between our faces. It would take the slightest movement to bridge the gap between us. He'd gotten this close the first night we met in Esteban's tavern—the same night he'd helped me. My eyes lifted to his, but his focus was on my lips. Those thunderous depths churned with something unfamiliar, and for a moment, I thought he might kiss me.

"It's wonderful to see you smiling," Keiran said.

I stiffened at the sound of his voice and took a step away from Caelus. With a deep breath, I turned to face Keiran. He stuck out among those dancing in his white-and-black finery. People shot looks at the three of us. Most lingered on Keiran, but he ignored them, offering his hand to me.

"May I?" he asked Caelus.

Caelus placed his hands above my hips once more, and my heart raced. "That's for Eira to decide." His breath coasted against the sensitive skin of my neck.

Keiran's eyes filled with confusion. Was this part of Caelus's act?

Regardless, it seemed rude to decline. I hoped I wouldn't ruin Caelus's plan. "Of course!" I said, and I prayed I didn't sound too enthusiastic.

"My sister has had her eye on you," Keiran said to Caelus, gesturing to a table where a woman sat toying with the rim of her glass. She winked in our direction before taking a sip of her drink.

"It would be uncouth to keep her waiting." Caelus placed my hand in Keiran's. "Take care of her," he said before he retreated.

Keiran began leading me through the next dance. I wasn't sure if the dance was simpler than the one with Caelus or if Keiran avoided complex movements to save his feet. The reprieve offered me a chance glance at Caelus dancing with Keiran's sister.

She was as striking as Keiran and Vinnie, in a violet dress that hugged her curves.

Her head tilted back, causing her hair to nearly reach her hips, and she laughed at something Caelus said. My stomach tightened.

"Your friend is quite the gentleman," Keiran said. "I believe Jenny finds herself taken with him."

Keiran wasn't wrong, but that caused the tightness in my stomach to squeeze harder.

"And you appear happier than before," Keiran said.

I tore my focus away from where Caelus and Keiran's sister danced. "Do I?"

"The Eira in Dusmir didn't smile or laugh quite as often."

Keiran twirled me, then pulled me close. He smelled of the ocean on a stormy night, the scent wrapping around me. I blinked up at him, not sure what to say.

His hand gently squeezed mine. "Leaving that dismal city of Dusmir has brightened your soul."

"I suppose it has."

Keiran's gaze drifted past me as if lost in thought. His eyes met mine, and I swore he looked like he was conflicted. In a blink, it was gone. "Was my father helpful yesterday?"

"He was. He also introduced me to Thalia."

"That sounds like something he'd do." The planes of his face softened, making him appear younger, the love for his father clear. "It's rare to see him nowadays. Rarer for him to be able to assist, even if indirectly. I'd like to think it brought him great joy."

I hoped it did too.

We continued through the dance, and I managed to avoid

stepping on Keiran's feet. While some of the muscle memory was returning, I was certain he could tell I lacked experience. His face hardened, his gaze lingering behind me. A tap on my shoulder made us come to a halt.

"I'd love a dance with such a beautiful lady," Perrin's venom-laced voice said from behind me.

Keiran's eyes met mine, a question in his gaze.

I turned and faced Perrin. He wore a tailored burgundy waistcoat over a long-sleeved shirt. With his well-trimmed beard, he looked ever the gentleman, but there was a coldness to his amber eyes. Perrin knew who I was, and while that didn't matter as long as I found Teeg, I wanted it to stay between us.

"But of course," I said, placing my clammy hand in his.

He pulled me toward him, his other hand landing on the small of my back. The music picked up again, light and melodic. Perrin began leading, spinning me away from where Keiran stood. "Have you reconsidered what I asked of you?" he asked, breaking the silence.

I thought back to that night and glanced around for Caelus, but I didn't spot him among the dancers.

"Hoping the king's pet will save you? He won't risk it."

My eyes darted to his. "Have you considered he's here to simply enjoy himself?"

Perrin grinned. "He has been. But his actions are always purposeful. There is a greater reason for his presence, and you're not telling me."

"To help me," I said. That was the agreement, after all.

Perrin appeared to ponder that for a moment. He leaned in and whispered, "But that's not all he's here for, is it, Lady Quinn?"

I caught sight of Caelus where he now sat with Keiran and Jenny. His gaze was fixed on Perrin and me as we moved across the dance floor.

"Why does it matter to you?" I asked.

Perrin's movements were rough compared to Caelus and Keiran. He guided me through a spin and jerked me into his hard chest, his gloved fingers digging into my hand. "I'll offer you a trade, Lady Quinn. You've been asking about Lord Ebonhammer. Perhaps I can help you."

My eyes snapped to him once more. "What makes you think that?"

His grin grew colder and unnerving. "I have loyal ears everywhere."

Had someone heard when I'd asked Ina? Or maybe Thalia? I couldn't remember anyone else being around to overhear on either occasion. But he was correct twice now. That didn't mean any of the information he would give me would be truthful, though. "I won't tell you anything."

"Even if it concerns a certain child?" he asked.

My grip tightened around Perrin's hand, my muscles tensing. We would have come to a halt if he didn't continue leading me through the movements. "I have no reason to believe you."

He laughed. "But can you be certain of that, Lady Quinn?"

I couldn't be. And that was the problem. But he was asking me why Caelus was here instead of Caelus himself. There had to be a reason. "Why is it you need me to tell you about him?"

He glanced at where he sat. "Because he possesses a talent that you do not, which makes him exceedingly difficult to track or overhear," he said, ire coating his words.

"Then why not ask him yourself?"

His eyes narrowed, filling with annoyance. "You believe you hold the upper hand. But you've forgotten I can inform the entire city of your identity. It'd be the talk of the festival. I'm sure it'd be quite difficult to find the boy with everyone's eyes on you."

I didn't doubt him. And he'd do it all without telling me whatever it was he knew about Teeg. It wouldn't justify giving up Caelus's reasons for being in the city. But if Caelus didn't know where his sister was, then neither would Perrin. Right?

"Make your choice, or I will make it for you," he said, the music winding to a close.

I was running out of time. Teeg was the Golden Child. He had to be found before he ended up being used the way I had been. "He's looking for someone," I blurted out.

"You know who. Spit it out." His voice grew impatient.

"What will you do?" I asked again.

"It's none of your concern."

My heart raced. Caelus wouldn't let any harm come to his sister; I was certain of it. If we worked together, we could find her—protect her. But it didn't make my choice any easier. Perrin was the closest I'd come to answers about Lord Ebonhammer and Teeg. "His sister," I whispered, and prayed to whatever gods would listen that it wasn't a mistake.

Perrin grinned. "Travok Ebonhammer seeks immortality. The boy may be of use to him." He bowed, taking my hand in his, kissing the top of it. There was a pinch of pain along the skin, and I jerked it away. He grinned up at me. "I'll offer you a little bonus as well. The man who escorted your family from the city didn't do so with the sole intention of fucking your aunt. Travok should know more, however."

He straightened and strolled toward away, pulling a fur-lined coat from a rack and exiting the building.

I stood frozen where he left me on the dance floor. The start of a new song throbbed dully around me.

18

Perrin's words thundered through my head, and I twisted the lotus necklace Marus had given me around my fingers. *Would Perrin lie about Lord Ebonhammer's search for immortality?* Dwarves had long lifespans, often reaching the age four hundred years old. But for what purpose did he need the Golden Child? Malik had said Teeg would be powerful, but what was he truly capable of?

Caelus stepped in front of me without a sound and guided me toward the back exit with a hand on the small of my back. We stopped before the door, and the air filled with citrus around us.

With a finger under my chin, he steered my eyes to his. "What did he say to you?"

I swallowed hard. "He knew about Teeg. And my aunt and cousin," I said.

Caelus's gaze narrowed. "Exact words," he demanded.

I clamped my eyes shut and repeated what Perrin told me, keeping the part about being Lady Quinn to myself.

"That man does not give information for nothing in return. What did he want?"

My chest tightened, and nausea welled up. As soon as the words had left my mouth, I'd regretted them. I didn't want to tell him what I'd offered and lose his trust. Especially after all he'd done to help me so far.

But I had to tell Caelus—he deserved that truth. It was the only way to keep his sister safe now.

I met his callous gaze. "He wanted to know why you're in the city," I started. "I told him you were helping me."

"What else?" he asked, voice clipped.

I pressed my lips together and took a shaky breath. "That you're looking for your sister."

His fist clenched at his side. "Does he know where she is?"

I shook my head. "He wouldn't tell me anything else."

Fury filled his expression, and I couldn't blame him. I'd betrayed the trust he'd placed in me and put his sister in danger, but I hoped that by telling him, Caelus could stop whatever Perrin planned to do.

"I want to help," I said.

Emotions warred in the dark depths of his eyes for a moment. He leaned in and whispered, "We will pretend nothing has happened for now. Keiran and Jenevieve are waiting." He took my hand in his, that tingle shooting up my arm at his touch. Despite knowing Caelus had every right to be angry with me, his touch—that feeling I couldn't quite explain—eased the anxiety building in my chest.

He led us toward where Keiran was seated at a table in the corner.

"How wonderful for you to join us!" Keiran said. He gestured to the chair next to him. "I was telling Caelus about a tournament being hosted by a family friend as a part of the festivities."

I gave Keiran my best smile and sat next to him.

"However, our eldest brother is competing, so I'm not sure one can call it much of a tournament," he continued, sighing.

Caelus sat next to Keiran's sister, propping an ankle on his knee.

She giggled and said, "Ranvald doesn't know his strength. Otherwise, he'd know better than to compete at all."

"Jenevieve has also offered to take care of our attire for Ebonhammer's ball," Caelus said, no sign of what I'd told him present except for the tense set of his shoulders. "She's apparently quite the renowned seamstress."

Jenevieve surveyed Caelus. "With an excellent eye," she said with a wink. "And I told you to call me Jenny."

My stomach tightened, a sour taste coating my tongue, and I forced a tight-lipped smile.

"I'm surprised that he's even hosting a ball," Jenevieve started. "The king and his Dawn Conclave don't care about engaging with citizens. They split the Quinn land between Whistlemane and Ebonhammer instead of appointing a replacement." She sighed, poking her glass with her finger. The entire thing frosted over. "It hasn't done the people any favors." Her gaze slid to me, her icy-blue eyes curious and examining. It was like she knew more than she let on. But there was no way she could know who I was.

But Perrin does.

I clenched the soft fabric of my gown under the table and looked out at the dancing patrons. My parents had loved Mythbel. But I hated knowing the people my parents had once presided over suffered because I'd stayed hidden.

"Eira?" Caelus said, his voice pulling me away from my thoughts.

"Yes?"

"Would you like to meet Ranvald?" Keiran asked.

"Actually, I wanted to see Thalia," I said. If anyone could offer me a place to hide away from Caelus for now, it'd be her. I pushed away from the table and stood.

Keiran offered a wave and said, "Until we meet again, my friend."

I returned his farewell and headed for the exit. Caelus followed me, and I twisted the lotus necklace around my finger once again.

I made it a few steps outside and attempted my best smile before turning to face Caelus. "You know, lovers aren't joined at the hip either," I said, referencing his earlier statement. "You should go with them." Caelus had been competitive when we'd played the festival games, so I hoped it would be an enticing offer. Or at least one that let him pursue his search for his sister.

He studied me, crossing his arms and tapping a finger on his bicep. "While someone who claims to be unbeaten has me curious, we need to talk."

"About your sister?" I asked, even though I had no right to know after what I'd done.

He nodded, but Keiran and Jenevieve stepped outside before he could say more.

"Bring him back in one piece," I said, giving Caelus a gentle shove toward them. I made my escape to the Temple of Evryn.

PAST THE SHIMMERY PATH that led to the grassy clearing above Evryn's temple, I stopped to take in the grand statue of the dragon god Evryn. The statue of him at the temple of Ahrea had been of his human form, so I was in awe of the massive dragon before me and its bejeweled eyes.

But I could only stand and admire the god of abundance and virtue for so long while guilt ate at my insides.

I wanted to give Caelus space, but I wasn't certain that had been the right move. I wasn't certain telling Perrin about his sister for a scrap of information about Teeg was the right move either. That information could be false or even lead to nothing. But my own desperation won out.

I headed inside the temple to find Thalia. I knew nothing about Perrin, and that needed to change. Hopefully, her gift of knowledge would be helpful.

A few acolytes nodded in greeting or smiled at me. I returned their pleasantries and made my way to the library. Inside, I relished the scent of books and parchment. *I'll have to bring Marus here.*

I searched the massive rows of shelves for her cozy nook. It took longer than I hoped to stumble upon the mass of stacked books hiding Thalia, where she lay in an oversize chair. She didn't notice me until I cleared my throat.

"Oh!" She sat up, placing her book to the side. "I was certain that you planned to never come back. Not that you weren't friendly," she added. "But with your power block and uncertainties, it didn't plant any seeds of confidence."

I raised my brows. "I wasn't sure I'd have time, but—"

"You need help?" she finished with a smile.

I did my best to smile back and nod. Thalia's gift of knowledge might be even more valuable than the power of the Tempest, and I wondered how often people attempted to use or manipulate her.

"I'm sorry," I started.

Thalia giggled, revealing dimples. "What for? I enjoy helping when I can. Sit! Do you want some tea?" She gestured to the table on her left. "Oh, but it might be cold."

"Cold is fine," I said, sitting across from her.

She busied herself pouring tea for us. "What can I help you with?"

I opened my mouth to speak but hesitated, not sure what to say. "Do you know of someone named Perrin?"

She paused, confusion flashing across her face for a moment. "It's a name I've come across a few times. But it was in Ryseer. Almost like a local legend." She dropped a couple of sugar cubes into the cup and passed it to me. "Supposedly, it's someone who's been around for a few centuries. Could be a name that's been passed down, but I read one tale implying a fey blood curse made him immortal as long as he drank the blood of others."

"A fey blood curse?" Could Lord Ebonhammer be seeking that curse for immortality? It made the most sense, given what Perrin had said—but how did that involve Teeg?

She shrugged. "That part may be fiction. Hard to say. Fey used to practice curses before they were outlawed. The name stopped popping up after a while."

"But nothing in Tiruhm?"

"Do you have reason to believe I should have read tales of him here?"

I took a sip of the overly sweet, room-temperature Moonlit Passion tea. An infusion of citrus and floral notes coated my tongue. "I met someone who claimed to be Perrin. He seems to know the man I've been traveling with, so I've become curious."

"Why not ask your friend?"

I stiffened. She was right. If Caelus's sister could be in danger because of me, he should be the one I was asking. "His presence was . . . unsettling. I wanted to look into him myself first."

She pondered that for a moment, then said, "If it's the same Perrin, it'd make sense to feel that way. In the stories from Ryseer, he led an elite underground network of thieves. They stole anything of high value, and Perrin found the highest bidders."

I frowned. Why would Caelus's sister be important to Perrin if he specialized in finding buyers for rare stolen items?

"Not what you were hoping for? If you told me what exactly was going on, I might be able to give you more information."

I shook my head. "No, it helps. I'm just not sure what to make of it yet."

She smiled. "You're welcome to ask me anything. After all, we're both Divine. I know it's not an easy life."

I returned her smile. "Thank you."

She bounced up. "Now, how's it going with using your powers?"

I stayed with Thalia for a while longer. She guided me safely through using the tempest, as she had the first time we met. When I stood to leave, she led me outside, and we said our goodbyes. I headed toward my aunt's home, the sun only beginning its descent.

The Perrin in Ryseer could be the same or wholly different from the one in Tiruhm. The only connection was the fey blood curse and

Perrin's mention of Lord Ebonhammer seeking immortality.

And then there was Teeg. *Gods, protect him and Caelus's sister.*

Caelus was unlikely to be at my aunt's house yet, and he'd probably want to talk more about Perrin. But I wasn't sure where that tournament Keiran had mentioned was located. There couldn't be many places in Tiruhm to accommodate, so I made a turn to head toward the outskirts of the city.

"Eira! Here I was thinkin' it'd be hard to find you, and I would have to wait around at your aunt's," called out a familiar voice.

I turned to see Esteban ambling toward me down a crowded street. I smiled and rushed to him, people continuing past us. Kneeling, I squeezed him into a hug, his beard prickling against my cheek.

He patted my hair and chuckled. "It's only been a few days, girl." He took a step back. "But you look . . ." He smiled and shook his head. "Anyway, where's that boy they sent with you? Crown's guard, wasn't it?"

My shoulders tensed. "He's busy at the moment."

His brows raised. "I thought you were looking for that boy for Malik."

I gave him a sheepish grin. "We are, but it's not as easy as I hoped."

He crossed his arms. "I could've told you that, girl. Surprised he didn't."

I didn't mention that Caelus had told me as much. "It's a bit convoluted, but we have a way. There's a perfect opportunity."

"A perfect chance ain't usually so perfect."

"You don't even know what it is yet."

He laughed. "Let's go, then. You can tell me what I've missed."

When we reached my aunt's home, I helped Esteban with his belongings. He brewed a spiced tea with smoky undertones—Sunfire Spice, my mother's favorite—and we sat in the den. It was no shock when he pulled out a flask and poured golden liquor into his cup while I added honey.

I told him about what we'd learned and the plan Caelus had formed, explaining the yearly Frostfire Festival going on in the city and ending with how the plan involved Caelus and me attending together. As a couple.

"This plan is ridiculous. How in the world is he even meant to get you this 'audience'?"

I frowned, not sure how to answer. I'd come to trust what Caelus said he could do. My stomach turned. *Then why did I tell Perrin about his sister?*

"And what if he can't? Are you two going to go snooping around in that castle? Just the two of you? And what about your identity? Parading yourself around is bound to get you noticed."

I slumped and looked down into my teacup. The warmth of it had faded, but I liked it that way. Esteban posed fair questions—questions I hadn't even thought to ask. Each one revealed another answer I didn't have. The more Esteban brought up flaws in the plan, the more I wasn't so sure going to the ball was the best idea. But what other options were there?

"What if . . . What if someone *did* recognize me?" I asked. Because Perrin had. He knew exactly who I was the instant he saw me—likely before that moment too.

Esteban didn't answer, and I looked up at him. His expression was blank, but I could see it in his usually warm eyes. The idea saddened him. He knew how much it scared me to have people know—how people might resent that I'd run away and hidden, scared of how much would be expected of me. Being a Divine and the lost heir to House Quinn—each would compound the other. The king might even expect me to join the Dawn Conclave.

"Then it would be time to deal with the consequences," he said finally.

But neither of us knew the full scope of what those consequences could entail.

19

Esteban and I continued chatting, and he told me the Copper Jackals had been investigating the glowing jade-like stone in the catacombs beneath the temple. The stone contained an enormous amount of esprit. Their current theory was that it housed souls as well, but they'd yet to discover for what purpose. He also updated me on the temple. With Marus as high priest, the Temple of Ahrea was thriving unlike it had with Klareth.

A thud sounded in the foyer, cutting our conversation short. Caelus was collapsed on the floor, his back against the floral wall. Esteban sighed, claiming he needed food and a stronger drink, and left me alone with him.

I knelt in front of Caelus. His eyes were closed, and his breathing was slow. *He's asleep.* I admired the planes of his sleeping face despite the beginnings of a bruise forming around his eye. A faint scar marred the otherwise-smooth skin near his left brow. I reached out and glided my thumb against his cheek, that tingle winding up my arm. Guilt weighed down my stomach all over again. "I'm sorry," I whispered.

He leaned into my palm, sending flutters through my twisted stomach.

I started to pull my hand away but let it remain.

"Keiran's brother doesn't pull his punches," he muttered.

I smiled, and I barely had to envision a thread of life forming between us for the lightning to move in slow arcs from my hand and across the dark bruise forming.

The bruising began to fade, and his shoulders relaxed. He smiled.

"I thought you weren't going to participate," I said.

"I hadn't planned to."

"What made you change your mind?"

His eyes peeled open and met mine. That callousness from before was gone, but I couldn't be sure if it was due to his injured and exhausted state. "To clear my mind," he stated.

My heart sank. He'd taken part in the tournament because of me, then. Because he'd been angry and probably worried. And rightfully so.

"We still need to talk," he said, but his eyes fluttered closed for a moment, only to open again. It was taking everything he had to stay conscious.

"We will," I promised. "But right now, you should get to bed. You'll wake up sore if you stay here."

He seemed content to stay where he was, not saying anything in response and nuzzling my hand while arcs of lightning played along his cheeks.

"Let me help."

He smirked. "As you wish, Tempest."

The flutters in my stomach were at odds with the tightness in my chest. Had I mistaken that anger in his eyes at Forgesong? He was acting as he usually did, other than reiterating that we needed to talk about what happened. "How hard was your head hit?"

He laughed, but it spun into a grimace. "He certainly broke a rib."

My esprit receded and I stood, offering him my hand. He took it and pulled himself up, stumbling a step. I draped his arm around my shoulder to support his weight and steady him. He guarded his midsection and groaned in annoyance at the foot of the stairs.

The world around me shifted, and I fell onto a fluffy bed. Caelus held himself up above me, an arm on each side of my head, one of his legs between mine. His eyes widened. "Guess I was a little off," he breathed.

I swallowed. "Seems like it."

I stared up at him and the way his perfectly messy hair fell forward, nearly brushing my forehead. My body flushed from the heat radiating off him and a desire I'd been ignoring. All he'd have to do was lower himself and our lips would meet. But I didn't deserve that from him after what I'd done. And once everything was over, we'd be going our separate ways.

"Did you know your lightning tickles?"

"What?" I asked, breathless.

One corner of his mouth rose. "It's warm too. Almost too much." He shifted and brought one of my hands up to rest against his cheek once again. "But your hands grow cold, calming the heat."

I shook my head. The people I'd healed in the past were for Malik. I never saw them again, and they were often in such awful condition that I doubt they cared how it felt. They probably weren't even aware.

"It's soothing," he said, his thumb caressing the back of my hand.

He stared down at me for a moment, warring emotions I couldn't make out playing on his face. He sat up in one quick motion, sliding to the edge of the bed, and removed his shirt, all as though he hadn't said moments ago that he had a broken rib.

My body chilled at the sudden absence of him.

I stood from the bed, not sure what to do or make of what he said. I glanced at him and couldn't tear my eyes away. Along his taut, muscled abdomen, another bruise was forming, extending nearly the entire length of his left side. This one was dark, the blood already pooling into a light blue-black hue beneath the skin, the edges tinged with yellow. Several ribs had to be broken from a blow like that.

"How could an ordinary person do that?" I muttered.

He leaned back onto his palms, wincing with the movement. "Esprit."

"Right," I said. It'd been used to augment the strength of the one who'd landed that blow, making it deliver a heavier impact. Selena could do the same, though she refused to demonstrate it for me.

I stepped forward and placed my hand along what I guessed to be the center of the bruising. That thread connecting us sparked to life immediately, and streaks of azure wound from my hand to his abdomen and side. I wondered if it was because I'd healed him several times now.

It was difficult to concentrate after what he'd said about my lightning. It moved along his skin, and his eyes fell shut.

I bit my lip. His mood was better than it had been at Forgesong, so I asked, "Have you learned anything about your sister?"

His body stiffened. Instinctually, my thumb moved back and forth to soothe him. He let out another groan, this one different from the one he'd made at the bottom of the stairs. My body heated at the sound, and I was thankful his eyes remained closed.

"Travok has her," he said, voice husky.

My mouth went dry, and I halted. "Because of me?" I asked, voice trembling.

"I don't know."

My hand grew cold against his warm chest. The warmth was welcome, and the color of his skin was returning to normal. Once the last of the healthy color returned, I took a step back.

Caelus's jaw flexed like he wanted to speak but wasn't sure what to say, at war with himself once again. He pitched forward, and even sitting on the bed, he was almost as tall as I was while standing. Our gazes met.

"Eira!" Esteban called out, shoving the door open. His eyes widened briefly, and he cleared his throat. "I didn't know you were busy."

My face burned hot enough that I was certain it'd melt off. It might have been preferable, even though nothing was happening between the two of us, but I knew Esteban. I turned toward him. "Right. You should feel better now," I said, not looking at Caelus.

I made for the exit, and Esteban stepped to the side, letting me pass. His soft footsteps trailed after me. Caelus said nothing as I left the room, Esteban a step behind me. The door clicked shut on a citrus wind.

My mind raced to piece together what had occurred with Caelus. I couldn't tell what he was feeling. Those conflicting emotions gleaming in his eyes didn't help either. But Travok had his sister. I'd do whatever I could to help him if he'd let me.

I stopped in front of a door in the hall on the opposite side of the villa from where Caelus was—the room Esteban would be staying in.

"Why you didn't question his plan is clear as day," Esteban said beside me.

I pushed open the door and asked, "And what does that mean?" Not that I didn't have an idea what Esteban might think, but I wanted to hear him say it.

"You're falling for him," he said, stepping into the room.

I laughed. Bright everflame lanterns flickered to life, revealing minimal dust coating the surfaces of the furniture. Eying the room, I said, "That's rather presumptuous." There were the basic amenities—a bed, bedside table, armoire, and an adjoining bathing room, just like every bedroom in the villa. The musty scent would hopefully be gone after it continued to air out tomorrow.

He let out a boisterous laugh of his own. A rather excessive reaction, given the topic. "I've known you since you were a child, girl. While I may not have always been there and certainly missed some years, I've seen you fall in love. It may have been with food, drink, or animal, but your face is always the same."

My face? I stepped over to the open window. "So you think I love him?"

He laughed again. "Not yet. But you're falling for him, and that's only a step away."

I had no right to fall for him. I'd be falling for a lie, for one. A relationship and actions that were lies. There was no guarantee the man I'd come to know—the kindness, the banter, the charm—were real. It all seemed too easy for him to slip into, as if he were accustomed to morphing into a character to achieve a goal. *An actor.*

"We should have your eyes examined," I said finally. "And once we find Teeg, Caelus and I will go our separate ways. He'll be gone. There's nothing to fall for."

Esteban shot me a look that told me he didn't believe a word I'd said.

20

"What's your plan if you get caught sleuthing?" Esteban asked Caelus the next morning. They'd been going back and forth—more like arguing—about the plan for the ball for over an hour.

"If we have to go 'sleuthing,' I assure you we won't be found," Caelus answered.

"You can't assure that any more than someone could the weather."

I had enough of listening to them debate every detail and stood from the couch. I made for my aunt's garden to get a much-needed break from their bickering. Neither commented on my exit. I wondered if they even noticed.

Caelus and I still hadn't talked about what had happened at Forgesong. Truthfully, I wasn't ready to have that discussion. There wasn't anything I could say to Caelus to make it better or take it back. It didn't matter how much I wanted his forgiveness; he didn't owe me an apology. The most I could do was help him if he'd let me.

I opened the door and took a deep breath, inhaling the sweet aroma of the various flowers blooming despite the dusting of snow. The guilt in my stomach eased only slightly in the fresh air. Whatever esprit Aunt Celeste had weaved kept them safe from the chill of the mountain. She favored jasmine, and I always thought it was in honor of Evryn.

It was the first time I'd come out into Aunt Celeste's prized garden since we'd been staying here. I'd been avoiding it because at one time, I envied her esprit. She could grow and maintain any flower or plant, even the ones not native to the climate of the cold mountain city. It was a beautiful power that I'd wished for when I was young. Once I'd received my gift, my envy multiplied.

I closed my eyes and let tendrils of lightning flow along my body. Peeking at the streaks gliding across my arms, I realized it was a bit ridiculous to have not seen the beauty in my power.

I continued to free the tempest within, my focus on not harming my surroundings. I'd been working on it when I had free time, as Thalia had instructed. The electric blue-white energy coiled down my legs and feet and back up, not scorching any of the blades of grass it met.

I tried moving a nearby garden rock with air. So far, when I'd tried, I hadn't been able to release my power and use air at the same time. Either the lightning faded or air never manifested. Caelus would've likely known how to manage both, but I doubted he was in an instructing mood.

When the sun had nearly reached its peak, the door behind me that led back into the den creaked open. Footsteps crunched behind me, but I didn't turn around, sure it was Esteban. If it'd been Caelus, I was certain I wouldn't have heard a sound and citrus would be in the air. Waiting for Esteban to speak, I tried once again to focus on moving the rock while maintaining the arcing energy, despite his presence.

His pacing sounded behind me.

I did my best to ignore it, but the rock wasn't budging.

Esteban's footsteps continued to rustle along the grass as I tried again and again.

Nothing.

I turned to face Esteban, giving up and letting the lightning wither away. "Something on your mind?"

"His plan is that of a fool."

I took a seat on the stone bench beneath a large red-flowering tree. "And what would you change?"

"For starters, a backup plan for if you don't win that silly event. And what happens if you win, get in, and someone recognizes *you*? Because I'm certain you haven't discussed that with him," he said. "And why in all of Marunia did you plan on acting out being in a romantic relationship with him? You'll end up hurt."

"It doesn't have to be romantic." Though that was exactly the kind we had agreed on.

"And what of this gnome? The foolish boy says he's helping him attend but claims he's incapable of doing the same for me."

I blinked. "Stumbleduck?" He must have mentioned him after I left. "He never said anything about him coming."

Esteban let out a grumble of disapproval. "Of course," he sighed.

"Help me in the kitchen. I can't take much more of this without food."

I nodded and followed Esteban. Cooking was how he relieved stress. But what else hadn't Caelus told me?

CAELUS LET OUT A long sigh, his back to the flame in the fireplace. "Alston is a part of the plan, like it or not. It was a part of the deal as my informant for when we win the invitations."

We'd reconvened in the den after eating, and I tried to occupy myself with the book I'd brought with me—my mother's favorite story. But I'd been barely able to pay attention to it with all their arguing.

I lowered the book at the mention of Alston—the name Caelus had called Stumbleduck before. "Speaking of him, you never mentioned we'd be helping him get inside the castle too," I said from where I sat on the couch.

He gave me a look, and I swore he was about to say *You never asked.* He seemed to think better of it and leveled his gaze at Esteban.

"And why does he want to attend?" Esteban asked.

I'd only met Stumbleduck briefly. He'd thrown an explosive metal toy at us. He wasn't exactly a subtle person. I'd hoped that meeting would be our last.

Caelus's jaw tightened.

"You don't know?" I asked.

"He has a history with Travok. Once we're inside, Alston won't be our problem."

"If he can attend, I think you can pull some extra strings, boy."

Caelus crossed his arms. "And what makes you think I have more strings to pull?"

Esteban shot me a look of annoyance before narrowing his eyes back on Caelus. "So, you haven't figured out how you're getting this Alston in either?"

Caelus's hands squeezed against his upper arm, and he began pacing. A finger tapped against his bicep.

Esteban appeared to be right.

Caelus continued to pace, placing a hand on his hip. He'd likely paced the same way when he'd come up with all this—the plan Esteban was now questioning every detail of. I was learning how much of it I hadn't known.

But I wanted Esteban with us at the ball too. Having someone else we could trust there—someone who could act like we belonged—would be a benefit. It would also ease my mind to have him there as a reminder that we'd be going home as soon as we found Teeg.

Esteban huffed a sigh and slid out of the armchair he'd been sitting in and headed for the foyer. I shoved my book to the side and followed him. "Where are you going?"

"Forgesong is assisting with the Frostfire Ball. I'm friends with the owner. Since the boy doesn't have answers, I'll call in a favor."

"That fixes one problem," Caelus muttered behind me.

Esteban spun around, shooting a glare past me to Caelus. "It fixes both of your problems, boy. I'll get that old gnome in, but you'd better be right about him."

"Will you be back before the contest?"

He shot me a grin. "Wouldn't miss it, girl."

Esteban exited the front door, leaving Caelus and me alone. I headed back to the den, stopping in the doorway. He was back to pacing, his brows pinched together.

"Your sister . . ." I started, wanting to get whatever conversation he wanted to have over with.

Caelus paused, his head snapping to me.

I shifted my feet under his intense gaze.

"Have you met with Perrin before?" he asked.

"Once."

"When?"

I folded my arms over my chest. "He found me. It was when I was headed back from the Temple of Evryn. He wanted to know the reason you were in the city."

"Yet you didn't tell him why then."

I nodded.

"And somewhere along the way, you valued vague information about Teeg and your family over my sister."

I narrowed my eyes. "I valued both, otherwise I wouldn't have told you at all."

"If you valued both, you wouldn't have said a damn thing to Perrin."

I took a step back. I'd regretted telling Perrin immediately and wished I hadn't. He had to know that.

"How is it you know so much about him?" I asked.

He averted his gaze. "That's not your concern."

I sighed and grabbed my book from the couch. "If you're going to withhold what you know, there's nothing left to talk about. Conversation over." I left the room, planning to avoid Caelus until Esteban returned.

And Esteban made it back like he'd promised he would—an hour before the treasure hunt event was to start. He stumbled into the villa, cheeks rosy. He explained that he and the owner had caught up over drinks. Caelus had to carry him upstairs before he tumbled down them.

It was going to take a miracle for him to be fit enough to take part in the event, and no amount of healing would help him recover faster. I'd tried once after he'd had a particularly lively night at his tavern, to no avail.

Unfortunately, I'd planned to ask Esteban what the city of Tiruhm treasured to use as a hint of what we might be looking for. Between last night and his questions about Caelus's plans, there hadn't been an opportunity before.

Caelus came downstairs moments later. "You seem . . . displeased," he said, descending the last few steps.

Displeased was a nice way of putting it. "What gave it away?" Thankfully, practicing with my power had the storm inside me dulled; otherwise my rising annoyance might've caused it to slip through. Thalia's earring might be to thank as well, but I wasn't sure and wasn't willing to find out.

There was a slight twitch at the corner of his lips, but he didn't answer me. "Think your luck has run out?" he asked.

I narrowed my eyes. Talking to him wasn't easy. I thought we'd avoid each other until it was time to leave. But winning the event was important. Leaving out any details he knew that might help us win would hinder him as much as it would me. "I guess we'll see," I said, heading for the kitchen. Wine. I needed wine. But unlike Esteban, I could control myself.

I could only assume Caelus followed me, since I wouldn't hear his footsteps if he had, but the faint scent of his esprit told me he did. I pulled out one of Aunt Celeste's more expensive bottles of red wine. When I turned, he was there, leaning against the kitchen doorway. I clumsily removed the cork, and he wisely didn't remark on my choice.

Once I had a glass in front of me and took a long drink of the sweet wine, he said, "Vinnie the Storyteller writes riddles every year for festivals across the kingdom. They're usually vague. Otherwise, it'd be too easy to make guesses and have a winner immediately. They'll elaborate on the rules once they announce the game."

He was being friendly. After our argument, it was admittedly surprising. I wasn't certain it would last. But we needed to work together. I swirled the wine in my glass. "And what stops someone from accidentally participating and winning by being in the right place at the right time?"

"I'd guess an enchantment will be placed on all those who arrive to take part and hear the rules firsthand."

My skin recoiled at the thought of having an enchantment placed on me. The last one had been the *tenebrae*-like bond Klareth forced onto me. The very one that had marked her as a protector, even though she was anything but. Caelus made it all sound so easy, like always, and I hoped it would be.

21

Before we left, I checked on Esteban. If he was aware I'd been present, he certainly didn't show it. There was no telling how much he'd drunk to get that intoxicated. Annoyance burned in my veins. He'd promised to help, but now he couldn't. Not that it changed much. Caelus and I had planned to do this without him before he arrived in Tiruhm. It'd been smarter to plan it that way, I'd admit.

But now I was stuck alone with Caelus, a few feet from where Jenevieve stood on a floating wooden stage above the crowd. I glanced at him. He'd been friendlier shortly before he left, but after the miraculous failure of a conversation we'd had, I hoped Esteban could act as a buffer during the treasure hunt. At the ball, we'd be stuck together, though, so I had to learn to pretend we got along, even if he was irate with me for what I'd done.

My gaze shifted back to the floating platform—to Keiran and another young white-haired man I assumed to be Ranvald. He wore a sleeveless tunic despite the autumn chill, arms crossed and appearing more intimidating than a friendly host. Jenevieve rattled off information about it being the annual Frostfire Festival and how many years it'd been going on, leaving me about as bored as the man I presumed to be Ranvald.

Ranvald yawned on the stage, and Keiran laughed. Jenevieve didn't falter, continuing. People were enthralled by her presence, listening to every word. The dress she wore begged you to pay attention to her and left little to the imagination, making it clear she was here to host the event. She'd likely roped Keiran and Ranvald into assisting her.

Caelus was among those enthralled. His gaze locked on the floating stage, listening to every word she spoke. That sour taste filled my mouth again and turned bitter. I frowned but kept my attention on Jenevieve and her brothers.

Keiran made eye contact with me and winked, a charming smile in place. I couldn't keep myself from returning the smile. In my periphery, I caught Caelus glance at me before he looked away. The muscle in his jaw tensed.

"Now, for tonight's event, you will be looking for treasures throughout the city. The treasure may be a physical object or the answer to a riddle." She took a breath. "There will be representatives present to identify our winners, including myself and my brothers." She looped her arms with Keiran and Ranvald. "But you only have an hour, so be quick. And remember, you must work alone. The first three to locate one of the treasures will win an invitation to Lord

Ebonhammer's Frostfire Ball!"

The surrounding crowd erupted in excitement.

"Now, without further ado!" she continued, the volume of her voice increasing to be heard over the crowd thanks to esprit. Jenevieve waved a hand above her, and violet esprit glittered from her hand down onto the crowd.

A roll of purple parchment, the same shade as Jenevieve's esprit, appeared in the air before me. I glanced around. Rolls of parchment floated in front of others too.

"You should all have your first clue in front of you. Good luck!" She winked, and the three onstage vanished in a violet cloud.

Everyone broke out into chaos, grabbing their scrolls and darting in every direction. I plucked mine from where it floated in front of me. A man knocked into me, and I stumbled back. Caelus steadied me and took my hand, sending those infuriating tingles up my arm. He guided me out of the fighting crowd. We made it to an alleyway, and he unfurled his roll and read it silently, tilting his head. When he finished, he looked at me, revealing nothing of what it'd said.

I unrolled mine and read:

> *The hero of legend faces western skies,*
> *pockets full of treasures and adventure.*

The line obviously referred to Valton and that I should head west. Easy enough, but how was I supposed to know what I was looking for after that? I looked toward Caelus, but he was already gone. *I guess we're not talking, then.*

I headed back toward Valton's statue and hoped he understood his riddle, unlike myself. It was an effort to avoid the crowd of participants, but once the statue came into view, I scanned the street and buildings west of it. For what, I wasn't exactly sure. But I found nothing that immediately stood out.

I studied the statue, unsure of what to do next.

Violet peeked out from the statue's pocket, and I circled it for a better view. It was another scroll. Did they expect me to crawl up onto it to reach the pocket? I wasn't sure if that was allowed, but before I could second-guess my decision, I pulled myself up and plucked out the scroll, quickly hopping down before anyone could notice me.

Safely on the street, I opened it.

Seek a balance struck in fire and ash.

I furrowed my brow, more baffled than I'd been before and unsure of where to search.

The previous scroll hadn't disappeared, though. I held them next to each other and faced west. The largest street in that direction was the major shopping district. With no other clues, I started down it.

Most of the storefronts were still open for guests who weren't taking part in the event. Frostfire Festival–themed items filled the stores. Candles, blue glass in the shape of a flame, sapphires inlaid in flame-inspired jewelry, and more. Every item I passed could have been a possible answer to the riddle.

A set of scales caught my eye. It was inlaid with sapphires to appear as though it had caught flame, and I considered that they may be the answer to the riddle for balance. But scales were too easy of an answer, especially since someone could buy them before they were found. I moved along to avoid being hounded by the shopkeeper.

A few stores down was an oddities shop. The oddest part of it was that there was no one interested in it. I stopped in front of it, looking at their wares through their window. There were incense burners in various and intricate designs. Beside them were rabbit feet, said to bring luck, and the skulls of crows. *Definitely odd.*

But what struck me was the ornate bird statuette. It was made of a gleaming dark stone that shone red or blue, depending on the angle. It made the bird appear as if it were on fire. "Beautiful," I murmured.

I started to walk away when the shopkeeper peeked out. She glanced at the statuette and said, "Phoenix caught your eye? Beautiful creatures. Shame the Mad King had them slaughtered."

"Phoenix?" I asked, eyeing the statuette again.

"Myth says when it's ready to pass on, it makes a nest of aromatic wood and sets itself aflame. From the ashes, it's reborn."

Could it be? "Can I look at it?" I asked.

She nodded, and I followed her inside. The smell was striking—a mix of preservatives and herbs that boiled in a pot in the fireplace. There were other strange trinkets and items available that I wasn't sure why anyone would want to buy.

She grabbed the statuette and handed it to me. Surely, if it was the answer, I wouldn't have to buy it—or at least, that's what I hoped. Spinning it around in my hands, nothing appeared special about it. There were no hidden compartments I could find that might hold another clue or note.

I tapped a finger along the surface. Whatever material it was made of wasn't one that I could easily break.

I let out a sigh.

There wasn't time to mess around with something that might not even be the answer. I started to hand it over to the woman, but she was gone. I turned, facing the burning fireplace. *Burns, and in the ashes, is reborn.* If I was wrong, I'd have no choice but to buy the trinket. It'd no doubt be ruined by the flame, but if I was right . . .

I knelt down and placed the statuette in the fire. The flames engulfed it, turning it a roaring blue before sputtering out. In its place was another roll of violet parchment. Smiling, I picked it up.

The shopkeeper appeared and clapped excitedly. "I wasn't sure you were going to get it."

"Me either," I muttered, opening the next clue.

Royal Frostfire's sight lights the way
through serene rainbow's light.

Rainbow? I thought over what I'd seen since I'd been in the city. There wasn't any sort of particularly colorful part of the city I could recall, aside from my aunt's garden and Forgesong. Most of it was steely and cold, aside from the festival decorations.

I rolled up the parchment and headed out into the street. Walking around was better than standing in her store, hopelessly waiting for some hint or memory to fall into place.

My pace quickened and I searched for anything rainbowlike, continuing west. I bit the inside of my cheek. The busy street faded into a stone pathway that led to a residential area. Would a clue or treasure be there?

"I'm guessing you didn't intend to lie to me when you said you wouldn't be taking part in the festivities?" Keiran's voice called out from behind.

I glanced over my shoulder at him, still not sure if I should check the residential area or turn back. There wasn't enough time for both. "It's a sudden development," I said.

He gave a light chuckle. "I would help you if I could, but I'm afraid my hands are tied as a judge."

I turned, deciding that the homes of others would likely not be the home of this city's treasure. "Jenevieve behind that too?" I asked, her name bitter on my tongue.

He fell into step beside me, grinning. "But of course. It's her show, after all."

Her show. Their family likely decided the events of the festival, then. How they managed to obtain three invitations to Lord Ebonhammer's ball was a question for another time. I took a left down a street, not really sure where I was headed, while keeping a lookout for anything bright or colorful.

Keiran followed.

"Vinnie is behind the riddles?" I asked, to confirm what Caelus had said before.

"His silver tongue is envied by many."

I smiled. If Vinnie wrote the riddles and their family ran the events, it might be a hint. They may not choose treasures *of* the city but perhaps things they themselves treasure *within* the city.

I continued until I stopped in front of the shimmery path that led to Evryn's temple. Moonlight shone down on the iridescent walkway, revealing a rainbow of color. Keiran smiled next to me when I stepped forward. I hoped it was confirmation that I was on the right track.

All that was left was to decipher the meaning behind the rest of the riddle. *Royal Frostfire's sight.* I looked around, landing on the statue of Evryn's dragon form again. The sapphire eyes caught on the moonlight and glinted as if a flame burned within them.

I unrolled the page again, reading over the clue.

"It's the eyes," I said. They were frostfire sapphires. An incredibly rare jewel that could only form from dragon fire.

Clapping sounded from the shadows.

I turned, only for the sound to shift to another spot. Keiran tensed next to me.

"It's been rather boring watching you bumble your way through this little game, Lady Quinn."

Perrin stepped forward, and my body went rigid.

I glanced at Keiran. He didn't show any recognition of what Perrin had revealed.

"Are you the reason Travok has Caelus's sister?" I asked, the question tumbling out of me. Now wasn't the time to consider the ramifications of what he'd just revealed to Keiran.

Perrin laughed, the sound turning my stomach. "And what if I was?" Before I could answer, he said, "I thought it would only be fair, given our arrangement, to inform you that the man who escorted your precious cousin and aunt from Tiruhm had a partner who will be present at the ball."

"What arrangement?" Keiran growled. I'd never heard him sound like that before. He sounded almost feral.

A viper's smile formed on Perrin's face. "Lady Quinn is now one of my informants, and in exchange, I provide her with details regarding her family."

"I didn't agree to that," I said.

"Your blood tasted exquisite, and fey deals are binding, after all."

The skin on the back of my hand where he'd kissed it chilled as if confirming his statement. The moment he'd taken it and that sharp prick flashed in my mind. But there hadn't been any sign of the ancient fey tattoos that appeared when fey made deals or used esprit. I rubbed the back of my hand. He'd somehow forced me into a deal with him against my will. *Could I attack him? Kill him?* I wasn't sure if that would solve anything or if it would just be another needless death.

There was a flash of light next to me, and I glanced at Keiran. He appeared as he always did except for the snarl on his face. When I looked back to where Perrin was standing, he'd disappeared into the shadows again.

A bell tolled, signaling the end of the hour.

"Shit! The eyes!" I spurred into action, starting for the statue. Without the invitation, there wasn't a next move.

Keiran grabbed my arm, stopping me. "Eira, you won the moment you identified the eyes. Now, tell me what's going on."

My shoulders slumped. There was no point in lying to him. He'd heard my name, even if he hadn't said anything about it yet. "He sought me out. Offered me information. I didn't know anything about this . . . this deal. Until now."

He pulled me into a hug, his warmth invading me. Tears threatened to spill over. I didn't realize how much I needed this.

"And what about your friend's sister? How is she involved?" he asked.

"I'm not sure." I mumbled into his chest. "Lord Ebonhammer has her, though."

He sighed, releasing me, and then raked a hand through his wavy hair. "Travok and Perrin are despicable people," he spat.

"What do you know about Travok?" I asked.

His face turned grim, and he searched my eyes. For what, I wasn't sure. His features softened. "You're bound to a dangerous fey, Eira," he said, ignoring my question.

"You know Perrin?"

He reached into his coat and pulled out a sealed envelope, handing it over. "I know *of* him. You need to be careful, Lady Quinn."

There it was.

My greatest secret.

What could I say to him? I reached for the envelope but hesitated to take it. "You're not angry? Don't want to know more? Have questions?" I asked.

He smiled gently. "Do I need to know?"

Keiran didn't seem shocked by the news. He took the revelation as if he'd always known. Then again, I was Divine—the Tempest. Was being the lost Quinn heir really that different? "You don't seem—"

He stepped forward, leaving almost no distance between us. "I trust you, Eira. You had your reasons. Share them whenever you're ready. But all I wish for is that my friends stay safe. You're doing what you must, and you're far from weak."

He was close—close enough to remind me why I'd had a one-sided longing for him for the first few months I'd known him. But that had been nearly four years ago. I swallowed. "What have I done to earn that trust?"

Keiran smiled. "You have a beautiful soul, Eira. You care, even when it doesn't benefit you. That is enough."

IN MY AUNT'S DIMLY lit den, exactly one invitation sat on the table between Caelus and me, along with my wineglass. I'd had two filled to the brim before he'd returned in an attempt to calm my nerves from the run-in with Perrin.

Caelus hadn't managed to figure out his clues. Given that there was only one invitation, it was all I could assume. But a part of me wasn't sure I believed that. After the time I'd spent with him, it seemed unlikely he couldn't figure out the riddles. He was smart, clever. Always planning.

But here I was, sitting in a room with him, neither of us talking.

If I hadn't won, what would we—I—have done? I had been counting on him to win, but I hadn't realized it until he showed up empty-handed and my heart sank. Maybe it was thanks to Ahrea's luck, like Thalia had implied. Luck explained a lot, but I'd been unlucky in so many ways too. Luck was such an unpredictable thing. Not something I could rely on yet something I always found myself with—like an invisible power, almost.

However, Caelus deserved to know what Perrin all but confirmed when he didn't answer that question. I was the reason Travok had his sister. And despite our earlier argument, I really hadn't intended to cause any of this.

How angry will he be? The answer was irrelevant because he deserved to know. Despite that, the words wouldn't come.

I plucked up the wine and took a long drink.

He appeared bored, leaned back in the armchair with an ankle propped on his knee, staring out the window. "You're nervous. Did something happen?"

My palms grew sweaty, and I clung to the stem of the wineglass.

Tell him. My mouth dried. I took another drink, swirling the sweetness through my mouth before swallowing.

He sighed.

I spun the remaining wine around in the glass, working up the courage to speak. He wouldn't wait forever.

I looked away, toward the fire. "I'm sorry," I said, barely audible over the crackle of flame. And I was. Because I missed the teasing Caelus. I hated that talking to him was difficult now.

He leaned forward, and I could sense the intensity of his gaze despite not looking at him.

I found myself fascinated by the way the flames danced. The way they were free in a way I wished to be. "Perrin found me again tonight," I said.

He tensed.

It was thanks to the wine that the words tumbled free. I repeated what Perrin told me about my aunt and cousin when Perrin and I had danced at Forgesong. And then told him how my run-in with Perrin tonight verified my suspicion that it was, in fact, my fault that Travok had Caelus's sister. I left out the deal I'd been forced into that left me as one of Perrin's informants. That wasn't Caelus's problem to deal with.

Caelus remained silent.

To his credit, he didn't appear livid like he had at Forgesong. Though the look of indifference on his face was worse. Like I'd transformed into a disappointment. It reminded me of the way Malik said my Divine title as though he expected more—that I'd be better somehow.

He ran a hand through his hair, the only sign of frustration— or was it anger?—behind the mask. He stood and said, "I'll see you tomorrow, Tempest."

"Where are you going?" I asked, standing too.

"Out." His tone was distant. Icy.

He vanished. The only thing left was the citrus in the air.

22

I stared at the dress Jenevieve had crafted. It had arrived that morning, but I hadn't put it on yet and we'd be leaving soon.

The blue fabric spread across the bed reminded me of the color of an ocean during a storm. It was open backed, wrapping around the neck from the front to support it. Slits came up from the sides to midthigh, leaving my legs partially exposed. There wouldn't be anywhere to conceal weapons.

But the neckline was the problem. It plunged, leaving cleavage in its path. It wasn't that I was self-conscious, but I wasn't certain that the dress would blend in, and the main part of Caelus's plan had always been to go unnoticed.

Jenevieve had also included shoes that laced up my legs with bronze ribbons, and I thanked the gods she had enough sense not to choose something I could barely walk in. There was also a bronze necklace decorated with sapphires and matching bracelets included with the dress.

I slipped it on, the silky fabric sliding against my skin. There wasn't any extra time to do my hair, so I grabbed a hairpin that belonged to my aunt and pinned back the left side. I quickly painted my lips a deep red; I'd lined my eyes earlier while debating the dress.

In the mirror, I looked over myself one last time. The color complemented my fair skin, and the bronze jewelry brought out the pink undertones, adding warmth.

Jenevieve's work was beautiful. It was probably the most beautiful gown I'd ever owned. Her skill as a seamstress wasn't an exaggeration.

Caelus had been absent since last night. I sighed, readjusting my hair. But all that was left was the ball.

A knock at the door caused me to jolt. I turned, saying, "Come in."

Caelus opened the door, and I froze, staring at him. He stared back with wide eyes.

The desire to apologize rose in my throat, but I bit it back.

He cleared his throat. His face slipped into that indifference he'd adopted. He adjusted the sleeve of his black coat decorated with bronze accents that matched my jewelry. It was cut close enough that I could easily imagine the muscles underneath when he moved. A waistcoat of the same shade of blue as my gown peeked out from beneath, with bronze swirls patterned throughout. If he had any weapons, they couldn't be seen.

"We need to leave," he said. His voice strained with the words, and I wondered if he hated that he'd agreed to pretend to be romantically involved with me.

But I nodded and followed him out of the room and downstairs. Esteban was already gone, likely preparing food and transporting alcohol to the castle with Forgesong's owner. I never asked how Esteban planned to help Stumbleduck inside, and it was definitely too late to change their plan.

Together, we headed for Lord Ebonhammer's iron castle looming in the distance. Lightning buzzed beneath my skin as a palpable silence settled between Caelus and I.

Two gatekeepers checked invitations at the castle gates. They were the same ones who'd turned us away the day we'd arrived and tried to request an audience with Lord Ebonhammer. The same ones I'd accidentally spilled drinks on when I'd been dancing with Caelus.

As we approached, Caelus linked his arm with mine. Now was the time to hope we were convincing, and I'd mastered acting the part of a romantic partner. I did my best to appear happily in love, despite my twisting stomach. I peeked at Caelus. He smiled, relaxed—the smile of someone unbothered. Acting obviously came naturally to him.

Once it was our turn, he handed the invitation to the dwarven gatekeeper. The dwarf looked between us. After a close examination, he looked back at Caelus. "Sure ya should be here?"

"Is there a problem?" Caelus asked.

The dwarf narrowed his eyes at Caelus and me. "Step aside. I won't be havin' you tryin' to assail Lord Ebonhammer with your petty questions."

My fingers clenched around Caelus's forearm. "You can't turn us away. Otherwise, what's the purpose of the event?"

People behind us began whispering.

"Is there a problem?" a deep voice from beyond the gate asked.

The man I assumed to be Ranvald stepped forward. He pulled at the collar of his well-tailored dark shirt in an attempt to loosen it.

The dwarf shrank back but said, "Sir, these two are only lookin' to cause trouble. They were here only a few days ago—"

Ranvald looked at me, his face remaining impassive. His gaze slid to Caelus, and the corner of his lips lifted. "I do believe my brother rewarded Eira with that invitation for her efforts in the event. You wouldn't want to disappoint a member of the Nythe family, would you?"

He shoved the invitation back at Caelus and mumbled, "Go ahead," while waving us in. Nythe wasn't one of the five High Houses, but the name clearly meant something to that dwarven guard.

Once we were past the gatekeepers, I said, "You didn't have to do that."

Ahead of us, Ranvald said, "Keiran would never let me hear the end of it if I didn't intervene."

I smiled.

Caelus glanced at me, a flicker of emotion I couldn't read passing across his face before it was back to his veneer.

We passed through an oddly barren courtyard into the castle. A thin layer of snow dusted the dark ground. The flora native to the mountain was unkempt and withered. It was as though the land had rotted and nothing could grow. Did Lord Ebonhammer not have a groundskeeper?

A dark stone path that nearly blended in with the soil led through the castle entrance, and we followed Ranvald through to the ballroom.

Inside the dark-iron room with black marbled floor, several people were already dancing and mingling. Metal lanterns decorated the tables and walls, casting the room in an ambient yellow hue. A geometric iron chandelier hung down in the center, an immaculate accent to the room. A second-floor balcony overlooked where people were dancing.

Ranvald strolled through the busy ballroom with ease, joining Keiran and Jenevieve. The three together looked stunning in their black clothing—a stark contrast to their silvery-white hair. They were accented differently, matching each sibling near perfectly. Keiran's clothing almost matched mine and had similar bronze decorations paired with sea green, while Ranvald wore a waistcoat over a shirt, hints of burnt gold and deep red–orange woven throughout like living flame. Jenevieve's tight-fitting dress was laced with bright silver with diamond jewelry. Based on the style, it was clear that she crafted their clothing for the event as well.

"Mingle until the lord makes himself present," Caelus said, tone flat.

Another look over those attending confirmed Lord Ebonhammer wasn't there yet. "Doesn't seem like what two people would do if they're madly and irrevocably in love," I teased in a whisper.

He sighed, conceding, and tugged me along with him.

I grinned up at him.

A muscle in his jaw twitched.

Now that we were inside, he looked more agitated than before. And gods, I understood why. Finding his sister took priority for him, where finding Teeg took priority for me. While we hadn't discussed it, I intended to do what I could to help him, though.

Arm in arm, we rounded the room, conversing with others. Caelus's performance was seamless, and he blended in with ease. He had no trouble discussing topics of politics throughout the kingdom, most of which surrounded who the crown prince may marry. Apparently, it was rumored that he would soon announce his engagement.

People chattered about Iker Ebonhammer coming of age for marriage, too, and producing heirs of his own one day. Some debated who would marry first: the crown prince or Lord Ebonhammer's son.

Meanwhile, I scanned the people there so far, and Perrin's voice rang through my mind. A *partner who will be present at the ball.* I wasn't sure how that information helped me. Caelus and I hadn't discussed what it could mean either. If only Perrin had even given me a descriptor of the person I should look for. Maybe he thought it would be obvious. But if I couldn't find them, Travok would know something about them, too, if Perrin was to be believed.

We encountered the owner of Forgesong, a young dwarven woman in a glittering purple gown. She recalled us, noting that we'd been seated with the Nythe family. I wanted to ask her why their family was well known in the city, but it didn't seem appropriate. Neither did asking where Esteban was. I hadn't seen him, but he was working for her during the ball. The last thing I needed her to worry about was her business's reputation being ruined because we distracted Esteban while he was helping her.

A few guests had obviously bought their way in. Every inch of their attire screamed wealth, from the unsightly number of jewels to their gem-inlaid attire. Groups of them gathered together, gossiping among themselves.

I spotted Ina wearing a modest lilac gown near a table of food with her husband, Gavriel. The last time I'd seen him was the day my power slipped and I accidentally killed Dorian. He'd aged more than his wife in the past several years. Faint lines marred his forehead, and his jubilant expression I'd always known had been replaced with one of disdain for those around him. It didn't stop Ina from grinning and looking as though she was having the time of her life. She'd always enjoyed parties. Dorian would have probably enjoyed them too.

Ina waved at me, her big brown eyes full of warmth and love. Her husband didn't look my way when she tugged on his coat and gestured toward me. He said something to her and then took a drink from his wineglass. Ina frowned at him. When she looked my way, she smiled again, her eyes now downcast.

I tore my gaze away from them, and Caelus and I continued mingling.

Most people we spoke with asked questions about our time in Tiruhm and if we'd been enjoying the festival. If anyone was surprised when Caelus inquired about Lord Ebonhammer's whereabouts or the state of affairs in the city, they didn't show it.

No one stood out that could be the person Perrin had mentioned. But if I couldn't find them, he'd said Lord Ebonhammer would know more. I just hoped he was right.

We eventually took a break from mingling next to a table of food. Delicate sandwiches and an assortment of bite-size pastries were stacked on tiers. Bottles of frostberry wine and barrels of dwarven ale were ready to be served by a gorgeous young fey woman who looked out of place among the attendees.

I grabbed one of the little sandwiches, popping it into my mouth, savoring the unique flavors and unable to place the type of meat. After a sip of wine, I ate a small pastry, the sweet scent of it calling to me.

Caelus, on the other hand, didn't seem nearly as intrigued by the food. His gaze was focused on a point, and I turned to face it. A man stood next to a pillar, fidgeting with the buttons of his dark coat accented with burnt orange, seeming wholly uncomfortable. His dark hair was cut short and skimmed the tops of his ears.

"I'll be back," Caelus said.

He started in the man's direction, and I stepped in front of him. "Let me help."

His eyes narrowed on me. "You've helped enough."

"Really? Because I think I could do more if you'd let me," I whispered.

Caelus scoffed and sidestepped me. I followed him.

Whatever he was about to do had to involve his sister, and while it may be my fault she was in this castle, it wouldn't stop me from trying to fix it.

We approached the pillar, and Caelus spun and pulled me behind it, pressing my back to the pillar's cool surface. "If we both disappear, it's suspicious."

An unfamiliar male voice said, "Not if you're playing lover boy effectively." The tone was teasing. Light. He had to be a friend of Caelus's.

"He's not wrong," I added.

"Oh, I like her," Caelus's friend chimed.

"Kenzo," Caelus snapped, looking in the direction of the voice on the other side of the pillar.

A laugh sounded.

His gaze fell to me. "I'll handle this. Without you."

"How will you stop me?" I asked.

He narrowed his eyes at me again. "Stop her if she tries to follow me."

The man stepped around the pillar, a smile on his face.

"You have to know I never wanted this," I said.

Caelus headed toward a door obscured by shadows without acknowledging me.

I took a step to follow. Kenzo blocked my path. I sidestepped, and he did the same.

"He'll be in a better mood if you let him sort this one out on his own."

I frowned. "I somehow doubt that."

It was understandable why he didn't want me involved, but it still weighed on me. I wanted to do more than stand around and look pretty. I whirled away from Kenzo, the fabric of my dress swishing along with me, and walked back toward the table of food. Kenzo's faint laugh sounded behind me.

I stood on my own for several minutes, every now and again meeting Kenzo's gaze. There wasn't going to be a way around him.

I glanced around for other entrances and exits I may not have noticed. Esteban peeked out of a servant's access tunnel, locking eyes with me. He gestured subtly with his head for me to come to him.

With a glance around to make sure no one was watching me, I slipped inside the servant's tunnel.

Esteban said, "This castle ain't right, girl. Come."

"What do you mean?" I asked, and followed him through the tunnels until we entered a storeroom.

Crates sat stacked along a wall with a few sacks of flour leaning against them. Spices lined shelves in glass jars. Nothing remarkable for a kitchen storeroom, but the space didn't smell of spices. It was off, as though something had begun to rot.

Esteban walked over to one of the smaller crates and lifted the lid.

My stomach roiled, and I stepped back. Inside were small arms, a leg, and a scarred torso. They looked human, or at least as far as I could tell, disembodied as they were. "What is this?" I asked, even though I suspected the answer.

"He's eating them, Eira. Malik has found dismembered bodies like this a few times now. Always in crates." His expression turned grave. "We need to get out of here. That crown's guard needs to inform the king. Let them handle it."

My eyes shot to his. "We can't leave. What about Teeg? How do we know he's been safe here?" I turned, storming back into the tunnel. "It was ridiculous to believe he would be."

"If you insist on staying, girl, there's one more problem," Esteban called, catching up to me. "Lord Ebonhammer is sequestering himself in his chambers. If you're determined to speak with him, you'll likely have to do something reckless."

I looked over my shoulder at him.

He shot me a glare and added, "Don't."

Careful not to be noticed, I exited the tunnel and returned to the ball. Caelus's friend raised a brow at me from several feet away, but I ignored him and headed for the table of food and drink. I poured a full glass of frostberry wine and raised it to Kenzo. I downed the entire thing and poured another and faced those who were dancing.

Without Caelus and his font of mundane conversation topics, I avoided the crowd, scanning for the best-possible escape to investigate the castle on my own if Caelus didn't return soon.

Teeg needed to be found.

I nursed my glass of bubbly wine. It did little to ease my worries, but at least I had something to occupy my hands.

Gods, if Lord Ebonhammer was eating people, was he behind all those who'd gone missing? Several of them had been children. And to what end? Why would he be eating people? Surely it wasn't for the taste. Nausea bubbled in my stomach at the thought.

For a better view, I wandered up to the balcony overlooking the ballroom, where people were chatting away from those who danced. I scanned the room below. There was an exit that led farther into the castle that was the most likely to lead me to Lord Ebonhammer, but it would take a lot of guesswork to find his room.

I dragged a finger along the railing, considering the idea, and turned to the portraits lining the wall. One for each of the Dawn Conclave—Whistlemane, Moonveil, Ebonhammer, Ashwin, and Quinn.

Travok and his family sat in the middle, the largest of the portraits, so that it could be easily seen even from below. The dwarf appeared proud, clad in dark-iron armor and holding a large war hammer. Next to him was his son, no older than a teenager, though his dwarven blood could easily mask his true age, but his pointed ears gave away a hint of fey heritage that came from his mother.

I approached the portrait of my parents—House Quinn. They looked different from what I remembered. Younger. My mother sat while my father stood beside her, a hand on her shoulder. A pin resembling a scale from a large serpent held my father's cloak in place. My mother wore a matching brooch.

Looking at my father was almost like looking in a mirror. It'd been so long since I'd last seen him. I'd never noticed how alike we were. I was the softer, feminine form of him. It really wasn't a stretch for Perrin to have figured it out so easily. We shared the shape of my nose, my full lips, and my eyes. The color of my eyes differed, though. One brown, one blue—something borrowed from both of them.

My mother looked over her shoulder, smiling up toward my father. Their love for one another was apparent even in paint. The love I remembered extending past themselves and into Mythbel before it burned. My life would have been different without that fire. They would be here. I would have never been forced to live with Aunt Celeste or ended up with that imitation of a *tenebrae* bond to Klareth.

"The swooning couple of House Quinn. Do you long for love?" asked a fey man wearing deep green. He stopped beside me, admiring the portrait. He sipped his wine, and his sleeve slid up and revealed faint scars around his wrist.

I shook my head, my gaze landing back on my parents. "No. The artistry is beautiful." Which was true.

He stood silent for a moment. "It is lovely. Such a shame they passed so young." Another moment of silence went by. "You and Lord Quinn share a resemblance."

My heart raced, and I clenched the glass of frostberry wine. "Oh?" I laughed. "I'm sure anyone with black hair would look similar," I said, smoothing the side of my dress. My gaze darted around for some way to extract myself from the conversation.

He peered at me, trying to get a closer look.

The smile on his ashen face sent a chill through me, and I shifted my gaze to the painting of the Ashwins to avoid his stare. The fey man in the painting had a long, thin, handsome face.

But I couldn't afford to admire the painting. I needed to excuse myself before he made some connection between me and my mother and father. The last thing I needed was everyone's eyes to fall on me. He didn't have proof, but the resemblance alone would be enough to garner attention.

I began to step away, putting space between us to escape before he noticed who I was, and collided into a hard chest.

"There you are," Keiran said with all the charisma I was certain won over his clients.

He placed a warm hand on my bare shoulder to steady me. I turned to face him and smiled, thankful for his interruption. Taking advantage of it, I said, "I was wondering if you'd ever be free from Jenevieve. Care to dance?" I wasn't particularly interested in dancing, but it was the perfect excuse.

Keiran smiled and took my hand. "I'd never refuse."

Together, we headed down the stairs back to the ballroom floor, and I hoped that the man wouldn't follow.

A server approached and took my empty wineglass. Keiran led us to the middle of the dance floor. With a hand on my waist and the other holding mine, he led us through the movements. I barely paid attention to the steps, my mind racing with thoughts of whether that man would put the pieces together and figure out who I was. What would he do with that information?

"Something on your mind?" Keiran asked me after several moments.

He knew my identity and hadn't made a big deal of it, so I gave him my best smile. "I was admiring the painting of the late Lord and Lady Quinn. There was only one other person paying respect to the deceased family."

Keiran lifted a brow and scanned the ballroom. "They passed too young."

"It's a shame they also lost their child in that fire," I said, keeping up the ruse for anyone who might overhear.

"I'm sure had she lived, she would have grown into a fine woman with a kind soul that they could be proud of."

I smiled at his words but was uncertain if I believed them.

We spun through the dance, and Keiran continued to watch those around us rather than me. After several moments, he leaned in and whispered, "Your friend is nowhere to be seen, and Lord Ebonhammer has yet to make an appearance."

In the middle of a crowd of people was far from the best place to talk about Lord Ebonhammer, but there was nowhere else.

Voice low, I replied, "It's complicated, but you wouldn't know why, would you?"

Keiran's eyes darted to mine, brows knitted together. "I'm afraid not. Are you going to continue with your plan?"

I nodded.

"Be careful."

Before I could respond, we spun, and I spotted Kenzo speaking with a dark haired girl. Her dress was a size too large. We spun again, and I lost sight of them.

A tap on my shoulder interrupted us. We paused, and I turned, facing Caelus.

He looked at Keiran, smirking, and took my hand, placing it on his shoulder. With a hand on my waist, he led me through a flurry of steps that put distance between the two of us and Keiran.

Caelus didn't meet my eyes and focused on a point I couldn't see behind me. I wondered if that girl had been his sister. From his resolute expression, he was far from in the mood to talk.

Once the song ended, he linked his arm with mine and led us toward a shadowy alcove. A tower of food clattered to the floor and drew everyone's attention. We made our escape from the ballroom through the exit that led deeper into the iron castle.

He untwined his arm from mine. We maneuvered upstairs and continued several feet before he turned and led us down another hall, this one made of the same black marble as the ballroom. A deep red rug ran down the center, masking our footsteps.

"Wait," I whispered, and ducked into the next room we passed. It was dim, lit only by a lantern and a few candles, but we were alone. "Did you find her?"

He crossed his arms and kept his eyes on the doorway. "Kenzo has her. She's well. Unharmed. They're leaving. Now I'm helping you, like I agreed."

A weight lifted off my chest. She was alive and safe. All that was left now was a chance to speak with Lord Ebonhammer and find out where Teeg was and what had happened to Aunt Celeste and Lora.

"I'm glad," I said.

"We need to keep moving."

I nodded and said, "Lord Ebonhammer . . . Esteban said he's keeping to his room. And he thinks Travok's been—" I swallowed hard. "Eating people."

Caelus's face contorted with disgust. "Then we're wasting time."

We exited the room and continued through the castle. Caelus led the way, weaving through the corridors. "I hope you know where you're going," I whispered. He didn't respond, but the interior transitioned to iron as we continued through the castle. The walls lacked decoration for function.

The floor transitioned from carpet to metal, and my shoes clicked with each step. Citrus scent stirred around me, and the clicking ceased. Caelus was able to subdue the sound using his control over air. No wonder he never made a sound.

It was too late, though. Armored footsteps started around the corner, growing closer. There wasn't a nearby room to slip in and hide in the straight hallway. Only a door at the very end, but we'd have to pass the turn leading to the corridor where footsteps clanked.

I checked behind us, but options were too far away to hide before we'd be caught.

An idea that Esteban would classify as reckless came to me.

I turned to Caelus. "Kiss me," I whispered.

23

Caelus's hardened expression cracked at my utterly ridiculous request, but it was he who originally suggested that a ball with everyone fancifully dressed was bound to have couples sneaking off to find somewhere private in the castle. It was as good of a cover as any.

He glanced toward where the clanking sounded and then strode toward me. I stepped back, a narrow table lining the hallway pressing against the backs of my thighs through the soft material of my dress.

Caelus cupped my cheek and kissed me with a fervent, urgent need, as though his very life depended on it. I kissed him back, knowing deep down I'd wanted to for longer than I'd admit. His lips moved against mine, and I knew I'd never have enough. Heat tightened low in my stomach. All sense of reality warped away.

His hand moved from my cheek moved to my nape while the other traveled along my side, sliding lower. My hands drifted over his chest until my arms made their way around his neck. Caelus groaned. I pulled back, breathless. He took that moment to draw my bottom lip into his mouth. A whimper escaped me, and, with a tilt of his head, he deepened the kiss with a sweep of his tongue.

I should have stopped him. It would have been the smart thing to do. The kiss was only meant to be a distraction, but I found myself lost in it. My body craved his touch—wanted him.

As if sensing my body's desire, he stepped forward, his fingers drifting down my back. His body pressed me harder against that narrow table behind me, the edge digging into the backs of my legs. His calloused fingertips slipped through the slits of my dress, featherlight and leaving decadent tingles in their wake. Warm hands caressed the back of my thighs, and he lifted me up onto the narrow table behind me. I gasped, and I swore he smirked against my lips.

My legs spread wide, and he situated himself between them, the hard length of him against my hot center. His grip on my thighs tightened, and my body flushed and ached for more—for him.

One of his hands released my leg and his fingertips traveled up my exposed spine. My body shivered at his touch, my back arching. My hands threaded through the soft strands of his hair, relishing each touch. He teased my lips. His hands wandered my body, avoiding my aching breasts. I moaned against his lips as he kept kissing me as though he never wanted to stop.

And I wasn't sure I wanted him to either.

"You two shouldn't be—" started a male voice, but he cut himself off, grumbling about drunken guests.

Caelus broke the kiss but didn't back away. His eyes remained locked on mine and burned, like thunder clouds ready to burst. Despite the guard's presence, Caelus appeared as though he'd rather still be kissing me. And I wanted him to, despite being undeserving of it.

He didn't bother looking at the guard. Voice thick, he said, "We got lost. We'll be on our way."

The guard mumbled and his footsteps retreated, but we stayed as we were for a moment longer, neither of us acknowledging the intensity of the kiss yet neither of us seeming quite ready to move.

Caelus inhaled deeply and took a step back, that look of indifference slowly slipping back into place. My hands slid free of his soft hair, leaving it disheveled.

My foggy mind dragged itself back to reality, and I pushed myself off the narrow table. My shoes touched down on the iron flooring, not making a sound this time.

I'd only kissed a few people, but none of them had left me wanting more. Romantic relationships weren't something I pursued, mostly because the risk didn't outweigh any benefits. At least, not before, when my life had been almost nothing aside from the stone halls of Ahrea's temple and Klareth's demands.

Caelus ran a hand through his hair, only making it more disheveled. My face flushed, and I glanced away. Even if my plan had saved us for the moment, the guard would still be around the corner. We needed some way to go unnoticed.

Caelus approached the corner of the hall where the guard had come from. I followed, keeping a short distance between us.

Voice still thick and quiet, he said, "Travok's chamber."

The doors creaked open, followed by the sound of a man and woman arguing in hushed tones.

As they grew closer, the man said, "Don't worry about Tooley. The labryn's skilled at mimicry."

The woman pleaded, "Don't work with a monster from the Abyss."

"Trust and all will be well, my dear."

The woman's voice was familiar, but I couldn't place it.

Their footsteps grew closer, and Caelus took my arm. The hall whirled away, and we were in front of the door at the end of the hall. He slipped inside, and I trailed behind him. The room was small and circular, containing a few shelves lined with books, a single armchair, and a spiral stone staircase leading down. He shut the door behind us without a sound, and I turned to face him.

"I thought doing that drained your esprit," I said.

Caelus peered down the stairway, his fingers wrapping around the protective railing. "It does."

"Ah, so kissing me was all about conserving esprit." He'd already been using it to mask me, and he'd said transporting another with him was draining.

His grip tightened. "Plans change."

I frowned. My fingers drifted to my lips. Had I misread the desire in that kiss? Maybe Caelus was just an excellent kisser.

I sighed and peered down the shadowy stairway beside him, but it was too dark to see past where we stood. "Should we go down?"

He continued peering down. Finally, he took a step. "There are still people outside."

I followed behind him and created a small ball of light. The little arcs of lightning struck the invisible barrier that trapped them, seeking a way out. Worn stone lined the stairwell. Wherever it led was older than the iron castle.

My mind drifted to the voices we'd heard.

Lord Tooley Whistlemane was another of the Dawn Conclave serving the king. The man said the Abyssal was good at mimicry. Was it copying Lord Whistlemane in some way? The king needed to know. Hopefully, the king had enough sense to get rid of an Abyssal posing as a member of his court.

Abyssals were monsters that ventured into the realm of Marunia from the Abyss. They varied in skill and strength. One that could shift and mimic a person would be powerful. Did Ebonhammer know? Maybe he'd been behind it, given his current eating habits. The Abyssal may have even been responsible for manipulating Lord Ebonhammer into eating flesh.

We traveled downward and away from our ultimate goal, and my worry for Teeg grew. But the closer we got to the bottom, that pull I'd felt all those nights ago in Ahrea's temple—the same pull as though a rope was tied to my waist—drew me downward.

At the bottom, we stepped into a dimly lit cavern. The orange glow of torches illuminated a desk covered in scraps of paper. Vials lined the back containing a luminescent green liquid.

In the center of the space was an altar with a jade-colored stone in the center. It was about the size of a large jewel, smaller than the one I'd seen in the Temple of Ahrea. "This is like the catacombs," I said.

Caelus took the stone into his hand and examined it. His face paled, and he dropped it. "It feels like . . . like death."

I crouched next to it and looked at it closely. The interior of the green stone swirled and shone like the liquid in the vials. "Could

Klareth and Ebonhammer have been working together? She would have easy access to . . ." I trailed off, unable to finish.

Caelus stepped toward the desk, looking through the papers atop it. "It's likely."

"We should take it," I said.

Caelus rifled through the drawers and came back with a small leather pouch. I scooped it inside and handed it to him for safekeeping.

"You'll tell the king, right? About Whistlemane and Ebonhammer?" I asked.

"Do you think I wouldn't?"

I shot him a glare.

He glanced above us. "It's safe now."

"How do you know?"

He started up the stairs. "My esprit allows me to hear better than the average person."

For him to hear that far above us was more than simply "hearing better than the average person." If his esprit could do that, what else could he do?

Caelus led the way back up, keeping our movements silent. It would be a matter of time before he ran out of esprit to mask us, though. We needed to get to Lord Ebonhammer and then make our exit before anyone took notice.

We emerged at the top of the stairs, and Caelus pulled out a dagger from underneath his coat. He motioned for me to stay back. Weaponless, I obeyed.

He crept toward the door leading out of the room. In one swift, controlled motion, he shoved the door open without making a sound.

He spun to the side, thrusting the blade up.

I peeked out, and his blade was pressed to a man's throat. He hadn't killed him. Not yet, at least.

Despite the sneer on the man's scarred face, he held his arms up in surrender. "Smart to come out first," he said.

But I knew that face—that scar and crooked nose weren't features I'd soon forget. Or the feel of his arms wrapped around me, pressing my arms to my body, leaving me with no way to defend myself besides my gift. "You tried to kidnap me."

Caelus gritted his teeth. "You should be dead."

"Seems the goddess of mercy spared me."

Caelus jerked the part-dwarven, part-fey man by the collar, and he guided him into the small circular room, keeping the blade at his throat. The door closed behind us on a phantom wind. Caelus shoved him against the stone wall.

The man's gaze shifted to me, and his smile caused that scar to appear jagged. "Seems you ended up here all the same."

Caelus pressed the dagger's tip farther, breaking the skin. A thin trickle of blood slid down his neck. He didn't show any reaction.

I narrowed my eyes. The man in front of me appeared familiar still. Not just because he'd tried to take me. "Who are you? And what does that mean?" I asked.

He chuckled, not seeming to care that it caused the tip of the blade to dig deeper and free another droplet of blood. "I'm sure you're familiar with my father. Travok Ebonhammer."

I took in the man claiming to be Iker Ebonhammer, son of Lord Ebonhammer. Iker bore a slight resemblance to his father in the painting above the ballroom. His unruly black hair and the shape of his jaw, the color of his eyes. Whoever his mother was, however, must have been fey due to his height and slight point to his ears.

"Perrin told me who you are. Said you might be useful to me," Iker continued.

My muscles tensed. Had Perrin told him about me being the Tempest or heir to House Quinn?

"Useful for what?" Caelus asked.

"My father. He's obsessed with longevity."

So Perrin hadn't lied.

"He's planning to head House Ebonhammer indefinitely."

My stomach turned. "How?"

"He discovered some ritual to sustain his youth by obtaining people's esprit. He's consuming their flesh." His nose wrinkled. "Even going so far as to use any left over to feed the castle. It started with adults just past childhood. When that became less effective, he moved on to those who were younger."

Bile burned the back of my throat. "The food at the ball."

His features turned grim.

I twisted, saliva building in my mouth. My skin grew clammy, and I leaned my head over the railing of the stairwell. The contents of my stomach came up, burning my throat. It'd only been one little sandwich, but to eat someone—a child.

A hand rubbed my back and another pulled my hair away, saving it from the vomit as I retched again. It was a miracle no one heard. I supposed I had Caelus to thank for that. His esprit likely kept us concealed in the room for the time being.

A thin coat of sweat covered my forehead, but I stayed as I was. A handkerchief appeared in my periphery, and I grabbed it from

Caelus's hand, wiping my forehead and then my mouth, the acrid taste lingering.

I faced Iker where he now leaned against the wall. He didn't seem surprised by my reaction—maybe he even assumed I'd eaten some of the food unknowingly. And, in a way, he'd done me a favor by telling me. Otherwise, the flesh of someone would have remained in my stomach to digest more than it had.

But now was my chance to ask questions. Yet all I could think of was his father. Iker had let this continue. "Did you try to stop him?" I asked.

He averted his gaze, not saying anything. It was enough of an answer that I didn't stop the arcing tempest from slipping free and slithering across my arms.

Shock passed over his face, and his eyes met mine again.

The last time we'd met, I'd held it back, afraid of my power, but as long as I didn't touch either of them, they would be fine. A part of me considered killing him, though, for allowing his father to continue consuming flesh—children—but I didn't want needless death. "What did he do with Teeg?"

Iker lifted a brow. "Be more specific."

"A boy. A little boy with brown curls, round cheeks." I held a hand, palm down, near my hips. "This tall." It took everything in me not to yell.

Caelus didn't say anything beside me, his focus pinned on Iker.

Iker narrowed his eyes. "Children meet one fate in this iron cage."

"Even the Golden Child? Klareth sent him here. I doubt it was to be eaten." Even as I said it, a fresh wave of bitterness filled my mouth.

"That high priestess and Father worked together. But I know

nothing of a Golden Child."

My mind raced with everything I'd learned. Klareth . . . She'd sent them here for Ebonhammer to consume. All so that he could use their flesh—their esprit—to continue living. What was I supposed to do? As a Quinn or the Tempest? Kill Travok? "Why haven't you killed him?"

"He was once a man I looked up to. A father one could be proud of."

And killing him would hurt despite the man his father had become. It would be hard to forget—harder not to hope he may change and become a decent man again. But it was too late for that. There was nothing Travok Ebonhammer could do that would redeem him. I prayed Thanally, goddess of death and spirits, was not kind to him in the afterlife.

"Take us to him. You can get us past the guards at his door," Caelus said.

Iker pushed himself off the wall and stepped into the hall, not saying anything.

We followed him. The lightning faded with each step; with each deep breath in and out, I regained a sense of calm. A sense of control.

Killing Travok should be easy—he was a child-murdering cannibal. But could I do it? Caelus had said that killing someone who ruined the lives of others was better, and maybe it was true. Because if he lived, he would continue.

But I still needed answers.

We rounded the corner to find two guards collapsed in front of Travok's doors, a crossbow bolt in the neck of each, blood pooling along the iron floor. Someone else had beaten us to him. I rushed into the room. *He can't be dead. Not yet.*

A lush rug lined the floor of Lord Ebonhammer's chambers.

Fine velvet couches and a cabinet of bejeweled decanters made up the sitting room. A stark difference to the bareness of the rest of the castle.

Another set of double doors led from the sitting room to the bedroom. A large canopy bed sat in the center. Lord Ebonhammer lay in it, and standing next to him was Stumbleduck. He'd wanted into the ball because of his history with Travok. We could have worked together if we'd known about his plans, but he held something in his hand. Something I recognized.

A small metallic toy man.

24

I moved toward the bed where Lord Ebonhammer lay, my steps remaining soundless thanks to Caelus. Stumbleduck hadn't noticed us. Yet. He was speaking to Travok, voice too low to make out.

I continued closer, stopping at the foot of the bed.

The dwarf in the bed looked nothing like what I'd imagined or the version I'd seen in the portrait. Thin, sallow skin clung to his bones, his muscles wasted. The frail man couldn't have weighed more than the blanket on top of him. Travok's sickly appearance didn't make sense. He was consuming youth to stay young. Healthy.

Caelus and Iker didn't come past the doorway leading into the bedchamber, both seeming to let me decide what to do—what to say. But I wasn't sure if the man in front of me was capable of speech.

Travok's head shifted, his sunken eyes gazing in my direction, but

I wasn't certain he actually saw me or if he just sensed that someone was there.

Stumbleduck glanced up at me, finally noticing that there were others in the room.

Disregarding Travok's appearance, I asked, "Where's the Golden Child? Where's Celeste and Lora Ortunis?"

Stumbleduck's gaze fell back to Travok, the metal toy still in hand.

Recognition flashed in Travok's cloudy eyes, the color near impossible to see beneath them. He opened his mouth to speak, but words didn't form, his body too weak. Yet I swore he mouthed, *Audric.* The name of my father.

I took a step back and twisted the bracelet I'd worn. "I thought you said he was taking youth?"

"More. I need more," came Travok's voice, raspy and near breathless.

Travok's son didn't have time to answer before Stumbleduck threw the metal toy at Travok with enough force that the head popped off and it exploded. Black smoke filled the room.

I raised my arms out of reflex, blocking bits of wooden splinters flying toward me. I coughed, my eyes and throat burning, my ears ringing. A gust of wind blew free loose strands of my hair, sending the smoke billowing away. Wind wrapped around me, creating a protective barrier, but not before sharp pain radiated from my side and my leg.

I screamed, but the sound was lost. I wasn't sure if it was from pain, shock, or surprise. Maybe all three. Strong arms scooped me up, and instinctively, I tried to shove away. The arms tightened around my waist and under my legs. Spring rain and citrus broke through the thick smell of smoke.

Caelus sprinted and I bounced in his arms. Any other time I would have marveled at the ease with which he ran while holding me. The ringing in my ears faded, and people shouted around us.

I coughed and hit Caelus's chest. "We need to go back," I choked out. I needed to know if Travok was dead, because I needed to talk to him. I needed to hear his answers.

"We can't go back. Everyone in this castle heard that explosion, and if anyone sees us, it'll be viewed as treason."

"This way," Iker said.

Caelus followed his voice into a tunnel. I examined my thigh as best I could in the dim light of the tunnel. A stray bit of wood was deeply embedded. Seeing it somehow caused a new flare of pain to shoot through it, and I winced. Caelus slowed his pace at that, but I couldn't tell where we were headed.

The tunnel looked similar to the servants' tunnels, but there was no one else present besides the three of us. Every few feet we passed the Ebonhammer emblem of a chipped mountain with a shooting star. It eventually ended at a stone wall. Travok's son stepped forward, pressing on a stone that opened a hidden door exiting onto a street.

Caelus didn't wait before barreling through. From what I could tell, it was an exit on the west side of the castle, past the walls.

Stumbleduck appeared a moment later, panting, a satisfied look on his face. He was covered in soot and specks of blood and wooden bits.

"You're coming with us," Caelus said, glaring at Stumbleduck.

To the gnome's credit, he didn't argue and began to follow.

"I have to go back," Iker said.

Caelus sucked in a deep breath and gave him a nod. He continued to navigate the streets, increasing his pace, and a few beads of sweat formed along his forehead. Stumbleduck managed to keep up despite his short legs. I tried to free myself from Caelus's arms, but his grip remained firm, not giving me an inch of room to escape his hold. Not that I would have made it very far with my injured leg.

We soon arrived at my aunt's house, and before Caelus could, I pushed the gate open with air and did the same with the front door, knowing his esprit must be nearly drained. Stumbleduck turned and headed for the den. Caelus didn't bother speaking with the gnome before heading up the stairs and into his room. He must have been confident Stumbleduck wouldn't leave the villa.

Caelus sat me on his bed and eyed the giant splinter in my thigh—though calling it a *splinter* was putting it lightly. Pain radiated from my waist, and I prodded at it. My fingers met a sticky, deep gash through a tear in the dress.

Caelus turned my face to his with a thumb and forefinger on my chin. "You're injured."

"I can tell," I said, eyes drifting toward my thigh again. "I'll be fine."

He sighed. His expression became somber—became real. "You don't have to be okay."

I blinked back tears. "You don't have to stay," I said, even though he'd brought me to the room he'd been using.

Caelus stood and made for his satchel of belongings.

I examined the cut on my waist. The tear I'd felt in the dress was gone, mended together by the esprit Jenevieve had most likely infused into it to enchant the fabric. I laid back on the bed and closed my eyes, my cheek and arms beginning to sting. If I touched either of them, I knew my fingers would come back smeared with soot and blood.

The plan had been stupid. Worthless. Lord Ebonhammer couldn't even answer my questions. I wasn't certain that he had been lucid. He could barely speak, and when he had, it'd been after mentioning taking the youth from others.

He'd said *more*. Even though he appeared moments from death, he'd wanted to eat that flesh. Would it have done anything? If there'd been an opportunity, would letting him consume youth have given him the strength to answer?

They were all questions that I'd never have answers to because he was gone. And between Travok's death and never finding the man Perrin had mentioned, I was no closer to finding Aunt Celeste and Lora either.

Stumbleduck likely had his reasons for what he did. Or at least, that's what I hoped. A part of me had wanted to kill Travok too. Partly for his role in taking Teeg but also for his role in the disappearances. I imagined he'd been taking people for a few years to steal their youth, if Iker was to be believed.

The bed dipped, and my eyes shot open. Caelus had returned with three lavender rose petals in his hand. His finger caught a tear I hadn't felt trailing down my cheek.

I blinked, clearing them away, and reached for the petals from Reina's rose. "I can take care of it."

Caelus's brow disappeared behind the hair that had fallen over his forehead. "Plan on pulling that out of your leg too?"

"I can wait for Esteban."

He pressed a petal to my cheek. "But I'm already here for you."

The stinging subsided, and I hoped the burning in my cheeks might be seen as coming from the petal. He was acting closer to himself. And I honestly wasn't sure what to make of it, what might send him back to acting cold and distant.

"I looked for information," he said. "Anything concerning your aunt and cousin. There was nothing about a man escorting them from the city that I could find."

My chest tightened. "Thank you."

He removed his fingertips from my cheek, the petal gone, and handed me another one. I took it and he turned away, giving me a moment to shift my dress. My thigh throbbed, sending new waves of burning pain up my leg with the movement. I pressed the petal to the gash on my side. Whatever magic was present in Reina's rose had also healed the cuts along my arms.

Once the petal faded and I righted myself, Caelus faced me again, eying the long wooden fragment in my thigh. I swallowed hard. It was unavoidable. But Caelus was right not to let me attempt to walk on the way back. There was no amount of preparation I could do for the added pain that would come. I took in a deep breath. "Do it," I said.

He gripped my thigh, and my body heated at the memory of those hands on my thighs—of our kiss. I closed my eyes, bracing myself. This would be nothing like that. Caelus gave only a brief warning before he jerked the wood from my leg.

I white-knuckled the sheet, trying to avoid shoving Caelus away. A cry escaped me at the sudden surge of burning pain. It was soon replaced by a cooling sensation, and the burning faded.

There was only a dull remnant of pain when I opened my eyes. Caelus was staring down at me, concern in his eyes mixed with longing. A longing I'd seen after he kissed me. But everything about us was for show. All for a night that was ruined the moment Travok Ebonhammer died.

There was a knock at the door, but Caelus didn't move. The palm of one of his hands was still pressed into my thigh. His thumb moved in a slow, tantalizing path over where the wound had been a moment ago.

The door burst open. "I heard a scream," Esteban called out frantically.

That made it the second time Esteban had barged into a room with Caelus and I—the second time it had looked like it could be more than it was.

A small laugh escaped Caelus, and he looked up at Esteban. "She's all right." He stood, his fingers slipping away from my thigh. "I had to remove the wood before her leg could be healed." He gestured to the abandoned bit of bloodied wood. "But her leg will be fine."

Esteban stopped by the end of the bed.

I sat up and examined my leg. There was nothing left of the wound except faint pink skin surrounded by blood. I slid through the blood-covered sheets to the edge of the bed and tested my weight on it. There was only the smallest twinge of pain in the muscle. Certain that it wasn't going to give out, I gave Esteban a tentative smile.

"I said don't do something reckless, girl!" Esteban looked me over, no doubt searching for any other wounds.

I started to hug him, but I was covered in dust and my own blood—maybe even some of Travok's. My body shuddered at the thought. "We found Ebonhammer, but before I could talk to him . . ." The words wouldn't come as it all sank in once again. Days had been spent planning how to meet him, and for what?

Esteban smiled, but it didn't reach his eyes. "Get cleaned up. There may be good news yet."

I BATHED AND SCRUBBED away the blood and debris from the explosion. When I emerged, the water was stained a brown-pink color.

From the top of the stairs, I could hear talking in the living room. When I rounded the corner, I spotted Kenzo and that woman from the ball. Caelus and Esteban were there, too, along with Stumbleduck on the velvet couch, looking as though he would drift off to sleep any moment.

Kenzo laughed at something the young girl said. She and Caelus turned to face me at almost the same time, and Kenzo's face lit up with delight.

My eyes darted between them. The girl and Caelus shared the same hair color and nose. Her eyes were a shade darker but similar enough to see the resemblance. "I'm sorry," I said to her.

She tilted her head, confusion on her face. She looked so much like Caelus; it was almost funny. Caelus whispered in her ear, and understanding replaced her expression. She smiled. "It wasn't your fault."

I started to argue with her, but Caelus said, "Corrin says she saw Teeg while she was in the castle."

"Where?" I asked her, hope bubbling up. I stood frozen in place, afraid that it might wash away.

"I only saw him. He was okay, if a little spooked, maybe. Someone took him away, but I didn't see who. They weren't alone. I heard one of them say something about Thistlewall and Lord Whistlemane."

My heart raced. No. Tooley Whistlemane might be an Abyssal or under the control of one. "We need to go," I said, starting to turn.

I collided with Caelus's chest. He'd left his spot next to his sister and placed himself in front of me. He grabbed my shoulders, squeezing gently. "Breathe," he whispered.

My inhale was shaky, but I held my breath a moment before letting it out, then repeated it until they were smooth, in and out.

"We need to think this through," he said.

It was the rational thing to do, but I'd spent all this time looking for Teeg, trying to do the rational thing. He needed help. With my power, I could get him back to safety. I'd be able to kill any Abyssal. Lord Whistlemane's role in all this was for the king to figure out.

But more than anything, I didn't want to wait. I didn't want to think it through. I wanted this whole thing to be over. Seeming to sense my racing thoughts, Caelus said, "I'll help you."

My eyes widened, meeting his. I hadn't expected that.

Caelus had no reason to continue helping me. He'd done enough. He had his sister. His job as crown's guard was done. The king would no doubt question why he'd taken so long to return as it was.

"But first . . ." He released my shoulders, looking past me.

I followed his gaze and landed on Stumbleduck.

"I hope you have a good fucking explanation for why you murdered a member of the Dawn Conclave," Caelus said.

"Then you better sit down, Tall Boy."

Caelus crossed his arms and waited.

I sat in the fluffy armchair across from Kenzo and Corrin. Anger didn't fill me, as I'd expected it would. Teeg wasn't safe, and that curbed whatever bitterness I had about Stumbleduck killing Travok Ebonhammer for now.

It helped that Travok was a cannibal and responsible for gods knew how many deaths too. Deaths that even Thanally herself couldn't have considered righteous.

"Travok killed my daughter," Stumbleduck started. "Unprompted. Unwarranted. The old fool wanted to expand and burned my home and many others to the ground." He pulled out the small music box I'd seen in his metal shack that was barely a home and started winding it. "The men he sent didn't even bother checking if anyone was inside. Melody burned up, not knowing why. I can only imagine the screams—the pain . . ." He released the little crank, and the music box began playing a slow, somber melody.

I suspected the homes had been checked and anyone home was taken for Travok's nefarious ritual, but I chose not to say that to Stumbleduck. He didn't need added grief.

Tears fell from his eyes, the fog gone from them for the moment. "I swore that I'd kill whoever was responsible. One by one, I've tracked and killed the men Travok sent. It took longer than necessary to learn who gave them the order. But I've devoted everything to ensure that man's death. He deserved every ounce of pain he felt."

Travok was responsible for so much suffering. More than people would ever know. The world was better off without Travok Ebonhammer in it. I agreed with what Stumbleduck had done—understood why he'd done it and didn't care that I'd been hurt. Physical wounds would heal.

I peeked over at Caelus. His face was a blank canvas, arms still crossed.

His sister had a hand to her mouth, and her eyes were glassy. Kenzo's face had turned grim. Esteban pulled out a flask and took a long drink.

"I'll help you find the boy," Stumbleduck said. "Teeg. If only to ensure another child doesn't suffer because of that man." His grip tightened on the music box until it was shaking.

"Okay," I said, not waiting for anyone else's response. While I might be able to kill an Abyssal with my power, I wanted all the help I could get.

"What will you do?" Caelus asked. "They won't let you walk right into Thistlewall."

"We'll find a way. Make a plan."

"Because the last one worked out so well," Esteban chimed in.

Caelus glared at him, and Kenzo snickered.

"Thistlewall is a well-fortified gnomish city. Most of it is underground. We'll have to tread carefully."

"I want to help too," Corrin said.

Caelus's features hardened. "You won't."

"I will! You don't get a say."

Caelus's hands squeezed against his biceps. "I do, I'm afraid. You're going home. Away from all this."

Kenzo's face fell.

"There's nothing stopping me from following you."

A muscle worked in Caelus's jaw. "Kenzo will."

She pitched forward, her hands slamming down on the coffee table. "You can't be serious."

"I am."

She looked at the man sitting next to her.

Kenzo held up his hands in mock surrender. "Don't look to me for backup. I agree with him. You shouldn't be involved." His gaze rose to Caelus. "But if the boy's in Thistlewall, it's not going to be easy getting in." He flashed me a smile. "You'll need the help."

I blinked. Then blinked again. "No, no. I can't ask you to help me. You don't even know me." I glanced at Corrin "And—"

He stood from the couch and stretched. "A friend of Caelus—of which he has surprisingly few—is a friend of mine. And as long as Corrin behaves, it'll be fine."

I looked between the two men. Caelus made no move to deter the offer or object to us being friends.

Kenzo's grin widened, delighted at my speechlessness. He began to step out of the room and stopped, glancing over his shoulder. "Is it all right if we stay here?"

I nodded. Aunt Celeste wasn't around to protest extra guests, anyway.

Corrin stood, chin up, and stomped out of the room, not even looking at Caelus as she passed him. Caelus sighed and followed her.

Esteban took a long swig from his flask. "Get some sleep, girl. It's too late to start planning anything. Wait till morning."

I nodded, and he stood, leaving me alone with Stumbleduck.

The old gnome tinkered with the metal music box, and it began playing again.

"There's likely to be an Abyssal in Thistlewall," I said. "You don't have to come."

He laughed, the sound hollow. "I'm old and have nothing else to live for, sweet girl."

There was a content smile on his face. He believed what he said, and I doubted he would take no for an answer. "I hope you find something new to live for."

THE FOLLOWING MORNING, ESTEBAN, Caelus, and Kenzo sat together at the kitchen table. Esteban shot down one of Caelus's ideas. Caelus furrowed his brow, thrumming his fingers along the table. Kenzo watched Caelus, grinning between bites of bacon.

"Climbing or using explosives to get in is a fool's way," Esteban said.

"If a labryn from the Abyss—and who knows what else—is what we're up against, do you truly think most of those people are still alive?" Caelus asked.

"If their plans hinge on a child born once every thousand years, I would imagine there are more defenses in place than before. Wouldn't want someone, like say a group of misfits, to come in and take the kid back."

"Most people don't know what the boy is. Having too much in the way of defenses becomes suspicious."

"Oh, but not if they're hidden," Kenzo added. It was the most useful observation from him I'd heard.

Instead of listening to the three of them, I left the house, restless. I doubted my absence would go unnoticed for long, but we couldn't sit around planning forever. I would have to hurry. There were people I needed to pay a visit to. Starting with Thalia.

25

I stepped down into the underground Temple of Evryn. The stone hallways were becoming vaguely familiar to me. It didn't take long to find my way to the library.

I needed to find Thalia to ask her about Perrin. He was the last person I wanted to rely on, but he had information coming to him somehow. Quickly. He'd found out Caelus and I were in Tiruhm within hours. And we'd need extra people if Thistlewall truly was well defended. Malik would come, but I needed some way to get a message to him, fast.

I had a feeling Perrin could do just that. But I needed to know where he was in the city. Thalia's information about Perrin selling valuables stolen by a group of underground thieves only went so far as a lead. I hoped she might know more. I could have asked Caelus, but I knew he'd refuse the idea without a second thought. Esteban likely would too. So Thalia was my best bet. And I had a favor to ask of her before we left the city.

I found her napping in one of the large armchairs with an open book in her hand. The book started to fall. I darted forward, grabbing it before it hit the floor. I flipped it over to the front cover, and the title wasn't familiar. *Fey Legends and History.* I smiled and shook my head, not at all surprised to find her reading about history.

I placed it on the small round table, not sure if I should wake her. Dark crescents framed her eyes. Maybe it would be better to come back, but without her help, I wasn't sure if I could find Perrin—I wasn't sure she could help me find him at all. I bit down on the inside of my cheek before turning to leave.

"Eira?" Thalia's sleepy voice called.

Turning back to her, I smiled. "Sorry. Did I wake you?"

She shook her head, stretching in her seat and reminding me of a cat. "Last night was a bit chaotic," she said.

"Really?" I asked, hoping I sounded interested. The disturbance in the castle and Travok's subsequent death wouldn't go unnoticed to the temple.

She pursed her lips. "You haven't heard?"

Feigning ignorance, I shook my head.

She readjusted in her seat and motioned for me to sit. "That's remarkable. I'm not sure I've ever heard news spread so fast." She continued to tell me about the explosion that occurred at the iron castle. The temple was called on to assist with ensuring none of the guests were injured, which included her help as Divine.

It was difficult not to squirm or react. "I stayed home," I lied, "so I haven't heard anything."

She didn't appear entirely convinced, but she didn't push. "Did you need something?"

My eyes drifted to her dark circles, then to her messy curls. "Are you sure you're okay?"

She grinned. "Of course! Let me help you!"

I hesitated a moment and then asked, "When I asked about Perrin before, you said he had a group of underground thieves. Surely they had some sort of hideout or meeting place. Did those stories mention anything like that?"

She frowned. "You're very interested in that man. Let me think." She closed her eyes for several moments before opening them again. They looked different—lighter, or maybe glowing, with a faint touch of gold beneath the hazel. "He used a front. Often pleasure houses or gambling dens. Sometimes a mix of both. The Ruby Lantern on the outskirts of the city is newer. I've heard rumors of women being sold there. But no one has been able to prove it to warrant further investigation."

My fists clenched in my lap. Perrin was awful. Yet Caelus was somehow well-enough acquainted to know that and didn't want to talk about it.

Regardless, the Ruby Lantern was the perfect place to start.

I pressed my lips together. All that was left was to ask Thalia for my favor, but she was clearly exhausted. I didn't want to put more on her by asking her to help with Corrin.

"Eira. I'm your friend. And with all due respect, you look as though your stomach is upset. Do you have something on your mind?"

I smiled. "Right." A nervous laugh broke free. "Well, there's something I'd like you to take care of. I'll be leaving the city soon. I was hoping you'd be able to help get someone back to at least Dusmir. But only if you don't mind."

She popped up from her seat. "Of course!"

I gave Thalia the instructions to my aunt's villa and explained that Caelus's sister, Corrin, would require a guide to Dusmir to ensure her safety. She jumped up and headed off, saying she would pack, and I started for the outskirts of the city toward the Ruby Lantern.

THE HOUSES ON THE outskirts of the city were older than the structures closer to the mountain. Most of the buildings were made of stone and wood. Repaired walls and roofs appeared to have been done with iron, though.

Eventually, I found the Ruby Lantern across from a tavern that was falling apart, with wooden sides reinforced by iron. The Ruby Lantern, however, looked out of place. Red everflame lanterns hung outside the building, but they were unlit. The outside was made from a dark-iron, though there were still stone columns along the outside. I wondered if it was to help it look more like it belonged—though it hadn't helped.

I stepped through the door, and pungent incense burned my eyes. Patrons glanced at me, but I ignored their stares.

People played cards while women in sheer red dresses I wasn't certain counted as clothing danced. Some sat in the laps of guests, flirting and caressing. The women all wore matching ribbons around their necks. A man and woman sat on a velvet couch, growing very close. Hands palmed breasts and drifted toward intimate places all throughout the establishment. But the wooden stage along the wall was empty.

Hoping it didn't show that I'd never been in such a place before, I refocused on the back counter where a voluptuous woman was polishing glasses. Her dress was the same as the red ones, but in black. Glass bottles of liquor lined the wall behind her, and the beautiful woman greeted me with a smile. She, too, wore a ribbon around her neck. From where I stood, I could see another set of stairs behind the counter that led down.

"I suggest looking elsewhere for work if you're going to fluster over what you've seen so far, honey," she said.

I cleared my throat. "I'm not looking for work. Do you know Perrin?"

She stilled. "Forget you ever heard that name," she whispered.

"I need to speak with him."

Her eyes darted toward a door that was visible on the upper level. The girl standing near it knocked lightly and stepped inside. "Perrin doesn't take customers, I'm afraid."

"Oh, I'm not looking for *that*. We had a deal."

Her lips pursed. "You should leave."

"I'm afraid I won't."

She narrowed her eyes and opened her mouth to speak again, but the door above swung open. Her mouth snapped shut.

Perrin leaned against the doorway, shirtless, and his lips pressed into a thin line.

A lock of my hair fell in my face from a citrus breeze. *That didn't take long.* I'd known there was a good possibility that Caelus might come find me. I hoped he wouldn't—or at least, that he would take longer.

Caelus stalked to my side, his gaze locked on Perrin.

Perrin stepped back, and then went inside the room, leaving the door open behind him. A silent invitation. Without waiting for Caelus, I started for the room. Caelus grabbed my forearm. "What are you doing?"

"Hopefully getting us help," I said, pulling my arm from his grasp.

Caelus huffed behind me, but I knew he followed from the lingering citrus in the air around me, even if I didn't hear his footsteps. The door closed on its own behind us. Lit candles scattered what appeared to be a bedroom. A desk sat in the center with nothing on it. Two velvet chairs sat before it.

Perrin sat in a throne-like chair on the other side of the barren desk, his mouth pressed to a woman's neck. She writhed in his lap, her soft breasts swaying. Moans escaped her red lips. My face burned at the sight, and Caelus crossed his arms, clearing his throat.

Perrin pulled away from her neck and his tongue flicked out, licking her bruised tan skin. He flashed Caelus a venomous smile, and then his eyes latched onto me. "How unexpected, Lady Quinn."

My heart thundered in my chest. *He didn't just say that. Did he?* My body remained frozen, unable to do anything but stare at him.

Gods, I'd been foolish. Of course the first thing he'd do would be say my name. The man seemed to thrive on chaos. My only solace was that he'd said it in a secluded room.

I glanced at Caelus, but his focus remained on Perrin, his body tense and ready to pounce. *What's he thinking?*

Being a Quinn was irrelevant since I hadn't claimed the name and people believed me to be dead. But the more people who knew, the riskier it was—the more likely it would end with me not having a choice and being forced into the role. That list of people was growing the longer I was away from the temple.

With a deep breath, I composed myself.

Perrin's gaze flicked to Caelus. "And you've brought my favorite lost asset with you."

I had no idea what that meant, but it was likely why Caelus had refused to talk about him. The tension in Caelus's jaw was the only indication that Perrin had struck a nerve.

"Celeste. Lora. You said they were escorted away. Tell me where." My voice came out shakier than I'd wanted.

I didn't think it was possible, but Perrin's smile grew more wicked. "How demanding. For someone who prefers to play dead, you certainly suit the role you so adamantly want to forget."

My fingers dug into my palms, and I took another deep breath. "I didn't find the person you told me about. So where are they?"

He tapped a finger on the chair's wooden arm, his other skimming against the woman's side. Her back arched at his touch, her short dark hair brushing her shoulders. "What do I get?"

I didn't want to give him anything, but our deal was for information. "Ebonhammer is dead," I tried.

He laughed, the sound cold—dark. "As if I didn't already know that. Everyone paying a visit since last night is talking about it. I doubt even an hour passed before it reached my doors."

"He was already dying," I tried again.

Perrin's finger stopped, and he looked intrigued. *Good.*

"How contradictory to all the information stating he was in good health. Why is it you say otherwise?" Perrin asked.

Caelus shifted closer to me, his upper arm brushing against me, and he shot me a concerned look. A silent warning to be careful.

I debated telling him about Ebonhammer leeching life through a cannibalistic ritual, but that information in the wrong hands would be devastating. The Ebonhammer name would be ruined if the public knew, and while I didn't know Iker well, he was probably better—maybe even good—for this city.

"He toyed with rituals. Sought a way to elongate his life, like you said. It didn't work out," I said, each word chosen carefully.

The woman in Perrin's lap shifted, and she whispered in Perrin's ear. Her hands slid down his muscled chest and dipped lower than I could see from over the desk.

"What sort of ritual?" he asked, ignoring her.

"I believe you've received more than enough information for the location of two people," Caelus interjected.

Perrin grinned. "The Wolf speaks."

Wolf?

Perrin tapped his finger again. The woman's arm moved in a steady motion, and his eyes hooded. I fought the urge to turn away. "To Lord Whistlemane with a redheaded man."

Lightning danced through my veins, prickling against my skin to be released. "Why?"

Perrin shrugged, unwilling to divulge any more information.

My fists clenched at my sides. Had the order come from Lord

Whistlemane, or had it been that Abyssal mimicking him? If it was a labryn from the Abyss, what did it want? Teeg, I could at least fathom. As the Golden Child, he'd be valuable for his esprit alone. But why two humans?

"How fast can you get a message to someone in Dusmir?" I asked.

He narrowed his eyes. "And why would I do that, Lady Quinn? Unless you have something else to tell me?"

I managed not to flinch at the emphasis he put on my name and let some of the lightning slip free, sliding over my skin. Harmless, but enough to be a reminder of who and what I still was. "Because we have a deal. If I plan to save them and die in the process, you'll lose an informant." The word tasted bitter in my mouth, but it was true.

Perrin's smile faded to a bored expression. "It would be an inconvenience. Not one I couldn't live without, however." His gaze shifted to Caelus. "Perhaps if you could ensure I'd go unnoticed in Ryseer . . ."

My jaw tightened. Going unnoticed in Ryseer wasn't something I could offer, but Caelus could. I didn't know enough about their history to understand why Perrin couldn't remain "unnoticed" in Ryseer, but allowing it had to be a bad idea.

"Why? You seem well off here. I'm sure the basement is already set up," Caelus sneered.

I resisted the urge to ask what Caelus meant, knowing deep down he was likely referring to that tidbit of information Thalia had mentioned about the possible unsavory business being conducted here.

Perrin snarled, displacing the woman who had been stroking him beneath the desk. She repositioned herself on the arm of the chair, pouting, her red-brown eyes narrowing on us.

"This brothel screams *well off* to you? This worthless city in the mountains is nothing."

Caelus smiled. It was different from the ones I'd seen before. *Wolf* echoed in my mind.

Perrin allegedly sold stolen valuables and more. Not many people came to Tiruhm, even less in winter. Business wasn't good, then.

"You have a confident smile for someone willing to let her die too."

Caelus's smile faltered at the corners, and he squeezed his biceps.

I placed my hand on his arm. Caelus shouldn't have to choose. I'd have to find another way to get a message to Malik.

Caelus's gaze dipped down to me. I shook my head, hoping he understood.

His stormy eyes flicked back to Perrin. "You may come back to Ryseer if you send Lady Quinn's message," Caelus said calmly.

Perrin thought it over for a moment. "I will send her message wherever she wishes, but you mustn't interfere once I return."

Caelus approached the desk and held out his hand. Perrin took it, and they shook. Caelus added, "As long as no one in Ryseer is harmed."

A flicker of glittering dark red smoke ensnared their forearms. Red swirls formed along Perrin's arm down to the tips of his fingers, like a tattoo—the ancient fey tattoos I'd only ever read about. But he'd been wearing long-sleeves and gloves when he'd forced me into our deal. *He hid them.*

The woman on the arm of the chair watched, intrigued. Her eyes almost looked red thanks to the smoke.

Perrin's fingers squeezed Caelus's hand, his knuckles blanching. "You've grown cleverer." He released Caelus's hand, but he may as well have thrown it to the side. "Write your message."

With a puff of that same smoke, a torn scrap of paper appeared in front of me, along with a glass dip-pen and inkpot. I jotted a message to Malik, doing my best to be vague while conveying urgency, and passed it to Caelus to add any additional information he deemed necessary.

Once he was done, he folded it in half and gave it to Perrin, who flipped it open and read it, and then the note disappeared from his grasp in a wisp of that red smoke. His mouth pressed against the woman's throat again, and I took it as a dismissal.

We emerged from that small room, a heavy silence falling between Caelus and me. Several eyes fell to us, and my guess was that few saw Perrin privately—if that could even be considered private. Before we'd even made it to the stairs leading down to the ground level, moaning sounded from the room behind us.

We weaved through the crowded city streets, and neither of us spoke. Once we were in the residential area leading to my aunt's house, the crowd thinned. Questions about Caelus bubbled in my mind. I knew he'd have questions of his own after our encounter with Perrin, though.

"How did you know where I was?" I asked finally, no longer able to bear the silence.

"Your friend told me, *Lady Quinn*."

The way he said "Lady Quinn" should have left me nervous that he knew my true identity, but instead it sent little shivers across my body. "Don't call me that," I said. Luckily no one around us reacted.

Caelus's hand grasped my arm. Air wrapped around us, sending wisps of my dark hair flying around my face. In a blur, we were surrounded by floral scents. His arms caged me against a stone wall. A quick glance revealed we were in my aunt's garden, hidden by a hedge of cherry laurels.

"Going to Perrin was dangerous," Caelus said.

I met his hard, thunderous gaze. "We needed a plan."

"Then you should have stayed and talked with everyone before running off."

"You would've stopped me."

He smirked, a hint of that wolflike smile I'd seen him give Perrin slipping through. "Correct."

"Because you worked for him?"

He chuckled, his warm breath caressing my cheek. "Perceptive—but not quite." His eyes searched mine for a moment. "My family needed money. Leaving him has left him less than forgiving. Especially after I had him exiled from the city." Then he leaned in and whispered, "We all have our secrets. Yours is safe."

My breath hitched, his proximity intoxicating. "And if he lied?"

"Perrin doesn't lie. Which is why it came as a surprise to me when Corrin told me she'd been captive for three days. Before you told him anything."

"What?"

He shifted, leaving one side of me free from being caged by him. I took a deep breath, but leather and spring rain engulfed me.

"It seems I owe you an apology, *Lady Eira.*" He twirled a lock of my black hair through his fingers.

My face flushed. "You shouldn't call me that."

He grinned. "I do believe you've told me that before. But you should know that my anger was never toward you."

I frowned, crossing my arms. "I'm supposed to believe that?"

He nodded, continuing to weave that lock of hair through his agile fingers. "I was angry, but never at you."

"It certainly seemed that way." That loathsome look in his eyes when I'd told him about Perrin flashed in my mind.

"My anger was at myself. At Perrin. At being unable to keep those I care about safe again."

Again?

"Even I struggle to rein in my emotions, *my lady*."

"Gods, you aren't going to stop, are you?"

He shook his head. "I'm afraid you make teasing you far too enjoyable."

I smiled, and his gaze dipped to my lips. That kiss flooded my mind, leaving my body hot despite the chilled air around us. He tipped forward, and I thought he might kiss me again, but instead his soft lips brushed the shell of my ear. "Travok's son is waiting for you. It seems he's interested in helping us. It only seems fitting to let you decide, Lady Eira."

26

We entered Aunt Celeste's villa through the garden door that opened into the den. Caelus followed behind me like a silent shadow. Voices came from the kitchen.

I pushed open the door leading into the kitchen. Stumbleduck sat eating at the breakfast table with Corrin across from him, pouting. Kenzo sat next to her with a grin. I was thankful for what she'd told Caelus—thankful it wasn't my fault she'd been captive. And if I was being completely honest with myself, my heart felt lighter. I prayed to the gods he and Corrin never had to go through something like that again.

Thalia sat at the head of the table, next to Kenzo and Corrin, giggling at the two of them. She sipped from her teacup and scanned the room. Her eyes glittered, taking in everyone. She looked between

Caelus and I, the corners of her lips twitching up. All pretenses that I hadn't been at the ball were probably gone.

Esteban stood on a stool, his waist level with the island he leaned against.

Iker took up the doorway exiting to the foyer. I kept my place from where I entered near the table with Kenzo, Thalia, and Corrin.

"Is there something you need?" I asked Iker.

He smiled crookedly thanks to the scars across the right side of his face. "I figured with my father dead and now that I am 'Lord Ebonhammer,' I would offer my assistance to you."

I bit the inside of my cheek. Caelus had said he wanted to help. So what he said didn't come as a surprise. I had to assume Iker knew my identity as Lady Quinn thanks to Perrin, but it wasn't information privy to everyone in the room. His help would be hard to refuse. "You know our plan?"

"You're going after the labryn pretending to be Lord Whistlemane."

I narrowed my eyes at his confirmation of what I feared. "The Abyssal pretending to be Lord Whistlemane . . . You wouldn't know more about that, would you?"

"My father kept me out of the loop. But I overheard. Abyssals are difficult to kill. You'll be needing help, want it or not."

Caelus sat on the edge of the table next to me, leaning back on his hands. He appeared bored, but I knew better than to think he wasn't paying attention.

"Your father was as much a monster as any Abyssal," I said. "And let's not forget the time you tried to kidnap me."

Iker chuckled deeply. "Because Perrin claimed you might be

able to cure my father of his *addiction*. Past Tempests have always been powerful."

"Eating people—children—because he feared death is not an *addiction*. It's repulsive. Your coward of a father didn't deserve the life he stole."

"Your disdain for my father is why I'm offering soldiers."

I blinked.

I'd known he despised what his father had become, but was he truly offering me help just because of that shared hatred? It was an appealing offer. But it would only be fair that the soldiers were told what they'd be heading into, and unfortunately, bringing random soldiers along would risk word of Travok's unsavory practices spreading. Anyone Iker sent with us could spread possible misinformation, compromise his status in Tiruhm, and send people into an uproar.

If the people learned a monster from the Abyss was lurking about and pretending to be a member of the Dawn Conclave, then they would distrust them all. That distrust would lead to worsening relations between them, the king, and the people. There wouldn't be any repairing their trust if that happened.

Iker had to stay in Tiruhm.

"How kind of you. But I can't accept," I started. "I assume there are concerns about a repeat of what happened at the ball," I said, shooting a look to Stumbleduck. He didn't notice.

Iker sneered. "I'm not a people person."

"The people here need you, and as Lord Ebonhammer, you don't get a choice but to consider them. They need you whether or not you're a 'people person.'" My stomach twisted at the words, knowing it could easily be me in his place—the one left with no choice if everyone learned the Quinn heir was alive. "We have all the help we need, anyway."

Esteban raised a brow at that. "Do I dare ask?"

Caelus scoffed from his seat on the table. "It was reckless, if that's your concern."

I shot Caelus a glare, and he smirked.

Iker growled, rolling his shoulders. "You're going to fight a monster and whatever contingent it may have brought with it. You can't stop me from following you."

I smiled, his words so similar to what Corrin had said last night. "You're right. But I can imagine the rebellion and panic in the city if they learned of your father's eating habits." My threat was hollow, but given he didn't know me well, I hoped that gave me an advantage.

Iker contemplated my words. The clinking of a fork meeting porcelain from Stumbleduck's eating broke the silence. Iker slammed his fist into the doorway and turned, leaving without another word.

It was better for him not to come, even if it was hard for me to accept that he thought I might publicize his father's misdeeds. But I couldn't shake the feeling I'd made the wrong choice in not allowing him to help us.

Before I could dwell on it, Esteban launched into a series of questions that had me confessing to each encounter I'd had with Perrin. He expressed concern over the deal I'd been forced into as an informant. It'd be easy for Perrin to demand I do something horrendous, regardless of the consequences, to obtain information for him. But we needed to alert Malik. To my surprise, Caelus agreed.

Once the conversation died down and everyone separated to

pack before we left, I headed back out into the garden for a breath of fresh air and a moment alone.

Thalia lay on the stone garden bench beneath a tree with vibrant red flowers peppered with snow. She'd forgone the dresses she usually wore for thick black pants and a coat with golden accents. She held up a book, reading it with one of her feet propped against her leg, her wavy honey curls spilling over the edge of the bench.

I bit the inside of my cheek. After confessing about Perrin, she would know I'd lied to her earlier. "I should apologize," I started.

She glanced at me for all of a moment before returning to her book. The gesture reminded me of Marus, and my heart ached to see him. *Soon.* Soon I would get to see him again.

"I suspected you hadn't been truthful," she said, turning a page. "No one goes without hearing news that big. That doesn't mean I think any less of you or that I don't want to help you."

I raised a brow.

She laid the book on her stomach and turned her head to face me. "Divine Tempests often bring about change, and change seems to follow you." She smiled. "It's been a bit messy, but I think you only want to bring good—be a light of sorts."

"You seem very certain," I said.

She giggled. "Of course. I have a . . . sense or maybe sight for things. Perhaps it's intuition, perhaps it's part of my gift." She shrugged. "But while I may have had a feeling you weren't entirely truthful, I have a few questions. Perrin, for starters. You actually met him and made a fey deal?"

I nodded, twisting a stray bit of hair. "More like, was forced into one."

She sat up and pivoted toward me from her seat on the bench. "Oh? Interesting. I've read that he often struck fey deals." Her features softened. "It's outlawed, so of course you didn't expect it." Her fingers thrummed against the book in her lap. "What of Travok Ebonhammer? There was clearly more to what happened than an explosion."

I explained to her what I'd learned from our time in the iron castle and the Abyssal. "I'm not entirely sure what to make of Iker yet either."

Thalia's head bobbed side to side as though she were weighing options. "It's unclear about Iker for now. He has always been a little . . . rugged. Preferred to do things his way, by himself." She frowned. "Travok allegedly caused the scar across his face. The fact that they didn't get along holds some promise for the future of Tiruhm."

"I hope. The people here deserve someone who cares more about them and their troubles."

Thalia smiled. "You should trust your decision. 'Luck is a boon that finds the bold,' as they say."

I laughed. "Sounds like something Ahrea might say."

Thalia saw something good in me—had believed I was favored by Ahrea from the moment we met—and I wanted to believe her. If I was going to save Teeg and my family, I would have to use my power against that Abyssal. Negotiating with it would be a mistake that would lead to needless deaths. Possibly even Teeg's.

"It wouldn't surprise me in the least if she believed it." Concern filled her eyes. "Are you certain it's wise to go after this Abyssal, though?"

"I have to," I said.

She smiled again, but it didn't quite meet her eyes. Thalia likely didn't think I should go—or maybe she wished there was more she could do to help. Perhaps both. Escorting Caelus's sister to safety wasn't a glamorous role, but I wanted to ensure Corrin stayed safe since Perrin was in the city.

"Everyone will be fine," I reassured her.

"Of course! Determination suits you. Let me help you practice some before you leave," she said, giggling.

I nodded, and she instructed me to use my lightning, even touching it while the arcs skittered across my skin and onto the grass. I protested, unsure of my ability to ensure she wasn't hurt by it.

She beamed when she remained unharmed, saying, "You've improved, just like I promised you would."

OUR GROUP GATHERED AT the stables at the city gate in the midafternoon. I stroked Kast's soft nose while he ate oats from my palm. Two rams—one for Esteban and one for Stumbleduck—were brought forward, though Stumbleduck would still need help to mount the ram due to his height.

Kenzo offered to help him, but Stumbleduck yelled nonsense about how he was an independent old gnome and didn't need help. Kenzo quickly backed away, hands up, mumbling, "Excuse me for offering."

Stumbleduck pulled out a contraption that transformed into a stool with a handle that shot straight up. Once mounted, he grabbed the handle, and the stool folded into itself with the press of a small button until it was only the size of a small plank. He then tucked it into a bag.

Thalia and Corrin mounted onto one horse each.

It surprised me to see Thalia capable of mounting on her own, unlike me. *I really need to learn to ride.* Unfortunately, it'd have to wait until I returned to Dusmir. Learning to ride on the way would only slow us down, and we needed to get to Thistlewall sooner rather than later.

Truthfully, riding with Kenzo was an option. I doubted he would mind, but it would feel like running away from my infatuation with Caelus. Infatuation I was never meant to have, because everything we'd done had been part of our act for the ball.

My traitorous body heated at the thought of being close to Caelus again. Neither of us had spoken about the kiss, not that there had been much time. At least not yet. I wasn't sure what people normally did after pretending to be lovers and kissing when it wasn't originally agreed upon. *Normal people don't go around pretending to be lovers with someone.*

Did he find the lines blurring between the reality of our relationship like me? It was most likely my body reacting to him. That made more sense than Caelus enjoying the kiss and wanting more. There wasn't even a *more* to have with each other.

I sighed and watched Caelus approach his sister. From where I stood, I couldn't hear what he said to her, but she crossed her arms, looking down at him from atop her dappled mare. Caelus glanced at me and opened his mouth, then closed it, running a hand through his hair. His gaze returned to his sister, and he placed a hand on his hip. His usual smug smile was replaced with a frown. He gestured widely, saying something else. Corrin narrowed her eyes at me and tapped her heels against the mare, urging it forward. The act caused Caelus to stumble back a step.

I couldn't suppress my laugh. Seeing someone who could ruffle Caelus out of his sureness was something I could have gotten used to. I almost wished she was coming with us, but it was safer for her this way. It would keep Caelus's mind at ease—allow him to focus.

My focus might have been the one in danger, though, because Caelus's head whipped in my direction, and his gaze heated. Even though I hadn't been able to hear him, he'd clearly heard my laughter and stalked toward me, the look on his face unamused.

"So, that looked like it went well," I said with a grin.

"At least it amused you," he said dryly, checking that everything was secured on the horse.

"Corrin isn't one to listen. Especially to Caelus," Kenzo said from the other side of Kast, where he tightened the straps along his horse.

I jumped a little in surprise. The corners of Caelus's lips tilted up.

"I can still go after them," Kenzo offered.

Kenzo going would be a kind gesture, but we needed all the help we could get. "Thalia assured me she will keep her from Thistlewall," I said.

"The two of them will be fine without you, Ken."

Now atop his horse, I could see Kenzo, concern on his face. "Suit yourself." He urged his horse toward the gate.

Caelus helped me up onto the horse, and then he swung up behind me. He urged Kast forward and the horse began moving. "I didn't get to thank you," Caelus said.

The heat of his body penetrated through the layers of clothing between us, but I longed for that closeness, unlike when we'd been traveling here. I mentally cursed my body. I glanced over my shoulder at him. "For what?"

"Ensuring Corrin's safety," he said. "I warned Thalia that Corrin has always been one to slip away and get into things that aren't her business."

I looked past the gate where a fine powder of snow covered the grass. They'd both disappeared. "Thalia's Divine. Her gift should come in handy for how to deal with Corrin." At least, I hoped it would.

He laughed behind me. The sound reverberated through me, and my body ached for him.

How am I going to make it to Thistlewall like this?

"I do believe you're right," he said.

27

We took several breaks on the way to Thistlewall, during which I practiced more with my esprit. Lightning gliding across my skin was beginning to feel more and more natural, but I avoided using it atop Kast with Caelus in case of a slipup. The breezes I mustered weren't nearly as powerful as the ones I knew Caelus could make, but it was progress.

Next to a flowing brook, I focused on a fist-size rock while lightning coated my skin, trying to move it. Still nothing. I wondered if it was even possible to wield both at the same time.

"You might burst a vessel with how hard you're staring," Esteban said.

I pictured the rock lifting seamlessly. Instead, it shot up in a jerky movement, and the bright azure arcs sputtered away. I groaned. "The labryn won't be easy to deal with."

"This plan . . . refusing Iker's aid . . ." He sighed. "I'm not sure it was the best idea."

"The more people who know about an Abyssal in Marunia likely taking the form of one of the Dawn Conclave, the greater the likelihood of panic. It'd also be good if the people of Tiruhm grew to like Iker."

"People didn't wholly dislike Travok."

"They accepted what they knew. Do you really think they'd love him or his son if they knew he'd been eating children?"

Esteban kicked a rock into the stream. "That's all well and fair. But assailing Thistlewall is rather ambitious, my girl. There could be innocents there too."

"Maybe. But the Golden Child—Teeg—is as powerful, or more so, than a Divine. He's in the hands of an Abyssal. He's young and easy to influence. So if being ambitious is what it takes to get him back before something happens to him, then that's what I'll be."

Esteban chuckled to himself. "You've grown in your time away from the temple."

I scoffed, turning back to the water. "Klareth would have had a field day with those shackles, I'm sure." Even speaking of them turned my stomach. I twisted a hand against my wrist, trying to wipe away the cool phantom sting of the iron against them.

Esteban took my hand. "I'm sorry there wasn't more I could do for you, girl."

I shook my head and focused on the rock again. "It doesn't matter. She's dead now."

Esteban remained with me while I practiced. He knew me well

enough to know that despite my words, the memory of those manacles would remain forever embedded in me.

Our break ended and Caelus assisted me in mounting Kast. The forest became denser the closer we came to Thistlewall, the snowy landscape tapering out into thicker green grass. We diverted from the worn dirt road, and howling sounded in the distance. Caelus's hands fell to my hip. Between the warmth of his body and the soothing circles of his thumb, I was lulled to sleep.

I WASN'T SURE HOW much time had passed when he shifted behind me and said, in a hushed tone, "You've been spending too much time with Corrin." The soft rumble of his voice pulled me out of my haze, and I shot forward, straightening myself.

Caelus's arm circled me, keeping me steady, as if he was worried I might fall. His grip loosened a moment later, but his thumb started rubbing those small circles again.

To my right, Kenzo laughed.

"What's so funny?" I shot at him.

His grin turned mischievous. "There's an audience almost every time Caelus and I train together. Most women would die to be so close to him. I'm surprised his looks and charms aren't winning you over."

"It takes more than a handsome face," I said.

"But you do think he's handsome." Kenzo winked.

"I—I'm not blind," I admitted, looking ahead in an attempt to hide my flushed face.

Caelus's chest brushed against my back, and I heard his failed attempt at suppressing his laugh. I looked at him over my shoulder. "Would you rather I thought you were hideous?"

His gray eyes met mine. He smirked. There was no way he hadn't known for a while that I found him attractive. Gods, the way I'd kissed him had probably said as much. There'd never been a reason to admit it openly. There still wasn't, but Kenzo coaxed it out of me all the same.

I huffed and faced forward again, and Kenzo laughed, tapping his heels against his horse. He quickly caught up to Esteban ahead of us, leaving Caelus and I alone.

We were quiet for a few moments, but Caelus's hand remained on my hip, thumb continuing those little circles.

I relished the feeling of him against me, breaking up the monotony of travel. Even if it was just his hand. The act was intimate—a closeness that'd built up in our time together. One I'd grown accustomed to but didn't know where it began and ended during our time *pretending*. I was growing to hate the word. But I didn't make him move his hand like I may have on our journey to Tiruhm. This way there would be little moments to remember after I returned to Dusmir and him to Ryseer.

I bit at the inside of my lip to suppress a yawn.

"You're draining yourself," Caelus whispered, his breath caressing my ear.

"I'm fine."

"You're using esprit every free moment you get. Rest or you'll be of little use when it comes to finding Teeg."

I frowned. He was right. And if Caelus and I didn't have to share a horse due to my own lack of ability, then we could have traveled faster. But we were taking our time to make sure the horses and rams rested enough, and to ensure Malik had a chance to join us. Caelus told me later that he had added a location to the note. I hoped that Malik had enough sense to bring more than himself.

"Don't let what Kenzo said bother you," Caelus said, breaking my thoughts.

"About you being handsome? It was a fortunate benefit of attending a ball with you."

He chuckled. "Fortunate for both of us, then. You were stunning in that dress."

"Oh," was all I could think of to say. *Thank you* would have been better, but I hadn't been expecting it. My lips curled upward, and my stomach fluttered. I'd known the dress was beautiful, but he thought so too.

28

The ball felt like a long-aged memory, but it'd only been a few days by the time we arrived at a dark wooden two-story hunting lodge with a veranda. Caelus said it belonged to the prince and was the location he'd indicated to Malik in my note. A small barn to shelter the horses and rams was on the property, and the surrounding cedar trees provided shade against the setting sun.

Thistlewall was only a couple of hours from here.

Esteban and Stumbleduck left to gather wood for a fire, and Caelus and Kenzo worked together to check the interior for anyone who may have found their way inside. I followed close behind them. They systematically checked each room. For what, I wasn't sure. But there wasn't even a speck of dust in the cozy interior. A worn couch with blankets and an armchair that was well loved sat in front of an enormous fireplace. The kitchen had everything we would need to prepare a decent meal and a dining table big enough for six.

"How often does the prince come here?" I asked.

Kenzo shrugged. "He has a fondness for leaving the castle."

Esteban and Stumbleduck returned and started arguing about the best spices for roasted meat in the kitchen. Caelus left to gather water for our mounts. Kenzo stripped away his weapons except for a knife that poked up from his boot.

Left alone with the three of them, I picked up one of his swords and stepped outside.

The sword was a bit heavier than the ones I'd used when practicing with Selena, and a little longer. Making a mental note of it, I unsheathed the blade and began going through a series of defensive exercises Selena taught me. Those training sessions at the temple seemed so long ago. I'd missed the methodical movements, missed getting lost in them and thinking of nothing else.

In my time at the temple, I hadn't been given an opportunity to develop many hobbies. Training with Selena had been my favorite pass time aside from reading whatever materials Marus provided. Otherwise, my day had been dictated by Klareth. Usually, activities meant to "serve the gods." The physical training had been a way to control my nerves and emotions—a way to keep me exhausted so my gift was less likely to manifest unexpectedly and hurt someone. Now I found all these days without that training left me wanting.

Kenzo stepped out and watched me from the veranda as I repeated the motions again.

I completed the exercise, and Kenzo approached with one of his other swords. "Seems like you could use a little help," he said.

I shot him a look and got into position again, like Selena had taught me. With the sheath of his sword, he lifted my elbow higher. He tapped my right foot with his. "Your stance should be wider."

I adjusted and started again. The movements came easier, and it was difficult to admit he was right. Missing my sessions with Selena over the past couple of weeks hadn't done me any favors, and I was thankful for his help.

"Better," he said when I finished.

"Would you spar with me? It's been a while, so . . ." It was better than sitting around thinking about how little I could do until we started for Thistlewall. Plus, it would be a chance to test myself against someone other than Selena, even if sword fighting wasn't my best skill.

Kenzo raised a brow. "You want to be ready," he hedged.

I nodded. *That too.*

He smiled and stretched, lifting his arms above his head. "Why not?" Kenzo unsheathed his sword and got into position.

Esteban and Stumbleduck's chatter from inside quieted, and I glanced at the window looking into the kitchen of the prince's hunting lodge. Their attention was on us.

"Whenever you're ready," Kenzo said, grinning with a cockiness that reminded me of Caelus. He rolled his broad shoulders, the leathers he wore creaking, and readied himself.

I inhaled deeply, focusing on the man in front of me. There was no denying the two men were attractive. Caelus might've been the more handsome of the two, but the women he'd said Kenzo teased him about during their training were definitely there to ogle at both of them.

On my exhale, I advanced a step. Kenzo retreated. I took another, and he repeated. With each step I took, Kenzo mirrored it with one of his own, maintaining his distance. I sucked in another deep breath and charged him.

Kenzo remained on the defensive, keeping space between us. I groaned, and he smirked. Feinting right, I swung. He predicted the movement, parrying the blow. The force of it shoved me back.

I shot him a glare, but he darted forward, swinging. I raised my sword, blocking at the last moment.

Kenzo struck again. I dodged, backing away. He closed the gap in a blink, grabbing my wrist, twisting it, and gaining control. My hand spasmed, dropping the sword.

"You could use more training," he said, releasing me.

Frowning, I plucked the sword from the dirt. "I'd be worried if you weren't better than me." I hadn't asked, but I assumed Kenzo was at least a member of the castle guard to know Caelus so well.

Readying myself for another round, I met his dark brown eyes.

Kenzo laughed, and I darted forward, slashing down. He blocked and stumbled back. "Fuck," he panted. "You almost had me."

I smiled. "Better pay attention, then."

Kenzo circled me. I watched for some tell of what he might do, but there wasn't one. He feinted left. I barely blocked it, spinning it away. But Kenzo didn't allow me to put any distance between us. He was fast, but not as fast as Caelus. I parried swing after swing, unable to gain any ground. He slowed, but I doubted it was from fatigue.

He sidestepped, leaving an opening, and I struck. Kenzo swung right, but I expected it and dodged, circling behind him. I kicked the back of his knee and he buckled, tumbling to the ground.

Kenzo dropped his sword and lifted his hands in defeat, laughing. "Guess I underestimated you a bit." He stood and clamped a hand down on my shoulder. "Not bad."

I grinned. "Thanks."

The sun had set, leaving only a half-moon for light. Howling sounded nearby.

"That's strange," Kenzo said, scanning the tree line. "Wolves normally avoid people in the wild."

Leaves rustled. "We should probably head inside," I said. A wolf likely wouldn't be a threat in present company, but it was better not to take any chances.

Kenzo nodded and picked up his sword.

Esteban stepped out onto the veranda. "Food's done," he called.

I sheathed my sword and started toward the lodge, Kenzo a step behind me.

An enormous ink black wolf tore through the trees, snarling. It stopped in the clearing a couple of feet away and turned its massive head toward us. Blue shadowlike flames sputtered from its paws. *An Abyss wolf.*

I stumbled back a step. Kenzo grabbed my arm to steady me and pulled out his sword. "Fuck," Kenzo said.

The wolf pounced. Kenzo sidestepped in front of me, and it collided with him, pushing him down on top of me. My breath was knocked away and my vision blurred. I blinked to clear it. Kenzo had managed to bring his sword up in time for the wolf to bite down on the blade instead of his torso.

My sheathed sword fell out of my hands with the impact, too far away to reach.

Sharp, flaming claws swiped down, and I hissed in a breath, gasping beneath Kenzo. Wet warmth slid down my left side and pooled at my hip. The stench of seared flesh filled the air. I couldn't cry out despite the growing burn, the intensity of it too sharp.

Kenzo shoved the wolf to the side. He grunted, pushing himself upright. Gripping his side, he staggered forward. I pushed onto my knees and reached out to steady him. Sticky warmth soaked my fingertips. Those burning claws had gotten both of us.

Kenzo held up that stupid sword to fend off the Abyss wolf. But he wouldn't be fast enough in his current condition if it pounced again.

I yanked the knife tucked away in Kenzo's boot, and I stood, gritting my teeth against the scorching pain. Kenzo kept the wolf in front of him. It circled us slowly, focusing on Kenzo. I threw the blade, hitting one of the beast's eyes. I stumbled and my knees collided with the cold grassy earth.

It yelped and then snarled at us.

A crossbow bolt shot into the thick fur and exploded. The Abyss wolf screeched in pain before a bright lance flew toward it. *Esteban.* It missed, piercing the dirt, and the bright-as-day lance faded away. With one last look in our direction, it growled and then darted back into the trees.

Kenzo collapsed in front of me, and I crawled over to him, ignoring the pain in my side that stretched to my hip.

Citrus filled the air, and before I could see Caelus, I said, "He's hurt."

Caelus glanced between where his friend lay collapsed on the ground and me a few feet away, helplessly trying to get to Kenzo—to heal him. His moment of hesitation passed as he gathered me into his arms and carried me to him.

I pushed away from Caelus, not caring that I nearly fell out of his arms onto the ground, and placed my palm on Kenzo's blood-soaked clothing. Closing my eyes, I pictured two threads of life connecting. There was a glimmer I latched on to, focusing on the rise and fall of his chest beneath my fingers. *He's alive.* I took a deep breath, concentrating, and pushed my lightning out from my hand and along the wound I couldn't see.

Kenzo's scream pierced the woods, and my eyes shot open.

That never happened.

Healing someone never hurt them.

Caelus clamped a hand over Kenzo's mouth, muffling his cries of agony, and tore Kenzo's clothing away with his other hand to reveal the deep gashes along his side. The edges were blackened, charred. Arcs of bright azure energy caressed the wound, and it was slow to close, but the bleeding was relenting. Where the claws had seared the flesh wouldn't mend, no matter how long the lightning slid across it, coaxing. The best I could do was mend the remaining skin and stop any bleeding, leaving behind a scar.

Once the wound was healed as much as it could be, I removed my hand, halting the flow of my power. Kenzo's screams receded, and his breathing steadied.

Esteban rushed over and clasped his hands around my cheeks, forcing me to face him. His face drained of color. "Are you all right, my girl?"

I nodded even though it was a lie. From my side down to my hip burned with every move, sending fresh waves of searing hot pain through me. But the wound wasn't as deep as the one Kenzo had.

He'd taken the worst of the slashing from the claws.

He's the only reason I'm alive.

Caelus returned, pressing what I suspected to be one of Reina's healing rose petals to my hip. The burning faded and didn't prompt whatever agony my esprit had caused Kenzo.

Esteban released my cheeks but didn't leave my side. "Gods, I thought you both might die." His voice was breathless.

I watched Kenzo's chest rise and fall. *He's still alive,* I reminded myself.

"The Abyss wolf. It was here because we're getting closer to Thistlewall, wasn't it?" I asked.

Caelus gritted his teeth. "Perrin read the note. I'm sure he gave away our location to the highest bidder. We need to get inside." He reached for my hand and steadied me on my feet. "I doubt there'll be more attacks soon. Whoever sent the Abyss wolf won't know they were unsuccessful for a time."

Caelus stepped away once he seemed certain I wouldn't collapse, and Esteban took his place. Caelus gathered Kenzo over his shoulders and headed inside.

Esteban kept hold of my hand even once we entered the lodge.

Caelus settled Kenzo onto the couch, pulling a blanket over his friend.

My head spun, and it was all I could do to stand straight, keeping my hand in Esteban's. Caelus used his skill over wind to propel himself faster than I could keep up. He stopped again in front of Kenzo with a bowl of water and a cloth and began to clean away the blood and dirt from him as best he could.

A laceration along Caelus's back caught my attention. Blood

seeped through his clothes. I fought the dizziness and took a step toward him.

Even if he didn't act like the wound bothered him, there were small signs. His movements were stiff and lacked the same smoothness I'd seen time and time again. I placed my hand on his shoulder to steady myself and made that healing connection instantly.

He placed his hand on mine without turning around, and said, "Later. Please."

I swallowed hard but nodded, unable to ignore the way he said *please*.

"I'll see you as soon as I'm done caring for him."

I nodded, and Esteban tugged me away. Each step up the stairs toward the bedrooms was heavier than the last.

29

Esteban helped me to one of the rooms on the top floor. Once inside, he headed straight for the attached bathing room and started drawing water for a bath. He left and returned minutes later with a tray of food and water, leaving it on the gold-accented desk parallel to the large plush bed.

Alone, I peeled away my clothing, letting it drop on the rug extending from under the bed, covering most of the floor with a sunrise design. I padded along the yellow-orange horizon until I stood before the floor-length mirror in the corner.

Three lacerations extended down at an angle from my left side to the front of my hip. The centers of the claw marks were cauterized by the fiery claws like Kenzo's wounds. Reina's petal Caelus used had staunched the bleeding. A few streaks of fresh pink skin peeked around the edges, but it would still scar. There was only so much an enchanted petal could do to heal a wound caused by an Abyssal, even if it was from one of Reina's roses.

Tears welled in my eyes. Not at the sight of what remained of the gashes—Malik had called on me to heal all sorts of injuries, so I wasn't uncomfortable in their presence—but because my ability to heal had a limit. If we faced the Abyssal impersonating Lord Whistlemane or anyone else, there would be wounds I couldn't mend—wounds that would linger from what was endured.

I'd healed people who shouldn't have lived. But with my help, they'd survived. None of them had been left with a physical scar. The wound left behind on Kenzo and the sounds of his screams, despite my efforts, twisted my stomach.

I turned away and headed for the bath, sinking into the hot water. I didn't move, soaking off the blood and grime. The bath water was tinted a reddish brown, flecks of dirt settling to the bottom. Silent tears fell, and I didn't bother to wipe them away. I wasn't sure how long I sat in that water, but it was losing its warmth. I washed away the tears and blood. By the time I got out of the water, it was cold.

I pulled on one of my flimsy nightdresses and glanced at the food Esteban brought. The roasted meat was cold, but I ate as much of it as I could stand with my knotted stomach, then sat in the plush chair staring out the window even though there was nothing beyond the dark silhouette of trees in the night, unsure of what to do. What to feel.

Rain spattered against the window, and levin strikes flashed in the sky. Seconds later, thunder boomed in the distance. My power purred beneath the surface as it always did during a storm. Thunder and lightning called to each other, wanting to play in the sky. The soothing hum of my esprit helped me sleep on rainy nights. Rain had become my favorite because of that, but thoughts of Kenzo kept me awake. And Caelus's injury.

There wasn't any more I could do for Kenzo besides letting him rest. But I hated the waiting.

The door creaked open, followed by the faint scent of citrus. With soundless footsteps, Caelus knelt in front of me. I smiled at the sight of him, despite myself.

His hair was damp and that spring-rain scent, his true scent, enveloped the space between us—amplified by the storm or from bathing, I wasn't sure. He'd changed out of his blood-covered clothes into a simple black tunic and pants to match.

Normally, I might care if someone entered while I was wearing one of the sheer nightdresses with thin straps that Klareth and Alissa had bought for me before I left the temple. But with Caelus I found I didn't care. It wasn't as though he hadn't seen me this way before, and he'd seen more of my body the morning after I'd killed the high priestess.

All I cared about was that I wanted to see him—needed to see him.

"Your wound," I said, not wanting him to think I'd forgotten.

His brows pinched together. "You look . . . drained."

I started to protest, but there was no way to hide the exhaustion I'd spotted beneath my eyes in the mirror.

He placed a warm hand on my mostly exposed thigh. "You should rest."

"I want to heal you."

He smiled and held up a lavender rose petal with his other hand. "I thought you might consider this instead."

The corners of my lips tilted farther up, and I took the velvet petal. Our fingers brushed, and a static charge passed between us. If Caelus noticed it, he didn't show it.

He stood and pulled over the simple wooden chair from the desk. With a quick tug, he removed his tunic. The muscles of his torso stretched with the movement. He sat with his chest to the back of the chair. My breath caught at the gash that ran from his right shoulder blade to nearly the full length of his back. The wound didn't have the same cauterized look as the ones Kenzo and I bore. "This doesn't look the same."

"I snuffed out the flames around the feet of another one, but doing so left me exposed."

I placed the petal against his wound, and the muscles of his back tensed. A warm glow formed around the petal, and it slowly sank down into his flesh. "You? Not fast enough?"

"Surprising, I know." He flashed a smirk over his shoulder, but it didn't hold the same lightness it normally did.

His skin mended itself back together beneath the petal, and the muscles of his back relaxed. "Did you manage to kill it?" I asked.

He shook his head. "It ran off. I'm guessing around the same time as the other one."

Lightning trickled from my fingertips and danced along the gash as if it were drawn to him, needing to stitch together the wound just as much as I wanted to. My power fell from me, and I didn't fight it, allowing it to add to the healing of the petal.

Caelus shuddered and groaned, tilting his head back.

My cheeks flushed at the sound that came from his throat, knowing he found bliss when I healed him.

It wasn't long before the wound was fully mended, leaving only the faint trace of new skin that would fade with time. I'd been distracted by the fresh wound when he pulled off his tunic, but with it healed, my eyes drifted to the faded scars on his back. My fingers traced the smooth, scarred flesh, and he didn't move as I trailed each one. Sparks continued to dance from my fingers, aching to restore his marred skin, the storm seeming to give it a mind of its own. But my lightning didn't heal scars. "There's so many," I murmured. *I never want him to have another.*

"My life wasn't always easy."

"And it's easy now?"

He shrugged, the muscles bunching and contracting under my fingertips. "Comparably."

My fingers skimmed the edge of a tattoo I'd noticed when we shared the room at the inn. "And this?" The design covered his upper arm, spilling onto his back. Swirls of ink that reminded me of sweeping winds spun toward his shoulder blade. From where I sat, I could make out the edges of what looked like a wolf staring back at me. He turned slightly, looking at the tattoo.

"It's a long story," he said, meeting my eyes over his shoulder.

I glanced out the window. "Sorry, I just . . ."

He turned to face me. One of his hands caressed my thigh, sending warm tingles through my body. The distance between us evaporated, and I became keenly aware of how little clothing I wore.

"Just what?" he asked.

I eyed his hand on my leg. "It's as though my power is attracted to you. Like a piece of it wants to be a part of you."

His lips twitched up. "But that isn't all, is it?"

His thumb stroked back and forth on my leg, leaving a trail of heat with each stroke. His smile was different. That lazy, patient one. Like the one he'd had when I found him collapsed in my aunt's foyer. *Does he know he gives away so much in those smiles?*

His eyebrows raised, and amusement lit his eyes. "I can't say that I do."

My eyes widened. *I said that out loud.*

He laughed deeply, the sound of it breathtaking.

I drew my leg to my chest and turned toward the window to hide my embarrassment—not that I could see anything past the dark, rainy night.

I was about to prop my chin on the heel of my hand, but his fingers slid under it and pulled my gaze to his. "You've been the sweetest dilemma since the moment you entered that tavern. One I couldn't escape and found myself unable to keep away from. One I've wanted to spend every moment with. Stunning to the point that I could barely look away."

My breath caught, and my heartbeat thundered in my chest. Heat spread from my cheeks down my neck.

"When I saw you and Kenzo . . . I froze. I knew Kenzo needed help—needed you." His fingers slipped away, sliding to the nape of my neck. He pressed his forehead to mine. "A senseless part of me wanted to take you and run. Keep you away from any further harm."

I'd seen the moment he'd hesitated. I wanted to reassure him, but my mind couldn't move past his words, that had my heart racing.

"Kiss me," I breathed, giving in to what I'd wanted for longer than I was willing to admit.

His storm-cloud eyes bore into me, and he pressed his lips to mine, tender and gentle and so unlike the kiss we'd shared in the castle. He pulled back far too soon, his hand releasing the back of my neck.

Caelus stood. "I should leave."

I pushed myself up from the chair. "Stay."

My gaze drifted over the tight muscles of his abdomen, and those indecent indents that dipped into his pants, before meeting his thunderous gaze. I knew I'd been caught admiring his body thanks to the smirk on his face. I didn't care, because the look in his eyes was the same as my own.

Caelus stepped forward, leaving a hairsbreadth between us. The sensitive peaks of my breasts brushed his bare chest with each breath, the thin fabric doing nothing to stop the friction. It was stupid to want him to stay. Stupid because I wasn't even sure what we could be. I just knew I wanted him.

I'd been falling since the day we met.

The burning silver of his eyes told me he wanted me too. Asking him to stay might have been reckless, but I stopped caring about that. Maybe it was selfish, but I didn't want to lose him when I hadn't even had him yet.

His lips brushed mine, a soft featherlight touch. Barely even a kiss. "What do you want, Eira?"

Not *Lady* or *Tempest*. Just Eira. I'd always been more than my titles to him, even when he used them. He used them more to tease me.

In answer, I pressed my lips to his with the same heat that boiled inside me, as I had in that iron hallway days ago.

His hands slid up my sides, brushing the edges of my breasts through the thin nightgown. He cupped my face, keeping the kiss gentler than I wanted, leaving room for me to reconsider.

But I wouldn't. I needed him. My body ached for him the same way the tempest within me was drawn to him.

I wrapped my arms around his neck, removing any lingering doubt of what I wanted from him. My fingers twisted into the soft strands of his hair, and, with a tilt of my head, I deepened the kiss.

Caelus groaned against my lips, his tongue sweeping into my mouth. He tasted spicy and sweet. His hands moved along the curves of my body, pulling me against the hard muscles of his chest. The evidence of his arousal pressed into my lower stomach, and his fingers tangled in my hair. He kissed me like he'd die if he spent another moment without doing so.

Caelus pulled away, panting, and rested his forehead on mine again, a hungry look in his eyes. "Tell me what it is you want." It sounded like a plea.

My eyes darted from his eyes to his lips, and I swallowed hard, trying to calm my thundering heart. "You," I breathed. "None of the pretending."

He grinned. "You were the only one who ever called it *pretending*." He kissed me again, and his hands slid down my back, cupping my ass. He broke the kiss, and his serious eyes met mine. "Say the word, and we can stop. Anytime."

I nodded, and his lips crashed into mine. He lifted me up, and my legs wrapped around his hips as I held on with my arms around his neck. His cock pressed against my wet center through his pants, and a whimper escaped me.

His chest rumbled with a groan, and the fiery ache in my core grew.

Caelus gently placed me on the bed. He settled himself over me, his lips gliding down my jaw to my neck.

His hot breath caressed my sensitive skin. "You're irresistible, the sweetest temptation."

My fingers caressed the muscles of his arms and shoulders. "You've resisted me so far," I said.

He chuckled, the sound deep and gravelly. His lips found my neck again, and more featherlight kisses trickled down to my collarbone. "Apologies, *my lady.*"

I slapped his shoulder, though not hard enough to hurt, and his laugh reverberated through me.

Caelus continued moving down my body, kissing the tops of my breasts before his lips returned to mine. He kissed me slowly, exploring, taking every inch I gave him. His hand palmed my breast, fingers teasing my peaked nipple.

I whimpered, craving more and exploring his taut body with my fingers, tracing them along his muscles. Wet heat pooled between my legs, begging for release.

Caelus's hands slipped under the hem of the frilly nightdress over my body.

I pushed a hand against his hard chest, and he immediately created space. "I've never . . ." I started.

He nodded. "Stop anything you don't like."

"And I don't take the contraceptive herb."

He chuckled, pressing a kiss on the sensitive spot below my ear. "I do."

I smiled, and he continued slowly, stripping the nightdress from my body and leaving me bare before him.

His eyes caressed every inch of my naked skin, lingering on my peaked breasts and the curves of my hips. His fingers brushed against the marred flesh, and he studied the claw marks. He dipped down, his mouth pressing against each one. "Never again," he said, his warm breath gliding over my skin.

He kissed his way back up my body, stopping at my breasts. His tongue worked in tantalizing swirls against my nipple, his hand teasing the other. Passionate need coursed through me. That teasing mouth moved to my other breast, drawing my nipple between his lips. One of his hands traveled down my body to between my legs. Agile fingers swept through my wet folds, and I felt the uptilt of his mouth against my skin. His fingers teased the sensitive bundle of nerves. My hips moved of their own accord, longing for more. His tongue swirled against a nipple, sending warm tingles down my body.

Caelus slid a long finger inside me. He pumped it in and out sinfully slow, his thumb maintaining that delicious friction—better than anything I'd ever done to myself. I wanted those fingers to move faster and chase my budding climax. He inserted another, and my hips undulated against his hand.

With a kiss between my breasts, he purred, "So stunning."

My back arched, and my head spun. Each stroke of his fingers left my body writhing. His thumb rubbed titillating circles on the most sensitive part of me while continuing to glide in and out, coaxing me toward release. My body collapsed against the bed, and his hand slowed as he began to map my body with kisses, making his way down between my thighs.

I fought the urge to close my legs reflexively, and his warm tongue slid between my folds and up to the tight nerves at my apex.

My fingers found their way into his hair, and my breathy moans filled the room. He continued to flick and tease, slipping his fingers back inside me, curling them, and I began spiraling.

I wanted more.

Gods, I wanted him.

My mind fragmented, and my hand gripped his hair as he sent me over the edge. I loosened my grip, the delicious waves of pleasure passing, and Caelus's fingers slipped out of me. But there was still an ache between my legs—a longing for him.

I pushed myself up, meeting him halfway, and my fingers found the clasp of his pants. Caelus helped remove them, and his long hard length sprang free. It throbbed, and I swallowed. The real thing was far more tantalizing than what I'd read about in books or overheard.

Caelus guided me back down to the bed and lowered himself over me. His lips found mine again, slow and gentle. A silent reminder that we could stop. That we didn't have to continue past anything I didn't want.

But I wanted everything.

He slid his cock between my slick folds with a groan. Then, slowly, he guided himself inside me. I winced at the slightest twinge of pain from the stretching to take him. He stilled immediately, letting me adjust before sliding in farther, and peppered me with sweet little kisses on my lips, my cheeks, and my neck, as if it hurt him to see me in the slightest of pain.

He paused once he was fully inside me, and I twined my fingers through his silky hair. With agonizing slowness, he pulled out to the tip. The muscles of his abdomen trembled as though it was a tremendous effort to go as slow as he was for me.

But the pain had passed, and I lifted my hips, encouraging him.

He thrust into me, still maintaining his slow pace.

I whimpered, "Please."

He kissed my forehead. "I think I enjoy your begging," he said, thrusting into me slowly.

I made a sound of protest, and he laughed.

"As you wish, *my lady*." He pumped his hips faster, sending waves of pleasure through me. He hooked one of my legs over his shoulder, thrusting harder. His pace quickened, and I was certain the others could probably hear us, if they hadn't already, but I didn't care. The sounds of our bodies coming together filled the room between my moans. Our mouths collided, and his fingers found my nipple, adding to the riot of sensations building and building. He buried himself deep into me again and again and created a wholly different storm within me.

Our bodies came together, and lightning flashed outside the window.

Gods. I wasn't certain I could ever have enough of him. How was I supposed to move about my day-to-day life once this was all over?

He shifted, hitting a deeper part of me, thrusting even faster than before and tipping me toward that edge. I reached my hand between us and circled that bundle of nerves until I was crying out his name, thunder booming outside.

He continued to pump into me, and I rode out the pulsing waves of my release. His muscles tensed, and he groaned against my throat, his cock twitching inside me.

I flushed at the sensation. *No one ever mentioned that.*

But there was some sort of addictive feeling in knowing what I could do to him.

He kept himself propped over me as we caught our breaths, skin slick with sweat. My arms stayed wrapped around his neck, unwilling to tear my gaze away from his. He pressed his lips against mine, quick and gentle; then he pulled himself out of me and went into the adjoining bathing room to clean himself up.

When he returned, I was dozing off. "*Lady* Eira, you should clean up before sleeping."

I groaned in protest, exhaustion settling in, and he chuckled. "Or I suppose I could help."

My eyes shot open at the thought of Caelus cleaning me, and I pushed myself up from the bed and quickly made for the bathing chamber. I emerged moments later to find Caelus relaxed in the bed, hands behind his head. He pulled back the covers, inviting me in. I settled next to him. His warm body pressed against mine, and he wrapped himself around me, his arm draped over my stomach. One of his legs lay atop mine. That exhaustion found its way back deep into my bones.

Caelus kissed my cheek and murmured something, but the word *sleep* was all I heard.

30

Caelus's solid arms encased me in a warm, comforting cocoon. His slow, steady breaths were the only indicator he was asleep. My heart fluttered at the sight of his relaxed face. I admired his strong jaw and how much younger he looked while relaxed.

He turned onto his back and pulled me so that I was straddling him, his hardened cock centered between my thighs. I yelped, and my blood heated with desire. "I thought you were asleep." I tried to ignore that my bare breasts were on full display in the morning light.

His gray eyes, bordering on silver, latched on to me as if he were memorizing my body. "You were making it hard with all your staring," he said, voice thick with sleep.

"Is that so?"

He smirked, gaze careening down my body once more. "Among other things." His eyes softened once they locked with mine. "How did you sleep?"

After exhaustion overtook me, nothing could have awoken me. The heaviness in my chest was lighter—the tenseness of my shoulders lessened. Being with him put me at ease, made me feel safe. I wasn't sure when it started. It could've been that first night we met.

I smiled. "Better. Maybe the best sleep I've had."

His calloused fingers pressed into the skin of my hips gently, and he smirked. "Happy to be of assistance, my lady."

I rolled my eyes with a sigh, but my smile remained. "You're having too much fun with that."

He laughed, and a knock sounded at the door, startling me. The eccentric tone of Stumbleduck's voice called, "That burly dwarf made breakfast! Best be quick, or you two won't have any!"

My face flamed, but Caelus remained content. That gnome announced to everyone that Caelus and I had spent the night together. I didn't mind them knowing I cared for him deeply—they'd learn, eventually.

It was the newness of it and of everyone knowing what we'd done—what they'd likely heard last night. I pulled the blanket up around me and groaned.

In one swift motion, Caelus pushed himself into a sitting position and pressed a kiss to my forehead. His gentle fingers pushed a loose bit of my hair behind my ear, his eyes lingering for a moment. "They won't know anything more than we shared a room, unless you want them to." A soft breeze caressed my shoulder. "Convenient tricks, remember?"

I wrapped my arms around his neck, grinning. "How silly of me to forget." And it really was. Of course Caelus would have used his esprit to keep everything we'd shared private.

We quickly dressed, and I chose the blue garb Selena and Alissa had gifted me prior to me leaving the temple, with black pants. I checked myself in the mirror and found that the earring Thalia had given me was missing. I searched around the room and even asked Caelus. He helped look, but neither of us could find it. My stomach grumbled, and I gave up, hunger winning out.

Downstairs, we sat at the dining table of the crown prince's hunting lodge.

Esteban, Kenzo, Caelus, and I sat together. Stumbleduck was nowhere to be seen. It took some modifications, but Esteban had adjusted a seat to be tall enough for himself.

I watched Kenzo, and he barely showed any signs of an injury. He'd found new clothes that were black, with a peek of sunrise orange, the color of the royal family. The clothes were likely left behind by the prince.

Esteban pushed a plate of dried apple slices, hard cheese, and bread in front of me.

I grabbed a piece of dried apple and popped it in my mouth, ignoring the mischievous grin from Kenzo looking from me to Caelus. So far, he'd been wise enough to keep whatever he was thinking to himself. Caelus's glare may have helped too.

If Esteban thought anything of Caelus and me sharing a room together, he said nothing. I knew that wouldn't last, since his trust in Caelus was thin at best.

Caelus picked at the measly breakfast before deciding on a bit of cheese. "While we wait for the Copper Jackals' arrival, I'm going to have a look at Thistlewall."

Kenzo's grin fell.

"I can go with you," I said.

He shook his head. "You should stay. Rest. Explain everything to Malik when he arrives."

"Kenzo or Esteban can explain. I don't need more rest."

His narrowed eyes met mine. "You've been training your esprit since we left Tiruhm and healed two people yesterday."

Guess he'd noticed.

"Your esprit needs to recover."

"He's right, girl. That power may be from the gods, but it's still finite. You need to rest."

I squeezed my hands beneath the table. "I feel fine."

"Not to seem like I'm teaming up against you, but are you well versed in the ability to go unseen?" Kenzo asked.

Quick and quiet steps were something I'd been working on with Selena, but that had been interrupted before I'd been able to make any meaningful progress. Otherwise, my only other experience was Lord Ebonhammer's ball, and that hadn't gone well. I doubted kissing to seem like we were lost would work in Thistlewall. Without Caelus's abilities to keep my steps quiet, we probably would've been caught.

"See?" Kenzo said when I didn't respond. "Let him do what he's best at. He'll be back before you know it, without a hair missing on his pretty head." Kenzo popped a dried apple into his mouth.

"And what if you need help?" I asked Caelus.

Caelus crossed his arms, remaining seated. "I believe I told you before that I normally work alone. Working with you has been a rare exception to the plan."

"Which is rather odd for a crown's guard, isn't it?" I asked.

Kenzo choked on his water.

Caelus sighed, standing.

Kenzo excused himself, and Esteban grumbled, "Be wise, girl," before scrambling down from his chair.

I stood and faced him once the two of us were alone in the dining room.

Caelus twined a lock of my hair between his fingers, a contemplative look taking over his features. "The king . . ." He ran his other hand through his hair. "I am a crown's guard."

"Then why does it seem like you're about to tell me you're not?"

He swallowed hard. "The work I do for the king isn't well known. My skills are well suited for discretion. Perfect for a king who worries about losing power. He sends me across the kingdom as he sees fit. Alone. But I'm not that different from Kenzo when I'm in Ryseer."

"You're a spy?" I asked.

"I suppose that's one way of putting it."

It made sense, given his control over air and wind.

"Working with people—with you—is still new. It's habit to go alone, but that doesn't change that it'd be more dangerous if you came. It's a strain on my esprit to mask both of us." He freed the lock of hair from his fingers and cupped my cheek. "I only plan to figure out what we're up against."

I hated his rationality, his ability to be logical. Hated it because I would be more of a hindrance than a boon, no matter how much I wanted to be the latter. And despite my protests that I was fine, my eyelids were heavy, and the usual buzzing tempest within was barely a murmur. I needed the rest, but the thought of him going alone or getting hurt for me, for Teeg . . . "You're right," I conceded. "But—"

His lips brushed mine, cutting me off.

"Promise you'll be safe."

"For you," he said, wrapping his arms around me.

I memorized his hard body pressed against all my soft curves.

Kenzo cleared his throat, and Caelus released me. He shot Kenzo a glare and said, "I'll be back by nightfall. Go rest."

I took a shallow breath before nodding.

Despite wanting to go after him, I obeyed and headed for the bed we'd shared. I wrapped the blankets encased in his spring-rain scent around me and drifted off quickly, hating that they were all right about how drained I'd become.

IT WAS EARLY AFTERNOON when I woke. There was little to do in the prince's hunting lodge. I admired the lavish craftsmanship of it. How it could be mistaken for belonging to anyone besides the royal family was a mystery. There were sunrise motifs scattered throughout the wood, paintings, and even the rug in the room I'd been using.

Bored, I headed for the stables, if only to have something to do outside of the lodge.

I sighed. I hated waiting, but that's all we could do. It was silly since most of my time at the temple had been just that. My day had been dictated by Klareth and whatever task or punishment she wanted me to endure next. But somehow, waiting for Malik felt like a lifetime. Waiting for Caelus was like a never-ending eternity.

All with almost nothing to pass the time.

In the stable, I found the beautiful chestnut gelding Kenzo rode. Kast was gone, and my heart sank. I'd known he wouldn't be here, but seeing the empty stall was different and renewed that feeling of helplessness I'd felt when I'd been asked to stay.

I patted the nose of Kenzo's horse and offered him a handful of oats. "I'm sure you're enjoying the wait, aren't you?"

He nudged my hand and ate from my palm.

Footsteps sounded behind me, and I spun around.

"It's me, you jumpy nincompoop," Stumbleduck said. Soot and dirt covered his hands and smeared his cheeks.

The gelding nudged my arm with his nose, searching for more oats. "You missed breakfast," I said.

"I'd eaten before you lot even thought about waking up. Managed to get some traps set up, too, in case any more of them flaming wolves try to come after us!"

I stepped away from the horse's eager prodding. "Nothing that will cause our friends to lose any limbs, I hope?"

"If they have any wits about them, no."

My brows shot up. "They need to arrive in one piece."

Stumbleduck waved a hand in dismissal and stepped out of the stables. "I trust your friends have eyes," he called out.

I frowned, following after him. "Are they marked? Because your little toy soldier wasn't very obvious before you threw it at me."

He scoffed and walked around to the back of the stable. "I threw it at Tall Boy. Knew he'd be fine."

"We were standing together."

Stumbleduck stopped in front of a spot of freshly dug soil that stood out among the green grass. "Boy's fast." He pulled out a metal pole no more than a foot long from the pack he wore at his waist and pressed a button on the side. The pole extended, and a handle formed at one end and the blade of a shovel unfurled at the other.

"What're you doing?" I asked.

"The poor soil is singing secrets at the top of its lungs! A nice little ditty about finding treasures and mysteries. Though most people don't rebury treasures they find."

I chose to ignore the more nonsensical parts of what he said. "You think someone buried something here? This is the prince's hunting lodge."

He began digging, shoveling pile after pile of dirt to the side. "All the more reason to dig, young lady."

I crossed my arms. Everyone was *young* to this gnome, and I couldn't tell how old he was from appearances. Maybe in his sixties, if he were human, but gnomes aged differently, just as the dwarves and fey. "Just how old are you?"

He flung more dirt away, and then he swiped away the sweat from his brow. Leaning against his shovel, he began counting on his fingers. "Three hundred and fifty-one."

My eyes widened. I was no more than a child in comparison to him. My mind raced, trying to recall information I'd read long ago about the average lifespan of gnomes. He'd outlived it by fifty-one years.

There was no way I could let him dig this hole by himself. I grabbed the handle of the shovel. "Let me."

Stumbleduck jerked it away from my grasp. "I won't have you

treating me like I'm some impotent old man!"

My hand fell away, but I stayed with him while he dug, silence falling between us.

It wasn't long before Stumbleduck paused and began prodding at something beneath the earth. He dropped the shovel to his side and brushed away the dirt until it revealed what was unmistakably a lifeless arm.

I gasped, a hand shooting to my mouth.

Stumbleduck picked up the shovel and began loosening more of the surrounding earth until we could make out the clear shape of a woman's body. She'd been buried prone, her back facing the sky. Someone had preserved the body. The skin had barely mottled or discolored and had remained mostly intact.

A seven-pointed star with a circle of whirling lines connecting the points was branded into the flesh. It stretched across most of the upper and middle back, the uppermost points between the shoulder blades. The mark was elegant yet horrid.

"Who did this?" I asked.

"Get back to the house. Tell the other two," Stumbleduck said, his nonsensical tone gone.

I opened my mouth to ask why, but the mark pulsed a faint green and faded back to a dark scar.

The air stiffened, permeated with a heaviness that clung to my skin. I clutched the moonstone-lotus amulet Marus gave me, my cool fingers trembling. My lungs tightened, and I struggled to take in a breath. I backed away, step after step, until I'd made it several feet. Then I turned and sprinted for the lodge, my feet digging into the mud.

Hooves thudded against wet earth around me, but I kept moving, heart thumping rapidly.

The autumn chill grew colder. The muddy clopping of hooves grew closer. I didn't bother to chance a look over my shoulder to confirm who it was. The dread and terror emanating from that mark compelled me to put as much distance between myself and it as possible.

Boots squelched against the mud behind me, and I pushed harder, my thighs burning with the effort. Arms wrapped around me and sent both of us colliding onto the wooden veranda of the lodge. A scream escaped me, and Selena, her braided strands falling forward, held my arms to my sides.

The door flew open behind me. "Is everything all right?" Kenzo asked.

Selena looked at him. "Depends. Has my friend gone mad?"

Malik's intimidating frame appeared behind her, arms crossed. He gave me a scathing look, but the image of that mark pulsing and the sticky feeling of dread that followed filled my mind. *Why did that pulse make me panic?*

"If she's gone mad, she's useless," Malik said, stepping past where Selena had me pinned.

Selena's head whipped toward him. "Don't sugarcoat it."

Kenzo asked, "Did something happen?"

A grunt sounded behind me, and the next thing I knew, Esteban was leaning down next to me. "Are you all right, girl?"

I inhaled deeply, catching my breath and calming my mind. "We found a body," I said between breaths. "There's . . . something on its back. I could feel it."

My chest relaxed, my lungs loosened—the sense of overwhelming fear leaving my body.

Malik's green eyes grew icy, connecting with mine. "Where?"

"Next to the stables. There's a mark. It's not . . . It's not just a brand."

He headed for the stables, not waiting for anyone else.

My fists clenched and unclenched. I swallowed hard, trying my best to forget that sense of dread—of hopelessness.

Esteban placed a hand on mine, and I met his worried gaze.

Selena shot me a concerned look and then released me. She offered me a hand. I took it and smiled thinly before following Malik.

Kenzo and Esteban trailed behind. Selena remained at my side, filling the silence by asking how I'd been and what had happened in Tiruhm. My answers were short, clipped.

I'm fine.

Teeg wasn't there.

Whistlemane is probably an Abyssal.

It wasn't that I was unhappy to see her. But it took all my focus to bring a sense of calm back to my body and gain control again. If it wasn't for all the esprit I'd drained, lightning would have likely been leaking from within me.

Stumbleduck faced our group. Behind him, another body lay next to the first one. The same mark on their back. Both appeared to be human—adults.

My feet shifted, and I rubbed my arm to soothe a chill that ran through me.

Malik bent low and examined the marks on the two bodies. "The mark is fey. It's preserving the flesh, but the soul . . . It's gone."

"How can you tell?" Selena asked.

"Esprit comes from the soul. With enough training, anyone can sense it. There's nothing left."

"But that mark," I muttered. "It felt alive." The mark pulsed as though it knew I'd been thinking of it.

Another chill ran up and down my back, and I crossed my arms to fight it off. That tightening started in my chest again. I fought the urge to back away.

Malik placed a hand on the closest body, and red smoke wrapped around his fingers. Bits of flesh on the corpse began to decay and then rapidly repaired itself. He jerked his hand away. "Fuck." The red smoke fell away, and his hand was burned. "Interesting. We'll take them back to the guild. Gh'ells may learn something."

A member of the Copper Jackals I didn't recognize came forward and gathered one body into his arms. I took a step closer and brushed my fingers against their arm. I tried to form a connection, but that thread didn't form as expected. There was no light to attach to. The soul was gone, just like Malik said, but there was something else. A jade-colored void. My vision darkened, and a chill filled my entire being, but I couldn't seem to withdraw.

A laugh sounded in the void, dark yet inviting.

"Eira!"

I blinked, and Kenzo was standing in front of me, hands on my shoulders. He'd been shaking me. I let out a gasping breath. "I'm fine."

He didn't look as though he believed me. "You're pale," he said, voice more concerned than I'd ever heard from him.

I gave him a weak smile. "I need more rest. Like Caelus said."

He conceded, his arms falling back to his sides. Selena gave me a sidelong look like she didn't entirely believe me, either, but we made our way back to the lodge, neither asking more questions.

31

It was an hour past nightfall. Caelus hadn't returned like he'd said he would. And no one acted like they were concerned except me. Not even Kenzo, and the two of them were like best friends as far as I could tell.

The only decent thing that Malik had done during our wait was send the two marked bodies back to Dusmir. The farther away they were, the better. I didn't want anything to do with those dreadful pulsing marks on their backs.

But Malik insisted we wait to make sure Caelus really wasn't returning.

The fire crackled in the living room, where I sat next to the window, peeking out for any sign of Caelus. "We need to go," I said.

Malik leaned against the front door, blocking it.

Selena and Kenzo gave me sympathetic looks from where they sat at the dining table.

I glanced at Esteban on the couch, and he shook his head.

I stood and paced the entryway.

Malik said, "You'll die without a plan. Fortunately for you, I don't let little incompetent Divines run off toward deadly Abyssals on their own." He shot me a cold, calculated look. "We wait for backup from the guild," he added, as if it were some sort of peace offering.

I glared at him and loathed to admit more people gave us a better chance against a labryn.

Malik had always been difficult on the best of days—an arrogant ass, putting strategy before anything else. Becoming the guild leader hadn't done that part of him any favors. While his esprit wasn't as powerful as a Divine's, he was one of few who came close. We had a chance together.

I gestured toward Selena and said, "She trained me. And I've been training with my power on my own."

"Ah, so it's yours now, is it? Wasn't that way a few years ago when I offered to let you join the guild—offered to train you—and get away from that temple bitch," he sneered.

"She was a child, Malik." Esteban said from the couch. "We all make mistakes as children."

He crossed his arms. "And apparently, even greater ones as adults."

"Mistakes I've been trying to fix!" Without the earring from Thalia to hold it back, lightning slipped from my fingers at my outburst.

He stalked forward, not threatened by the lightning.

I stood my ground.

"Except that's the problem, Tempest. You aren't fixing anything.

You're worried about someone else. Teeg wouldn't come first if you went to Thistlewall, assuming you didn't get caught or killed before you find either of them."

"I can find him and Caelus—"

Kenzo interrupted, "I could go with her. A small team would likely go unnoticed."

Malik turned to face him, a muscle in his jaw tensing. "Sending her with someone untested could end with the same result."

"Calling him 'untested' is quite rude. He does work for the king, after all," Selena chimed in. "And I could go too."

"No," Malik said with a finality that had everyone silenced.

Selena sipped her tea loudly, unfazed.

I looked to Esteban, hoping he would side with me, but he was facing the fire. He probably thought the whole idea of going to Thistlewall was reckless and wouldn't want me heading off into danger. Siding with Malik would be an easy choice for him.

Spinning on my heel, I slumped back down into the worn chair next to the window. The moon peeked out from behind a cloud, casting silvery light on the trees and the stable.

I couldn't shake that something was wrong. *Caelus should be back.* Something had to have happened. Sitting around and waiting wasn't the answer, despite what Malik thought.

I had to get to Thistlewall, with or without Malik. If I ran into the labryn, I had my power. Using it against a monster would be easier than a person. *I hope.*

And if I went, I could find Teeg—and save him.

Malik looked content to block the door all night if he had to, just to ensure I didn't leave on my own before he had a plan. I'd noticed a few of Malik's men stationed outside, likely guarding the exits. Little did they know, I couldn't ride a horse. So I'd need help or a lot of luck to escape the lodge.

Ahrea's luck.

Before I could consider the good and bad of my idea, I headed upstairs to the bedroom Caelus and I had shared, tapping Selena's shoulder along the way as a signal for her to follow me.

She didn't join me immediately, so once inside, I quickly braided my hair and grabbed my dagger, strapping it to my thigh. I wished I had a sword, too, but with no way of getting one without Malik knowing, the small blade would have to do.

I crossed my arms and paced while I waited, keeping a close eye on the window for any Copper Jackals who may be patrolling outside.

Selena tapped against the door ten minutes later.

"Come in," I said.

She stepped into the room, shutting the door behind her. With a few steps, she closed the distance between us. She kept her voice quiet. "So, you plan on leaving?" She gestured to the window in the room. It was one possible exit, but one Malik—and obviously Selena—would expect.

I nodded. "I need your help."

She grinned. "What's your plan?"

"I don't have one," I said.

I knew it would sound ridiculous to her, but if Ahrea favored me as Thalia thought, then luck might be on my side, even if it often didn't seem that way. Luck could be enough to get me to Thistlewall and help me find Caelus and Teeg, though.

Selena's grin fell. "You don't?"

I shook my head and walked over to the window. I hadn't spotted anyone in the moonlit woods so far. Either Malik didn't think I'd try to leave through the second-story window or whoever guarded this exit wasn't present.

My gaze slid to Selena.

If Malik didn't have anyone outside guarding this exit, that could mean he was counting on her to keep me inside. Except right now, I'd confused her with my lack of a plan.

"Any ideas?" I asked.

She sat at the desk on the opposite side of the room. "Yeah. Stay here. Let us handle this."

I sighed, facing the outside again. "I thought as much," I muttered, and then shoved open the window and tumbled through it onto the roof. Righting myself, I spun back around and placed my palm on the glass. Lightning spread from my hand. The glass shattered, spraying into the room.

Selena had only made it a few feet, so I hoped she'd be okay.

She lifted her arms, blocking the shards from her face. I spared a moment to ensure she wasn't injured.

It cost me.

She recovered and sprinted toward me.

I turned and darted over to the edge of the roof. "I'm sorry!" I yelled before shimmying down the trellis.

Glass crunched and wood groaned above me.

Before I made it halfway, a vine wrapped around one of my wrists. Selena's esprit. I grabbed the dagger and cut it away. That was all she needed to catch up. Above me, she started making her way down.

I let go, grunting with the impact, my knees nearly buckling.

Without wasting another moment, I raced for the stable. Selena had always been fast, but I prayed to Ahrea that I could be faster.

Footfalls squelched in the mud all around me. I pushed my muscles harder until they were burning.

The shattered glass had alerted everyone, and I cursed my decision to break it.

I spotted faint movement along the ground thanks to the moonlight and dodged a rapidly growing vine from Selena. Thick roots sprouted from the earth, shooting toward me. One caught my wrist, spinning me around.

I reached for my dagger, but this root was tougher than the vines. Another one snaked up, encircling my other wrist, incapacitating me.

"Fuck, Eira! Let me help you!" Selena called.

I wanted to believe her, but she'd encouraged me to stay. Her loyalty to the Copper Jackals—to Malik—was respectable, but I couldn't sit back and do nothing. I struggled against the rough root but couldn't break free. "Fuck luck," I muttered, lightning forming at my fingers.

A boom sounded in the distance. My head twisted toward it.

Kenzo tackled Selena to the ground with a wet thud. He pinned her and reached into his coat, pulling out a rope. With deft motions, he secured her hands behind her back. He pushed himself back up. "Keep still," he said, brandishing his sword. He cut through the root and grabbed my hand. "Let's go," he said, pulling me along with him.

Inside the stable, his horse had already been readied. "Were you going to go on your own?" I asked between breaths.

"I hoped you wouldn't be complacent," he said, helping me up. "Glad to see I was right." He climbed up behind me, and a moment later, the horse shot out of the stable. "Never thought you'd cause glass to explode in your friend's face, though. Made for a decent signal."

"I couldn't sit and wait." My hands gripped the horse's mane. "She wasn't hurt," I added.

"You're right to be worried. Caelus isn't easy to apprehend, what with his airwalking and all."

My stomach dipped.

Hooves pounded against the mud behind us, and I twisted around. A brown ram galloped after us, Stumbleduck atop its back.

Kenzo looked over his shoulder, grinning. "The little guy really pulled through."

I blinked. "That explosion?"

Kenzo nodded. "That was supposed to be the distraction."

"For what?"

"The hard-ass guild master."

"You didn't tell me."

He chuckled. "Hard to do when they weren't letting you out of their sight."

Smiling, I turned forward but kept my senses alert. Malik wouldn't sit back and let us go without trying to stop us.

Stumbleduck's explosion bought us time, but it wasn't enough.

More hooves against mud caught up to us.

Kenzo weaved through the cedar trees of Reina's Woods, using the darkness to his advantage. But they knew where we were headed. Losing them would be tricky. Selena hadn't held back to stop me before. I wasn't sure what lengths they might go to stop us.

A crossbow bolt whizzed past us. "Gods, they're persistent,"

Kenzo muttered. He turned right. "They're serious about stopping us. It'll be impossible to go unnoticed unless they fuck off."

"Do you have a plan?" I asked.

He called out to Stumbleduck, "Do you have any more of those explosives?"

Stumbleduck slowed beside us and reached into his bag. He pulled out two of those explosive metal soldiers.

I jerked the reins from Kenzo, pulling back enough for the horse to slow. "We're not hurting them."

"Do you want to save Caelus and the boy?" Kenzo asked.

"I do, but . . ." Was injuring members of the guild protected Dusmir the right thing? I'd healed several of them from fatal wounds. If I agreed to this, I could cause one of those injuries, and they wouldn't have me this time to save them.

Malik may never forgive me for it.

Hoofbeats grew closer. Kenzo said, "Eira! We can't wait around."

"Is there a way to detonate them on a timer?" I asked.

"Of course! What do you take me for?" Stumbleduck yelled.

"Plant them elsewhere. Away from them. It may convince them we went another direction. It'll get them off our trail long enough to gain some distance," I said.

"They barely fell for that before," Kenzo said.

"I won't sit by and risk injuring them as much as I won't sit by and do nothing to find Caelus and Teeg."

Kenzo sighed, then shouted instructions to Stumbleduck.

With a squeeze of Kenzo's thighs, the horse sped forward. Stumbleduck branched off from us. Kenzo laced through the trees and shrubbery, keeping us out of view. Crossbow bolts flew past, missing their mark.

Several minutes later, Stumbleduck rejoined us, a trail of fuse behind him. The remaining bundle in his hand rapidly shortened.

We veered in a new direction that I hoped was Thistlewall.

Stumbleduck grumbled.

I turned to see him struggling to light the fuse while mounted, and he was running out.

I said a quick prayer to Wrynal's twin before yelling, "Drop it!"

Stumbleduck mercifully listened. I willed lightning to my fingers, sending it toward the end of the fuse.

It lit, the flame skittering along the fuse toward the explosive.

Wrynal may be the god of war. But his sister, Renelle, was the goddess of mercy, and I prayed that she'd have mercy on anyone caught in the blast.

32

I thanked Renelle that neither Malik nor Selena had caught up with us. Yet.

A beautiful, deadly spiked bramble wall decorated with flowering vines stood before us, keeping us from entering. The name Thistlewall made more sense than ever before.

Short, presumably gnomish guards patrolled the wall, and night hid any obvious entrances or weak points. The only way in or out was through the front gate or climbing the wall. We circled the protected town from the trees to avoid being spotted.

"Do you know what you're looking for?" I asked.

"I hope I will when I find it," Kenzo said.

Stumbleduck rode beside us. I hoped he might have some idea about how to enter the gnomish town, but he offered no advice when I asked.

We stopped after Kenzo had made a semicircle around the wall, and he slid off the horse. I followed suit, nearly slipping in the mud, but Kenzo steadied me. I offered him a thankful smile, but he was watching the parapet. After a moment, he approached the brambles. I followed him, Stumbleduck remaining back atop his ram.

The tips of the spikes had been sharpened to a fine point—or maybe they grew that way, I couldn't be sure. Kenzo pressed a finger to a spike and jerked it back, a bead of blood pooling on his fingertip. "It's effective," he muttered.

I narrowed my eyes at him, taking his hand. "Did you think it wouldn't be?"

He watched the lightning cross from my fingers to his, the pinpoint wound vanishing in seconds. "You didn't have to do that."

I released his hand and gazed at the wall again. "I wanted to."

"We don't have many options. They won't let us in through the gate, I'd bet, and if they did, they'd likely throw us in a prison cell if they're following orders from someone other than Lord Whistlemane." He sighed. "I'd love to have Caelus's ability right about now."

I looked at the top of the wall and then back at the spikes. Their placement was near perfect for climbing. I could squeeze between them, maybe.

Kenzo's brows rose, his eyes glancing from the wall back to me. "Gods, no. We're not climbing that."

"Do you have any better ideas?"

Stumbleduck approached, no longer atop the ram. "Blow a hole through and be done with it!"

I considered the idea but shook my head. "Do you even have more explosives?"

Stumbleduck's eyes downturned. "Give me some time and I can whip together something with enough force to blow through it."

"Time we don't have," I said.

Kenzo placed a hand on his hip and shook his head.

"So climbing, it is," I said.

Kenzo groaned.

Stumbleduck looked between us and grumbled. "Don't be fools." He gestured toward the wall. "Thistlewall is gnomish. Gnomes aren't foolish enough to rely on a gate as their only way in and out, like you tall folk."

"You know another way?" I asked, hopeful.

He nodded. "Just have to find it."

Going off to find an underground entrance would take more time, but it would be safer. I looked at the spiked brambles again. The plan to climb them was less than wise, even if it was more of a direct route.

My eyes drifted to Kenzo. He was broad. Broader than Caelus. And while the spikes were spaced out enough that I could squeeze through and climb, there was no way he'd fit between them. And with the vines growing between them, there was a greater chance of getting tangled and tripping. A fall could be lethal.

I sighed. Time was running out before the Copper Jackals could catch up to us again, and thank Ahrea they hadn't so far. I only hoped no one was injured from that explosion. Malik hadn't been willing to risk lives for what he'd called a ludicrous rescue attempt. I didn't know what he'd do if I'd hurt any of them for this.

Kenzo and Stumbleduck seemed to be waiting for me to decide.

Luck may have gotten us here without Malik catching up, but I couldn't rely on it to ensure we'd survive the brambles. "Let's go," I said.

Kenzo's shoulders relaxed. "Thank the gods," he muttered, and we headed back into the dark forest where our mounts waited, the sweet floral scent of the wall fading with each step.

Stumbleduck led us through the trees and brush until the bramble wall was no longer visible behind us. We abandoned the beaten road and wandered through the dark forest for nearly an hour, and I wasn't certain Stumbleduck knew where to find this other entrance. At least Malik wouldn't be able to easily track us.

We approached two boulders overgrown with vines and bushes. Stumbleduck stopped and dismounted, pulling out a hunting dagger. He cut away some of the shrubbery, revealing a cave mouth hidden deep within, between a set of boulders.

Kenzo and I slid off the horse and followed him into the cave. Wet-earth scent filled the surrounding air, and darkness swept in around us. I took a deep breath and summoned an orb of lightning. Hues of blue-white shone against the makeshift stone steps that led down. Above us, the tunnel had been carved out of the earth itself. Support beams had been put in place every few feet.

"Is this an escape route?" I asked.

Kenzo shrugged and Stumbleduck didn't offer an answer.

A fork appeared in the path before us. One was too small for Kenzo and me. Stumbleduck turned left down the taller path, still barely tall enough for the two of us.

Gods, have I made a mistake?

We continued through the dank cave in silence. The only sounds were our breathing and our boots scraping against the earthen floor.

I brushed my fingers along the low, smooth dirt ceiling. We passed more small tunnels—ones an average human or fey child could probably squeeze through. But Stumbleduck continued through the larger tunnels, ignoring them.

I wondered if Stumbleduck grew up in Thistlewall or one of the other gnomish burrows that Lord Whistlemane presided over. I hoped so, because I knew little of the gnomish cities, and that knowledge could prove vital. Gnomes were often secretive, though, preferring to keep to themselves, despite being ruled over by King Olbecht.

The tunnels transitioned from dirt to light limestone, and my palms grew sweaty with each step. Finding Teeg and Caelus was the priority, but could we do it? Stumbleduck had assisted us so far, and I was certain he'd at least help so long as we were looking for Teeg after his story in Tiruhm. Other than his penchant for explosions, I wasn't sure how much help he'd be beneath the surface. Kenzo, however, was at least a castle guard, if not also a crown's guard. Our sparring match proved he was skilled. But would the three of us be enough?

I shook my head.

We didn't have a choice. We had to find them. Even if it was only the three of us.

The smaller tunnels became more abundant the farther we went, and cracks had formed along the stone walls of the path we took. We passed an open dark-iron door that reminded me of Travok's castle. I peeked inside; the room had been reinforced with iron. Shackles hung on the far wall, and metal grates ran along the floor underneath them.

I wrapped a hand around my wrist, soothing a phantom coolness that ran up my arm.

Stumbleduck didn't stop, though, and we continued past.

Everflame lanterns became evenly spaced along the wall, lighting the way through the corridors, and I let my ball of light fizzle out. The tunnels were barren otherwise. No spark of life anywhere.

Stumbleduck stopped in front of a three-way junction in the path. Only two were tall enough for Kenzo and I. Down one of those two paths, iron bars lined the walls, appearing to be a makeshift prison or dungeon.

Voices drew my attention toward the other path. I didn't wait on Stumbleduck or Kenzo before bounding toward the sound, certain that I'd heard Caelus.

At the end of the tunnel, I rounded the corner.

A woman in clothes like Caelus's—dark leather fitted over a deep orange tunic trimmed in gold—wrapped her arms around his neck in the middle of a dining area. She pressed her chest to his, her midnight hair swaying. Seconds felt like minutes as she leaned forward, whispering into his ear. With a turn of her head, she pressed her lips to his.

My heart wrenched, and a sharp pain ran through my chest. All those shared moments together meant nothing. How could I think they had? *Because I fell for his charm.* But had the charm been a lie? We'd barely known each other. In truth, I barely knew him. Maybe this was the real Caelus—the one Esteban worried about.

My hands squeezed tight, and my nails dug into my palm to keep the teeming lightning at bay.

Caelus shoved her away and faced me. "Eira!"

I didn't want to look at him and instead focused on the petite woman who'd kissed him. She turned to face me, too, and took a step forward, a satisfied grin on her red lips.

Caelus stepped in front of her, approaching me with a pleading look in his eyes.

I stepped back.

Hurt flashed across his face. But I didn't care. That flash of emotion could have been practiced. Feigned. *It wasn't real.*

My stomach twisted, and my eyes stung.

None of it had been real.

"She's pretty. Too bad," the woman said. She darted forward, like a shadow coming at me.

I ran, but only made it a step before a hand grabbed my wrist. Cold metal clasped around it, and I whipped around. My body froze at the sight of the rune-lined cuff around my wrist. The same runes I'd grown too familiar with—the same ones that lined the shackles Klareth used.

Cool sweat beaded along my neck and forehead. My body hadn't forgotten the burning from the lightning attacking me.

I jerked away from her, breaking free from her grasp, and ran. But she was faster. She grabbed my other wrist before I'd made it a handful of steps. The woman forced me to face her, and the cold iron cuff wrapped around that wrist too. She tugged on a chain that was attached to the shackles around my wrists—a leash.

My eyes darted to where she stood, then to Caelus. "Was this why you were working with Marus? To learn which runes she used?"

He didn't say anything.

The chain tugged again, this time pulling me to follow, but I didn't budge, keeping my eyes on his emotionless face. She jerked on the chain, forcing me toward her, and I stopped fighting her.

The woman led me through the tunnel I'd come from. Caelus started after us, but a wall of hardened shadow blocked him off. He pounded against it, the sound reverberating through the tunnels. The earth started to rumble, and the stone walls shook.

"Curious," the woman said, but she didn't stop.

At the junction, Kenzo and Stumbleduck were nowhere to be seen. If they were smart, they would've found somewhere to hide. If they did, there was a chance to get out of here.

She led me down the hall I'd seen before and into a dungeon. She shoved me into a cell with iron bars, and I was left alone to wait for what pain may come from the runes lining the shackles.

33

I slid down the cool bars of the cell, collapsing into myself. A makeshift bed sat in one corner, and the other had a bucket for relieving oneself, and I hoped I wouldn't have to use it. Hoped Malik might be on his way, even if he had every right to abandon me after the stunt I'd pulled.

And what did I accomplish?

I ended up caught, just like Malik had said. Maybe he was right not to believe in me or my abilities. Aside from healing, I wasn't skilled at using it. It didn't even cross my mind when that woman rushed toward me to defend myself with it. I'd been distracted, like he'd said too. The moment I'd heard Caelus's voice, I ran off without thinking.

"Eira?" called a small, familiar voice.

My heart thundered. I whirled toward the cell across from mine, chains clanking. My eyes burned at the sight of Teeg in the cell across from mine. *He's okay.* Dark circles lined his eyes like he hadn't been sleeping well. His shirt had a few smudges of dirt on the sleeves, and the bottoms of his pants were tattered. But he was okay.

Teeg was standing across from me, and he was alive.

Our eyes met, and a small sob escaped me. It couldn't be real. But it had to be. Gods, it had to be real.

My fingers twined around the iron bars, wishing I could tear them apart to get to him—to hug him and keep him safe. "We're going to get out and go home, all right?" I said.

He nodded. The everflame torch a few feet away illuminated his face in the faintest orange glow, but I caught a tentative smile.

I couldn't help smiling back. "Did you overhear anything?" I asked.

He wiped his face with his arm, dirt smudging along his cheek, and then his blue-green eyes met mine. They gleamed from the tears he was holding back. "They've been saying I'm special and taking care of me. Until they brought me here . . ."

Something changed if they'd been taking care of him. But what? "Who are 'they'?"

"Mr. Beris and Mr. Anwir."

My fingers trembled. "Are you sure?" I asked.

Teeg nodded.

But that couldn't be right. That would mean that Roan Beris and Gavriel Anwir had been working together—that they were responsible for all this. *Why?*

I'd seen Gavriel at the ball and assumed his distant demeanor was because of Dorian's death—because it had been me who'd killed him.

It didn't seem to matter that his wife, Ina, had forgiven me. But would that be enough for him to take a child? And for what purpose?

"Did they say why they brought you here?"

He shook his head. "They've been saying they need souls. I don't know what that means." His breath hitched. "Eira, I want to go home."

"We will," I promised. "Don't worry. I'm here now. Malik is on his way." I hoped that wasn't a lie.

Teeg calmed, giving me another glimpse of a smile. He retreated farther back into his cell, saying he was tired.

I released the iron bars and tested my power against the shackles, but there wasn't even a faint hum. These manacles didn't redirect lightning back toward my body either. Caelus must not have memorized the correct runes if the cuffs were only blocking it.

It was a small mercy knowing I wouldn't be writhing in pain, unsure how much time passed or what was going on around me. Teeg witnessing that from his cell across from me would definitely leave a mark.

I needed a way out, and I needed to forget Caelus. I examined the cell for anything I could use to pick the lock on the shackles or the cell door. But there was nothing. Not even a loose stone along the wall that I might be able to use as a distraction.

Frustrated, I plopped onto the grimy, hard mattress and lay back.

When I closed my eyes, images of Caelus and that lovely petite woman flashed in my mind, her lips against his. Less than a day had passed since his lips had been on mine and shared much more.

My heart twisted. Had I really been that naive?

Yes.

Between growing up with Aunt Celeste, naïve who'd pretended I didn't exist, and being sheltered in the temple, I was the perfect target for falling prey to his looks and his charms. I'd let him in because I thought I could trust him and instead had been used. Again.

Had he been planning to get me here? Had he known I'd come for him if he didn't come back like he said?

And what about Kenzo and Stumbleduck? They were both people Caelus knew. They helped me get inside Thistlewall. Was it something the three of them had planned, then?

I shook my head, pushing the thoughts away. Getting out came before worrying over that.

Esteban wouldn't sit still while I was missing. And even if he didn't know I was captive, he would push Malik to come after me. I knew Malik well enough to know he wouldn't allow Esteban to go alone.

I hoped they made it in time before anything more happened to me or Teeg.

With a sigh, I sat up and examined the manacles more closely. The tight cuffs didn't allow for much maneuverability with my wrists. Slipping my hands out didn't seem to be an option. The longer I scrutinized them, the more I regretted it. Sweat built on my brow, and my heart pounded. Memories of Klareth's punishments filled me. I closed my eyes and took a deep breath in and let it out slowly until my heart eased.

Groaning, I stood up and began to pace.

Citrus filled the cell. Caelus stood with his arms crossed in the middle of the small space.

"You shouldn't be here," I said.

"And brooding doesn't suit you."

"Leave."

He smirked and took a step forward. "You're rather ill-tempered. Again."

I scoffed. "You think I shouldn't be?"

"*She* kissed me."

"And I should believe it wasn't mutual?"

His lips pressed into a thin line.

My eyes drifted toward the iron bars of the cell, not wanting to meet his gaze.

Caelus stalked forward, pressing my back into the stone wall of the too-small cell. Two fingers lifted my chin so that our eyes met, but his hair fell forward, casting shadows that hid whatever emotion was trapped behind them.

My heart raced for an all-too different reason, and I could have sworn the tempest murmured within, trying to slip past the invisible cage keeping it locked away. I swallowed and tried to ignore the way my body relished being so close to him—the heat radiating from him.

I wouldn't make the same mistake of trusting him so easily. Not after that kiss with that woman. Not after I came for him, and he wasn't even in danger. And especially not after he allowed Teeg to remain here, knowing the dangers that might await him.

"She enjoys causing trouble," he said, voice low.

"Is that some lame attempt to convince me that you didn't want it?" I shoved my cuffed hands up between us. "Or am I supposed to believe you and that you had nothing to do with this?" I shook my hands, the chains clanking together.

His gaze dropped to the shackles, and a muscle worked in his jaw. "I had everything to do with ensuring you wouldn't be harmed."

My brows rose. Maybe he meant that woman couldn't use

runes, and maybe it was because of him that my blood wasn't burning. That didn't remove the hurt from him watching her place the shackles on my wrists—the terror that set in as the cold iron clasped around my wrists.

"Should I thank you, then?" I let out a bitter laugh and stomped on his foot.

Caelus winced, and his fingers slipped from my chin. When his face met mine again, he wore a wolfish smile, but I caught the flicker of surprise before it was gone. "Not yet," he murmured. "Almost got the better of me last time you were in a bad mood too. Too bad there isn't a dagger this time."

"Yeah, a real shame."

Those gray eyes drifted to my wrists, and a muscle jumped in his jaw again. "Roan and his associate brought Teeg here at the Abyssal's request."

My eyes widened. "Why are you telling me this?"

"The truth is complicated. But you were never supposed to be here."

I ground my teeth. "Malik said the same thing. So, when is someone going to explain to me what that means?"

"Roan and his cohort were working with the king."

"And what? I'm supposed to believe you? Do you think the labryn is working with him too? I doubt it. The king needs to be informed."

His body tensed and citrus filled the cell, and the faintest breeze was all that remained of Caelus.

I slid down the stone wall, fresh tears stinging my eyes. When I reached up to wipe them away, my wrist came free of the shackles, and the tempest stirred inside me.

I wanted to smile. I wanted to believe him. I wanted him to come back so I wouldn't be alone.

But he'd given me my way to freedom. There was no other explanation for how the manacles had been unlocked. And I hated that I wanted to smile because of him—hated that he was giving me reasons to think he could be trusted.

I picked up the iron cuffs and flung them at the far wall. They clattered against the stone. It didn't alleviate any of my anger or frustration the way I hoped.

Teeg didn't stir. He must have stayed asleep the entire time Caelus had been here. He'd always been a heavy sleeper, and he was probably exhausted.

But we needed to leave before someone noticed.

Pushing myself up, I focused on the cell's lock, praying it wasn't enchanted to repel esprit.

Caelus was the only reason I could use air well enough to even think of unlocking it. *Stop thinking of him.* I breathed in slowly to calm my mind and imagined a key slipping into the lock, shaping the wind. When I released the breath, the door opened.

In seconds, I'd done the same to the lock on Teeg's cell and rushed inside. I rubbed soothing circles along his back to wake him. "Time to go," I said.

"How did you get out?" he asked with a puzzled look.

"I'll tell you some other time," I said. "Promise."

He smiled and took my hand.

Together, we left the dungeon and approached the junction where I'd last seen Stumbleduck and Kenzo, everflame lighting the way. Teeg followed me down the stone path Kenzo, Stumbleduck, and I took when entering the maze of tunnels. I wished I'd paid more attention as we weaved farther and farther through the halls. The cracked-stone tunnels weren't special and had very few memorable markings for me to know if I was leading us toward the exit.

In a more familiar corridor—at least, I hoped it was familiar— voices drifted toward us. I ducked into what I assumed to be a supply room, Teeg a step behind me, and I slid the wooden door closed.

"You shouldn't be here," rasped a voice.

I twisted around, pushing Teeg behind me. A dark coppery-headed gnome was tied to a chair next to a glowing jade-like crystal. The crystal was taller than the gnome, just by a few inches, and like the others I'd seen, the inside of it seemed to swirl. It cast the dark room in a green hue.

"Who are you?" I whispered.

"Tooley Whistlemane. And not that Abyssal they have pretending to be me." He coughed as he finished speaking.

I stepped closer to get a better look at his pale, gaunt face. His body was thin, as though he hadn't been eating well. "Why did they restrain you?"

"Because I wanted nothing to do with this!"

I bit back a frustrated retort. "And what is 'this'?"

The door pushed open behind me, sending Teeg tumbling to the dirt floor. On instinct, I blocked Teeg with my body, cursing myself for not paying more attention to the sounds beyond the door.

Roan Beris stood in the doorway. His clothes were clean, and he wore an embroidered maroon coat over his tunic. With a smug smile, he said, "Tempest! How good it is to see you again. I didn't get a chance after I found my wife's corpse. With your infernal connection to that guild, I had to get out of Dusmir before Malik found me." His eyes narrowed on me. "But I always knew there could only be one person responsible for my dear Klareth's death."

"She killed Tryssa," I said, and Teeg's hands squeezed against my hip, clinging to me. I'd forgotten he didn't know, but there would be another time to talk to him about that. "She sent Teeg to that cannibal, Travok. Who's to say how many lives both are responsible for."

He straightened his lapels. "Ah, but it was always so much more than that. We collected souls," he said reverently. "Souls are powerful."

Lord Whistlemane scoffed behind us.

I narrowed my eyes. "And that was worth killing children?"

He growled. "Continuing our work is worth anything. And you, an orphaned girl who killed her childhood friend, unable to control your gift from the gods, wouldn't understand that."

Teeg tugged on my clothes, and I glanced at him. His eyes were wide, and his face drained of blood.

We needed to leave, and Roan wasn't a threat. He didn't have any esprit that I knew of. He was just normal human Roan. Curiosity got the better of me, though. "And how does Gavriel fit into this?"

"The father of your childhood friend. What better ally to have in all this? Once I learned of Travok's betrayal and needed to retrieve the boy, it was all too easy to convince him to assist me, if only to spite you."

My heart sank into my stomach. For Gavriel to involve a child . . . all because of an accident. My blood sparked, but I willed the storm to remain within.

"You must be thinking it'll be easy to outrun me with the boy. That you have an advantage over me because you're a Divine. But I believe your dear aunt and cousin have been missing, haven't they?"

That spark in my blood writhed with new life. "Where are they?" I asked through gritted teeth.

Roan stepped aside and into the hall, gesturing to that iron door I'd seen coming in. He grinned from ear to ear—a grin that never led to anything good—but I didn't move. I waited for him to be the one who stepped inside.

Seeing that I wasn't going to move, he walked in, and I peeked into the room.

I wished I hadn't.

From the doorway, I spotted Aunt Celeste and Lora in the previously empty manacles on the far wall. Their once-fine dresses were torn and tattered, splotched with blood. Cuts marred their bodies and their beautiful, nearly identical faces. Lora's blonde hair was matted with blood and grime. Aunt Celeste's head hung limp, unconscious. Lora's eyes met mine. They darted over to Roan and widened.

Fear replaced the shock in her gaze once they landed on me again. "Run," she rasped.

I stepped in front of Teeg, preventing him from taking in the sight and praying to the gods that the things he experienced wouldn't haunt him for the rest of his life.

"What did you do to them?" I bit out, ignoring Lora's weak command.

"Nothing more than they deserved for hiding the only living daughter of the Quinn family."

Lightning broke free along my fingers, and Teeg's hand found mine, squeezing it—a reminder that he'd never been afraid of me.

"I'll let you leave, but you can only choose one: your family or the boy."

I stepped over the threshold, and Teeg released my hand. "You can't stop me from choosing both."

Roan's grin didn't falter. He snapped and the sound of running water came from below the metal grates that lined the room. In front of Lora and Aunt Celeste, a shape the colors of night glimmered and began to form.

The shades of blue and black morphed together, the colors changing to gray. Skin stretched over muscle, forming into an enormous man's body. A single giant saucerlike eye stared back at me. That inky substance dripped from the golyath's arms. It wielded a mace far larger than any human could. The labryn had taken on the form of a golyath from the Abyss.

Teeg screamed behind me, and a hand shoved me farther into the iron room. I spun around, and Gavriel tugged Teeg away by the arm. He slammed the door, trapping me in the room with Roan and the Abyssal.

34

I jerked on the handle of the iron door, but it wouldn't budge. Heavy steps sounded behind me, and I turned to face Roan and the labryn. The monster stepped closer to Aunt Celeste and Lora.

Lora whimpered.

"What happened to choice?" I asked.

"The threat on my life was your choice," Roan said.

My lightning-coated hands clenched. I needed to buy time, figure out how to save them and Teeg. "What if I offer to help you?"

Roan held up his hand, and the labryn stopped its approach toward them. "You've taken my darling wife from me and Gavriel's son from him. Why should I believe you'd help me?"

Darling? Klareth certainly hadn't been very darling in the time I'd known her.

I scanned the room for something—anything—that might be used as a weapon while I considered how to respond. Everflame torches speared into brackets lining the walls. "Klareth needed me, didn't she?" I asked, gambling. "I imagine my cooperation would make your plans easier." I took a few steps closer to my family and one of the torches.

Roan glanced at them and the Abyssal, considering. It was enough to buy me a few more steps. *Almost.*

"Souls hold power. I'm sure you saw Travok's inefficient use of them," he spat.

Bile rose in my throat. "You mean the children he . . . consumed."

"He did more than that. He harvested the essence of souls. Absorbed their youth. Do it too much and the effect diminishes. But the Golden Child's soul, well, that would be another story."

My nails dug into my palm. Stumbleduck was right to murder Travok. "But you took Teeg before that," I said, taking another careful step toward my goal.

"Travok promised to share the power of the child's soul with Gavriel and I. He lied, so we took him. Brought him here where the plan would continue uninterrupted." He shot me a glare, and I froze. "Or so we thought."

"And you plan to use his soul for your own purposes?" Another few steps.

"You and the boy have powerful souls. A Divine and the Golden Child. By siphoning all that esprit into the crystals, we would gain a longer life—gain esprit of our own. Enough to bring back those you've killed, with a little help from the Abyss."

I halted. "That's impossible," I said, my gaze lingering on the hulking golyath form the labryn had taken. "Nothing from the Abyss helps anyone for free."

"Precisely why I'm helping it enter Anuvyn."

"The fey realm?"

Roan shrugged. "It's not my business to ask questions as long as I get results. So far, it has been very accommodating, but it grows impatient."

As if to emphasize his point, the labryn tapped its giant mace along the iron floor. Loud clanking reverberated off the walls.

I took another few steps toward the everflame torch. "Thanally punishes those who attempt to play with life and death."

Roan's brows furrowed. "You speak as if the gods truly care. They didn't stop you before you killed my wife, and they won't stop me from bringing her back!"

I lurched for the torch and pulled it free, ignoring Roan's shouts. His fingers snapped, and then the labryn swung its weapon. Before I could do anything, Aunt Celeste and Lora were splattered against the wall, nothing more than mushed heaps of flesh and blood.

The torch fell from my grasp and clattered against the iron floor. I fixated on the bits of flesh, all that was left of my family, sloughing down the iron wall—dripping from that mace.

Roan's laughter filled the chamber.

There would never be another pretty smile from Lora. My last memory of her would be of her raspy voice begging me to run. The shock on her face. Her whimper of fear when the labryn appeared. She and Dorian had been my only light after my parents' death.

And while Celeste hadn't been perfect, I'd hoped for a chance to reconcile. A chance to try to understand one another and the situation we'd both been in when she'd been forced to take me in. I wanted a chance to create memories with them that weren't bitter.

But they were gone.

I stood motionless, staring, tears trailing paths down my cheeks. Roan said something, but I didn't care. *This is all my fault.* If I hadn't thrown that dagger into Klareth's chest, they would've been safe. Roan wouldn't have involved them.

Teeg and I would still be in that temple, together.

Someone screamed, and arms wrapped around my waist, pushing me down. I rolled across the cold iron floor, and a swoosh sounded next to me—the sound of that weapon being swung.

Caelus held himself over me. Blood trickled from his mouth, and the sight pulled me from my stupor. My fingers glided down his cheek, through the blood trickling from his lips, and lightning danced along his face, mending an unseen wound. His eyes darted to the touch, and then they met mine again, and he smirked. "I'm glad you're not hurt, my Tempest," he murmured.

I didn't get a chance to respond. The golyath's mace flung him away. He collided with the wall and groaned on impact.

It came down toward me next.

My heart pounded and I rolled, dodging it. I scrambled to get myself up. A clang sounded behind me where it struck the iron floor. I turned to face the Abyssal. It stood beside the dented floor and snarled at me.

I chanced a glance at Caelus.

He lay next to the now-open exit, motionless but breathing. A dark puddle of blood pooled beneath his head. My power urged me toward him, and I darted.

Heavy steps chased me. A glance over my shoulder showed Roan was nowhere to be seen. He'd run away like a coward, leaving me with the Abyssal.

I needed to heal Caelus, but the steps only grew closer. There wasn't time to mend him with the Abyssal right behind me. I needed it distracted. Whirling around, I came face-to-face with the labryn.

It hurtled toward me. Azure tendrils formed at my fingertips, and I shot a bolt of lightning toward it. The hit landed, sparks skittering across the iron room, and the monster roared. My stomach turned at the scent of burnt flesh filling the room.

Oozing ink-like blood spilled onto the floor.

I spun back to Caelus, assessing him. His breathing came in short bursts, and fresh blood trickled from his lips.

Heavy footsteps started toward us.

"I need more time," I muttered, and yanked Caelus's sword free from the sheath at his hip and faced the labryn's golyath form again.

A shape began to take form from the hissing pool of blood on the floor. In seconds, the night-black substance shaped into an Abyss wolf, sputtering blue flames at its feet.

My grip tightened around the sword. I had to keep them away from Caelus.

Both the wolf and the labryn's focus remained on me, thankfully. I ran to the opposite side of the room, skirting out of reach of the massive mace. Both followed me, mercifully ignoring Caelus. I came to a stop on the other side of the room and thanked Renelle.

The hulking one-eyed form the Abyssal took darted for me, hauling back the oversize mace. The wolf was a step ahead, claws clicking against the iron floor. It pounced in my direction. The labryn swung. I sidestepped and fell onto my back.

The massive Abyssal roared and flailed its weapon. I rolled to my side, evading one strike, and scrambled to my feet, narrowly avoiding another. The wolf howled and raced toward me. But I couldn't dodge them both. The wolf's fangs sank into my leg. Lightning sputtered from the wound, frying the wolf from the inside out. It seized and yelped, falling lifeless next to me.

The labryn roared again and heaved the mace down. I jerked my leg free and staggered out of range, the blow barely missing me.

How am I supposed to kill this thing? I couldn't even get close thanks to the huge weapon.

I panted, my body tired from the relentless evading. The Abyssal swung, his mace slamming into my stomach and knocking me against the far wall. I coughed up blood and slumped to the floor. *I can't let it kill Caelus.* My body moved, leaning forward, the blood of my family sticking in my hair. I pushed against the floor to stand, my hands slipping in the mess that remained of Aunt Celeste and Lora.

Its large hand wrapped around my torso, picking me up, and squeezed. Caelus's sword fell from my grasp. The hand grew tighter, and my ribs cracked. My lungs burned, longing for air.

Spots filled my vision, and I knew I was going to die.

I wasn't skilled like Selena or Esteban.

There was never a chance that I could've killed this Abyssal on my own.

A twist of voices whispered in my mind. *Embrace your gift.* That's what I'd been told by Thalia and Caelus. But there was another voice. I'd heard it once before in the temple. I thought I'd imagined it out of desperation.

Lightning rippled from my body and skittered across the labryn. Its grip loosened, and I dropped to the cold, hard floor. I braced my broken ribs and coughed, taking in deep breaths, each causing a sharp ache to shoot through me.

Blue-black ichor dripped from its hand and formed inky fur—another Abyss wolf, smaller than the last and without flaming claws, sprang toward me.

Lightning surged from me, but I wasn't worried about Caelus. The tempest wouldn't harm him as long as I didn't want it to.

When my lightning made contact with the iron, it cascaded along the floor and walls of the iron room toward the only sources I willed it. All that pent-up energy, never unleashing, because I spent years wanting to be normal—trying to pretend to be normal—just needed a target.

The creature bellowed, the form it took fading into that inky fluid. It tried to reform, a large arm springing out of the substance, only to wither again. The night-black puddle slid toward the grates lining the room—an escape. I willed the lightning to ripple through the puddle of its shapeless form.

The wolf that formed from the blood was gone, rejoined with the labryn's liquid form.

The puddle smoked, boiling. I didn't stop until there was nothing but a stagnant dark unmoving ichor on the floor. The iridescent sheen was no longer visible and instead seemed to absorb all the surrounding light.

I took a tender breath, glancing at Caelus. His breaths were still shallow. I pushed myself up, pain sinking into each movement. I stumbled toward where he lay on the ground.

"Wake up, you poofing idiot," I murmured, pressing my hand to him. Without a thought, the lightning darted from me, covering him like a cocoon. His breaths grew stronger, and after several minutes, his eyes fluttered open.

"Eira," he murmured.

My head spun, a wave of lightheadedness overtaking me. I fell forward and a fierce pain penetrated the dizziness. Caelus caught me, and my vision faded, my power humming beneath the surface in his presence.

35

My eyes sprang open, and I sat up from a worn table I'd been placed on. I didn't recognize the room, but from the layout, it appeared to be a dining space within the network of tunnels beneath Thistlewall. Chairs lined another table a few feet away.

"You're awake," Caelus said next to me.

My power pulled toward him, but I slid off the table on the side opposite him. The pain in my leg was gone, and I suspected that if I looked, the wound from the wolf's bite would be healed. "You saved me," I said.

"Should I not have?"

It was a loaded question. I hadn't forgotten that woman's lips pressed to his, and I wasn't sure if I could forgive him. "I need to find Teeg," I said, stepping out into the hall. It was familiar, but the near barren stone hallways offered nothing to help identify where I was.

Caelus didn't say anything, following me through the tunnels.

I found the iron door where I'd fought the labryn. Roan had escaped. I loosed a defeated sigh.

Across from that room was where I'd met Lord Whistlemane. I pushed inside, the green glow of the crystal illuminating the space. He remained tied to the chair. "Lord Whistlemane needs help," I told Caelus.

He hesitated, giving me a once-over, before leaving my side, untying the gnomish member of the Dawn Conclave.

I approached the crystal, placed my palm along the smooth surface, and gasped. The souls trapped inside writhed and warred, their suffering filling me. Their unjust murder left them angry and twisted.

Caelus placed his warm hand on my shoulder, anchoring me. "What happened?"

"What is this?" I asked Lord Whistlemane, ignoring Caelus.

Tooley Whistlemane looked from me to the crystal and back, eyes weary. "They've been collecting souls to power their resurrection project."

Within the crystal swirled a lighter green substance so much like the one I'd seen the night I'd woken up in the catacombs of the Temple of Ahrea. "Can it still be used?"

He nodded. "No one should practice using souls of the dead."

I released lightning along the crystal. Cracks spiderwebbed across it, and the glow faded. The light green soul essence spilled through the fractures, losing their light as well.

Give them peace, Thanally.

As if in answer, a sense of well-being washed over me, warming my chest. I smiled and clutched the moonstone lotus Marus had gifted me. I rubbed my finger across the smooth center stone to find it cracked as well. Holding it up, the stone was missing a piece and the silver outline of the lotus was bent and crooked, most likely from when the labryn had been squeezing me.

I frowned at the broken amulet and stepped outside, my job done, and continued to search for Teeg.

Caelus was there in an instant. "You can't run away, Tempest."

I glared at him. "I haven't forgotten what happened."

Footsteps barreled against the stone floor toward us, and I took on a defensive stance. Caelus stepped in front of me, a hand on the hilt of his recovered sword.

Selena rounded the corner, her tight braids now pulled back. She slowed, eyes landing on what remained of my wounds, the mess of my hair, and my blood-stained clothes. Her brows furrowed and lips thinned. "You should've listened!" she said between pants.

"You appear to be well," I said, thankful the glass and the explosion hadn't harmed her.

Her fury faded, and she laughed. "Honestly, I'm almost proud of that stunt you pulled. Esteban is furious, but he'll be glad to know you're alive and mostly well."

"Have you seen Teeg? He was with a half-fey man, Gavriel. Or maybe Roan?"

"I found Teeg and got him to Malik, but there's been a complicated development."

I raised an eyebrow at her.

"It'd be better if you saw for yourself."

I followed Selena, though Caelus was still unwilling to leave my side.

Admittedly, I had saved him just as he saved me. I hadn't wanted him to die, and my body moved on its own—was compelled—to save him. But he'd go back to Ryseer, and I'd go to Dusmir, never to see each other again, and my heart ached at the thought, despite all that had occurred.

"What happened after you left?" Selena asked. "It took us a while to find these tunnels, but you had that gnome with you."

"I . . ." I wasn't sure what to say. I'd been captured but found Caelus. Finding him had been the plan, but Selena didn't need to know all the messy details when it came to the hurt and betrayal.

"Roan was responsible for taking Teeg," I said finally. "He delivered him to Ebonhammer before he knew about Travok's plan to kill and consume him for himself. After that, Roan took him with Gavriel's help. They planned to tamper with life and death, and I'm to blame."

Selena stopped and gave me a wide-eyed look. "You?"

I gave her a half-hearted smile. "I lost control of the tempest when I was young and it killed Gavriel's son. And Klareth . . ."

She nodded. "You killing anyone sounds ridiculous. Guess the bitch finally pushed you to your limit."

I gave her a thin smile. "She murdered Tryssa in front of me." The crystal below the temple flashed in my mind. Had Klareth been gathering souls beneath the temple too? For what purpose? "I don't regret it. But Dorian . . ."

Selena wrapped her arms around my neck. "He's probably smiling down at you, proud that you killed that bitch."

She smelled of sweat and lilacs, but I didn't care. I smiled, wrapping my arms around her in return.

We continued forward, and I could feel Caelus's stare on me.

Light shone at the end of the tunnel, and I glimpsed the dawn sky peeking through. Chattering grew closer. Soon I'd be with Teeg, and I would go home.

Caelus pulled me to a stop and Selena glanced back at us with a questioning look. Lord Whistlemane didn't bother stopping and started up the steps.

I gave her a nod, and her lips pressed into a thin line before going up the makeshift steps out of the cave.

Once she was out of sight, I faced Caelus. His eyes stayed on the steps a moment longer before meeting mine. The light shining into the tunnel made his gray eyes appear darker than usual.

Caelus stepped forward and twirled a dark lock of my hair around a finger. "You've accepted your gift," he said.

I stepped back, my hair falling through his fingers. I'd expected another apology or an explanation, but not that. "Is that all?" I asked.

He glanced at the exit again and took a deep breath. "There's one last thing I need to tell you."

My heart sped up, and my mouth dried.

"I was sent to Dusmir by the king. For you."

"What do you mean?" I asked, taking another step back.

He opened his mouth to speak again, but he was cut off by concerned shouts.

"Prince Alpheus! It's dangerous. You shouldn't rush down into unknown tunnels!"

36

An impassive mask slipped over Caelus's face.

A man around my age bounded down the steps two at a time, ignoring the shouts behind him. A cloak billowed around him in the sunburst orange of the royal family. Dawn light pouring in through the tunnel haloed him with each step down.

He stopped in front of Caelus and me.

Unsure of what to do, I bowed.

The prince laughed and said, "That's unnecessary, Tempest."

I cleared my throat and straightened.

Caelus took up a position beside me. "Prince Alpheus. How unexpected," he said, tone dry.

I glanced at him, unsure of what to make of the prince's presence and Caelus's familiar tone. The two shared an indignant look, and I began to wonder if they didn't like one another.

"I was informed by a mutual friend of your situation," Prince Alpheus said. "Thought it best to pay a visit."

I rolled my eyes.

It shouldn't have annoyed me that the prince wouldn't divulge information in the company of a stranger, but I was tired of secrets.

He gestured up the steps. "But let's get out of this putrid cave, shall we?"

I nodded, and Caelus and I trailed after him.

The exit of the cave mouth had two guards stationed on each side. The surrounding forest was filled with guards on horseback garbed in the royal crest—a rising sun.

Selena, Malik, and his group of guild mates shifted their feet and busied themselves with their horses. Among them was Teeg. He laughed at something Selena said, and I smiled, tears rimming my eyes. The fact that he could laugh after everything he'd been through and seen was a miracle of the gods. With him safe and Klareth gone, joining the guild might not be so bad.

Seven Abyss wolves lay dead, along with people I didn't recognize. The Copper Jackals' night had been arduous in their efforts to get to me and Teeg. I said a quick prayer to Thanally for each dead guild member.

Prince Alpheus headed for his retinue of guards, but I headed for the Copper Jackals.

Malik shot me his signature piercing look, but I didn't care what he thought of me running off on my own. Without him, I'd found Teeg, and it was admittedly thanks to his efforts that Teeg got to safety.

Teeg beamed up at me, pushing past Selena and another woman—the one I'd healed so long ago. I knelt and wrapped my arms around him. He squeezed me and sent a shooting pain through my sore rib cage.

"Did you beat that monster?" he asked.

I squeezed him back. "Yeah. There's nothing to worry about. We'll go home and see Marus, okay?"

His grin grew wider, and he returned to Selena.

"You reckless girl!" Esteban ground out behind me. He pulled me into a tight embrace, and I yelped in surprise.

His warm whiskey scent enveloped me. A heaviness lifted from my chest and renewed fatigue settled in. "Don't ever do that again," he whispered.

"I'll do my best," I promised.

Esteban pulled away, meeting my eyes. "Selena told us what happened. You did good, girl." He patted my shoulder before walking off to join Malik and the others. I pushed myself up, and my eyes met Caelus's. He was speaking to the prince, probably informing him of what had happened.

The prince caught the direction of his gaze and turned to face me, grinning. He waved his hand for me to come forward. Knowing better than to defy the wants of the Crown Prince, I obeyed.

I stopped a few feet from where the two of them stood. In the growing light of the morning, Alpheus was handsome, with a strong jaw and gold-flecked eyes. The rays of dawn seemed to be drawn to him, leaving him bright and warm. I wondered if it was an effect of the blessing of the Sunburst Throne.

"I hear you slew a labryn. Excellent work."

"It almost killed me," I said, truthfully. It wasn't as though it'd been a pleasure or easy. Adrenaline fueled most of my actions.

"Eira is skilled when the moment is right," Caelus supplied.

I shot him a glare, but he didn't seem to notice.

The prince, however, did, his eyes darting between us. Prince Alpheus's smile fell a fraction.

"You must have traveled quite the distance to arrive in time to offer assistance," I said.

"Ordinarily, yes. The Refulgent is to thank for our hasty arrival."

Before I could ask how, he gestured to Caelus. "He tells me he assisted you in your search for the Golden Child. Is that correct?"

I glanced at Caelus, but he still wore that emotionless mask. "He did."

"And Lord Ebonhammer and Lord Whistlemane have been killed or injured, respectively?"

My muscles stiffened. "What are you implying?"

A thoughtful look passed over his features. "It could be seen as treasonous to some, Divine or otherwise."

"As I'm currently unsure of all the information you've been given, Prince Alpheus, Travok was eating children to gain their youth. His death isn't regrettable, but I had nothing to do with it. As for Lord Whistlemane"—I took a step back and gestured to the gnome resting against a rock, drinking water—"he can confirm that neither I nor my companions were involved in harming him."

Stumbleduck shouted, "Unhand me or you'll see your dungeons gone up in smoke next! You fools can't even prove anything. Whose word are you listening to?"

The guards said nothing against his protest. They tugged Esteban along beside Stumbleduck. Esteban gave the prince a seething look before the two of them were shoved into a carriage, hands restrained behind them.

My lightning was nothing more than a buzz at the sight, completely drained. "They had nothing to do with Travok Ebonhammer's death. Release them."

The prince smiled, but it didn't reach his eyes. "Forgive me. I believe you, personally, are not responsible for Travok Ebonhammer. Unfortunately, it is out of my hands whether they go free." He held up his hands in feigned innocence. "Their capture and return to Ryseer comes from the king. You'll have to discuss it with my father."

I turned back to the carriage and spotted Teeg sleeping in Selena's arms. He would be safe with them. Malik and Selena would see to it.

I faced Caelus and Prince Alpheus again. Caelus's lips were pressed thin, and the prince appeared displeased by the situation at hand. *He could be an ally.*

"How might I gain an audience with King Olbecht?" I asked.

"That should be simple enough, Lady Eira Quinn. You're to become my wife and queen of Valaryn. You shall be able to gain an audience with him nearly any time you wish."

My heart pounded in my ears and my mouth fell open. That couldn't be. I'd just gotten my freedom. Now I was going to be caged to the Sunburst castle by a marriage I didn't want.

A deep, throaty laugh sounded behind me—the one I'd heard when I touched the body marked with a seven-pointed star.

I turned, and a silhouette of jade flame stalked toward me. The green fire parted enough to make out the sharp features of a fey man.

Sweat coated my palms and the back of my neck. I took a step back, colliding with a hard chest. Shrieking erupted around me. Dread and terror flowed from the flame, and a weight filled my chest.

A hand grabbed my arm and pulled me back. But the flame grabbed my other arm, yanking me into it. The fire didn't burn, but another hand found my back, and a scream tore through my throat. Clothes and flesh burned. I writhed and jerked, trying to free myself. The pain was too much. My entire body *boiled* from the inside out, and a deep, gritty voice broke through my mind.

You've interfered enough, Tempest. Time to make your soul mine.

To be continued . . .

ACKNOWLEDGMENTS

Ah! I can't believe it this book is done. This book is special in my heart, and there are so many people that, without them, it would have never happened.

First, I should start with Lucas, Brandon "Fro," and Beau "Ozzy." Without them, this story wouldn't exist in the first place, despite the immense reimagining on my part.

And I especially have to thank Jake. I'm sorry I had to change Caelus so much, but I hope you love all the moments you ultimately inspired.

I dedicated this book to my mom, and that's truly not quite enough for such an amazing woman, but it's a start, for sure. And without my brother, A. J.'s, constant encouragement throughout my life to pursue my hobbies and interests with passion, I wouldn't be the person I am today.

Thank you to my wonderful critique partners: Alyssa Green, Lana Staux, and Kasey LeAlma. Each of you provided me with constant love and encouragement. If I'd never met you three, this book may have never happened. I cannot thank each of you enough, and words can't accurately describe how much each of you means to me.

Without my amazing beta readers, Alex, Vixen Avery, and Zarmeen S., The Tempest's Soul wouldn't be where it is today. Thank you from the bottom of my heart for your kind, constructive feedback.

And thank you to Rachel at Enchanted Ink Publishing, especially for catching every echo! You've helped make this book the very best it can be, and I am truly grateful.

Then there's you, reader. Thank you for taking a chance on *The Tempest's Soul*. It means the world to me.

ABOUT THE AUTHOR

Brittany M. Riley is a fantasy romance author who adores fantastical worlds, intriguing plots, and, most importantly, swoon-worthy romance. In her free time, she's an avid gamer and can often be found online gaming with friends. When she isn't writing or gaming, she's probably taking courses, napping or busy scrolling through Instagram or TikTok.

WWW.AUTHORBRITTANYMRILEY.COM

Follow Brittany on social media!
@AUTHORBRITTANYMRILEY